Picture Day

Sarah Sax

ALFRED A. KNOPF

NEW YORK

All rights reserved. Published in the United States by Alfred A. Knopf, an imprint of
Random House Children's Books, a division of Penguin Random House LLC, New York.

Knopf, Borzoi Books, and the colophon are registered
trademarks of Penguin Random House LLC.

RH Graphic with the book design is a trademark of Penguin Random House LLC.

Photographs on pages 282–285 courtesy of the author.

Visit us on the Web! rhcbooks.com

Educators and librarians, for a variety of teaching tools,
visit us at RHTeachersLibrarians.com

Library of Congress Cataloging-in-Publication Data is available upon request.
ISBN 978-0-593-30688-8 (trade) — ISBN 978-0-593-30687-1 (pbk.) —
ISBN 978-0-593-30689-5 (lib. bdg.) — ISBN 978-0-593-30690-1 (ebook)

The text of this book is set in 12-point Brinkley Yearbook.
The illustrations were created digitally.
Book design by Sarah Sax and April Ward

MANUFACTURED IN CHINA
10 9 8 7 6 5 4 3 2 1
First Edition

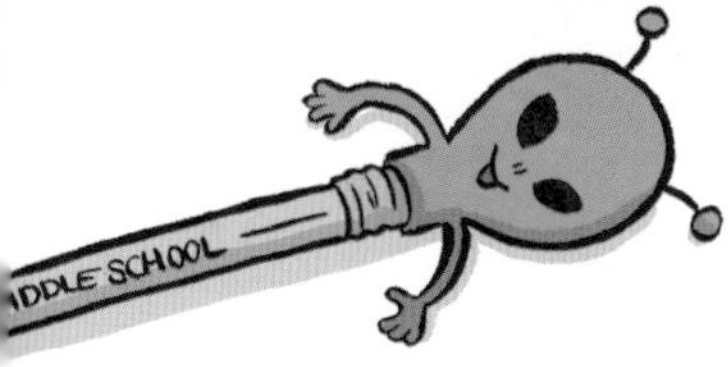
IDDLE SCHOOL

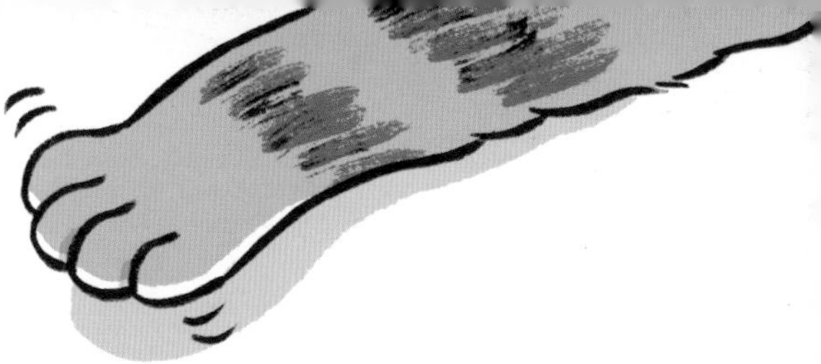

To my fellow
Hixson Middle School
Sailor Scouts:
Jennie, Sarah,
Celeste, and Maggie

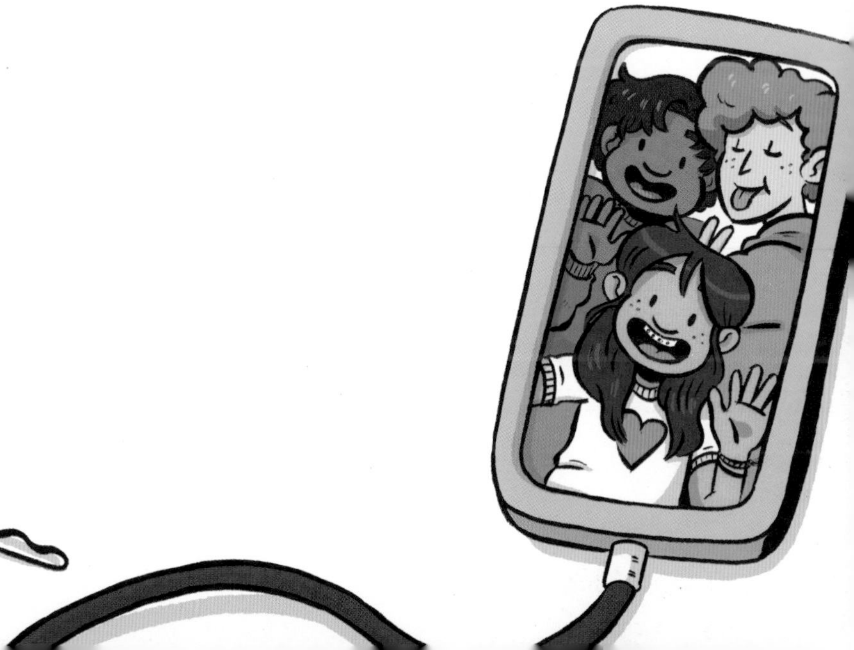

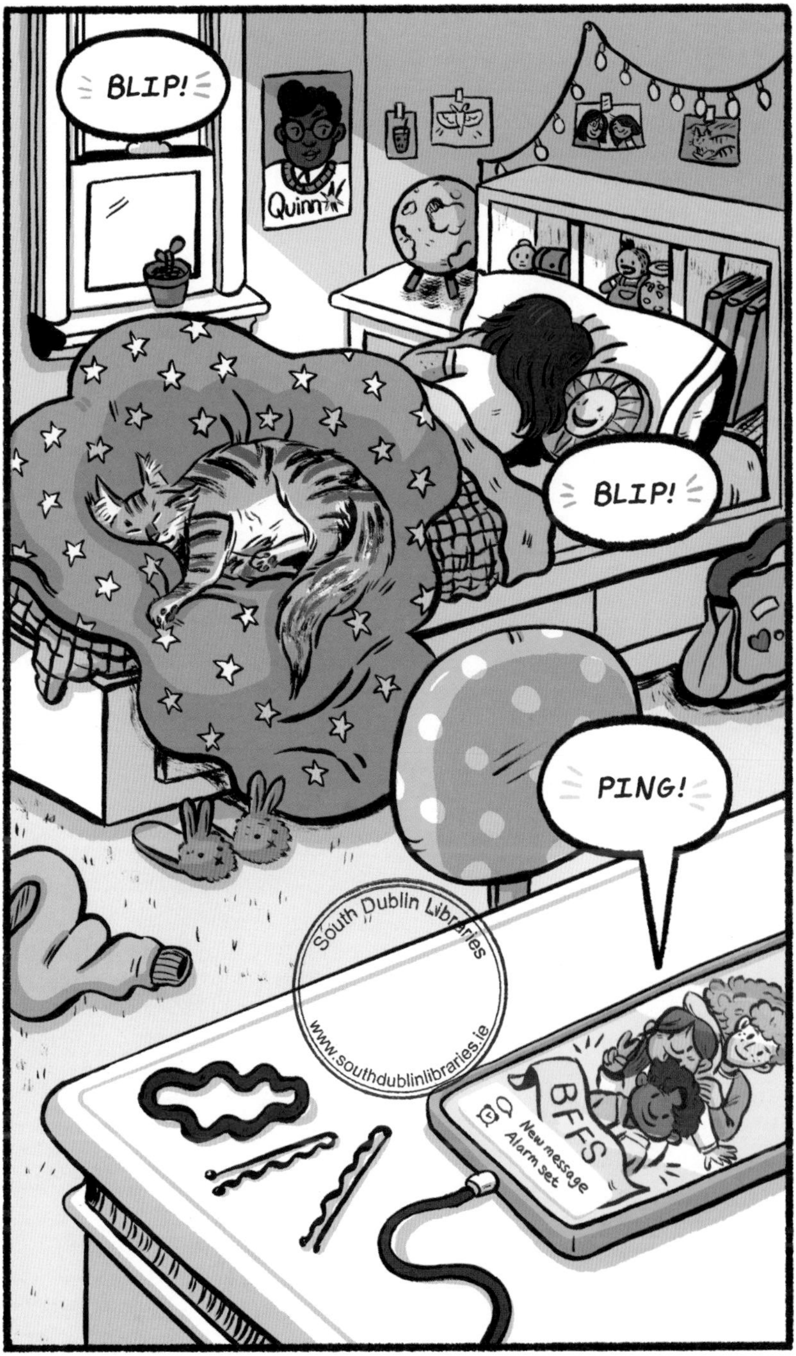
BLIP!
Quinn
BLIP!
PING!
BFFS
New message
Alarm set

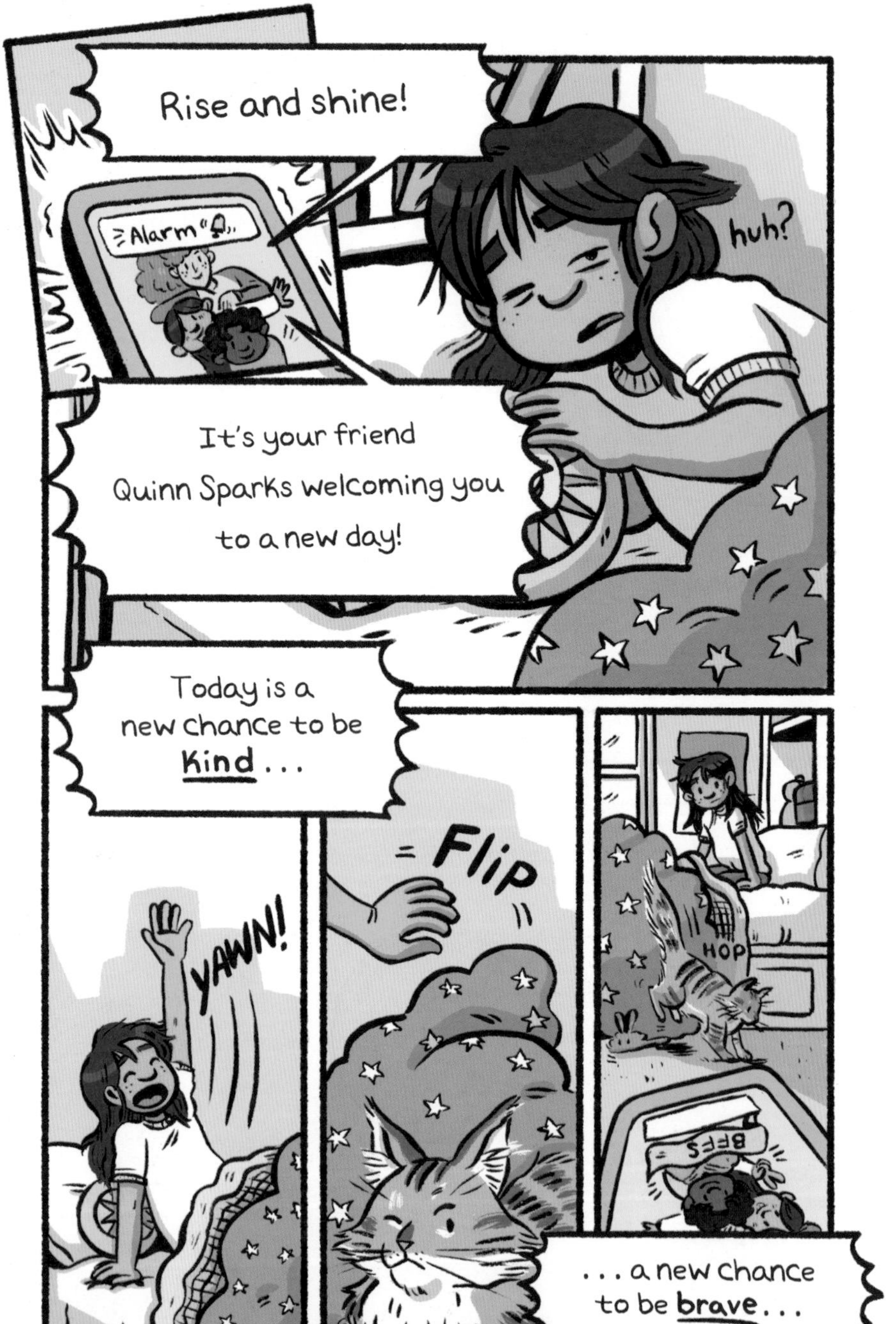
Rise and shine!
Alarm
huh?
It's your friend Quinn Sparks welcoming you to a new day!
Today is a new chance to be **kind** . . .
YAWN!
Flip
HOP
BFFS
. . . a new chance to be **brave** . . .

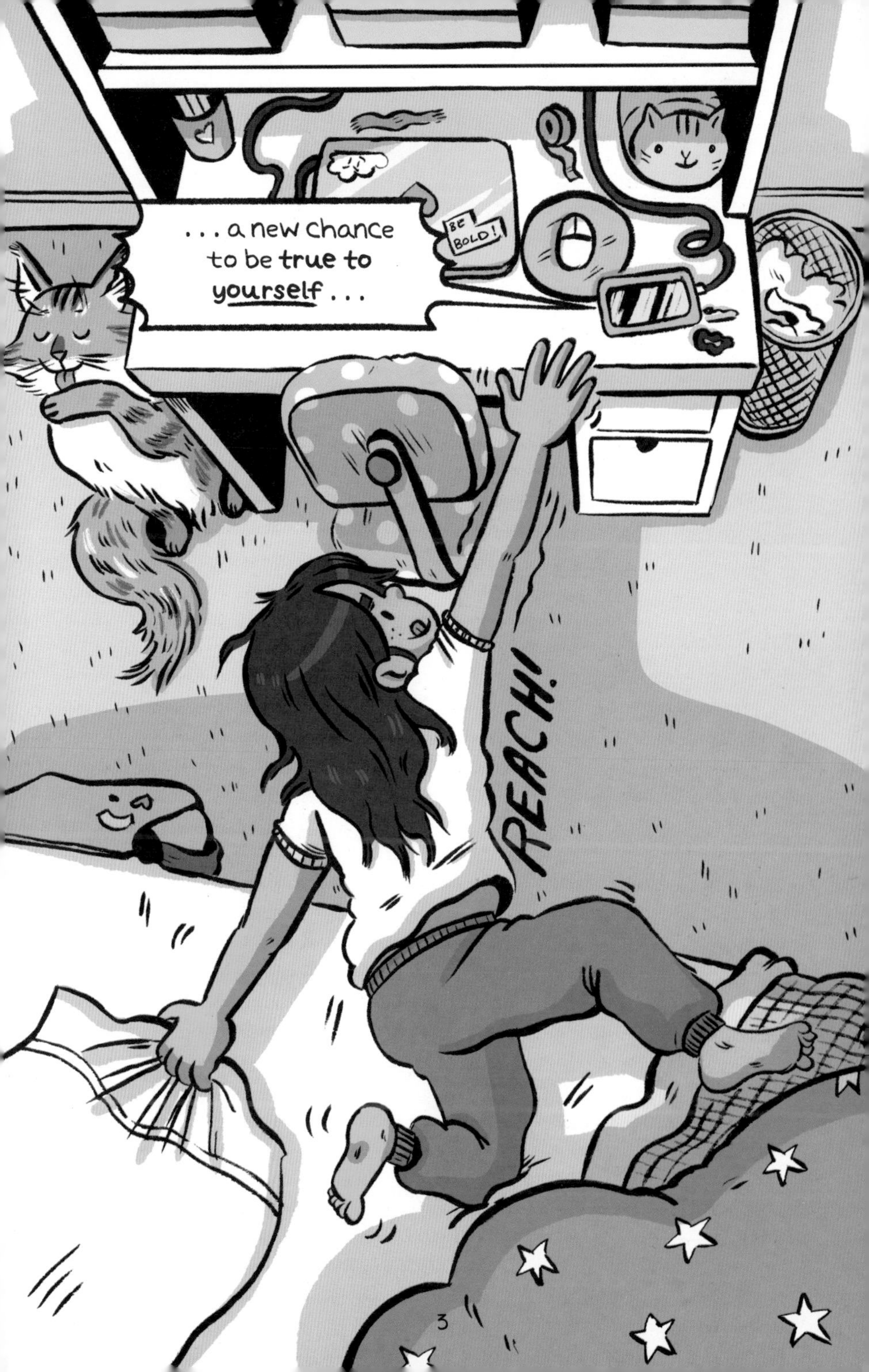
. . . a new chance to be **true to** **yourself** . . .
BE BOLD!
REACH!

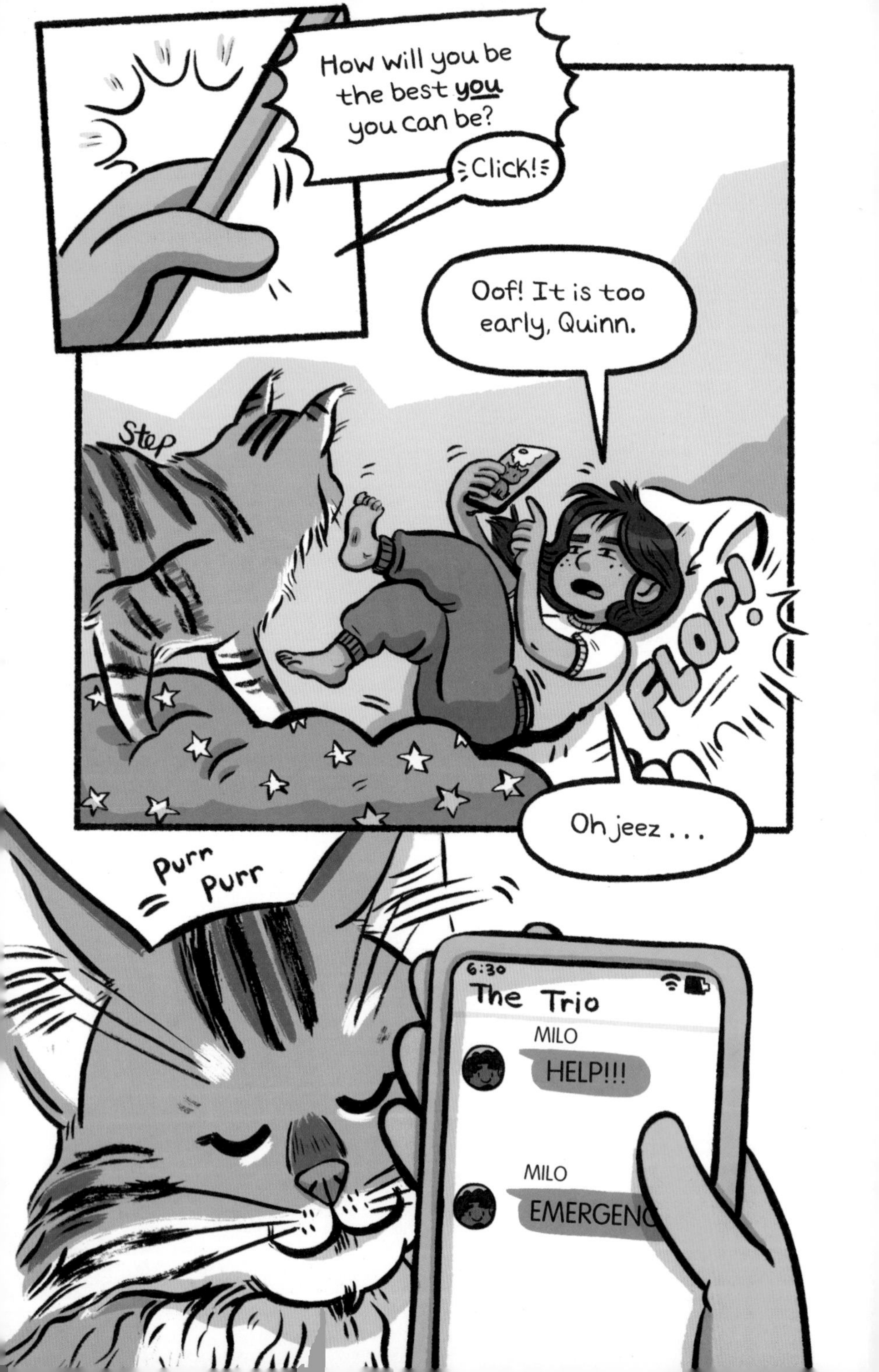

How will you be the best you you can be?
Click!
Oof! It is too early, Quinn.
Step
FLOP!
Oh jeez . . .
purr purr
6:30
The Trio
MILO
HELP!!!
MILO
EMERGENC

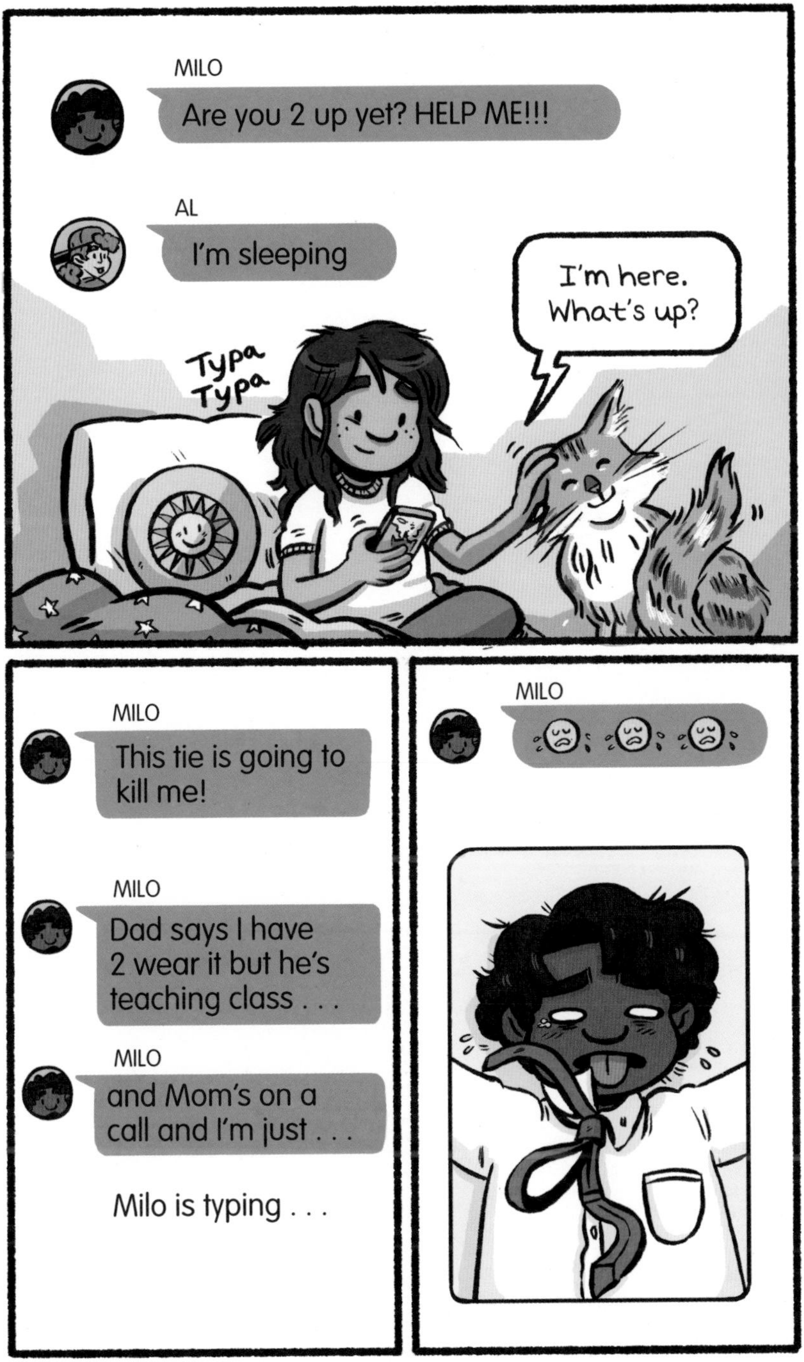
MILO
Are you 2 up yet? HELP ME!!!
AL
I'm sleeping
Typa Typa
I'm here. What's up?
MILO
This tie is going to kill me!
MILO
Dad says I have 2 wear it but he's teaching class . . .
MILO
and Mom's on a call and I'm just . . .
Milo is typing . . .
MILO

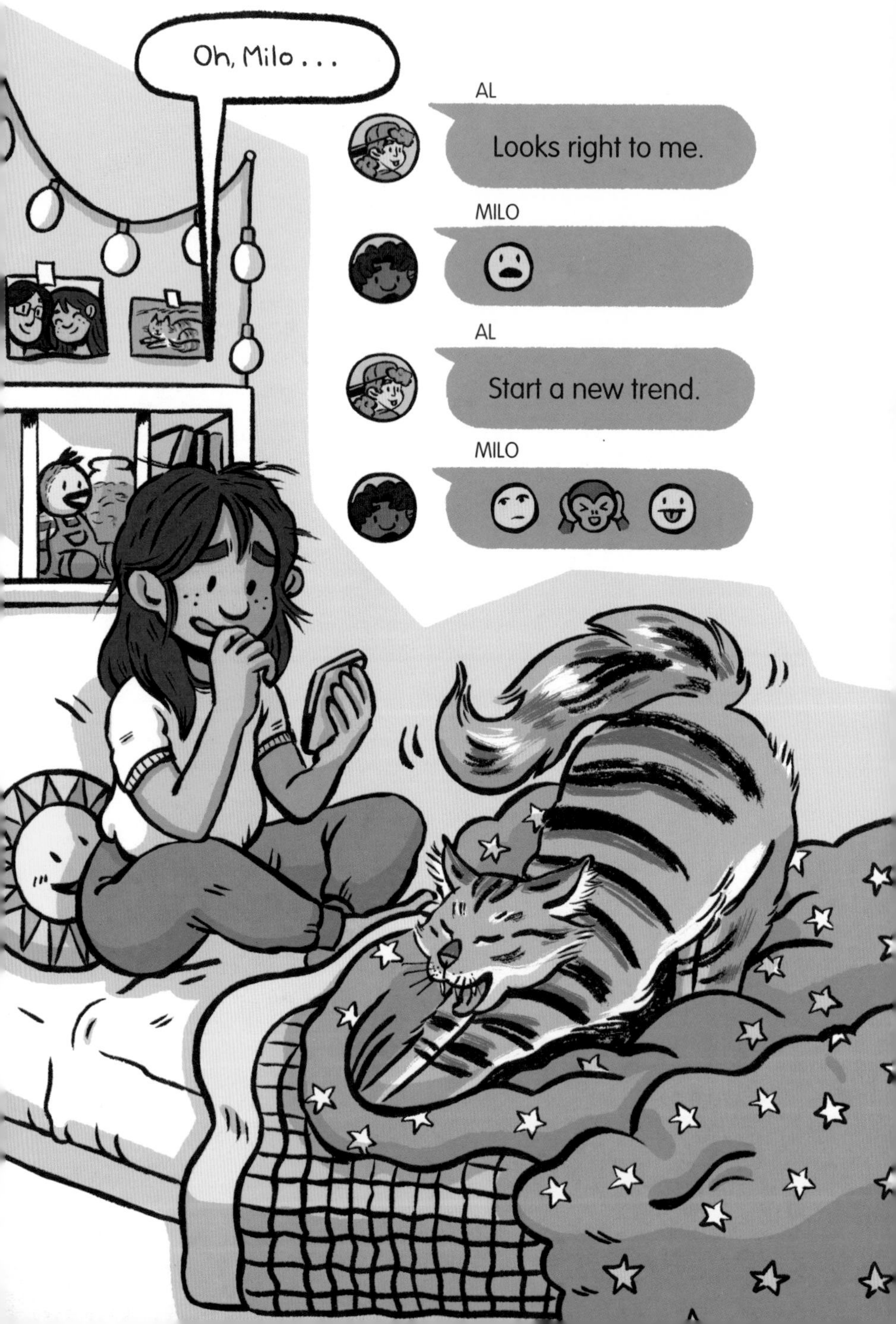

Oh, Milo . . .
AL
Looks right to me.
MILO
AL
Start a new trend.
MILO

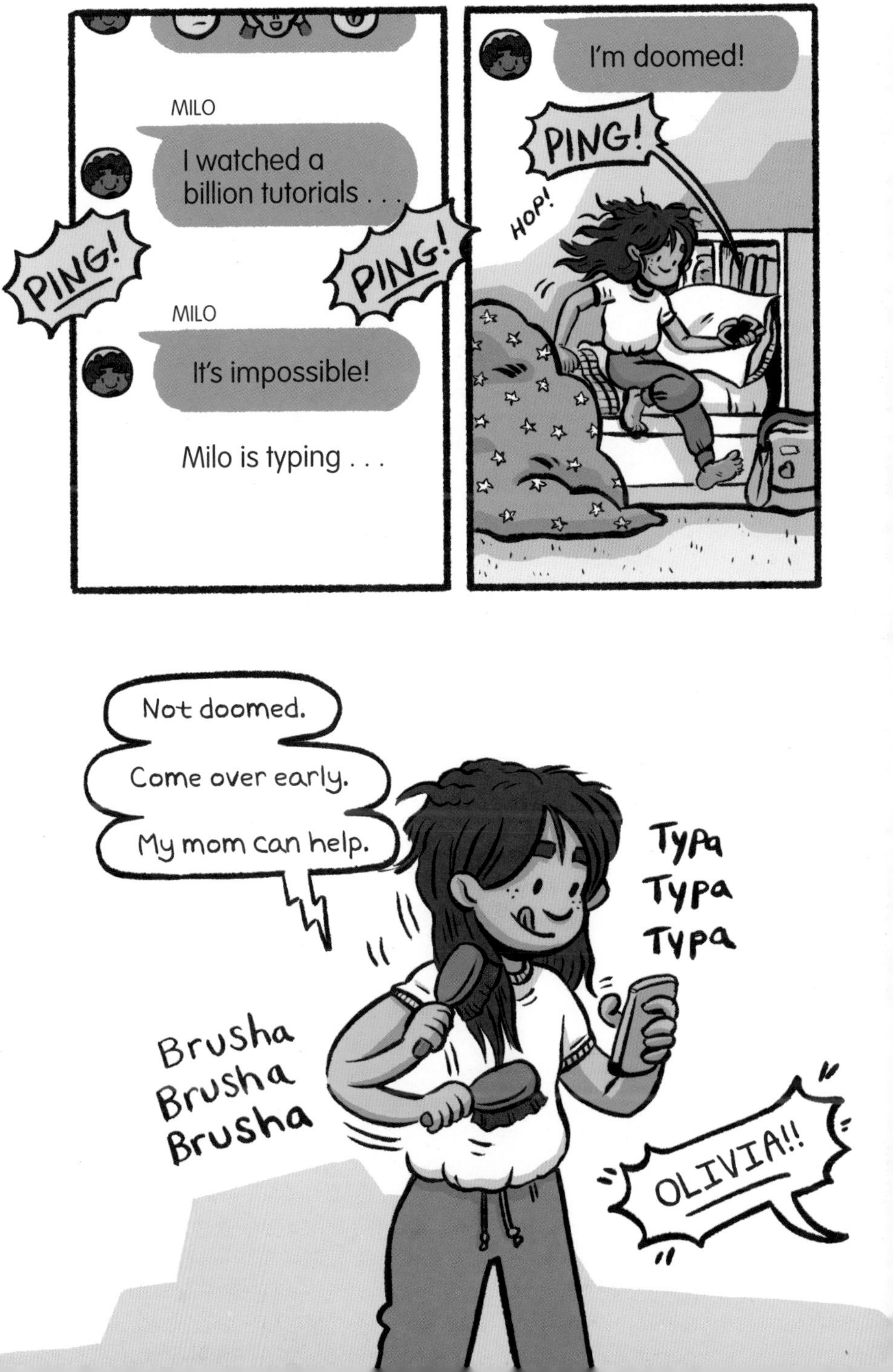
MILO
I watched a billion tutorials . . .
PING!
PING!
MILO
It's impossible!
Milo is typing . . .
I'm doomed!
PING!
HOP!
Not doomed.
Come over early.
My mom can help.
Typa
Typa
Typa
Brusha
Brusha
Brusha
OLIVIA!!

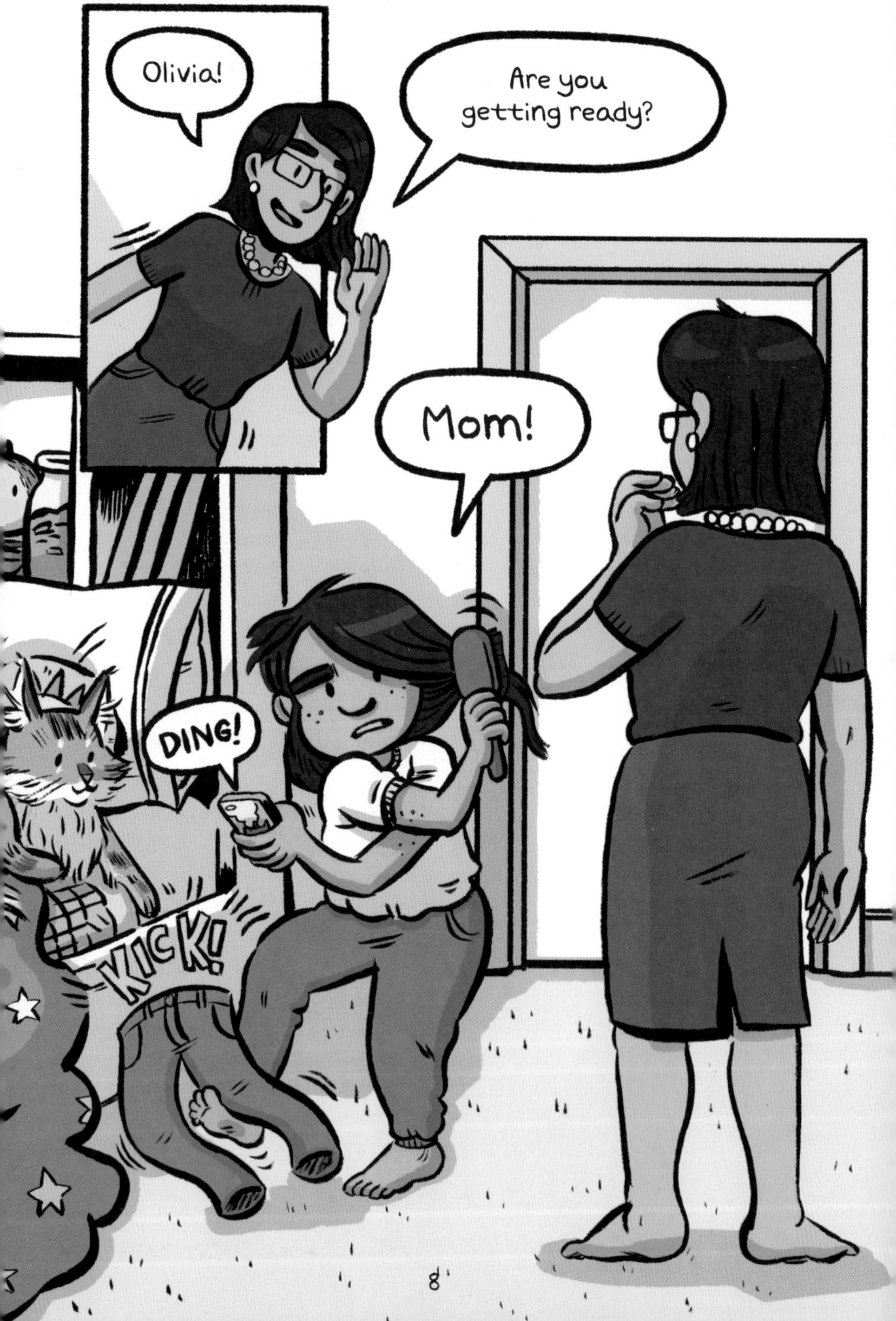
Olivia!
Are you getting ready?
Mom!
DING!
KICK!

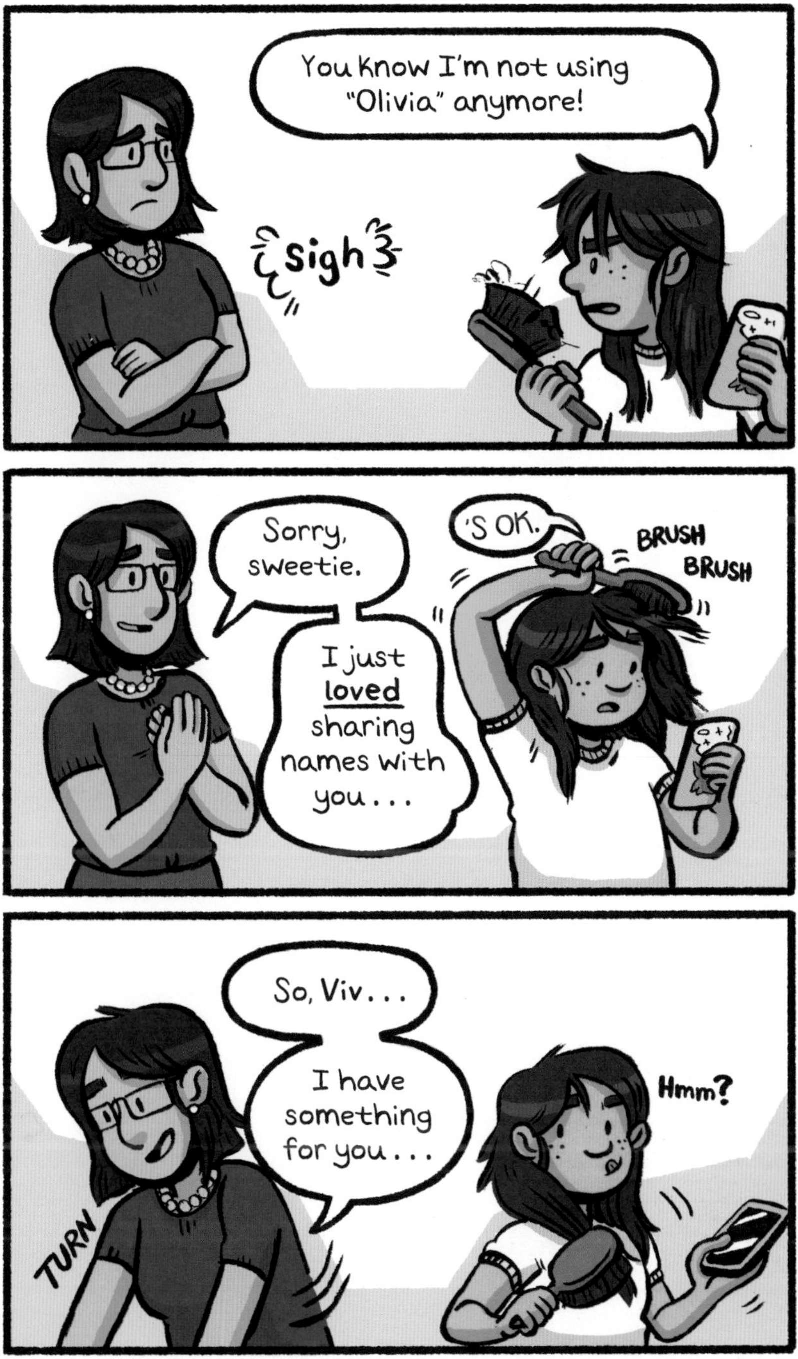
You know I'm not using "Olivia" anymore!
Sigh
Sorry, sweetie.
I just **loved** sharing names with you . . .
'S OK.
BRUSH
BRUSH
So, Viv . . .
I have something for you . . .
Hmm?
TURN

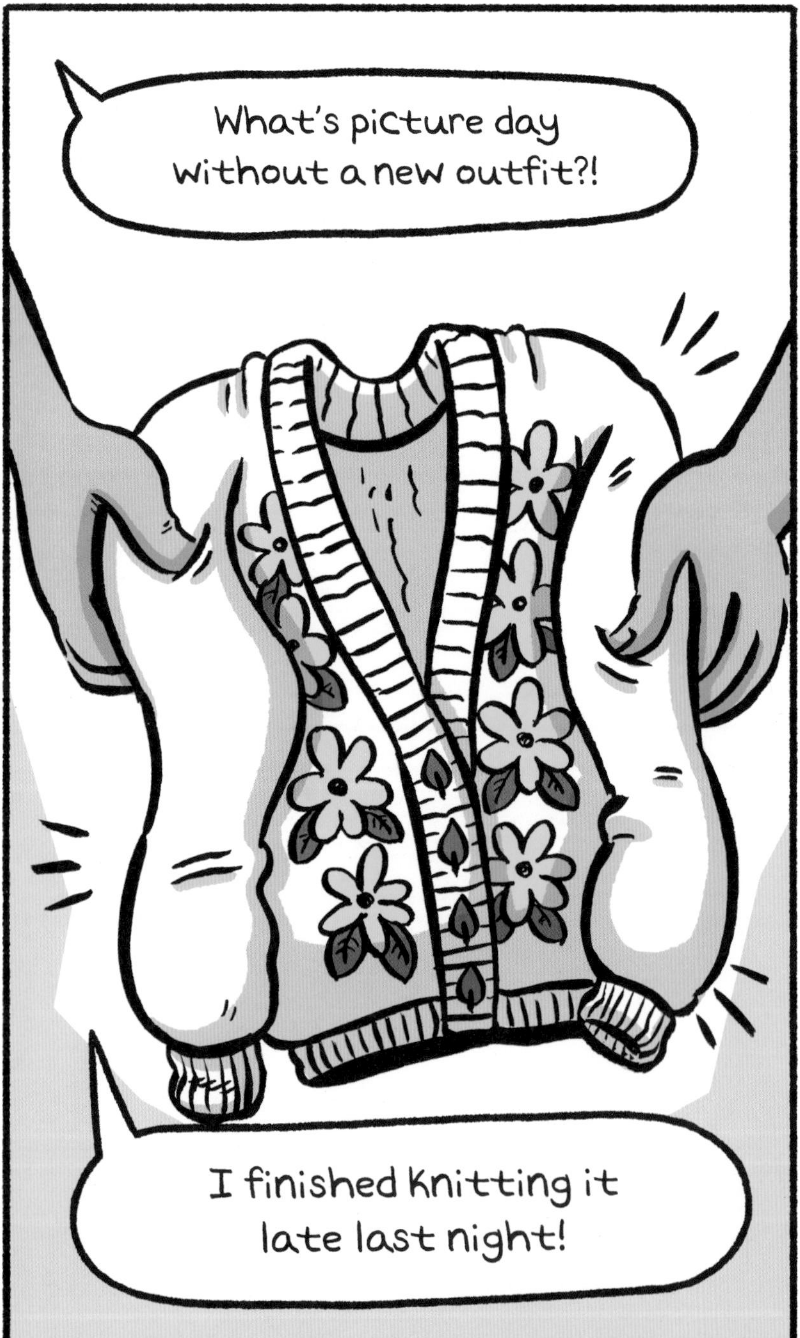
What's picture day without a new outfit?!
I finished knitting it late last night!

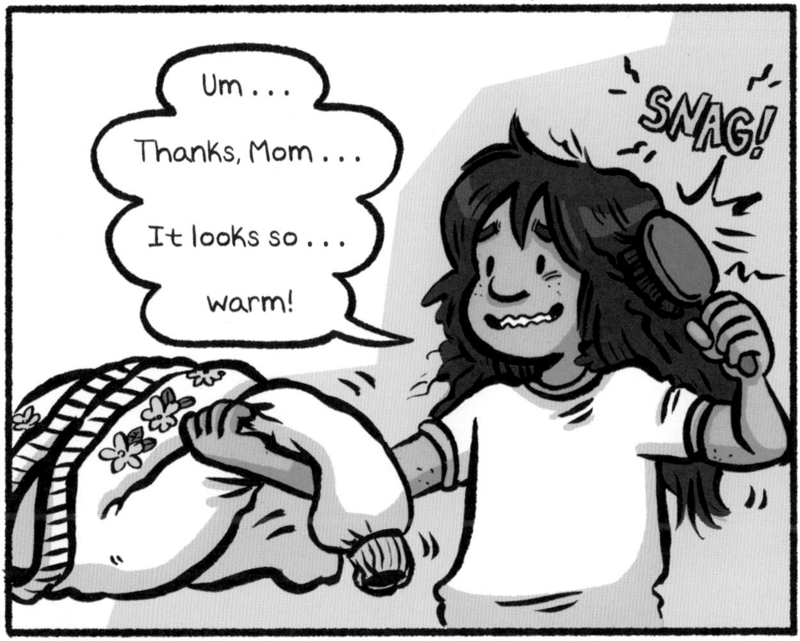
Um . . .
Thanks, Mom . . .
It looks so . . .
warm!
SNAG!

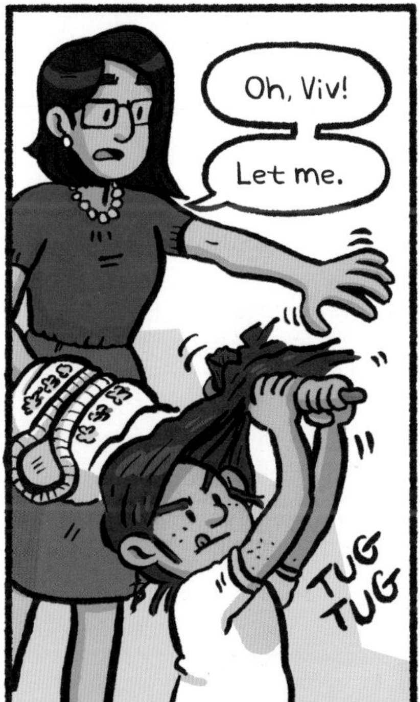
Oh, Viv!
Let me.
TUG
TUG

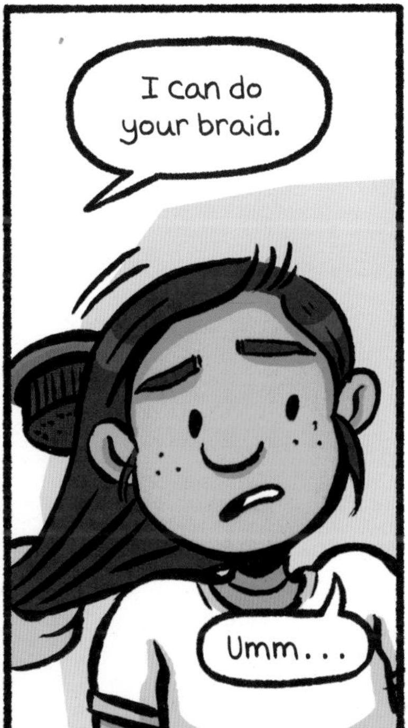
I can do your braid.
Umm . . .

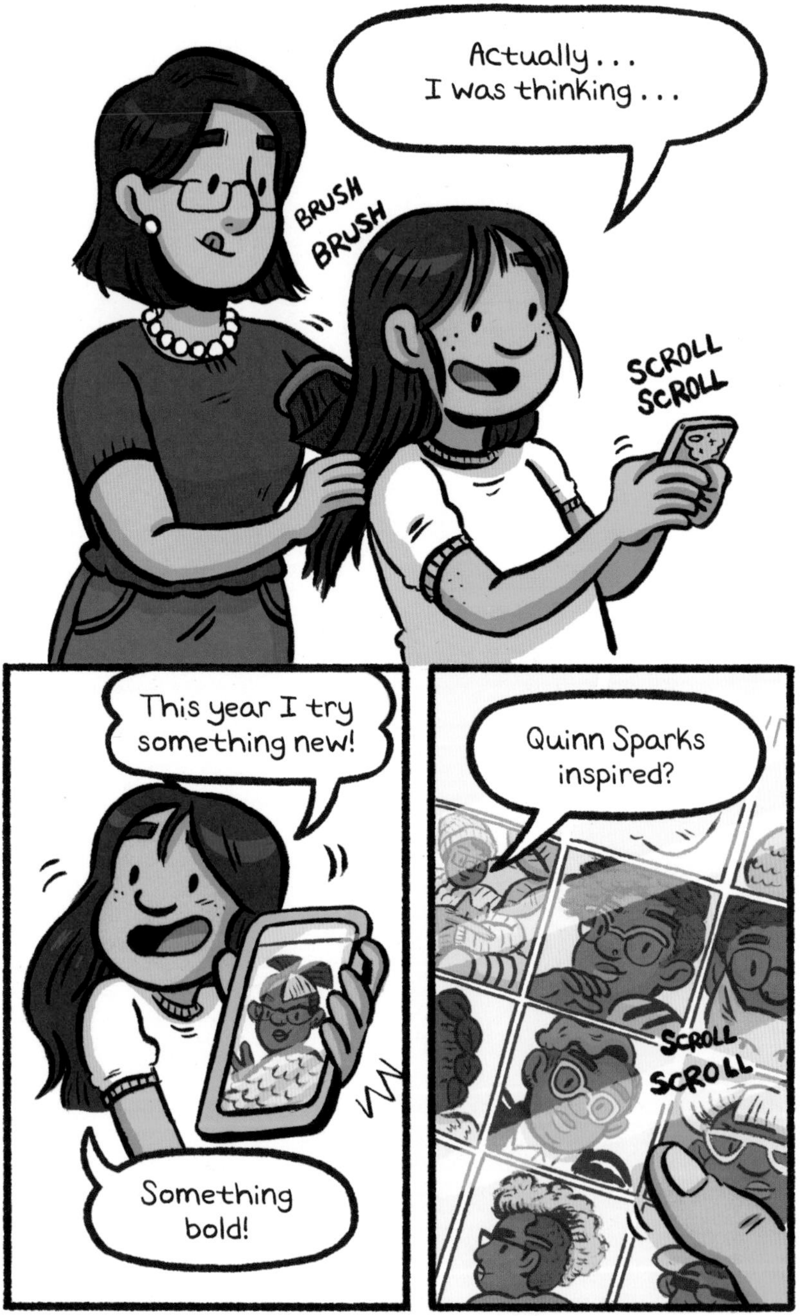
Actually . . .
I was thinking . . .
BRUSH
BRUSH
SCROLL
SCROLL
This year I try
something new!
Something
bold!
Quinn Sparks
inspired?
SCROLL
SCROLL

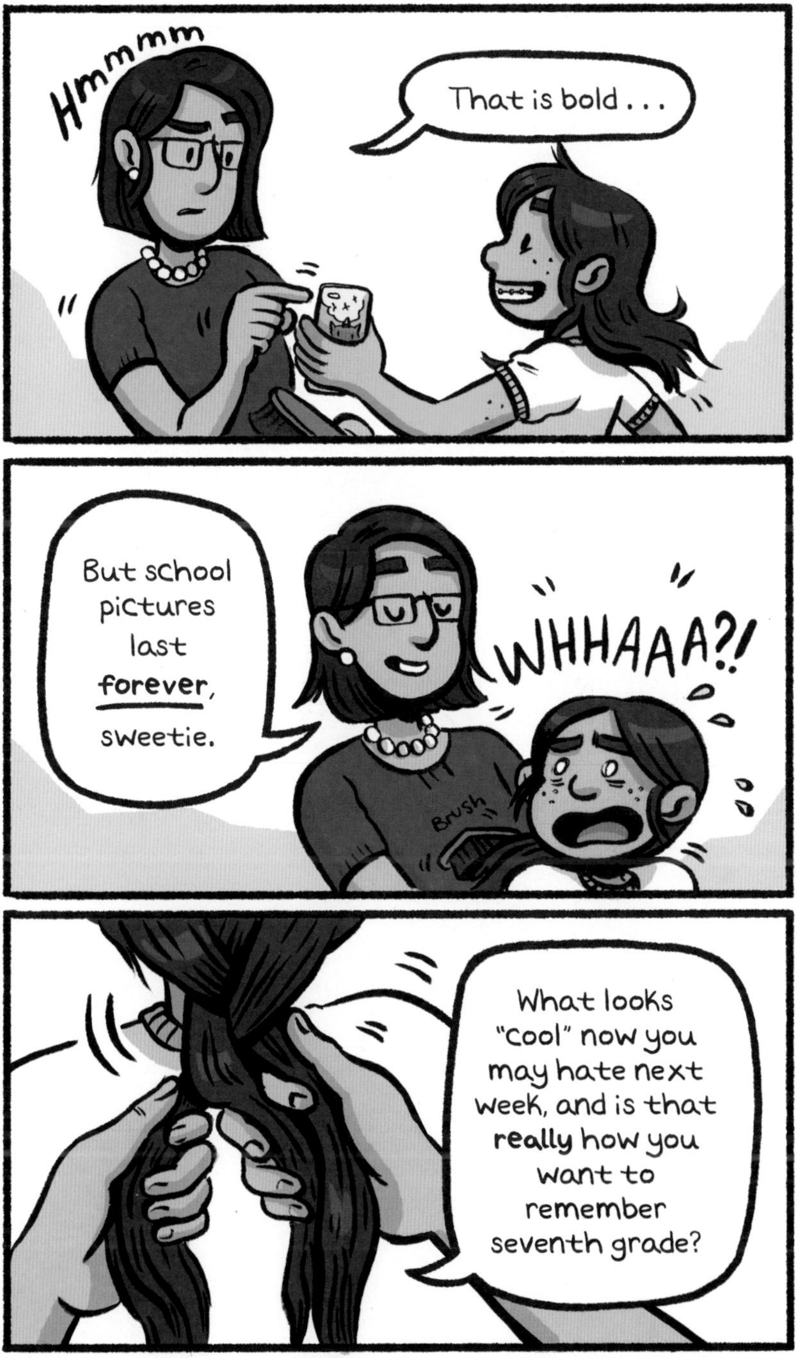
Hmmmmm
That is bold . . .
But school pictures last **forever**, sweetie.
WHHAAA?!
Brush
What looks "cool" now you may hate next week, and is that **really** how you want to remember seventh grade?

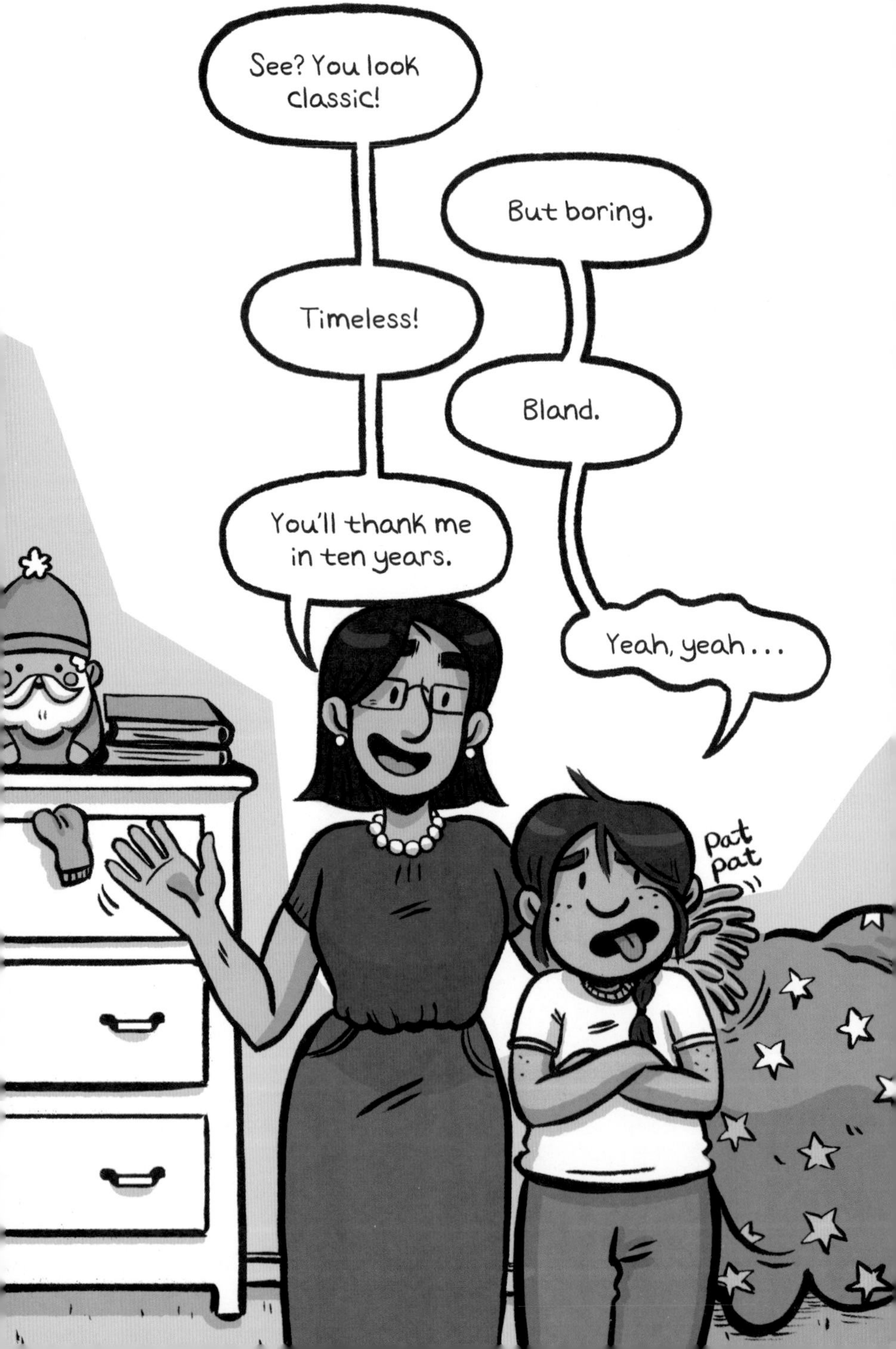
See? You look classic!
Timeless!
You'll thank me in ten years.
But boring.
Bland.
Yeah, yeah . . .
pat pat

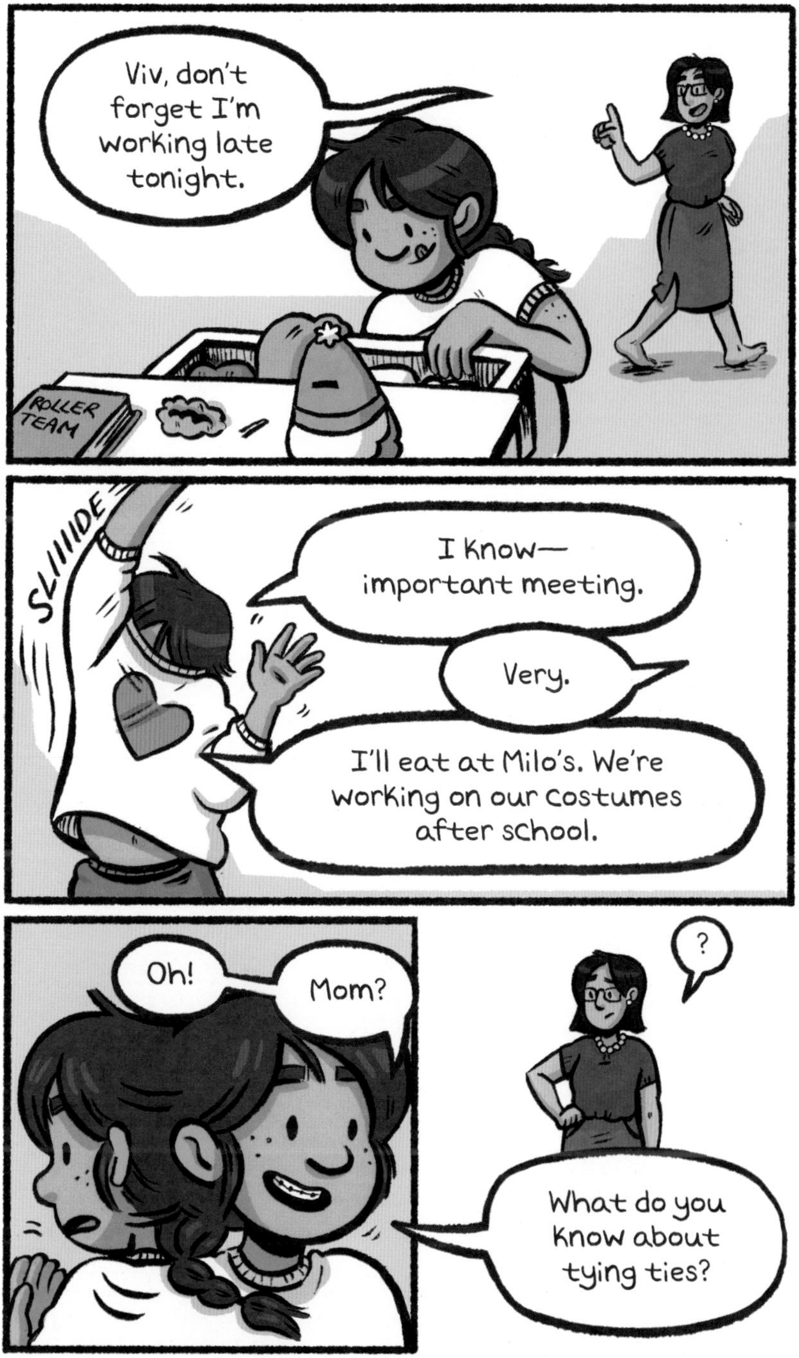
Viv, don't forget I'm working late tonight.
ROLLER TEAM
SLIIIIDE
I know— important meeting.
Very.
I'll eat at Milo's. We're working on our costumes after school.
Oh!
Mom?
?
What do you know about tying ties?

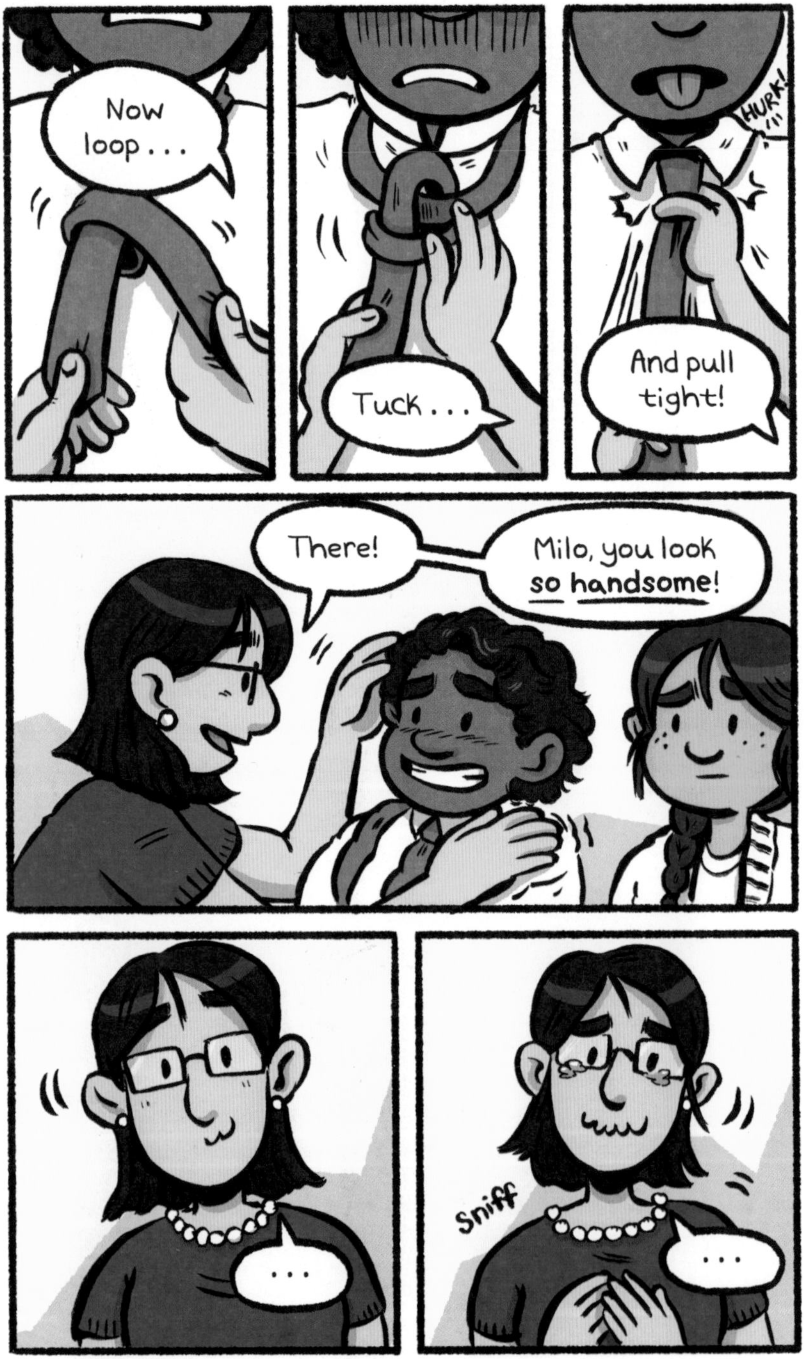
Now loop . . .
Tuck . . .
HURK!
And pull tight!
There!
Milo, you look so handsome!
Sniff
. . .
. . .

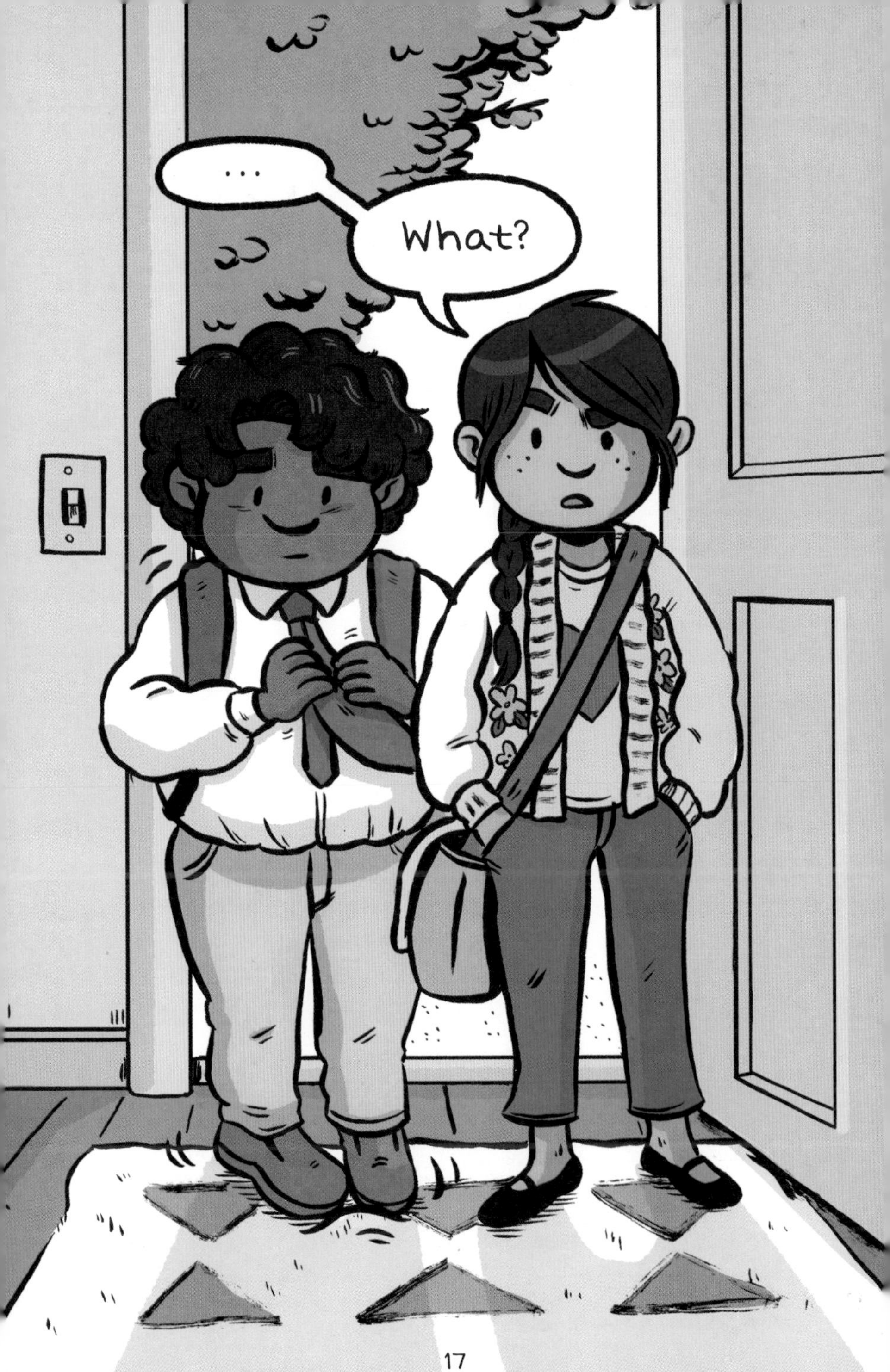
...
What?

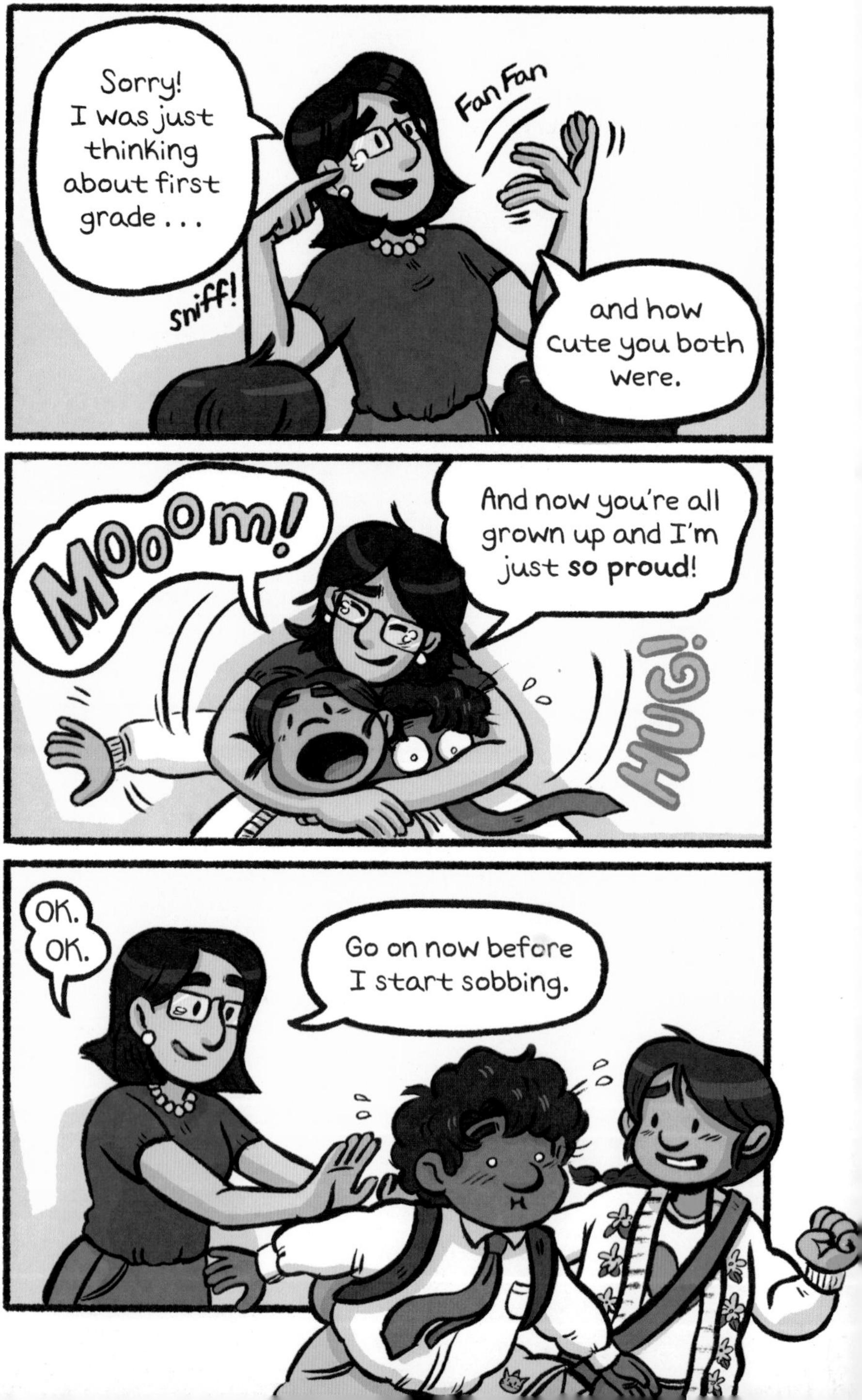
Sorry! I was just thinking about first grade . . .
Fan Fan
sniff!
and how cute you both were.
MOoOm!
And now you're all grown up and I'm just **so proud!**
HUG!
OK. OK.
Go on now before I start sobbing.

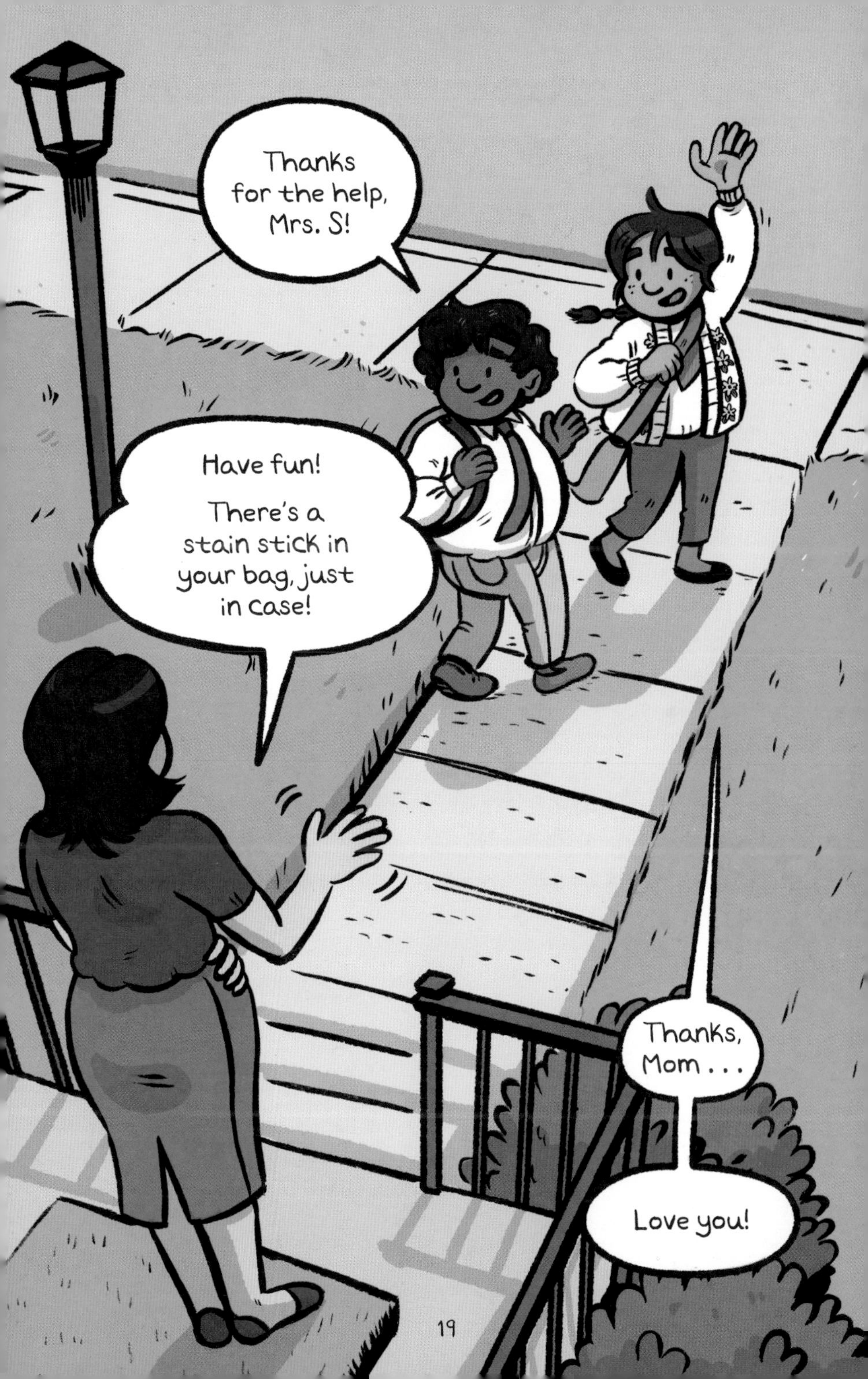
Thanks for the help, Mrs. S!
Have fun!
There's a stain stick in your bag, just in case!
Thanks, Mom . . .
Love you!

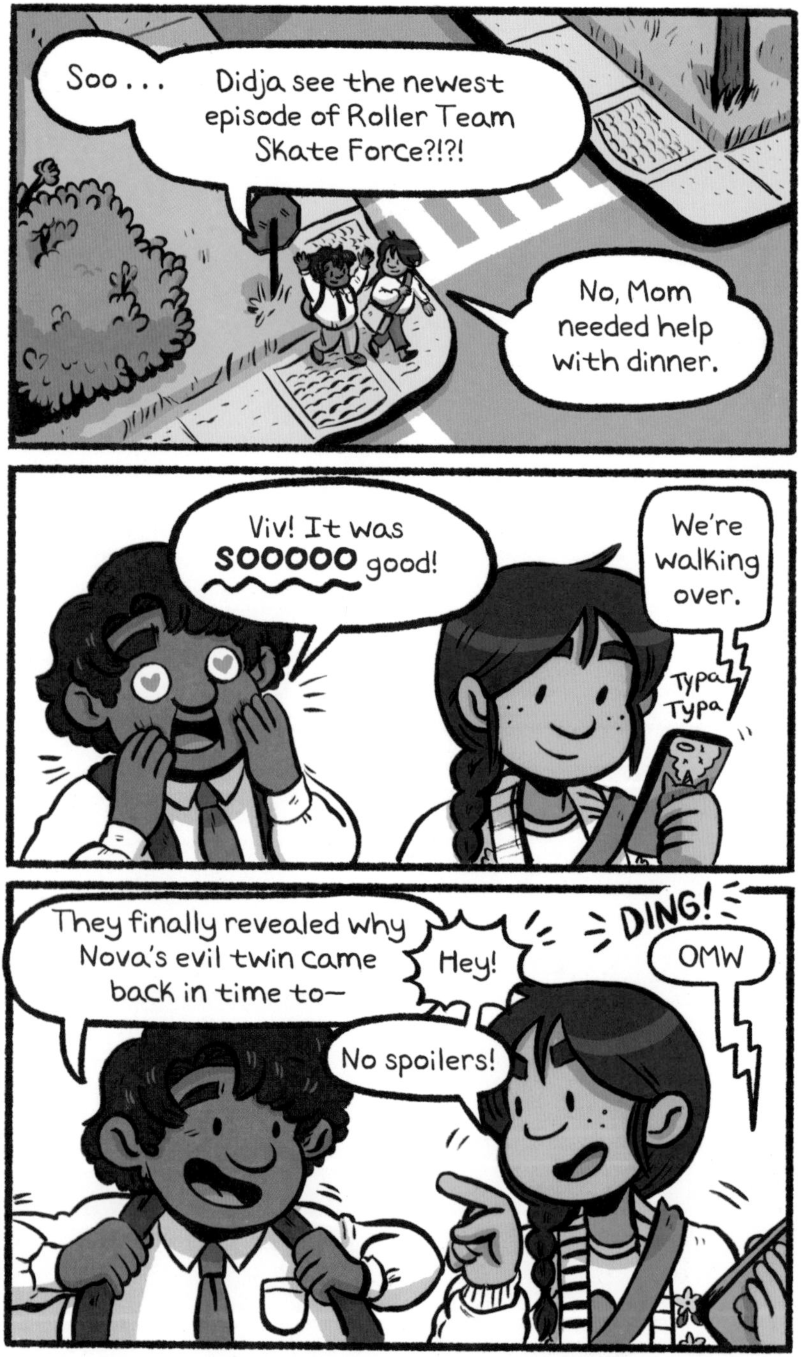

Soo . . .
Didja see the newest episode of Roller Team Skate Force?!?!
No, Mom needed help with dinner.
Viv! It was SOOOOO good!
We're walking over.
Typa Typa
They finally revealed why Nova's evil twin came back in time to—
Hey!
DING!
OMW
No spoilers!

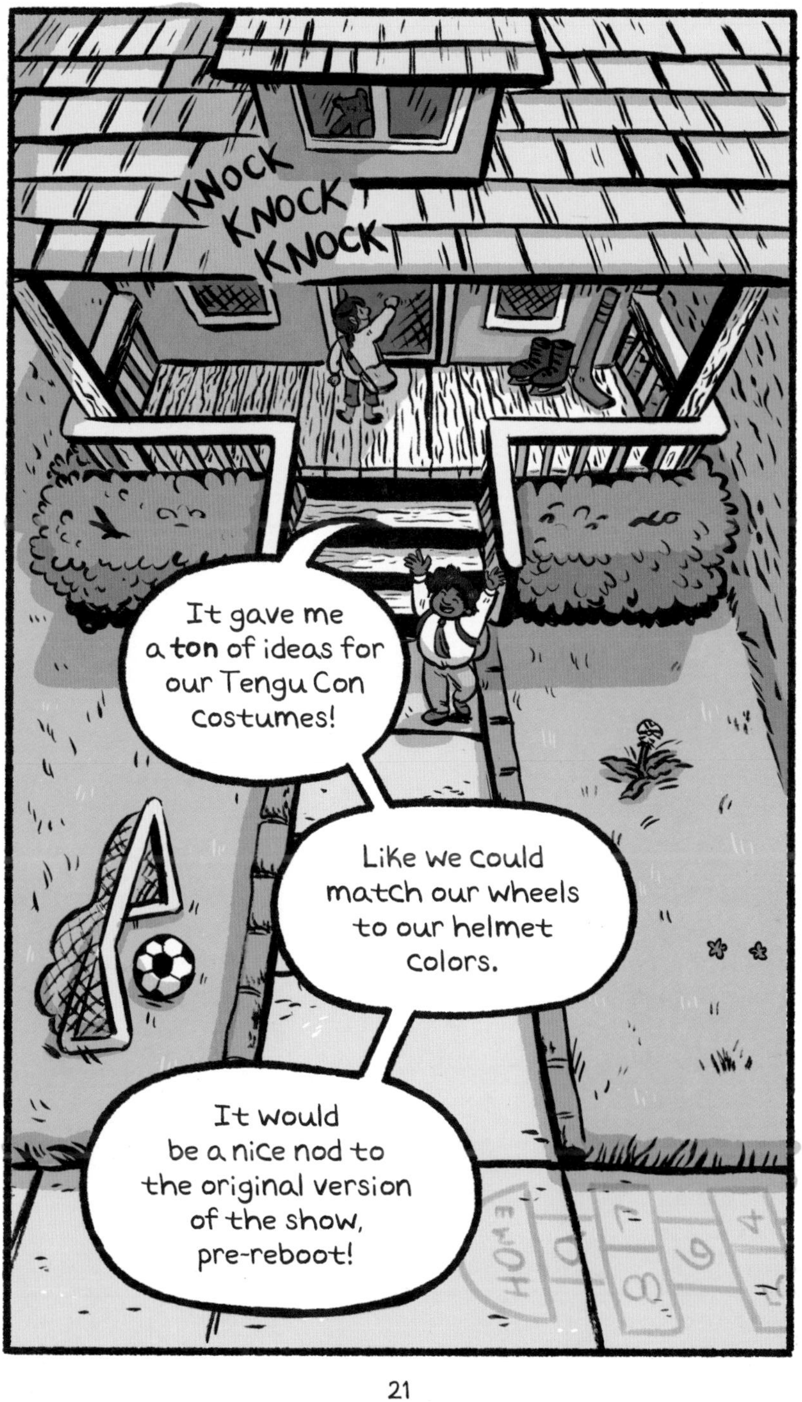
KNOCK
KNOCK
KNOCK
It gave me a **ton** of ideas for our Tengu Con costumes!
Like we could match our wheels to our helmet colors.
It would be a nice nod to the original version of the show, pre-reboot!

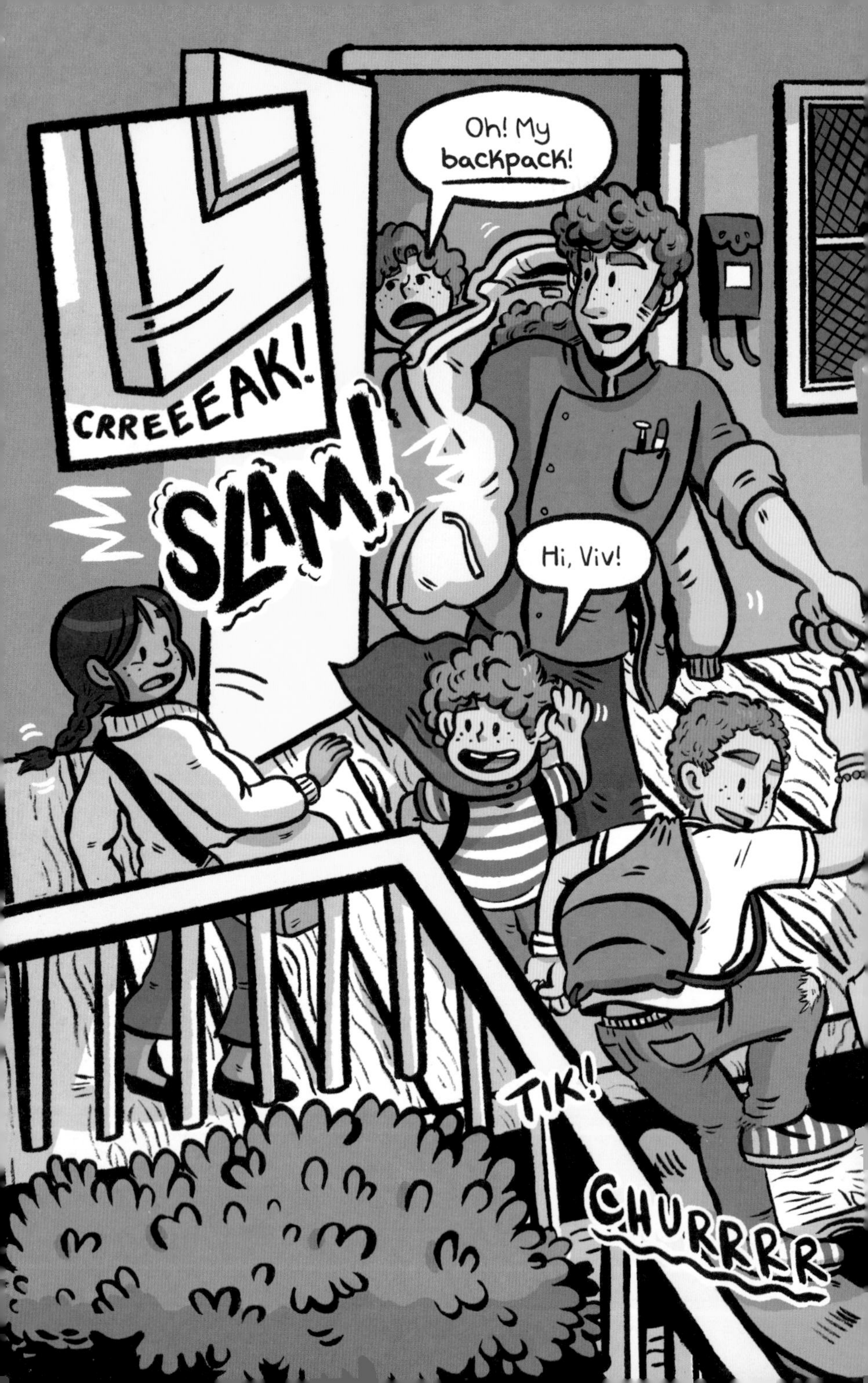
CRREEEAK!
SLAM!
Oh! My backpack!
Hi, Viv!
TIK!
CHURRRRR

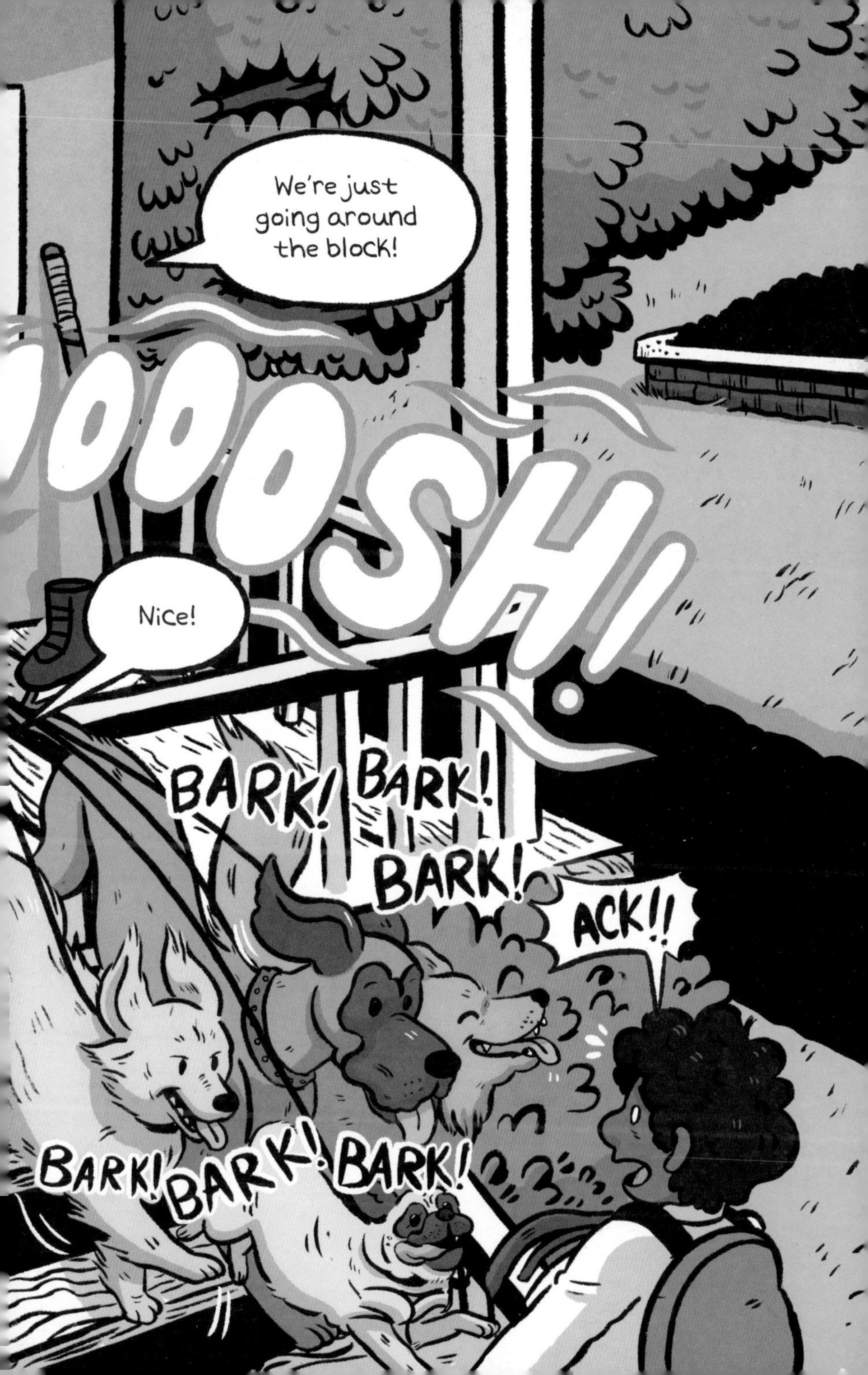
We're just going around the block!
OOOOSH!
Nice!
BARK! BARK!
BARK!
ACK!!
BARK! BARK! BARK!

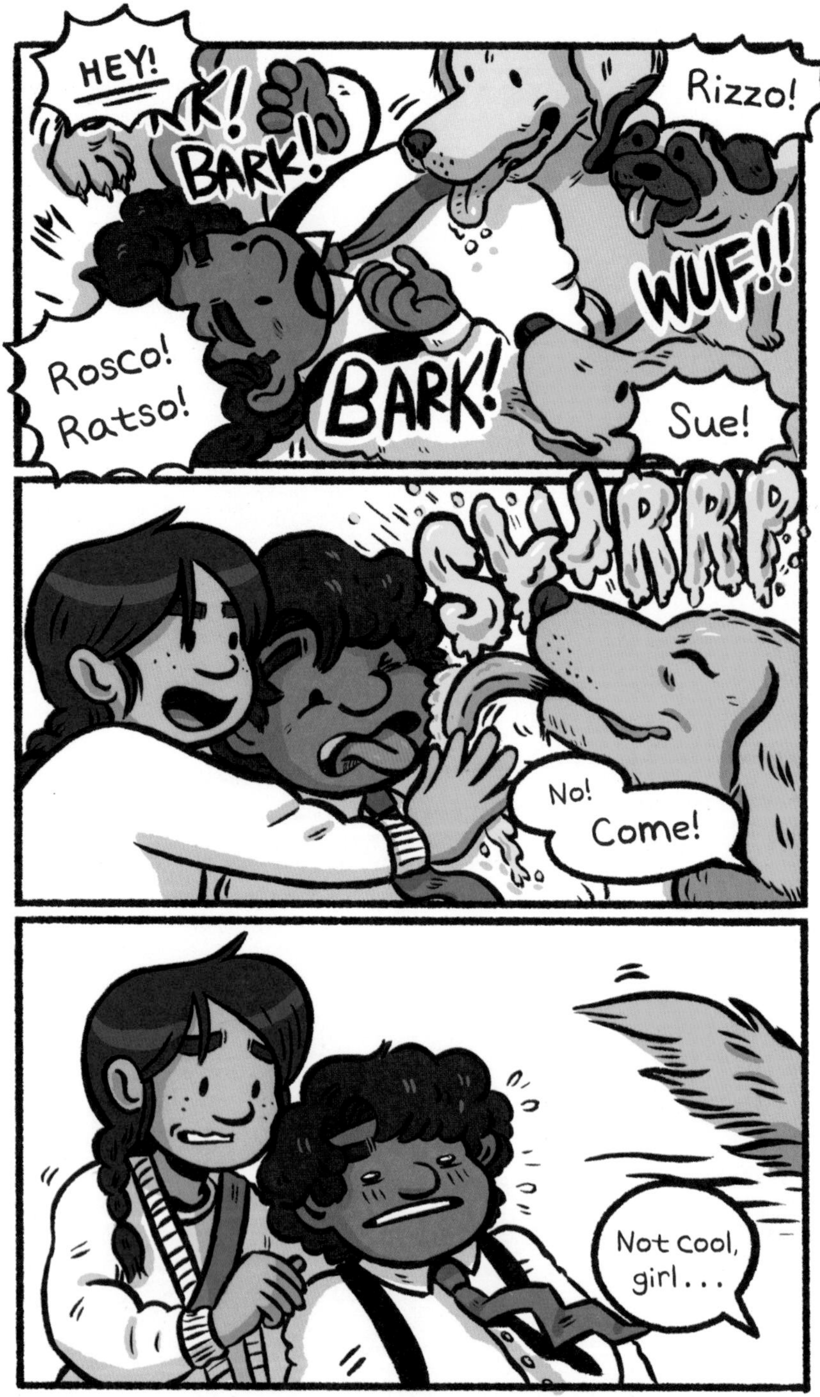
HEY!
...K!
BARK!
Rizzo!
WUF!!
Rosco!
Ratso!
BARK!
Sue!
SLURRP
No!
Come!
Not cool,
girl...

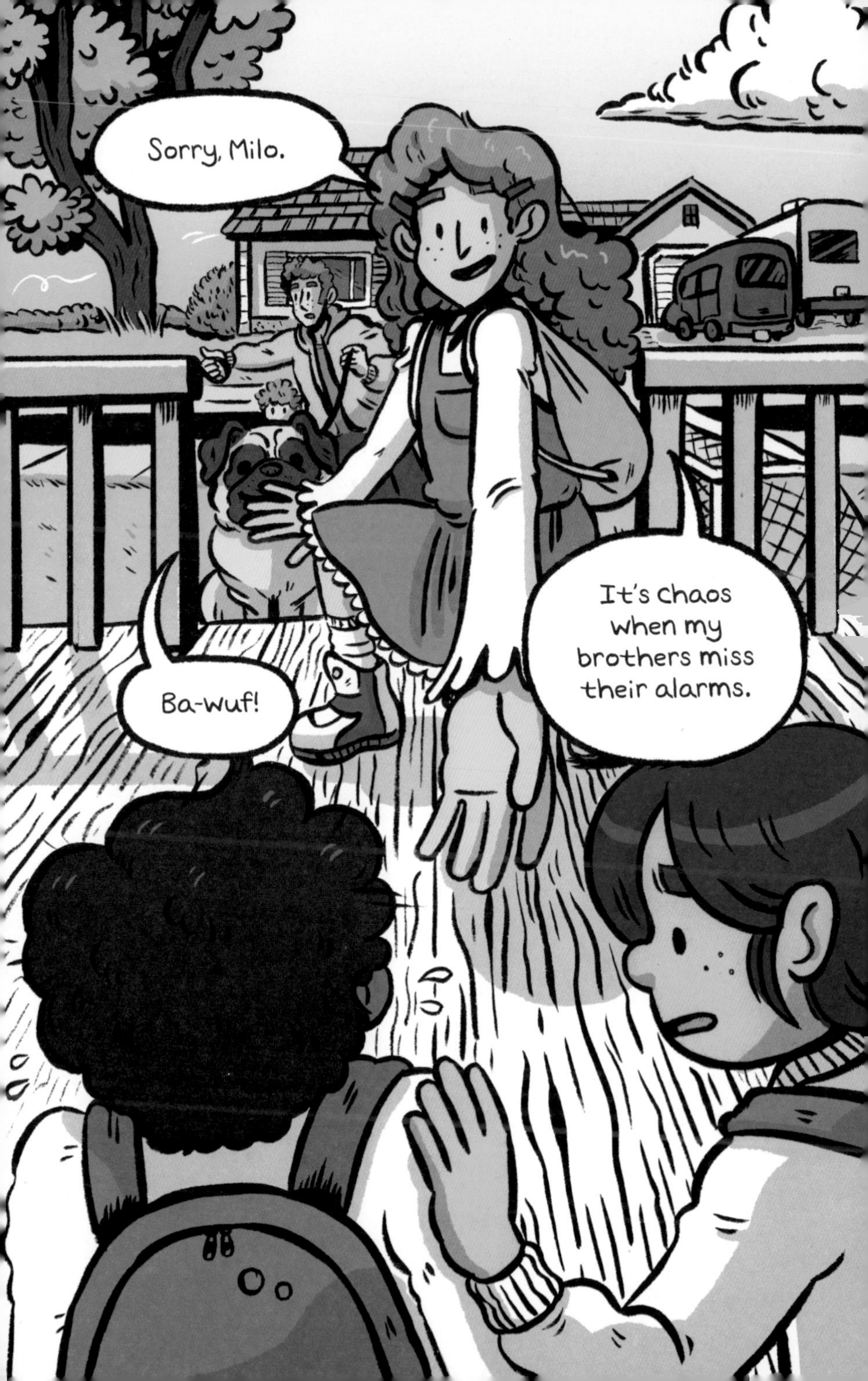
Sorry, Milo.
Ba-wuf!
It's chaos when my brothers miss their alarms.

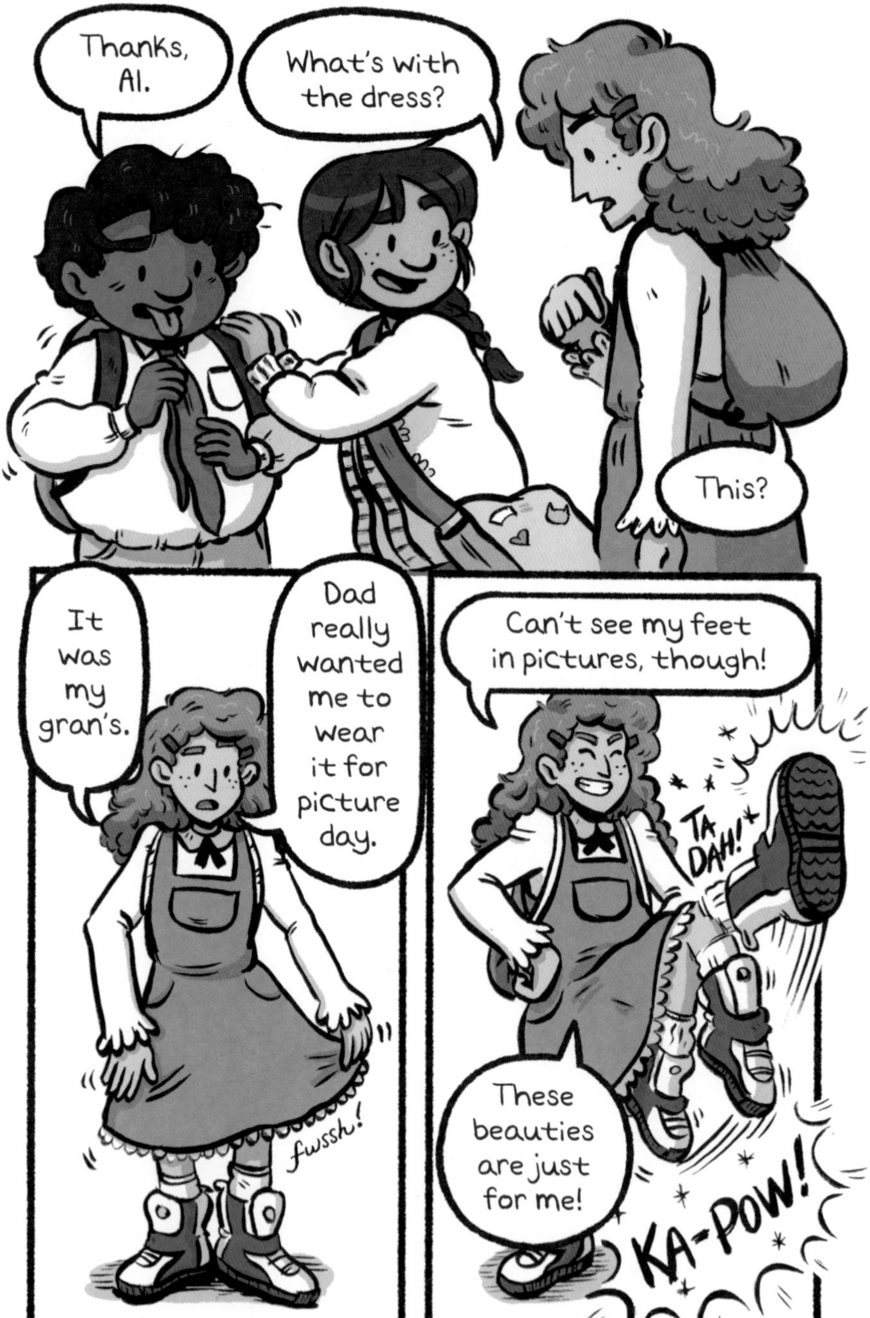

Thanks, Al.
What's with the dress?
This?
It was my gran's.
Dad really wanted me to wear it for picture day.
fwssh!
Can't see my feet in pictures, though!
TA DAH!
These beauties are just for me!
KA-POW!

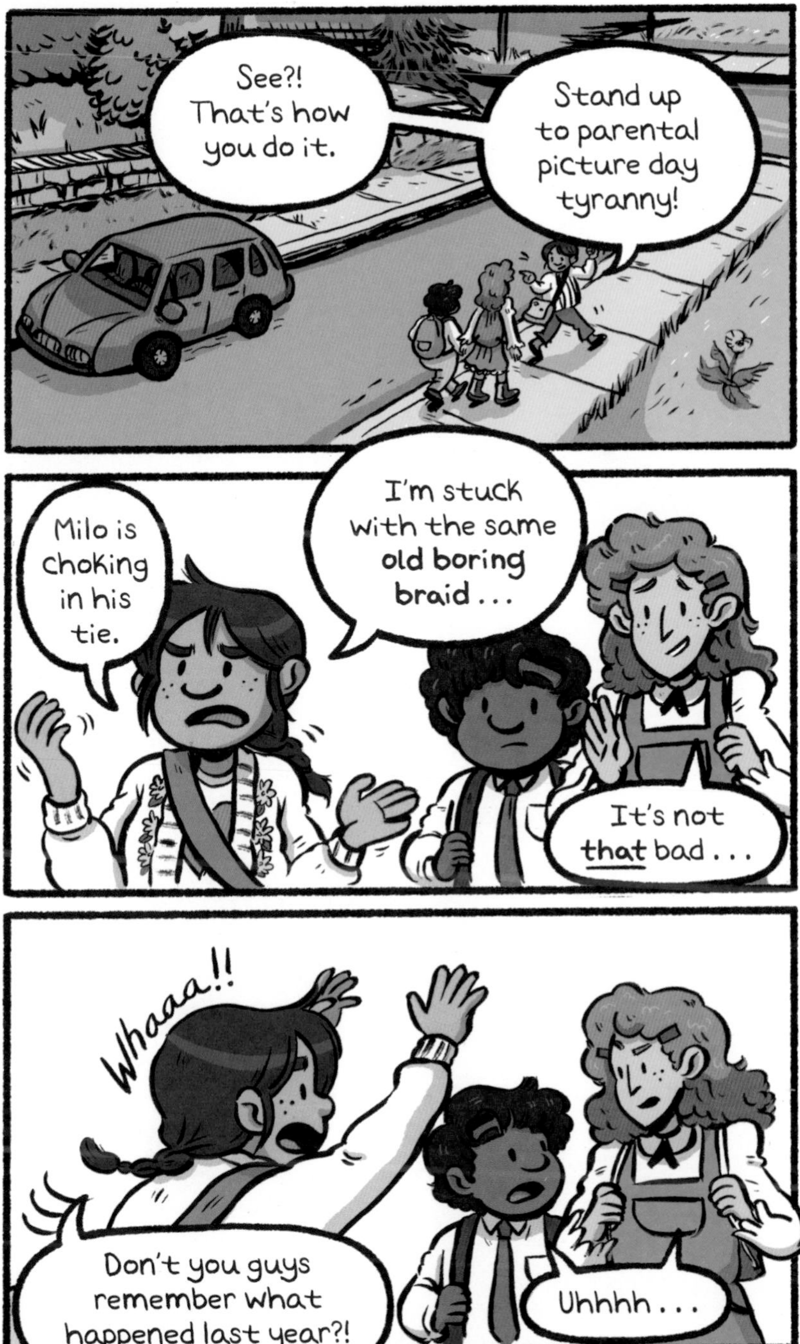
See?! That's how you do it.
Stand up to parental picture day tyranny!
Milo is choking in his tie.
I'm stuck with the same **old boring braid** . . .
It's not that bad . . .
Whaaa!!
Don't you guys remember what happened last year?!
Uhhhh . . .

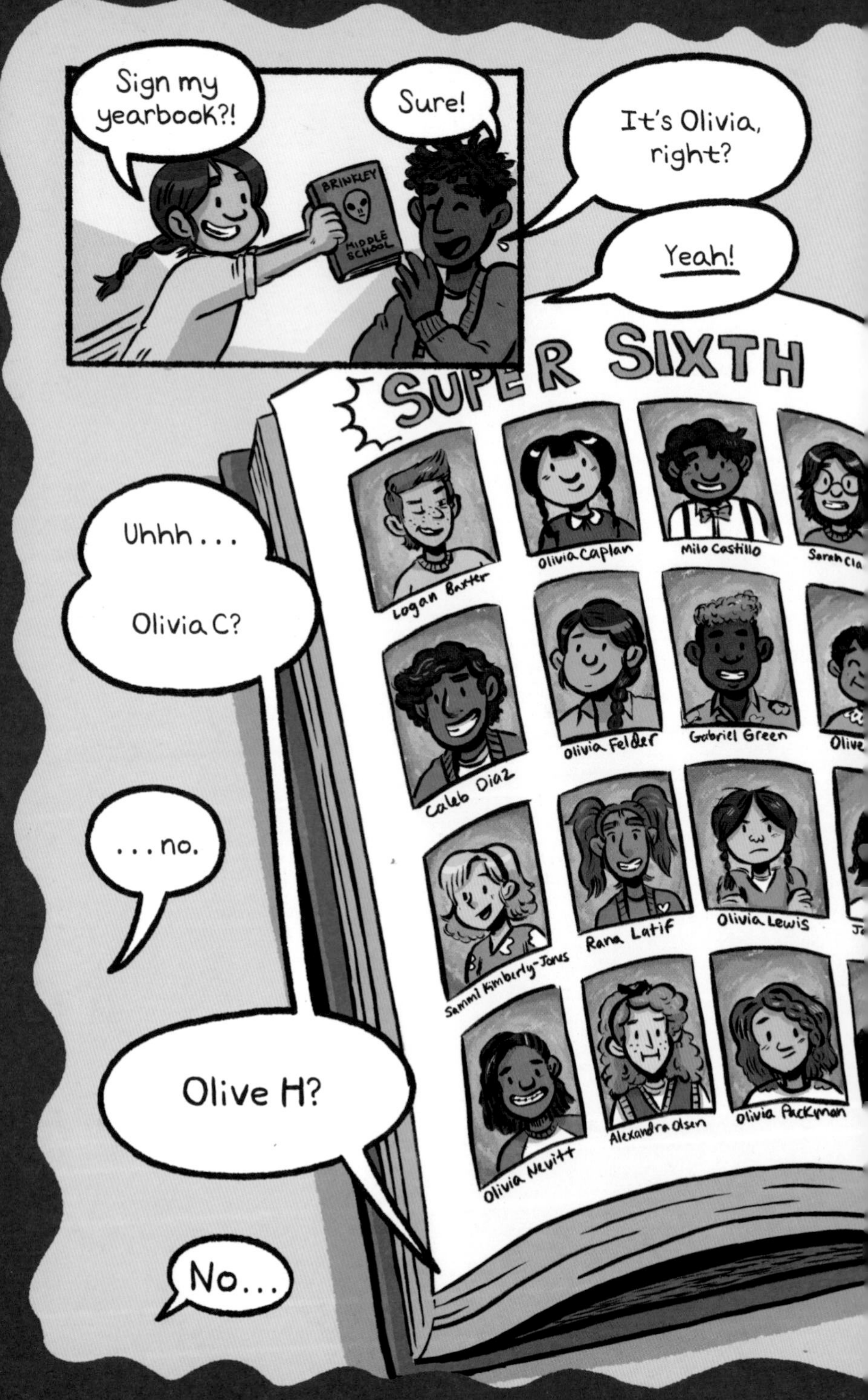

Sign my yearbook?!
BRINKLEY MIDDLE SCHOOL
Sure!
It's Olivia, right?
Yeah!
SUPER SIXTH
Logan Baxter
Olivia Caplan
Milo Castillo
Caleb Diaz
Olivia Felder
Gabriel Green
Sammi Kimberly-Jones
Rana Latif
Olivia Lewis
Olivia Nevitt
Alexandra Olsen
Olivia Packman
Uhhh . . .
Olivia C?
. . . no.
Olive H?
No . . .

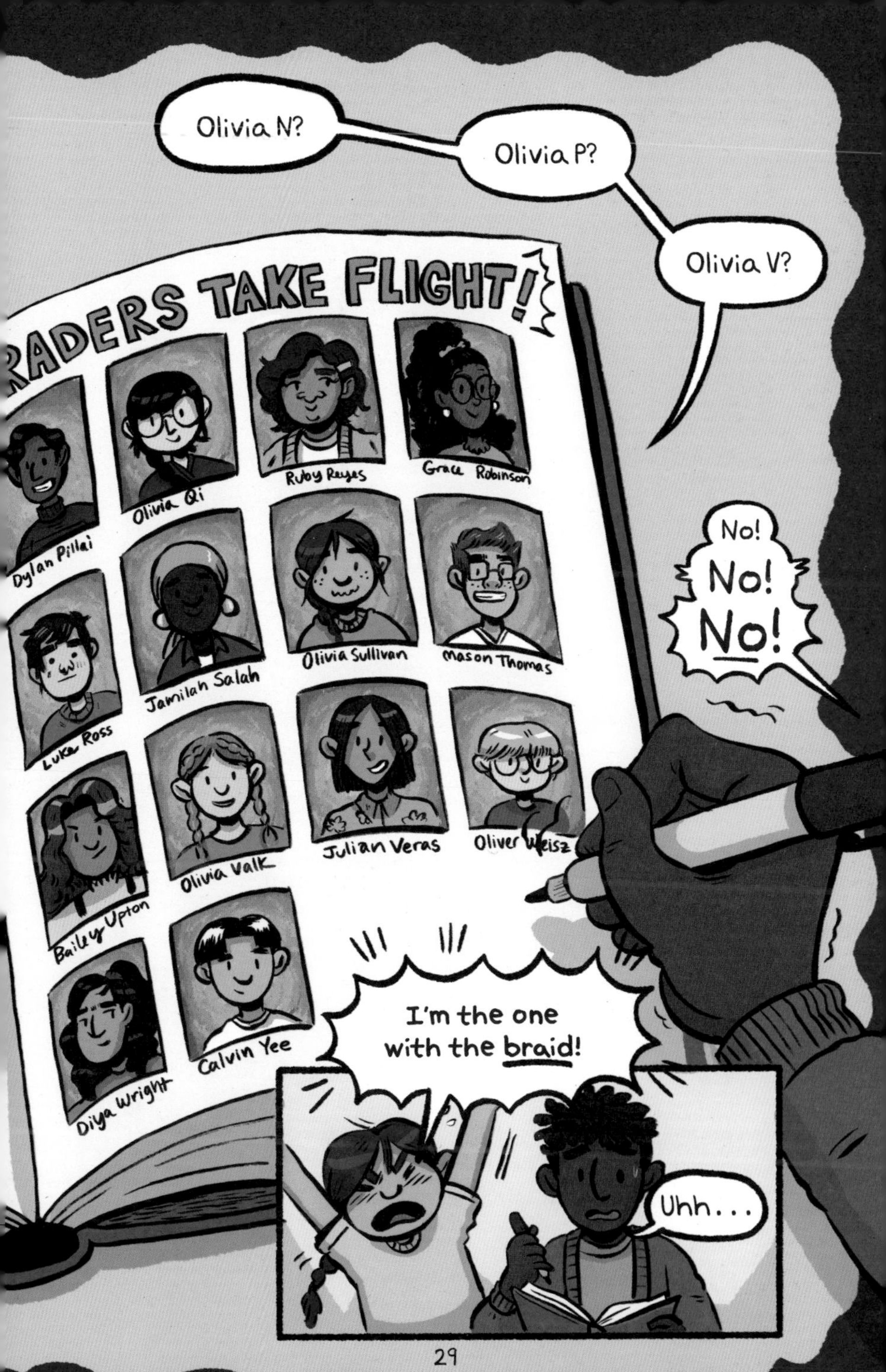
Olivia N?
Olivia P?
Olivia V?
RADERS TAKE FLIGHT!
Dylan Pillai
Olivia Qi
Ruby Reyes
Grace Robinson
Luka Ross
Jamilah Salah
Olivia Sullivan
Mason Thomas
Bailey Upton
Olivia Valk
Julian Veras
Oliver Weisz
Diya Wright
Calvin Yee
No! No! No!
I'm the one with the braid!
Uhh...

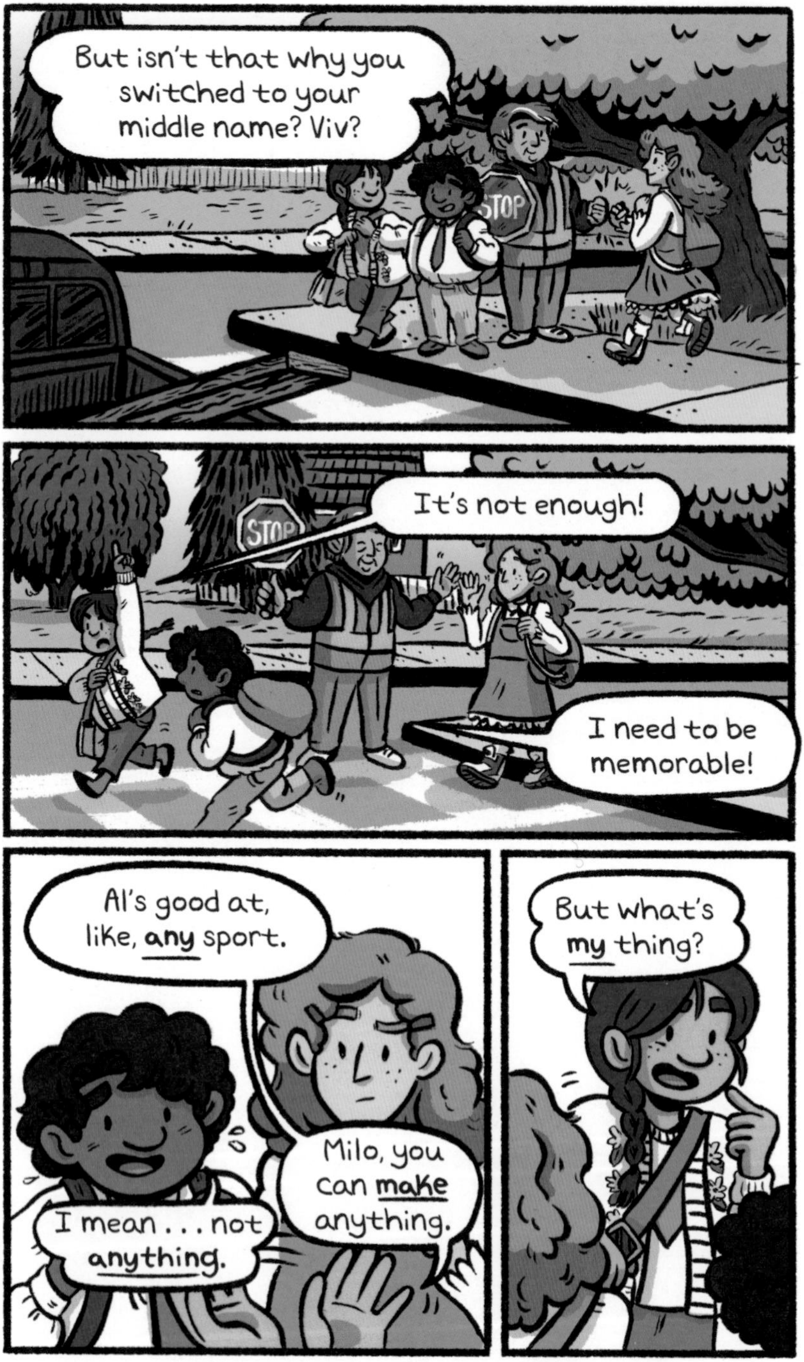
But isn't that why you switched to your middle name? Viv?
STOP
It's not enough!
STOP
I need to be memorable!
Al's good at, like, any sport.
Milo, you can make anything.
I mean . . . not anything.
But what's my thing?

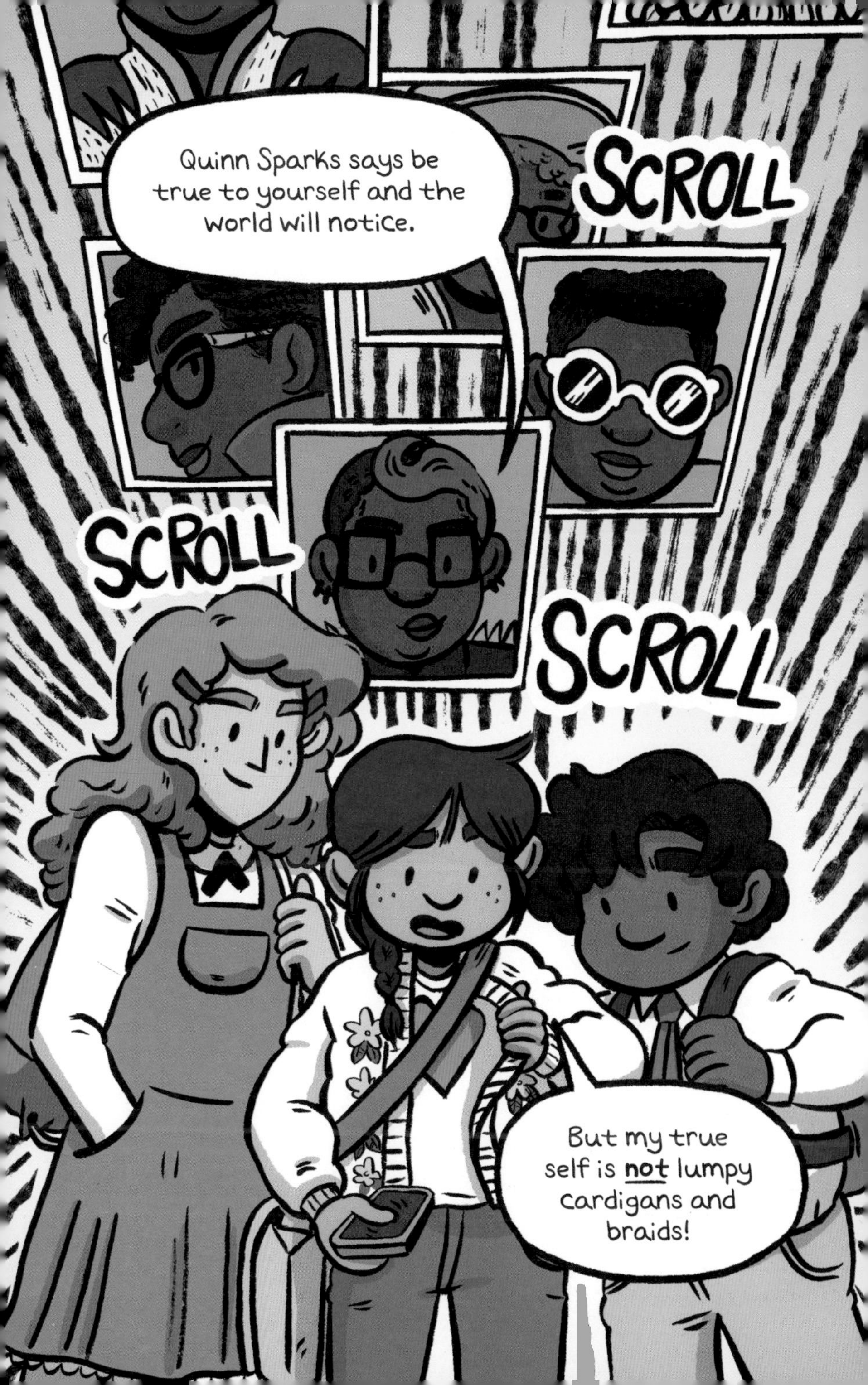
Quinn Sparks says be true to yourself and the world will notice.
SCROLL
SCROLL
SCROLL
But my true self is not lumpy cardigans and braids!

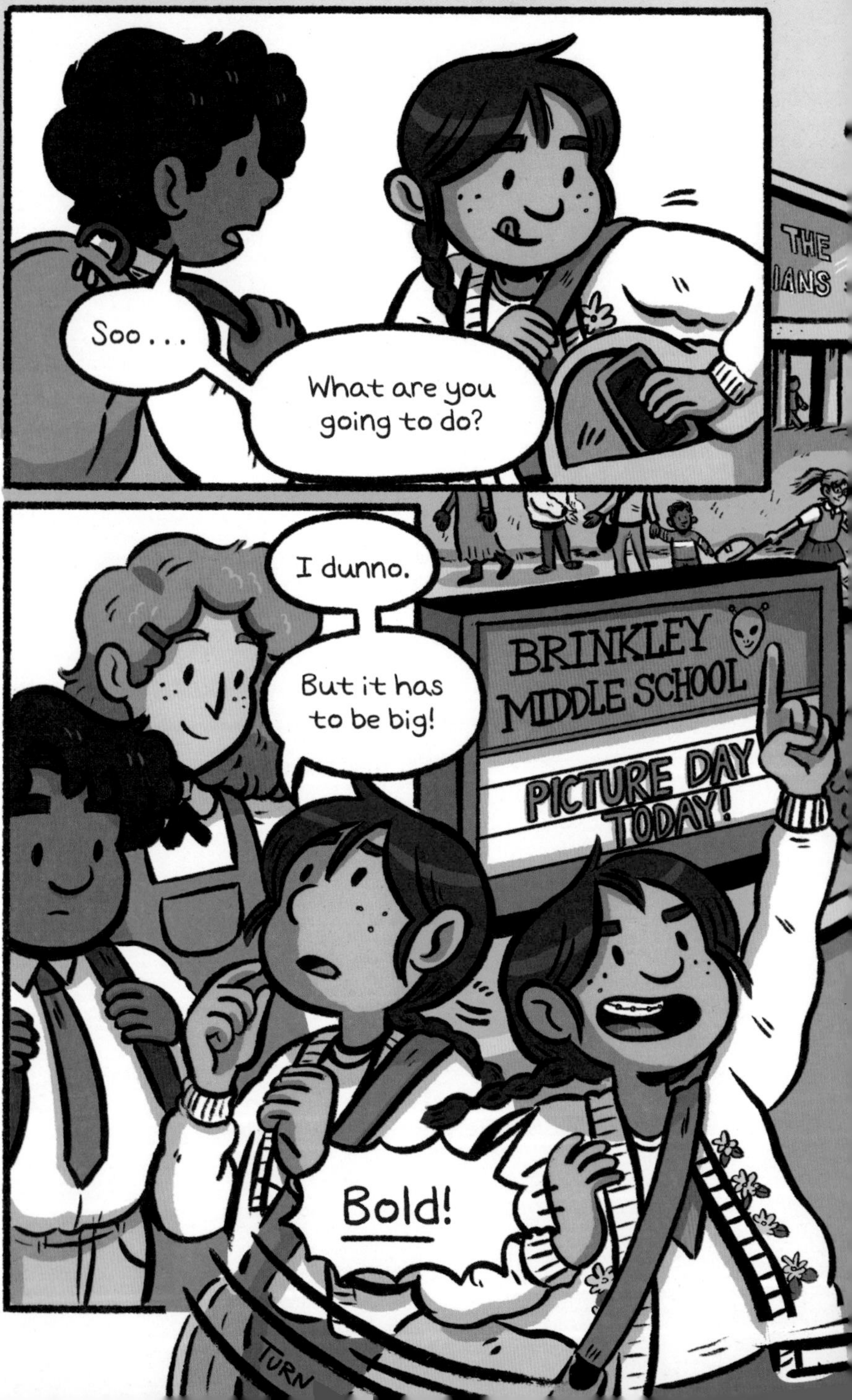
THE
IANS
Soo . . .
What are you going to do?
I dunno.
But it has to be big!
BRINKLEY MIDDLE SCHOOL
PICTURE DAY TODAY!
Bold!
TURN

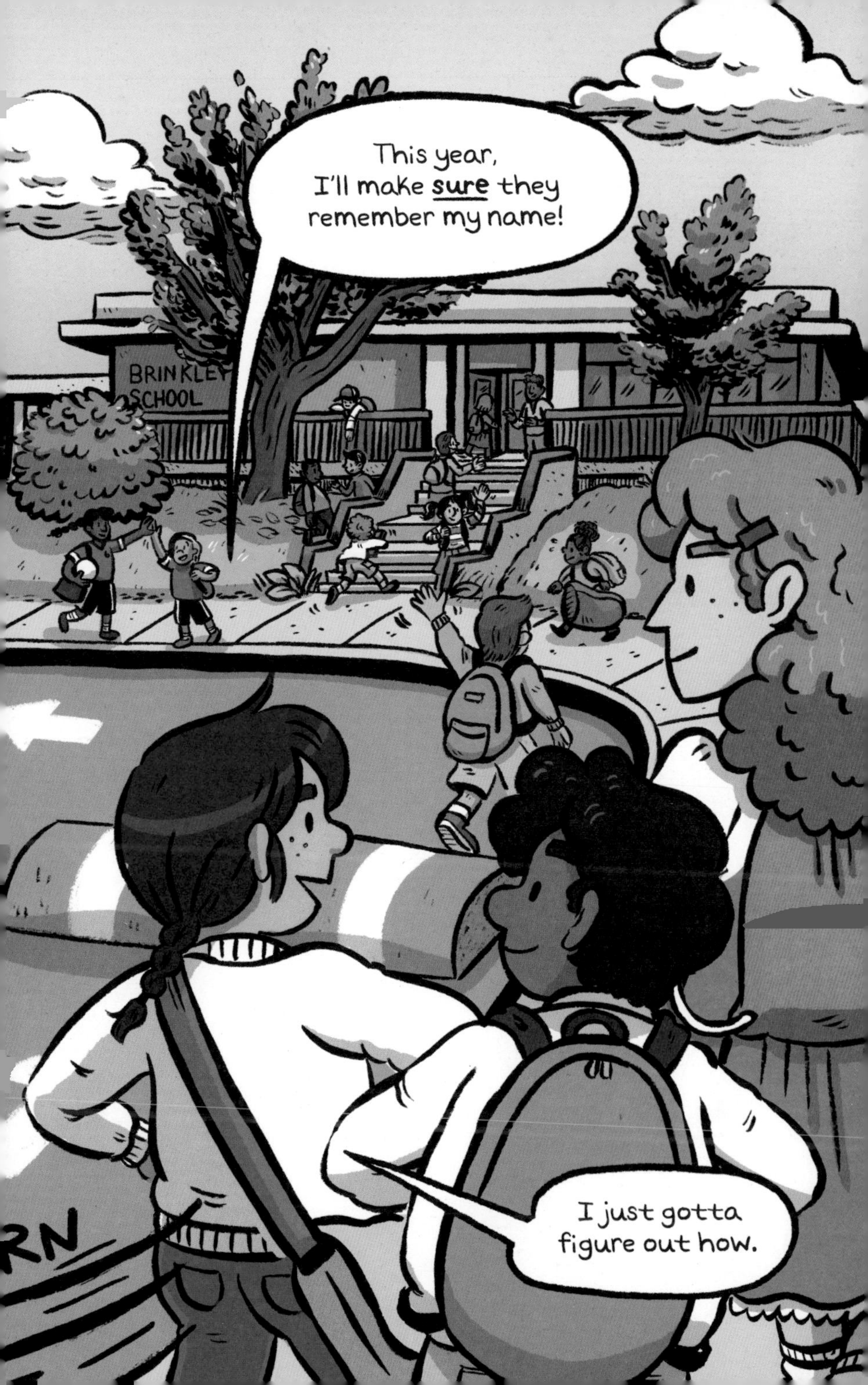
This year, I'll make **sure** they remember my name!
I just gotta figure out how.
BRINKLEY SCHOOL

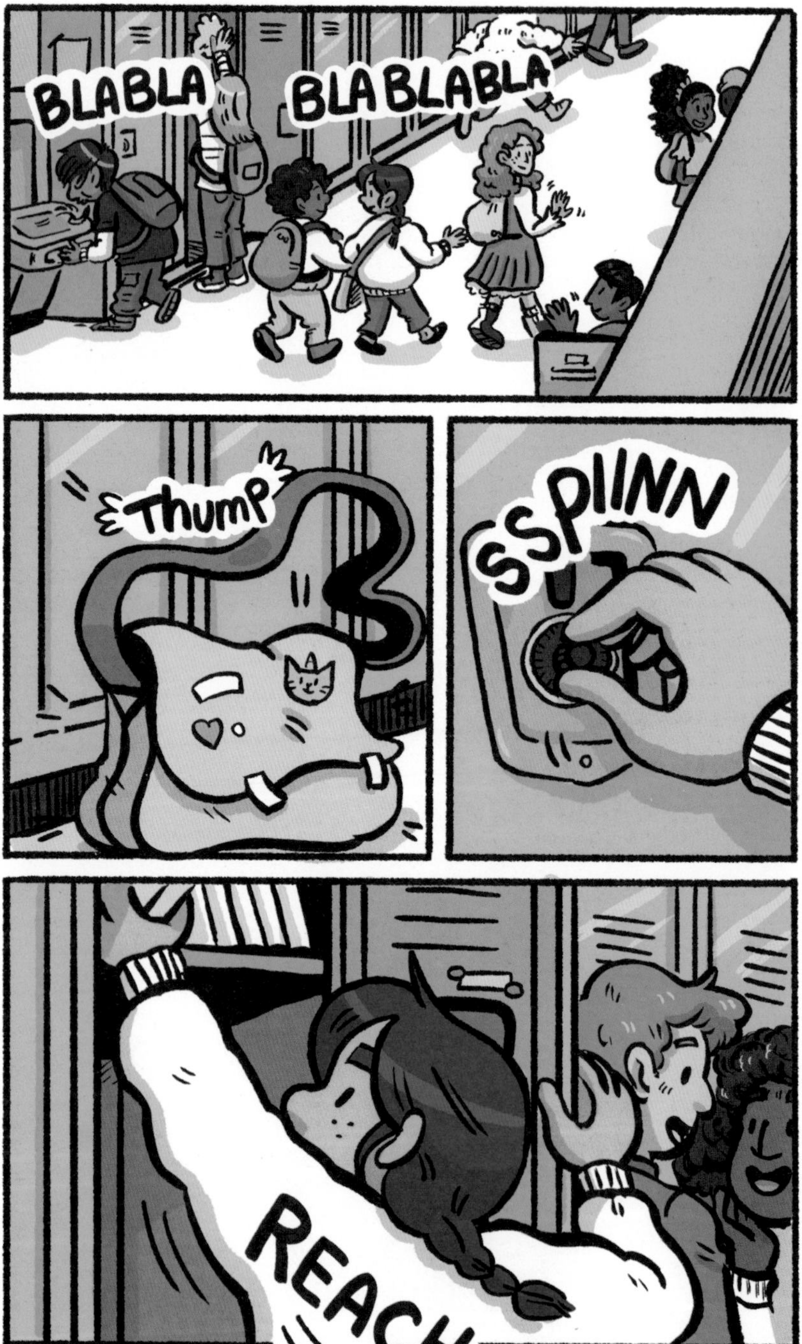
BLABLA
BLABLABLA
Thump
SSPIINN
REACH

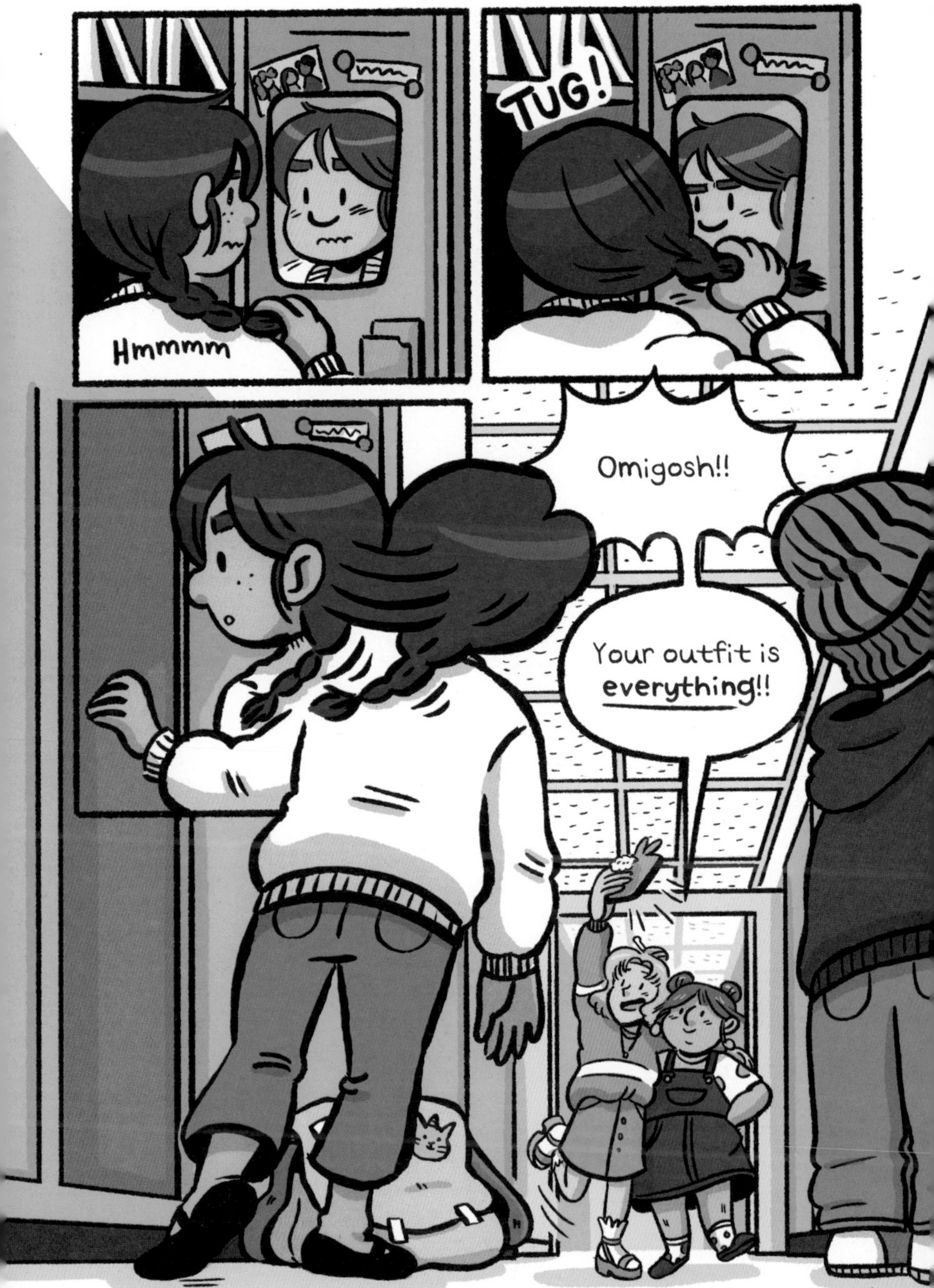
Hmmmm
TUG!
Omigosh!!
Your outfit is everything!!

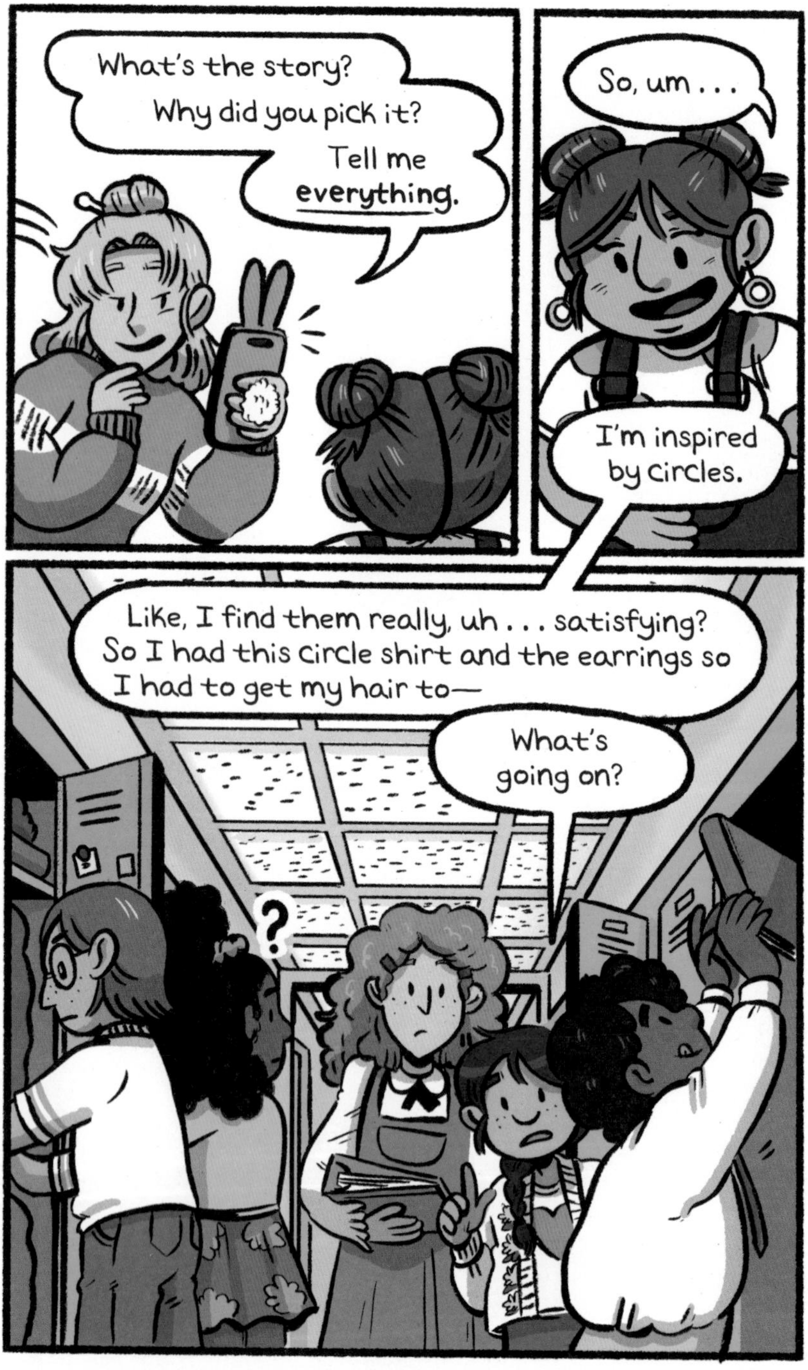
What's the story?
Why did you pick it?
Tell me everything.
So, um . . .
I'm inspired by circles.
Like, I find them really, uh . . . satisfying? So I had this circle shirt and the earrings so I had to get my hair to—
What's going on?
?

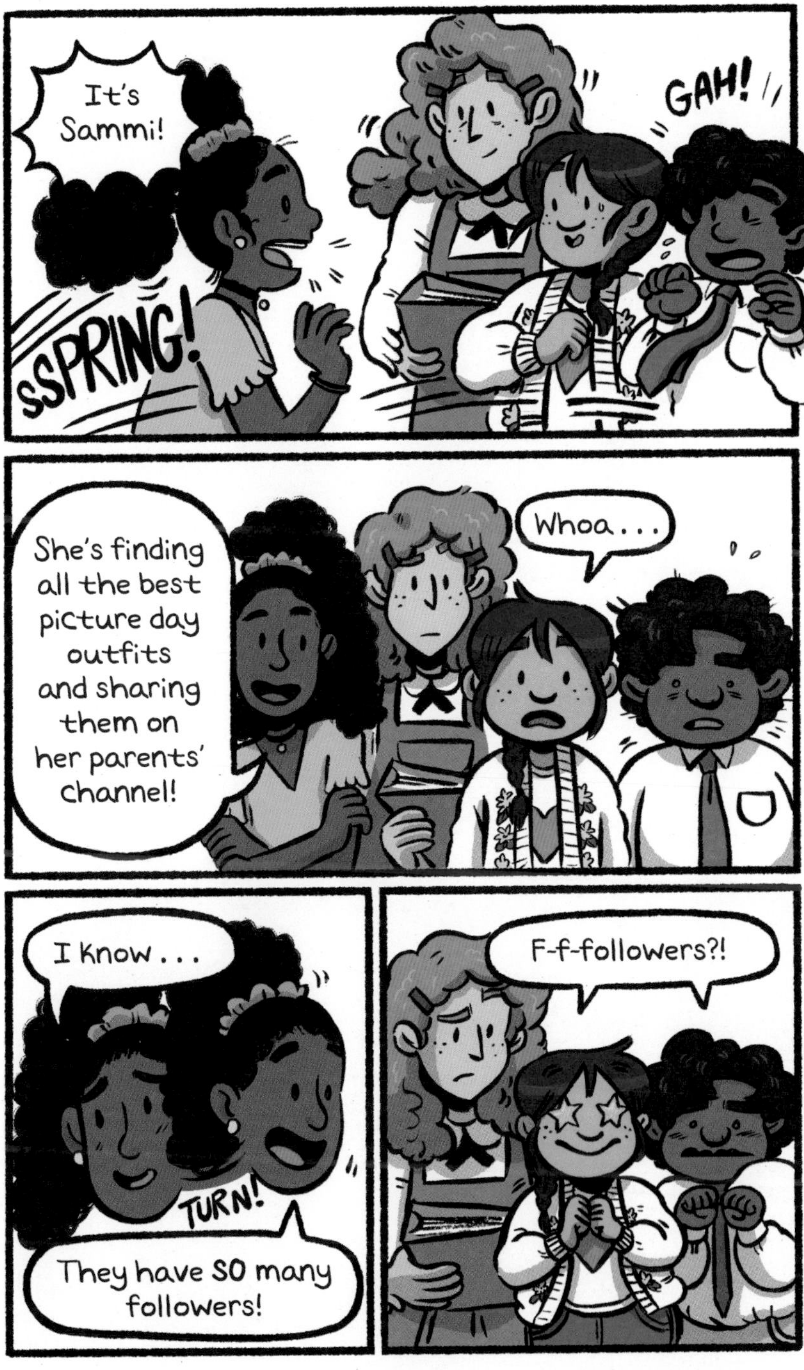
It's Sammi!
GAH!
sSPRING!
She's finding all the best picture day outfits and sharing them on her parents' channel!
Whoa...
I know...
TURN!
They have SO many followers!
F-f-followers?!

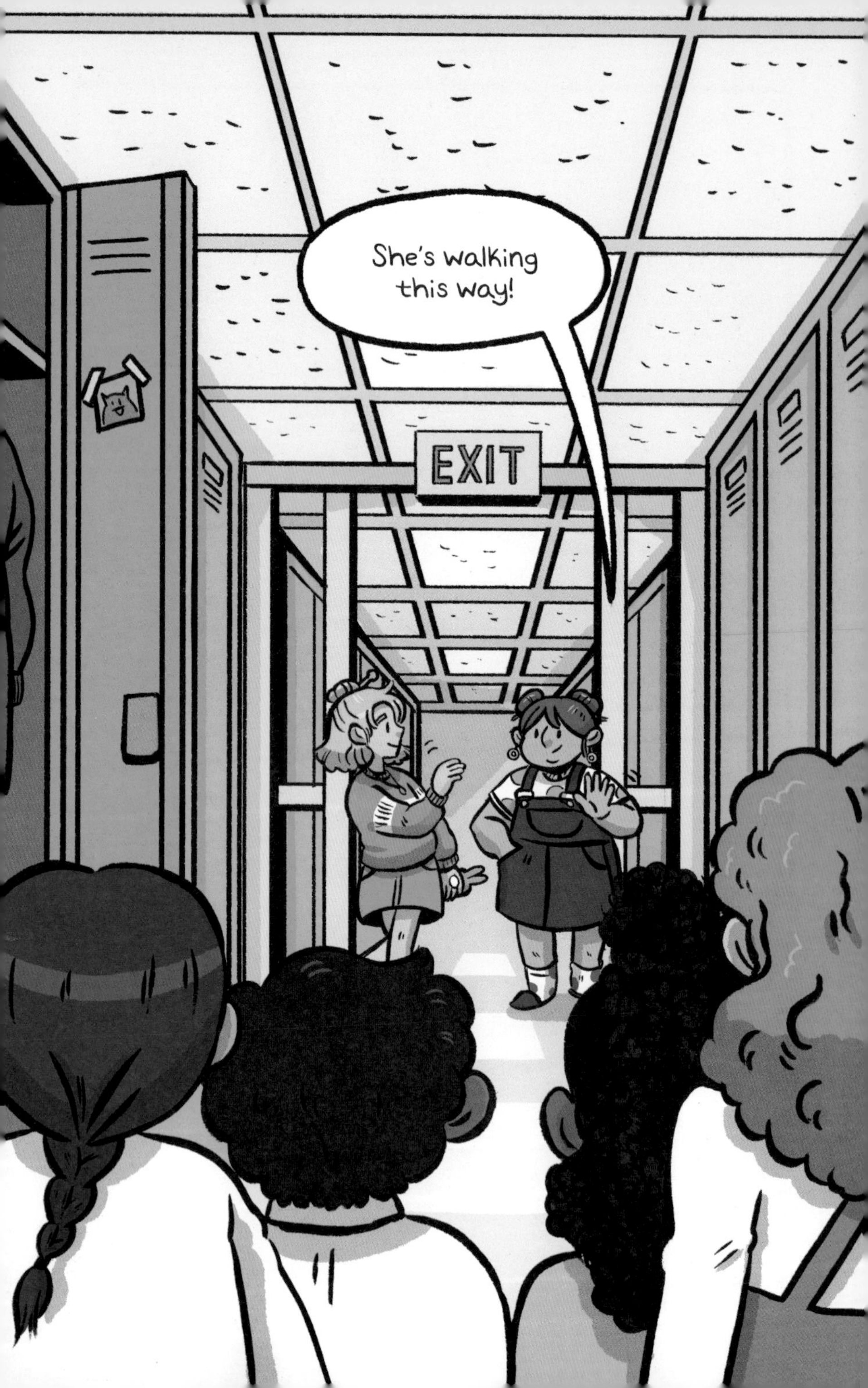
She's walking this way!
EXIT

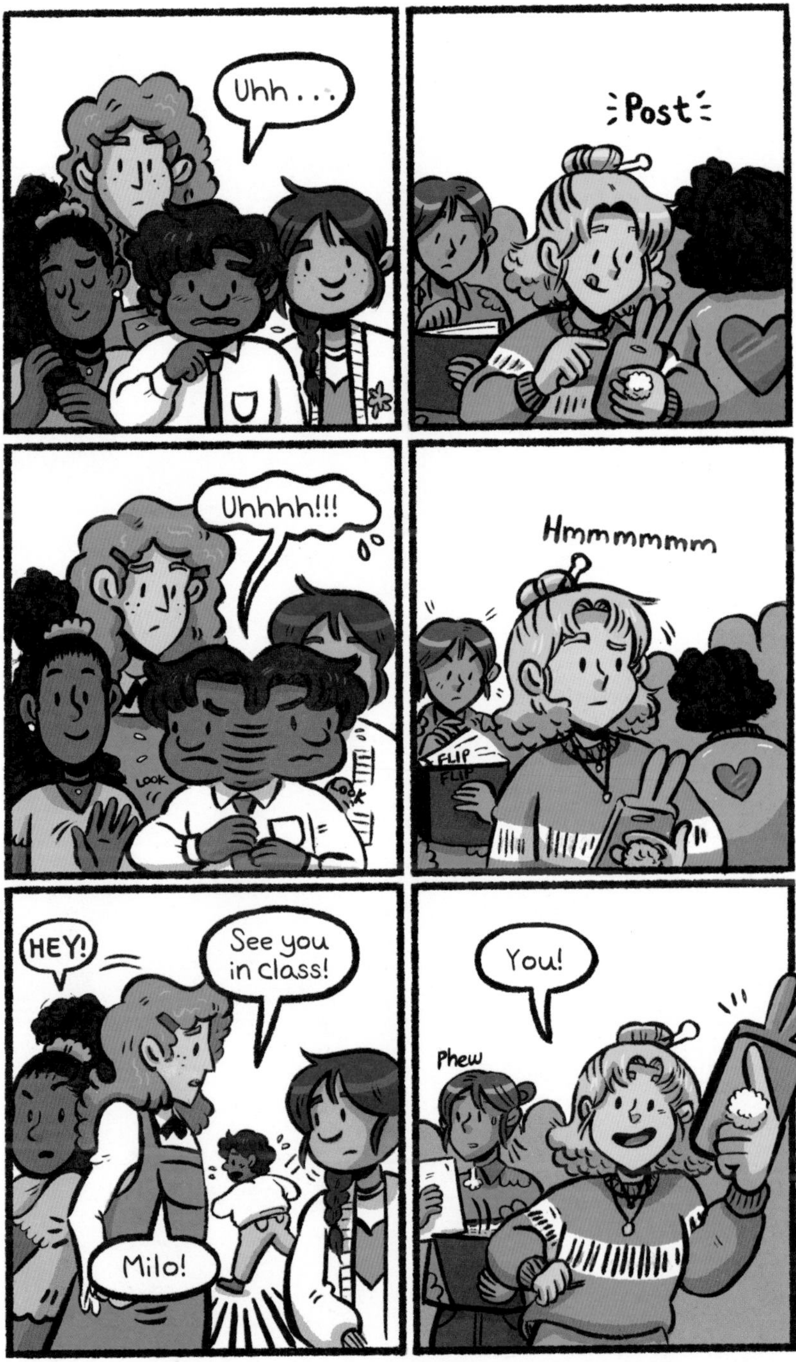
Uhh...
Post
Uhhhh!!!
LOOK
LOOK
Hmmmmmmm
FLIP
FLIP
HEY!
See you in class!
Milo!
You!
Phew

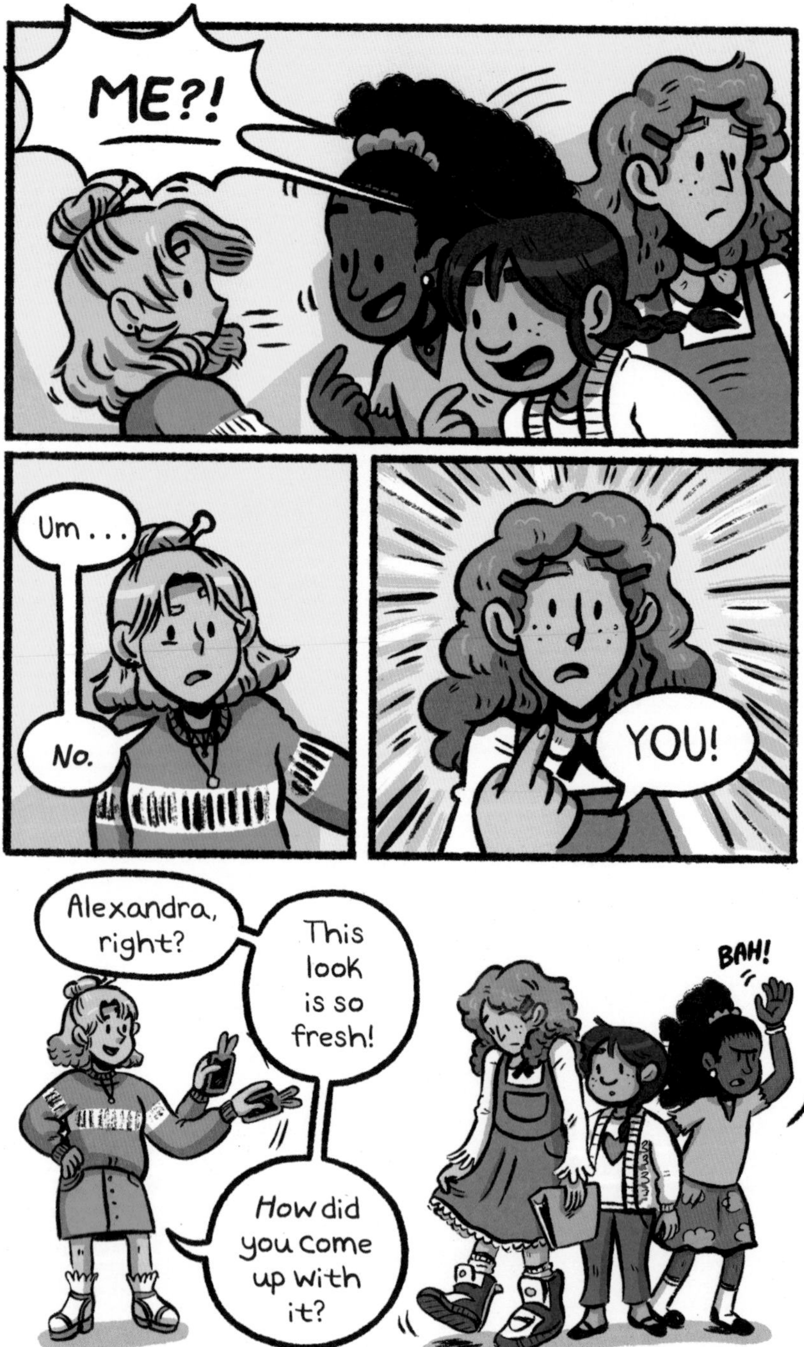
ME?!
Um . . .
No.
YOU!
Alexandra, right?
This look is so fresh!
How did you come up with it?
BAH!

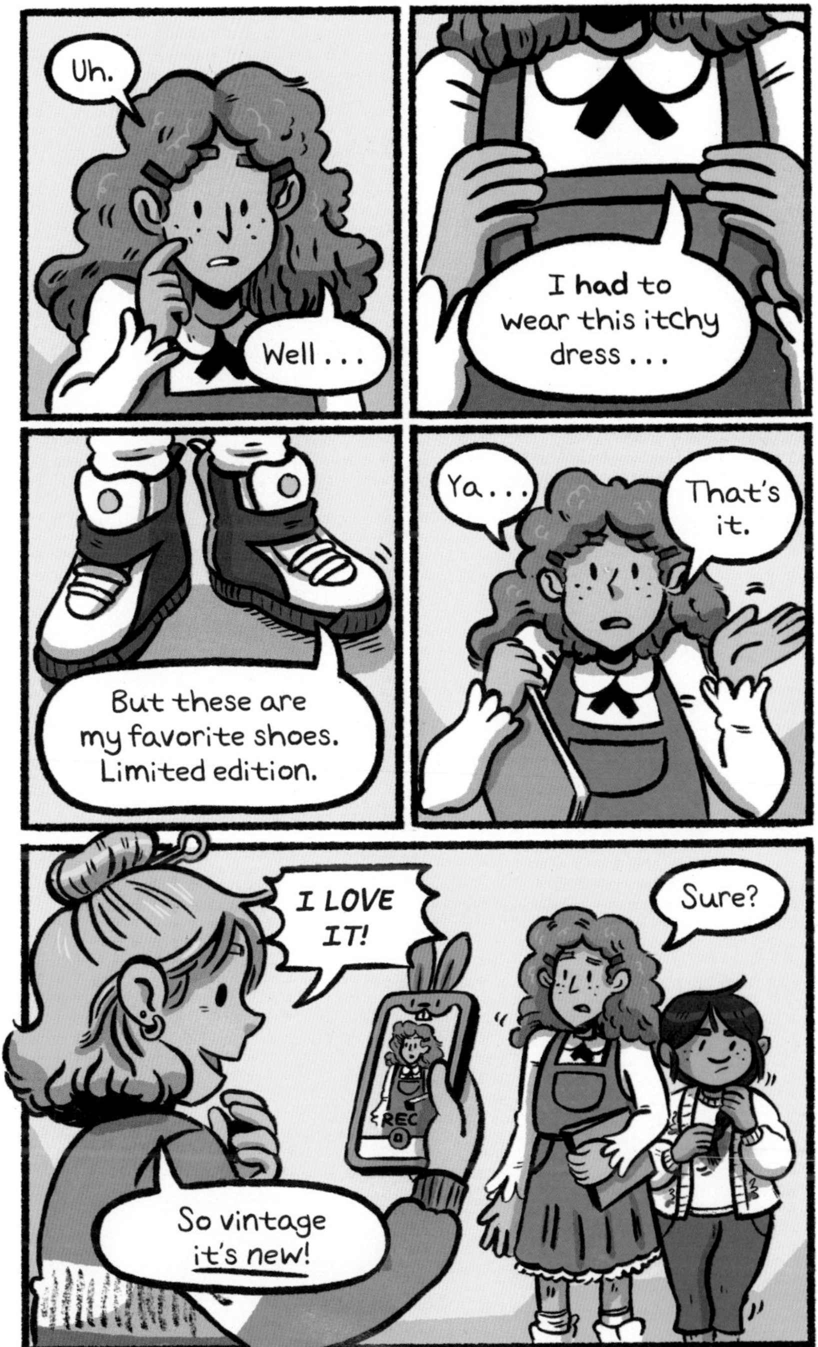
Uh.
Well . . .
I had to wear this itchy dress . . .
But these are my favorite shoes. Limited edition.
Ya. . .
That's it.
I LOVE IT!
So vintage it's new!
REC
Sure?

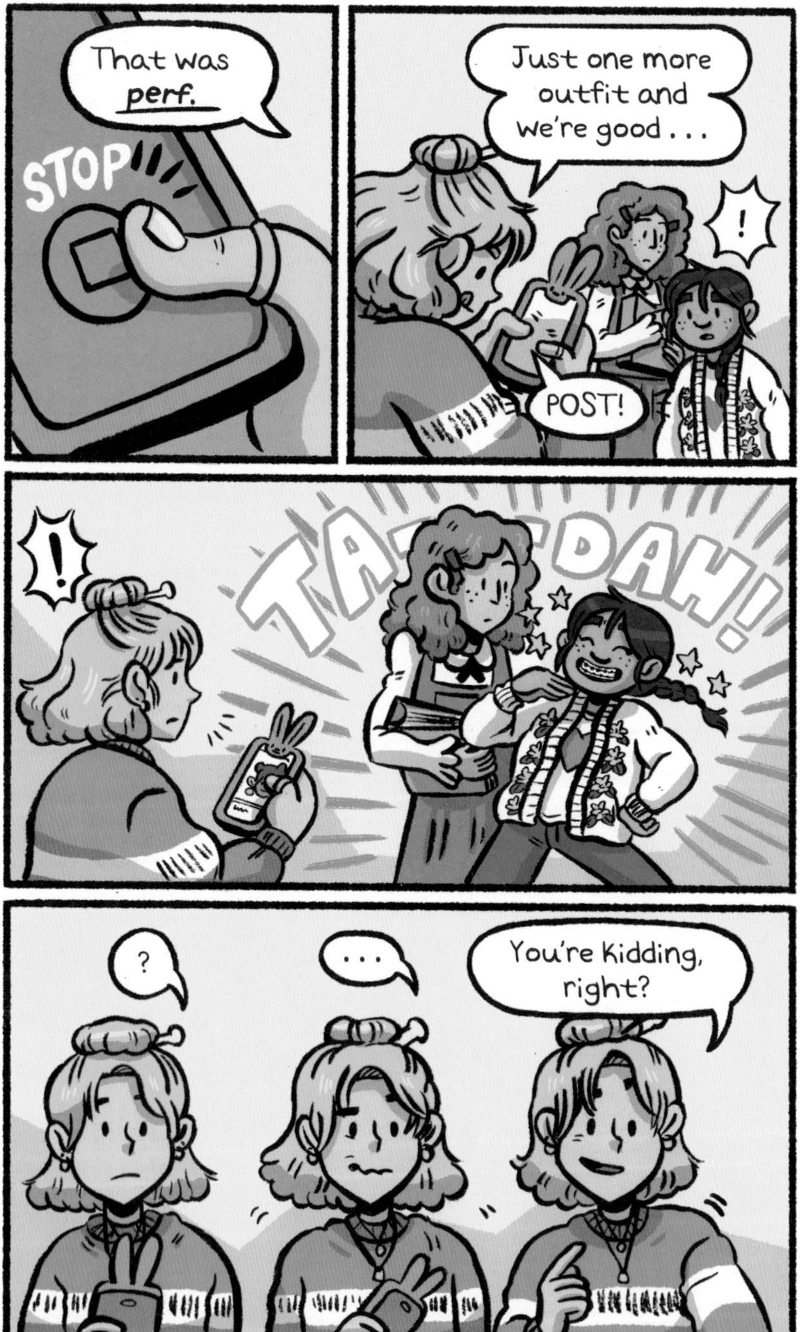
That was perf.
STOP
Just one more outfit and we're good . . .
POST!
!
!
TA-DAH!
?
. . .
You're kidding, right?

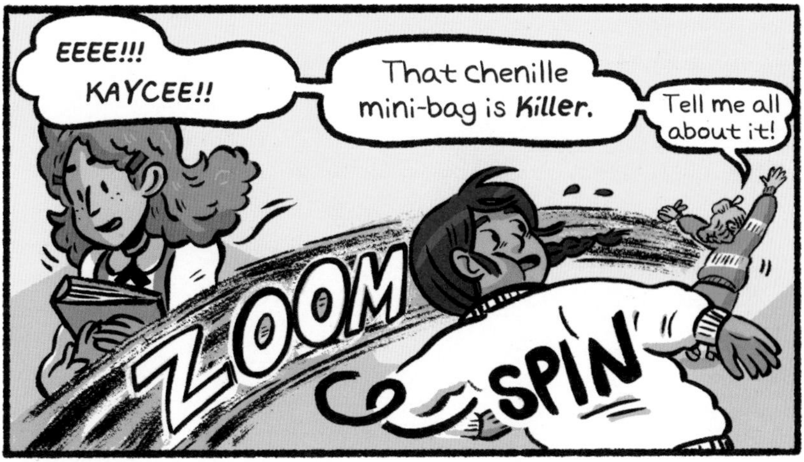
EEEE!!! KAYCEE!!
That chenille mini-bag is **Killer.**
Tell me all about it!
ZOOM
SPIN

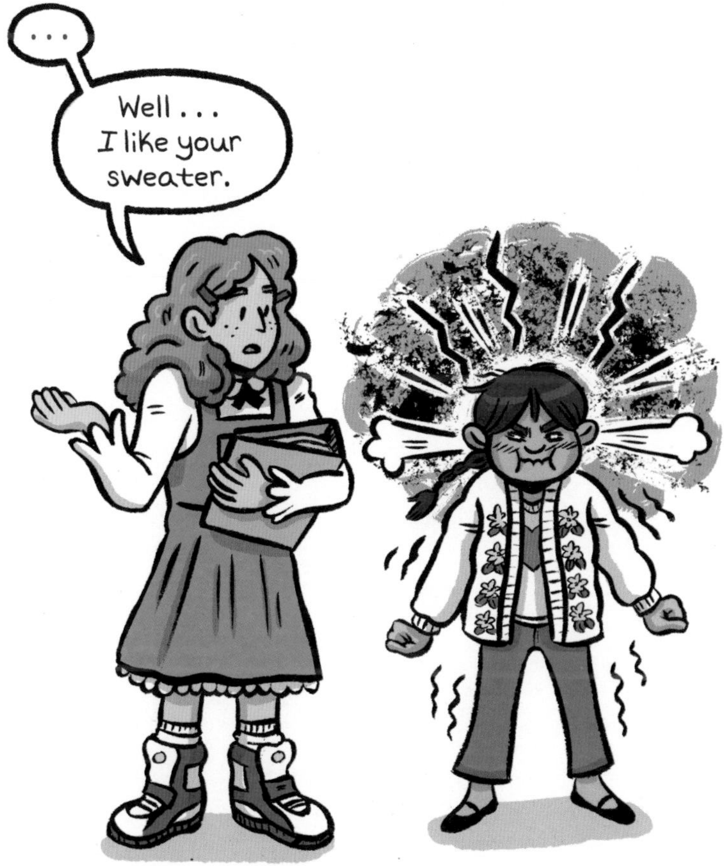
. . .
Well . . . I like your sweater.

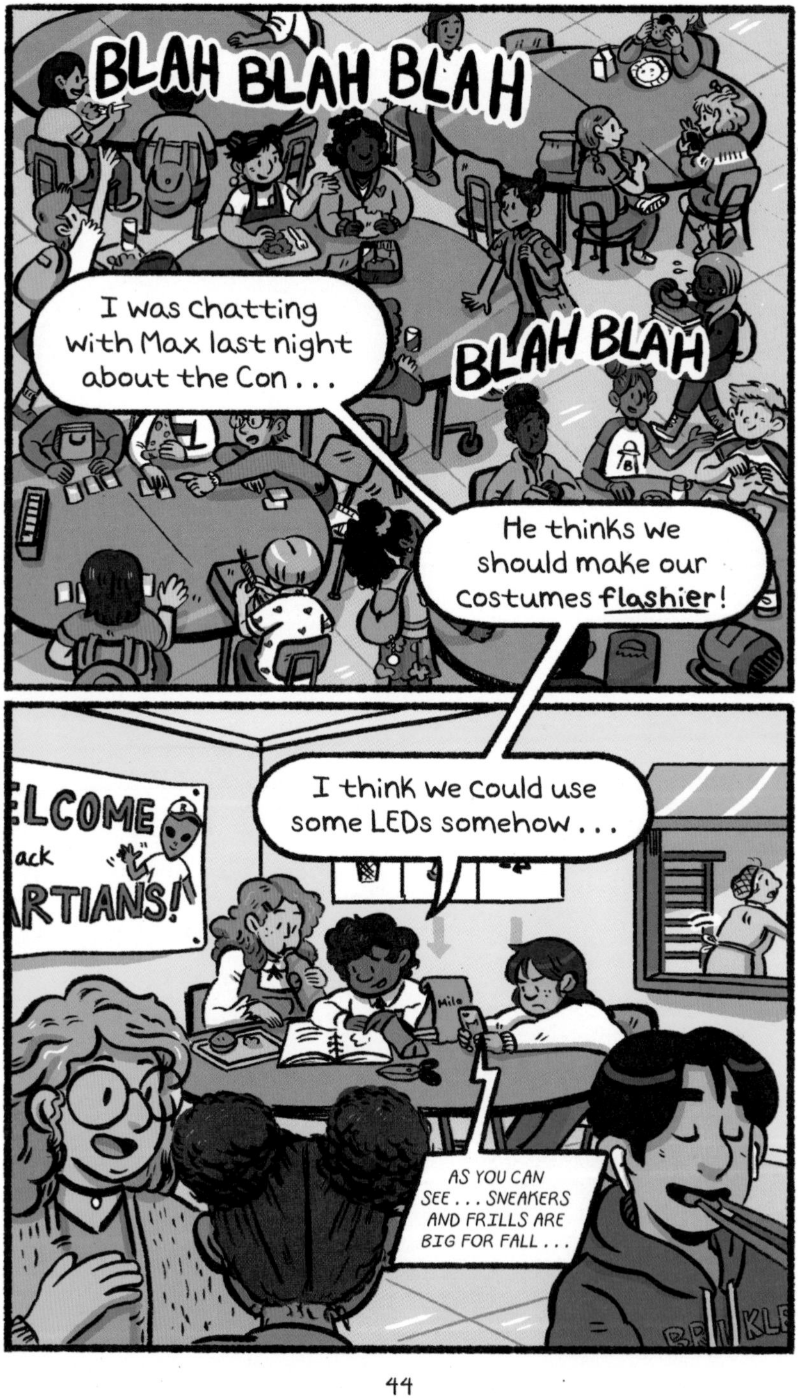
BLAH BLAH BLAH
I was chatting with Max last night about the Con . . .
BLAH BLAH
He thinks we should make our costumes flashier!
ELCOME
ack
ARTIANS!
I think we could use some LEDs somehow . . .
Milo
AS YOU CAN SEE . . . SNEAKERS AND FRILLS ARE BIG FOR FALL . . .

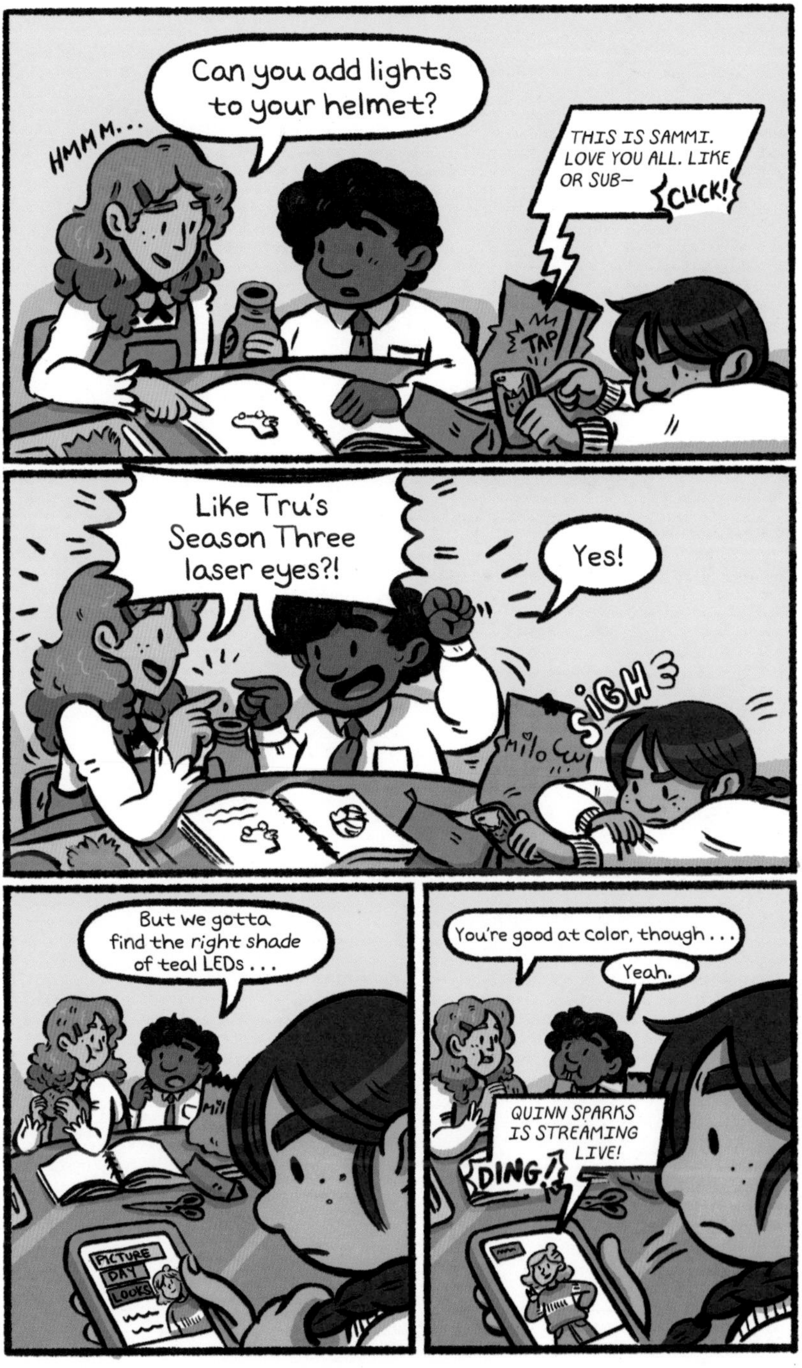
HMMM...
Can you add lights to your helmet?
THIS IS SAMMI. LOVE YOU ALL. LIKE OR SUB—
CLICK!
TAP
Like Tru's Season Three laser eyes?!
Yes!
SIGH
Milo
But we gotta find the right shade of teal LEDs . . .
PICTURE DAY LOOKS
You're good at color, though . . .
Yeah.
QUINN SPARKS IS STREAMING LIVE!
DING!

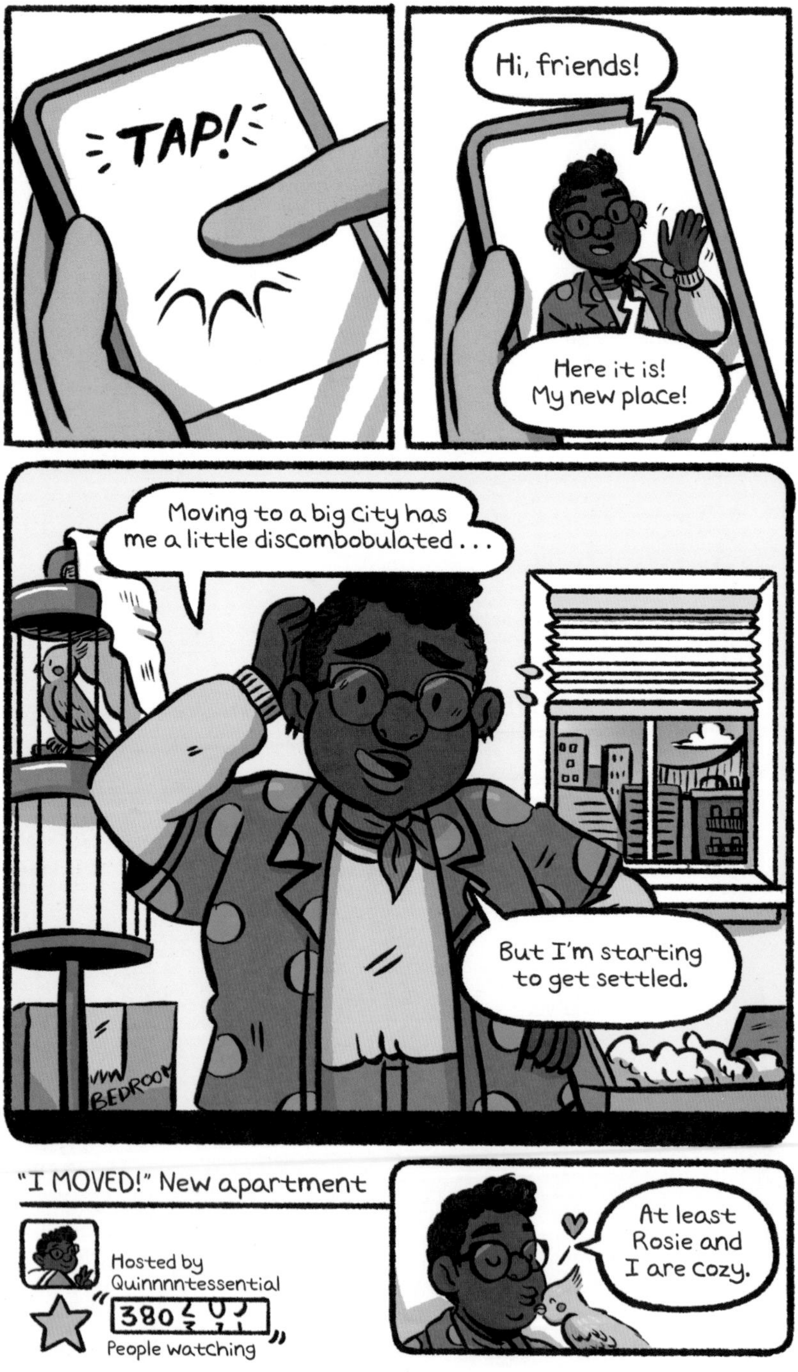
TAP!
Hi, friends!
Here it is! My new place!
Moving to a big city has me a little discombobulated . . .
BEDROOM
But I'm starting to get settled.
"I MOVED!" New apartment
Hosted by Quinnnntessential
380
People watching
At least Rosie and I are cozy.

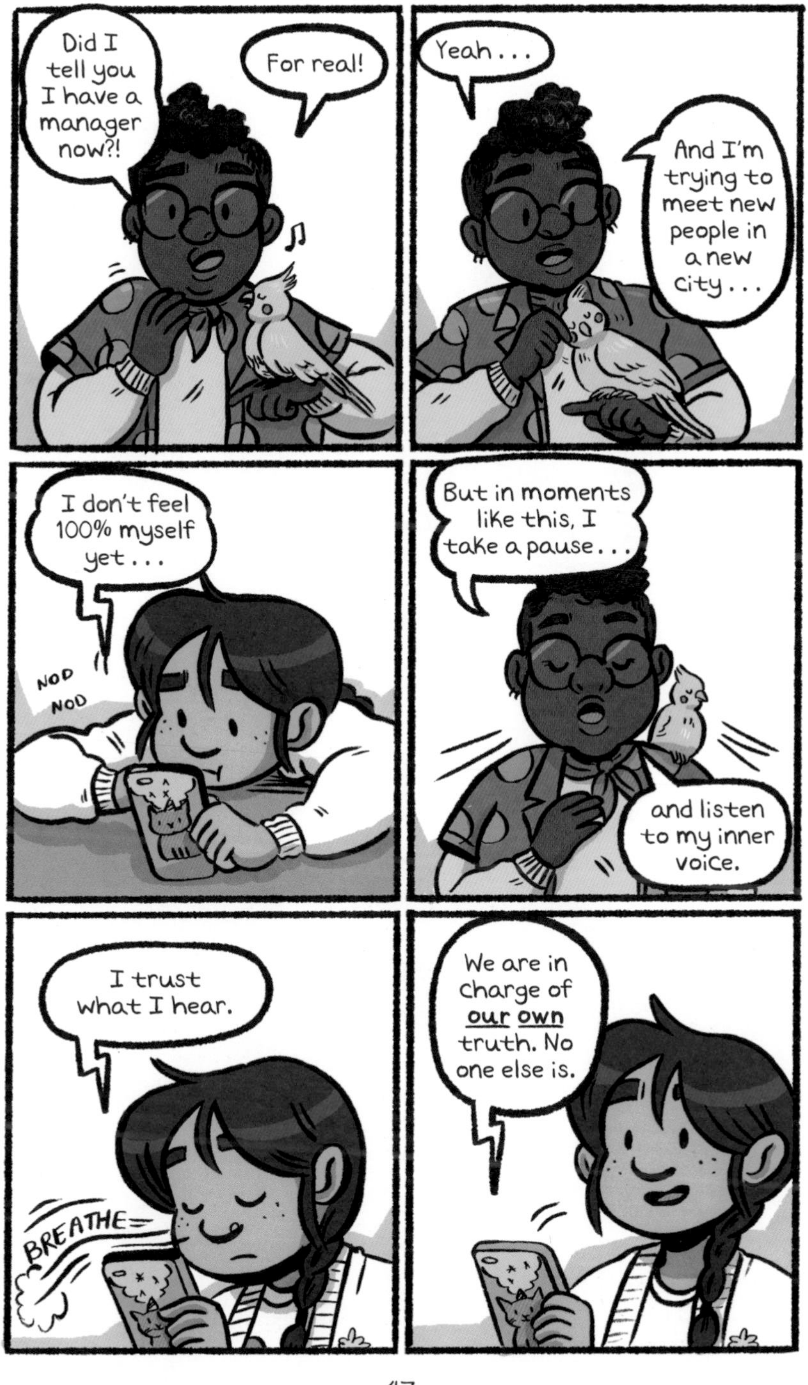
Did I tell you I have a manager now?!
For real!
Yeah . . .
And I'm trying to meet new people in a new city . . .
I don't feel 100% myself yet . . .
NOD NOD
But in moments like this, I take a pause . . .
and listen to my inner voice.
I trust what I hear.
BREATHE
We are in charge of **our own** truth. No one else is.

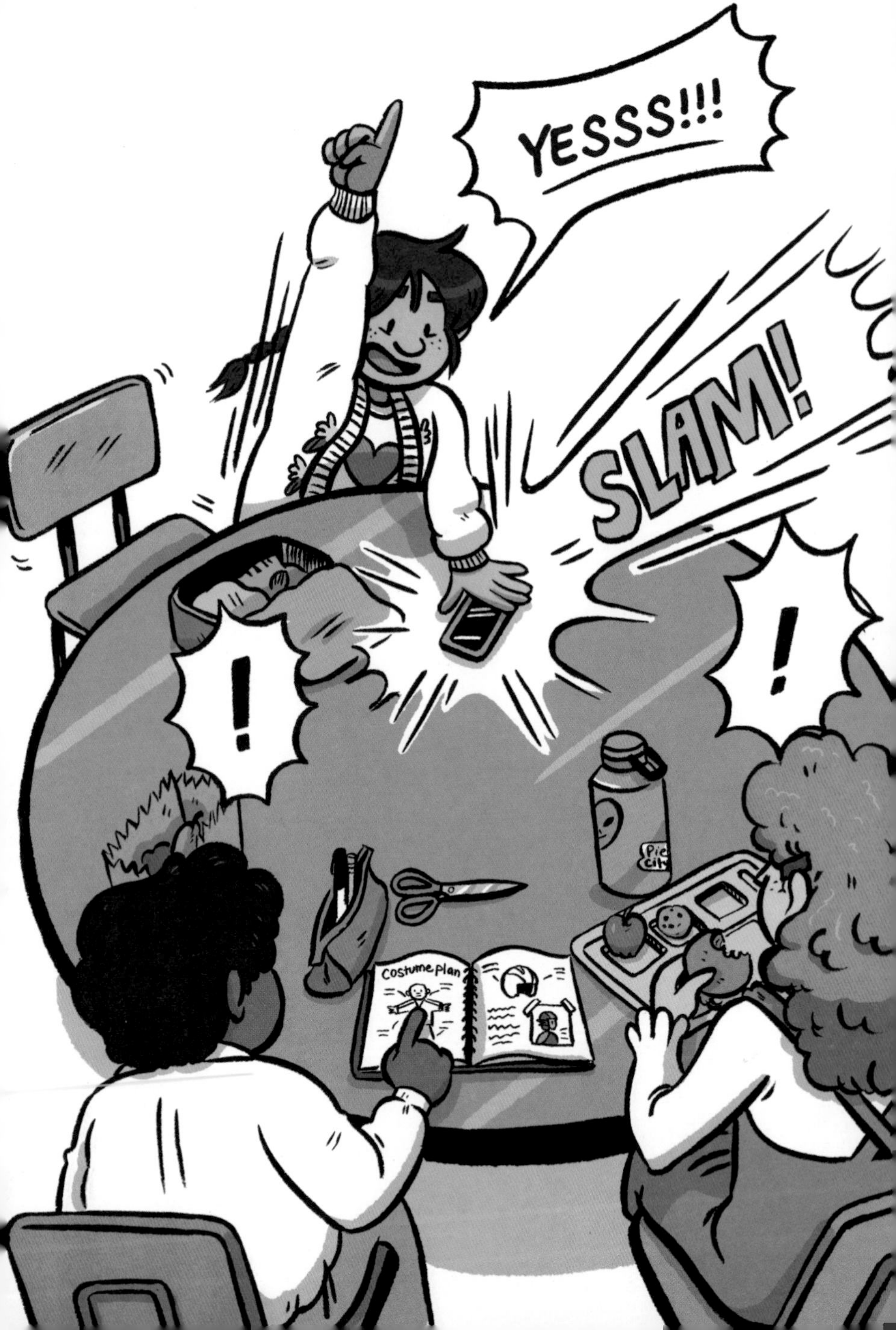
YESSS!!!
SLAM!
!
!
Costume plan

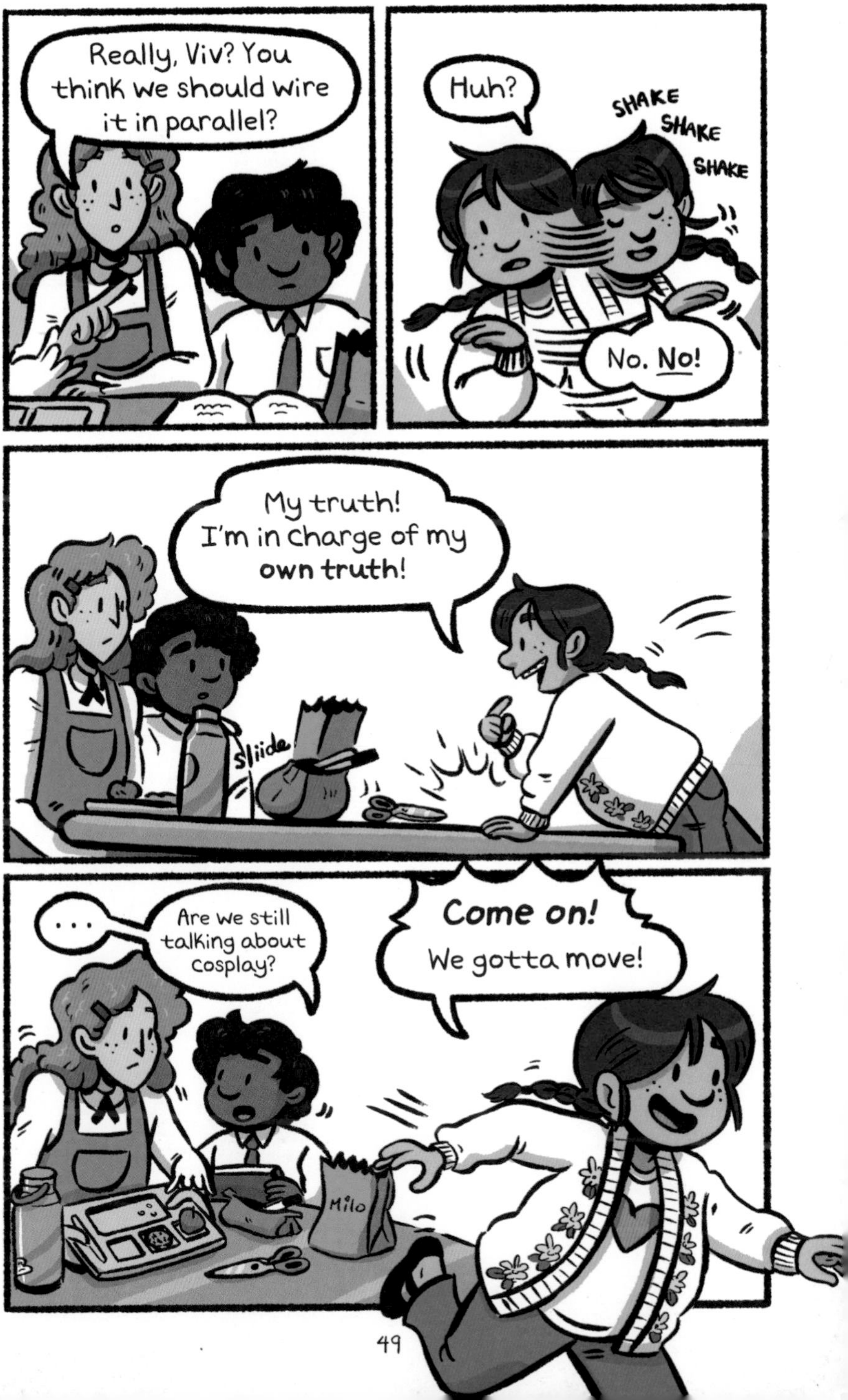

Really, Viv? You think we should wire it in parallel?
Huh?
SHAKE
SHAKE
SHAKE
No. No!
My truth! I'm in charge of my own truth!
Sliide
...
Are we still talking about cosplay?
Come on!
We gotta move!
Milo

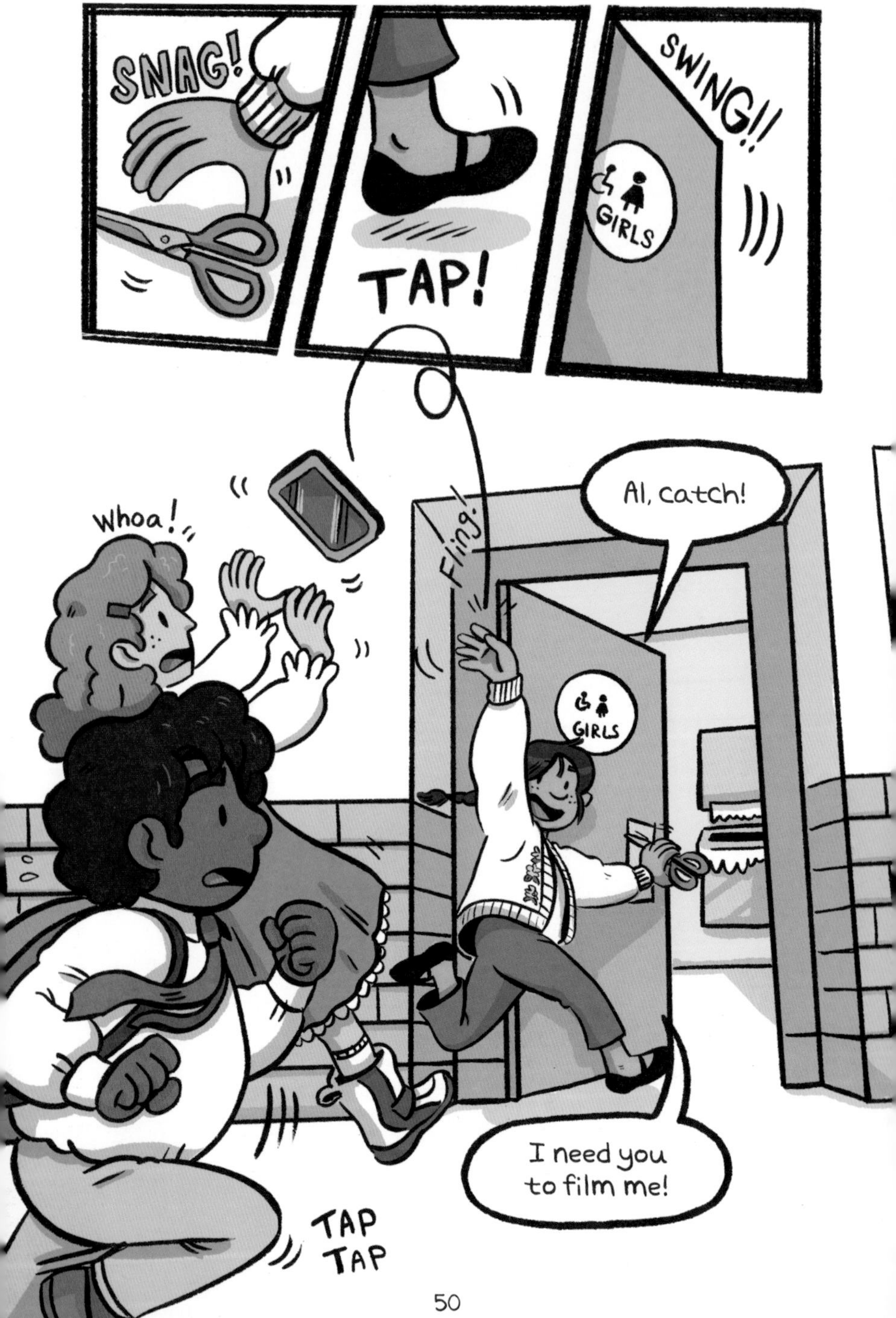
SNAG!
TAP!
SWING!!
GIRLS
Whoa!
Fling!
Al, catch!
GIRLS
I need you to film me!
TAP
TAP

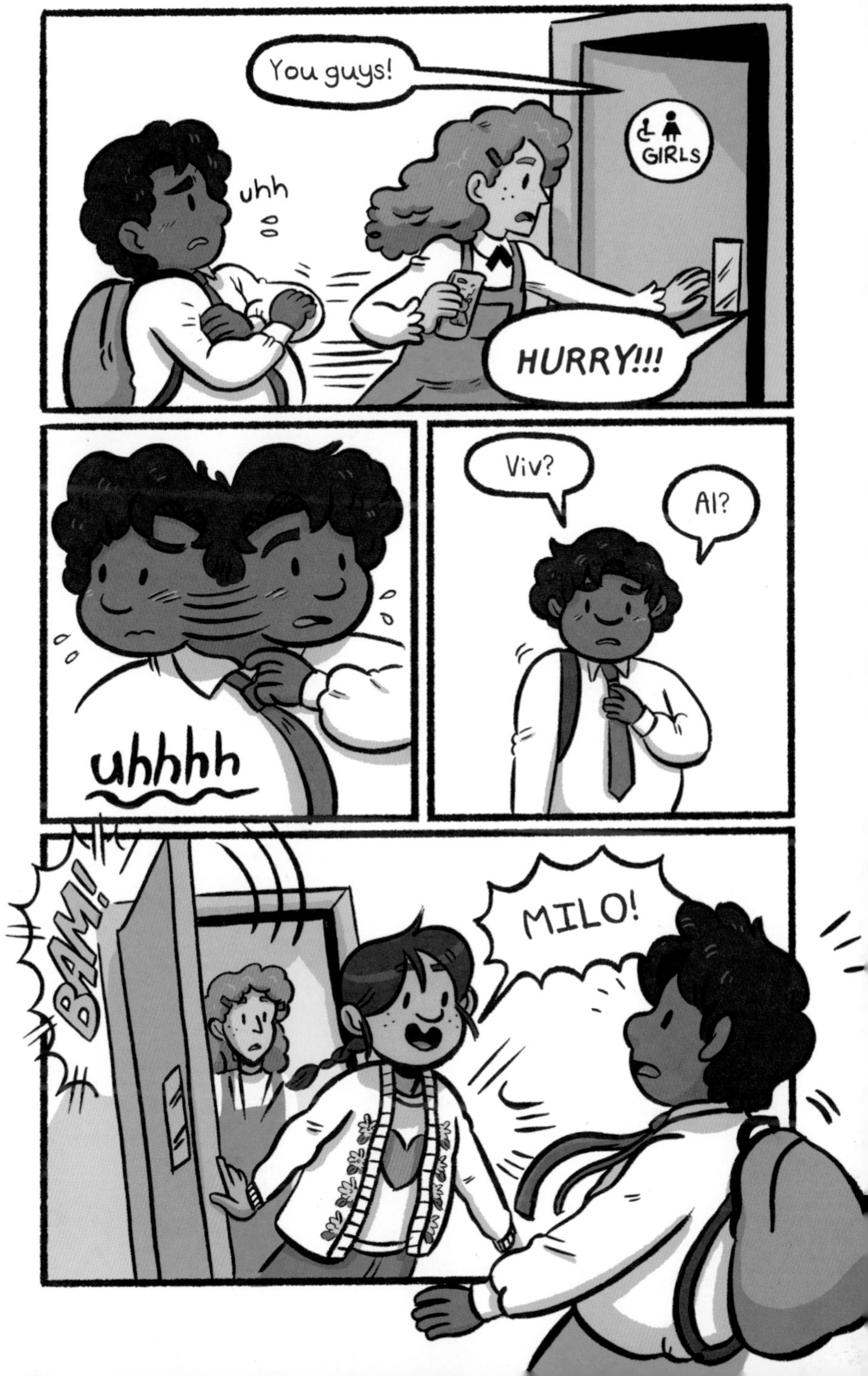
You guys!
uhh
HURRY!!!
uhhhh
Viv?
Al?
BAM!
MILO!

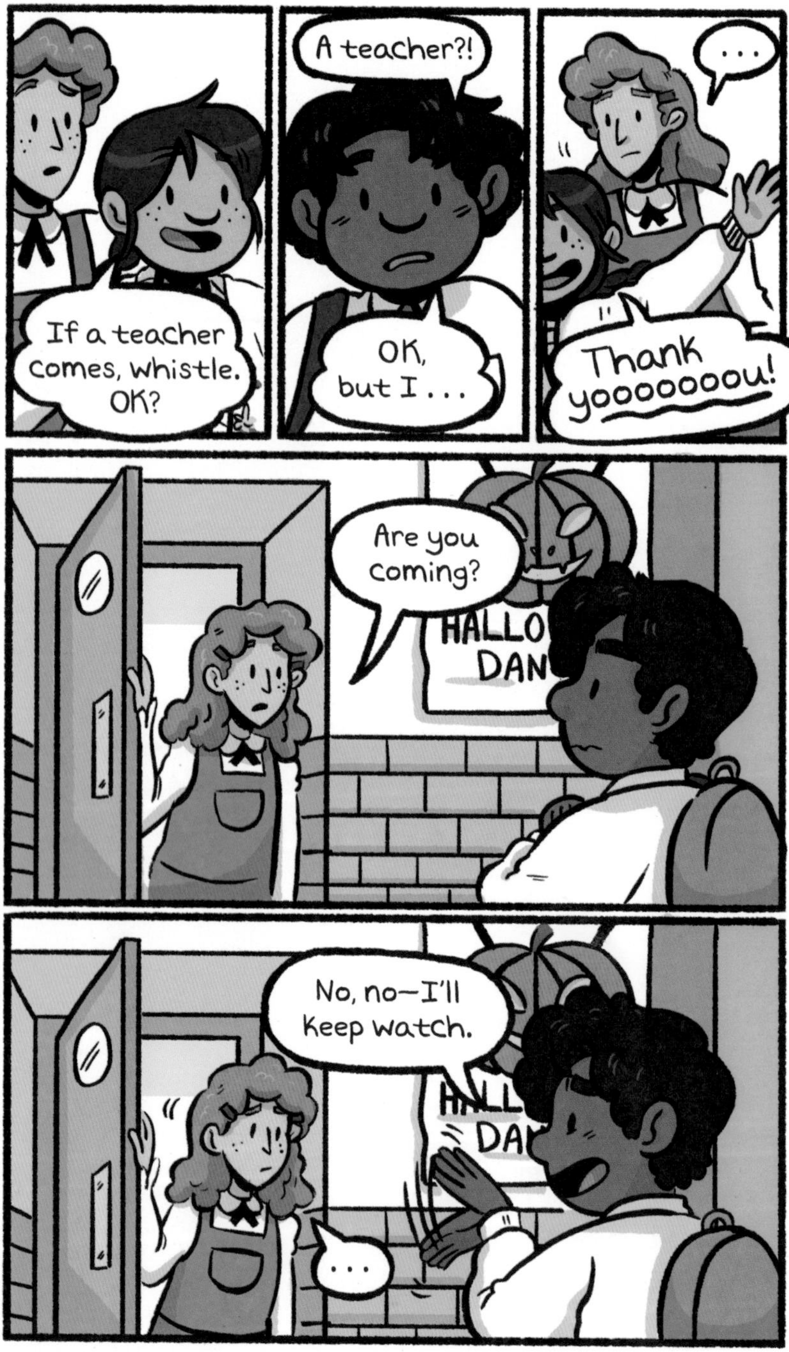
If a teacher comes, whistle. OK?
A teacher?!
OK, but I . . .
. . .
Thank yoooooooou!
Are you coming?
HALLO
DAN
No, no—I'll keep watch.
HALL
DA
. . .

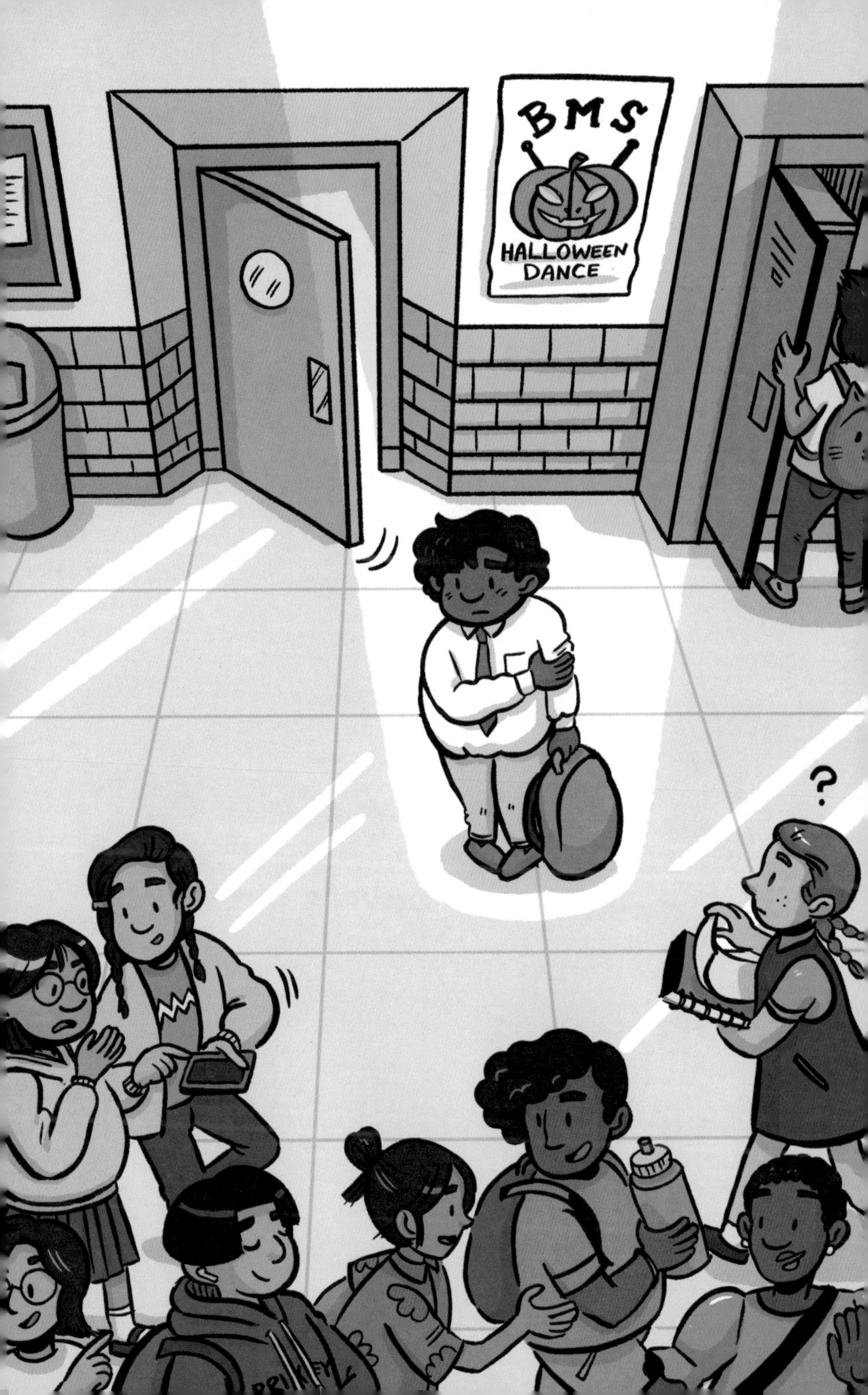
BMS
HALLOWEEN
DANCE

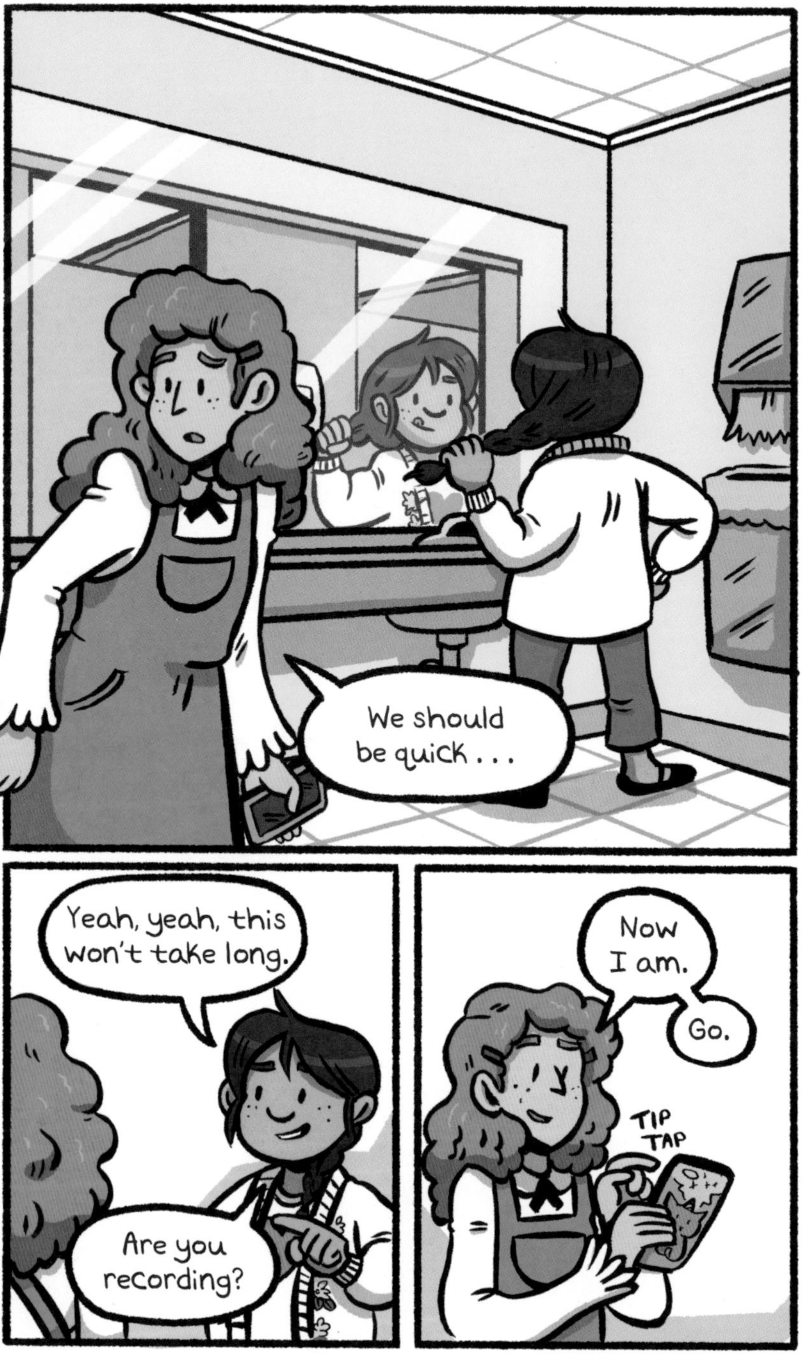
We should be quick . . .
Yeah, yeah, this won't take long.
Are you recording?
Now I am.
Go.
TIP TAP

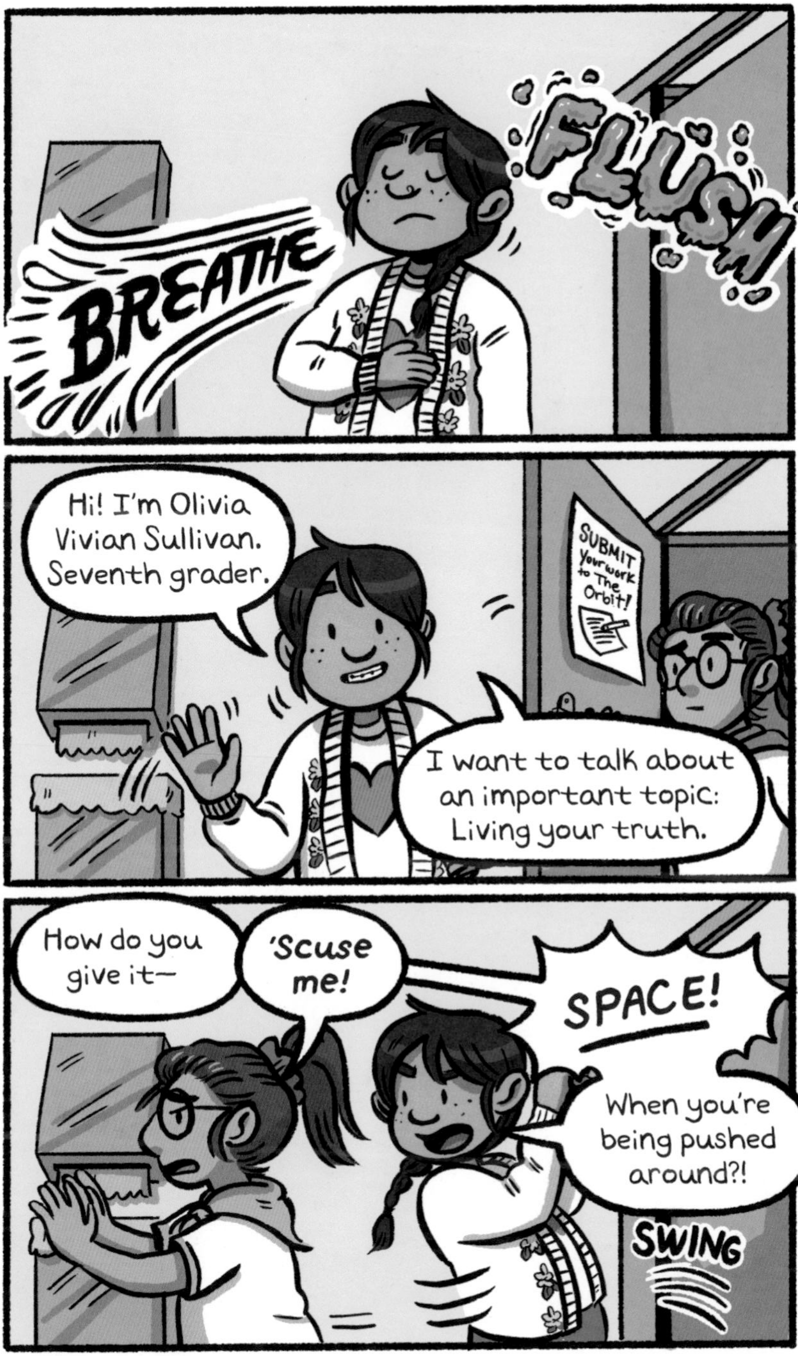

BREATHE
FLUSH!
Hi! I'm Olivia Vivian Sullivan. Seventh grader.
SUBMIT your work to The Orbit!
I want to talk about an important topic: Living your truth.
How do you give it—
'Scuse me!
SPACE!
When you're being pushed around?!
SWING

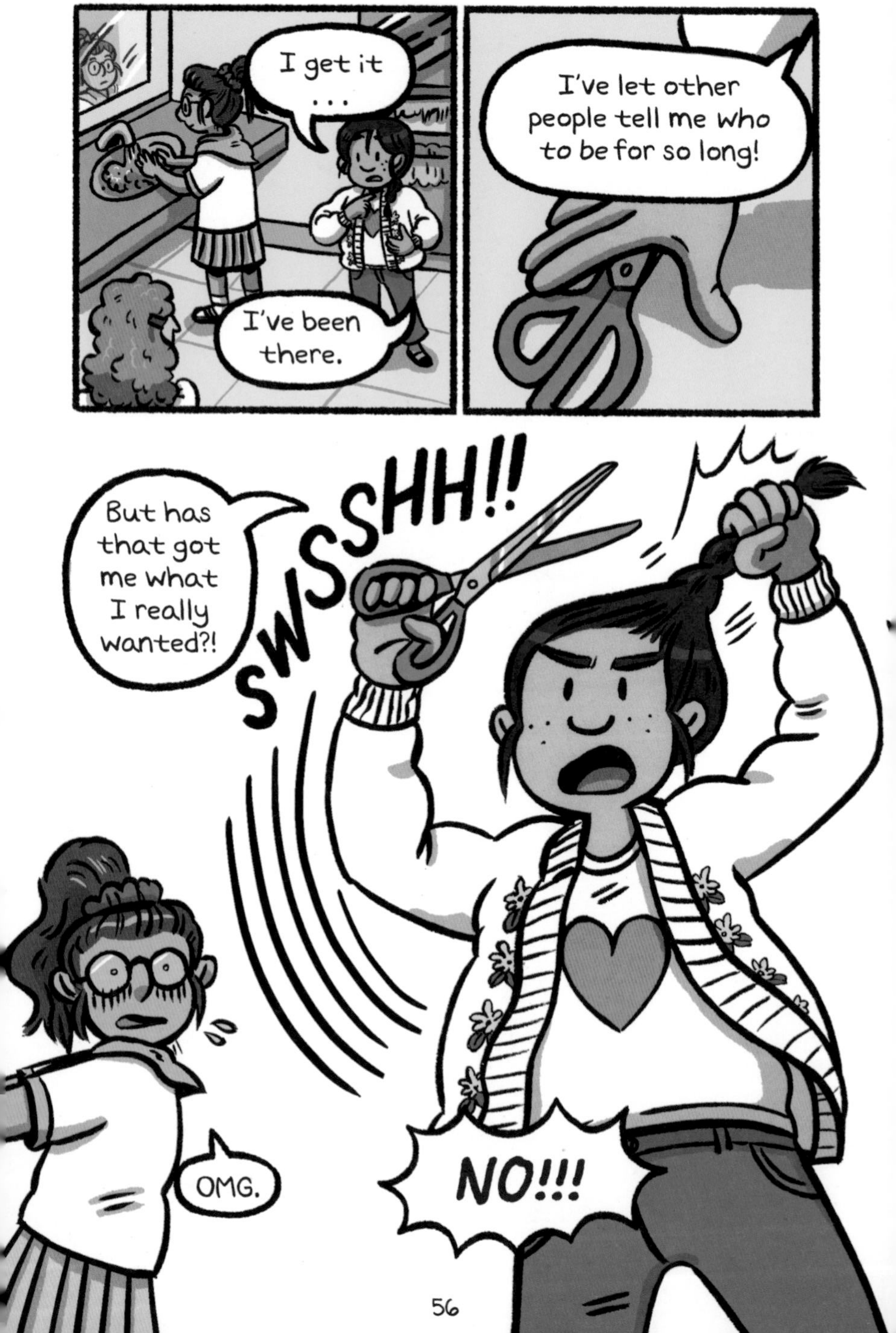
I get it . . .
I've been there.
I've let other people tell me who to be for so long!
But has that got me what I really wanted?!
SWSSHH!!
NO!!!
OMG.

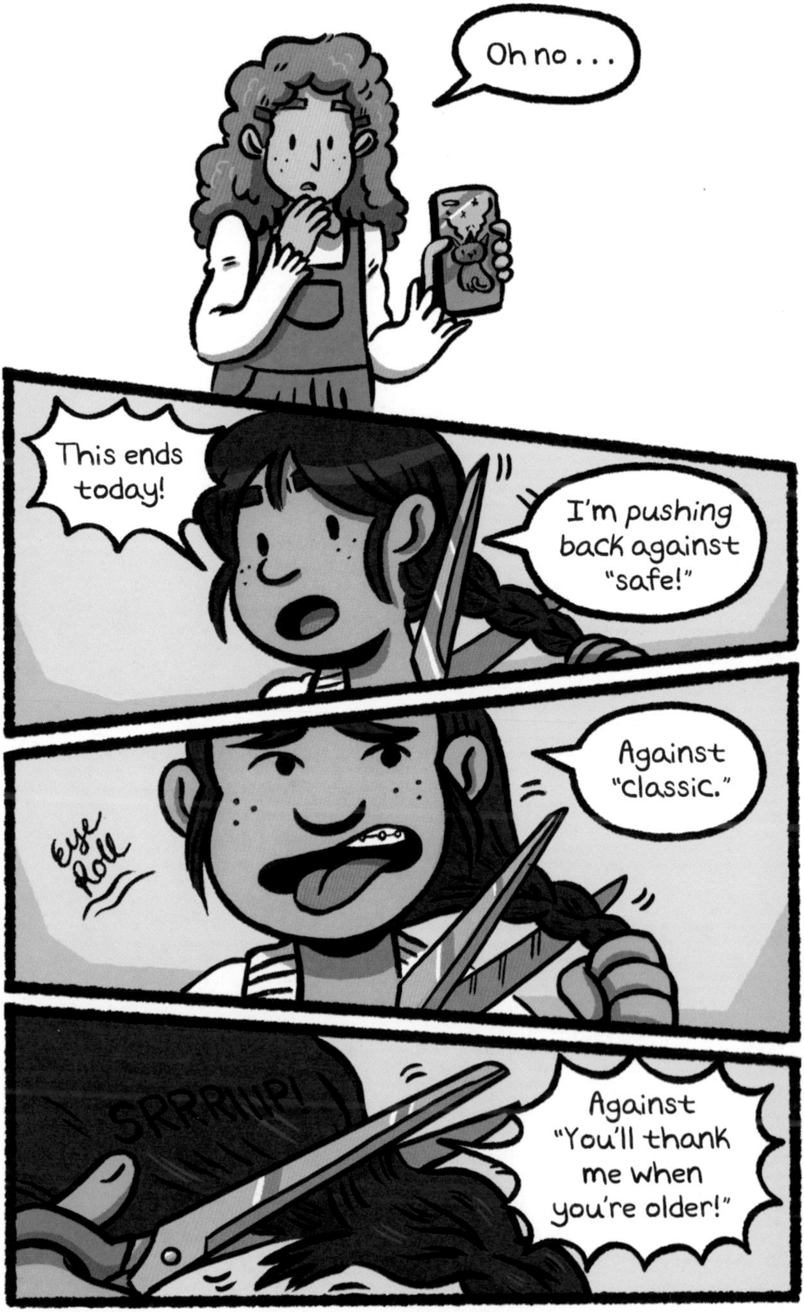
Oh no . . .
This ends today!
I'm *pushing* back against "safe!"
Against "classic."
Eye Roll
SRRRIIIP!
Against "You'll thank me when you're older!"

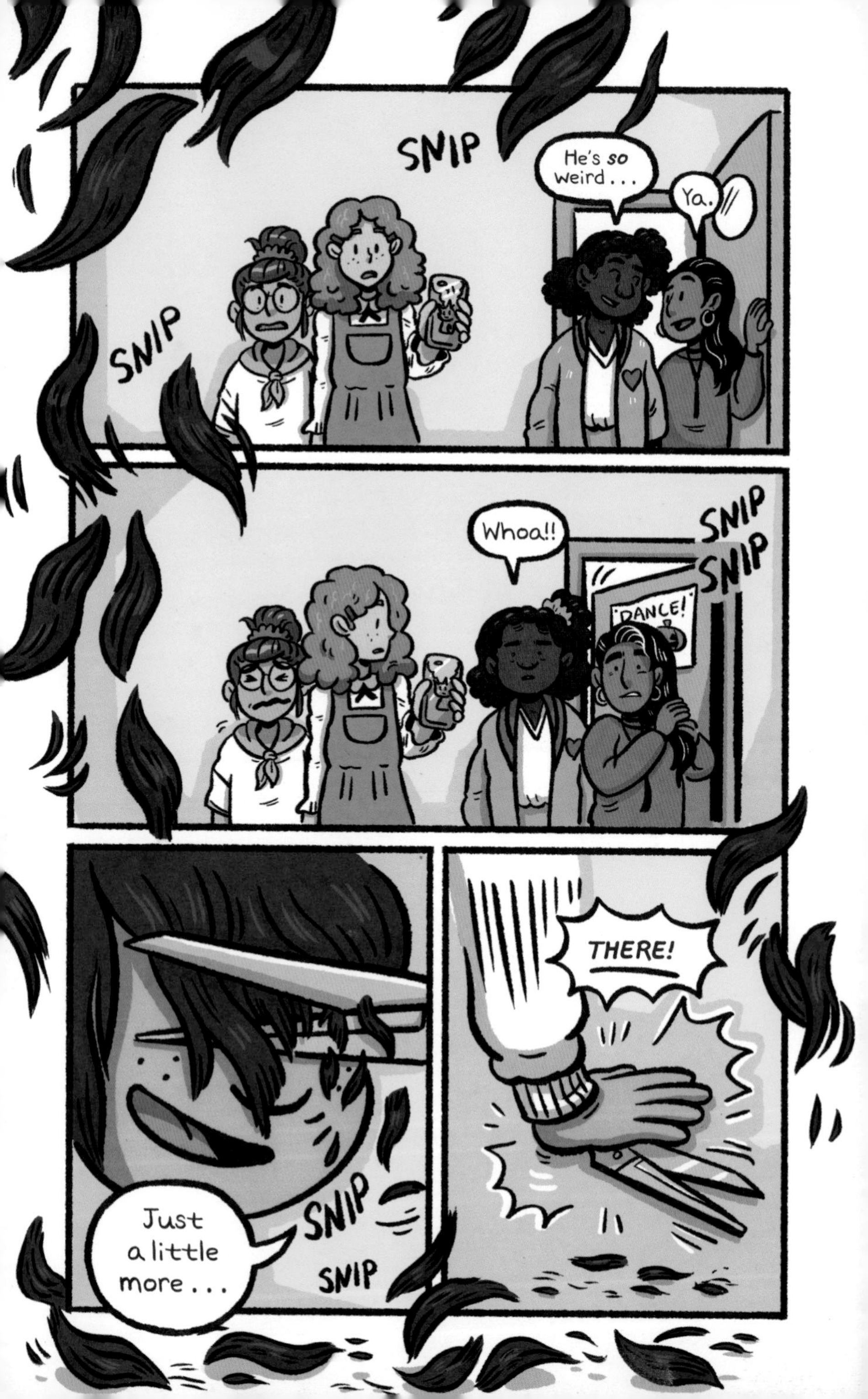
SNIP
He's so weird . . .
Ya.
SNIP
Whoa!!
SNIP
SNIP
DANCE!
THERE!
Just a little more . . .
SNIP
SNIP

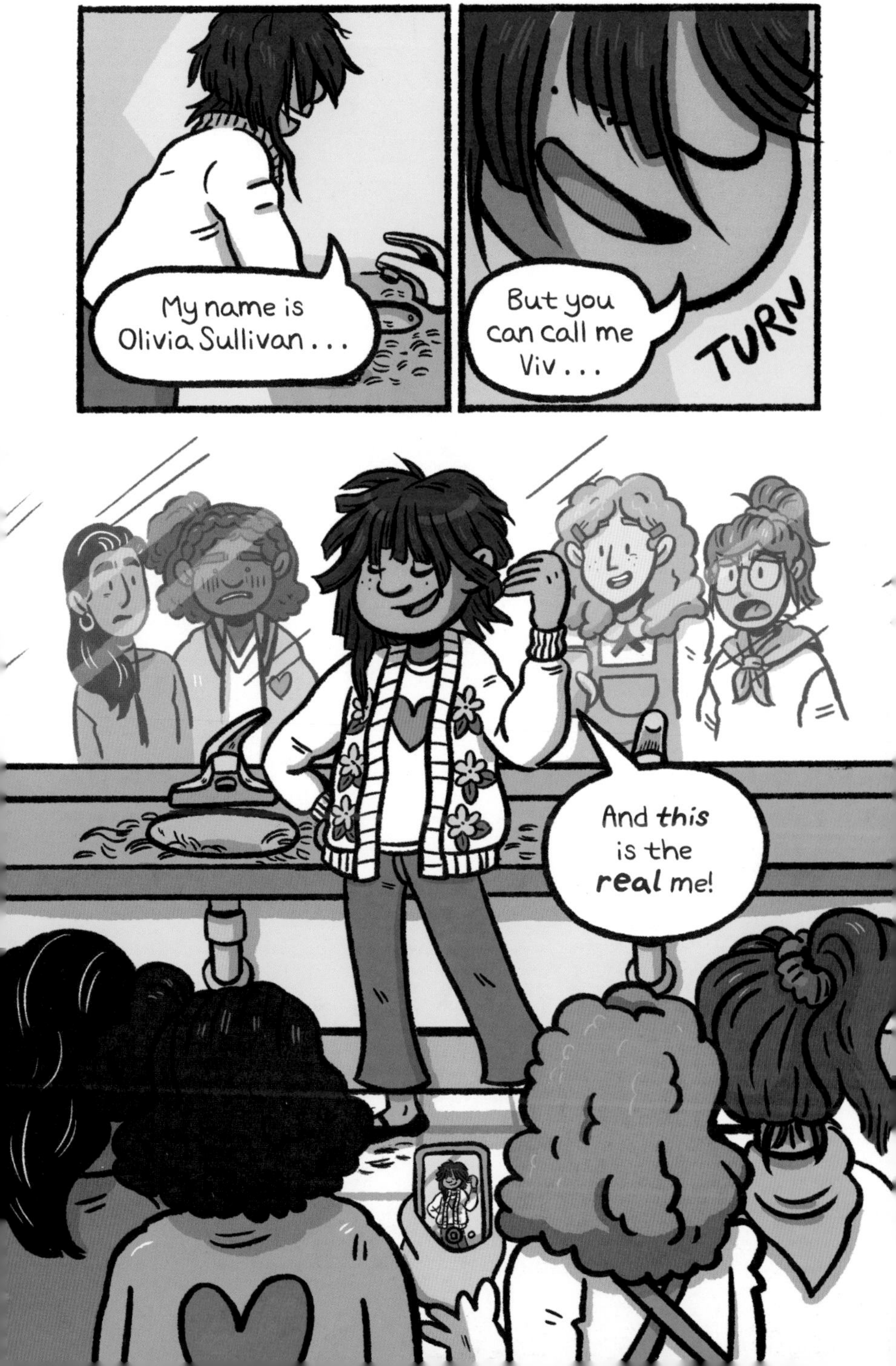
My name is Olivia Sullivan . . .
But you can call me Viv . . .
TURN
And *this* is the **real** me!

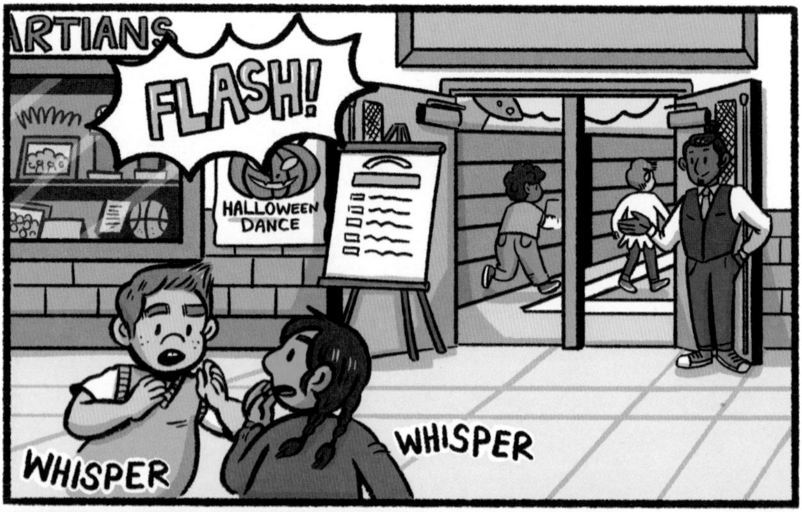
ARTIANS
FLASH!
HALLOWEEN DANCE
WHISPER
WHISPER

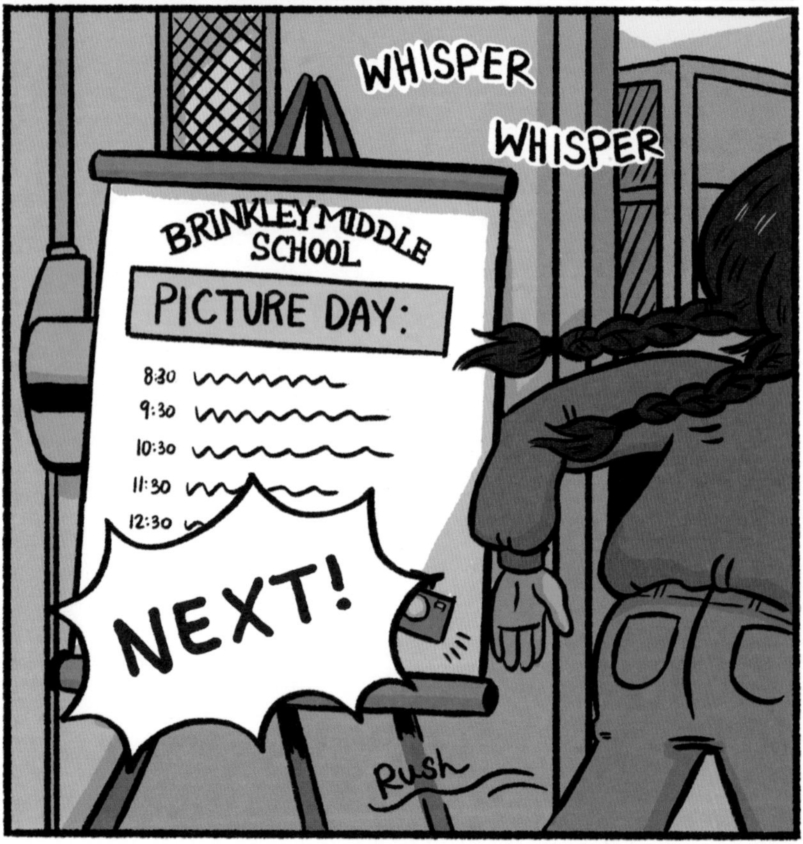
WHISPER
WHISPER
BRINKLEY MIDDLE SCHOOL
PICTURE DAY:
8:30
9:30
10:30
11:30
12:30
NEXT!
RUSH

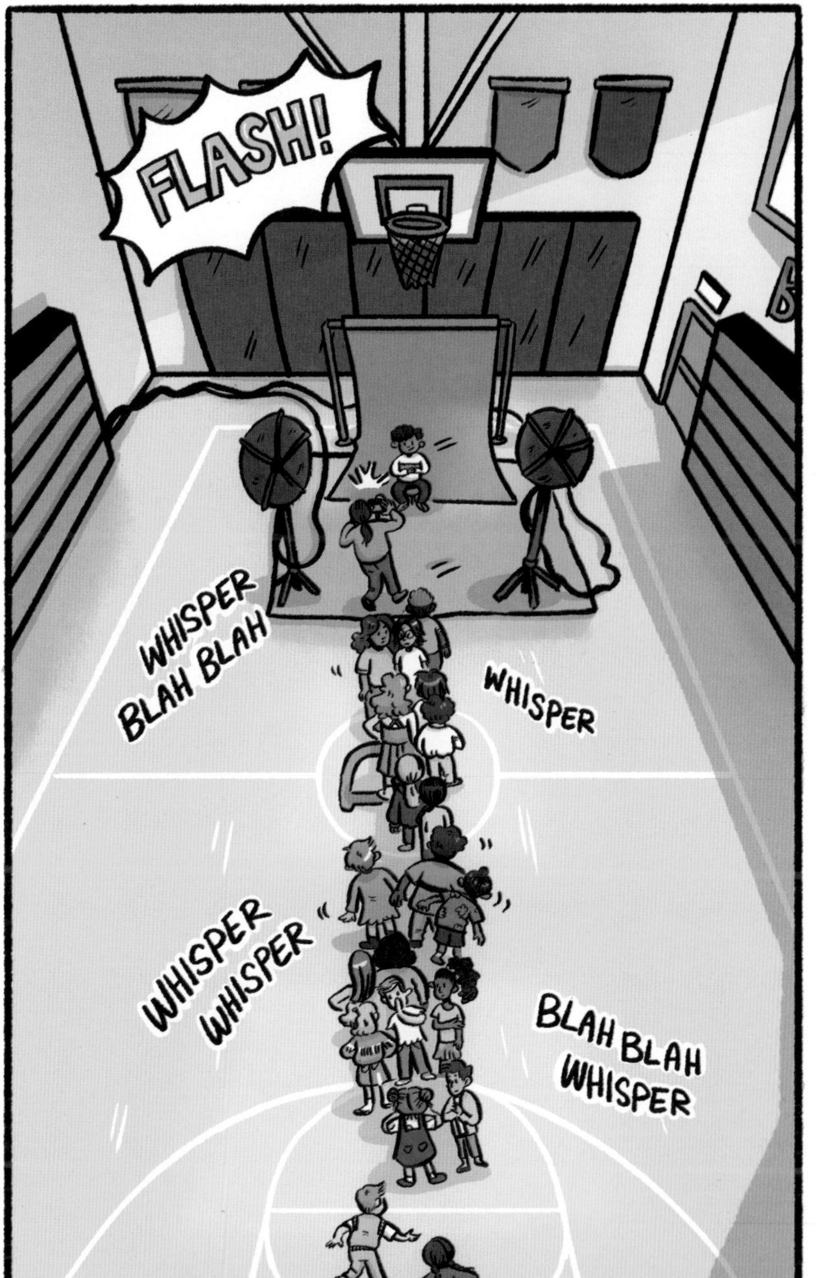
FLASH!
WHISPER
BLAH BLAH
WHISPER
WHISPER
WHISPER
BLAH BLAH
WHISPER

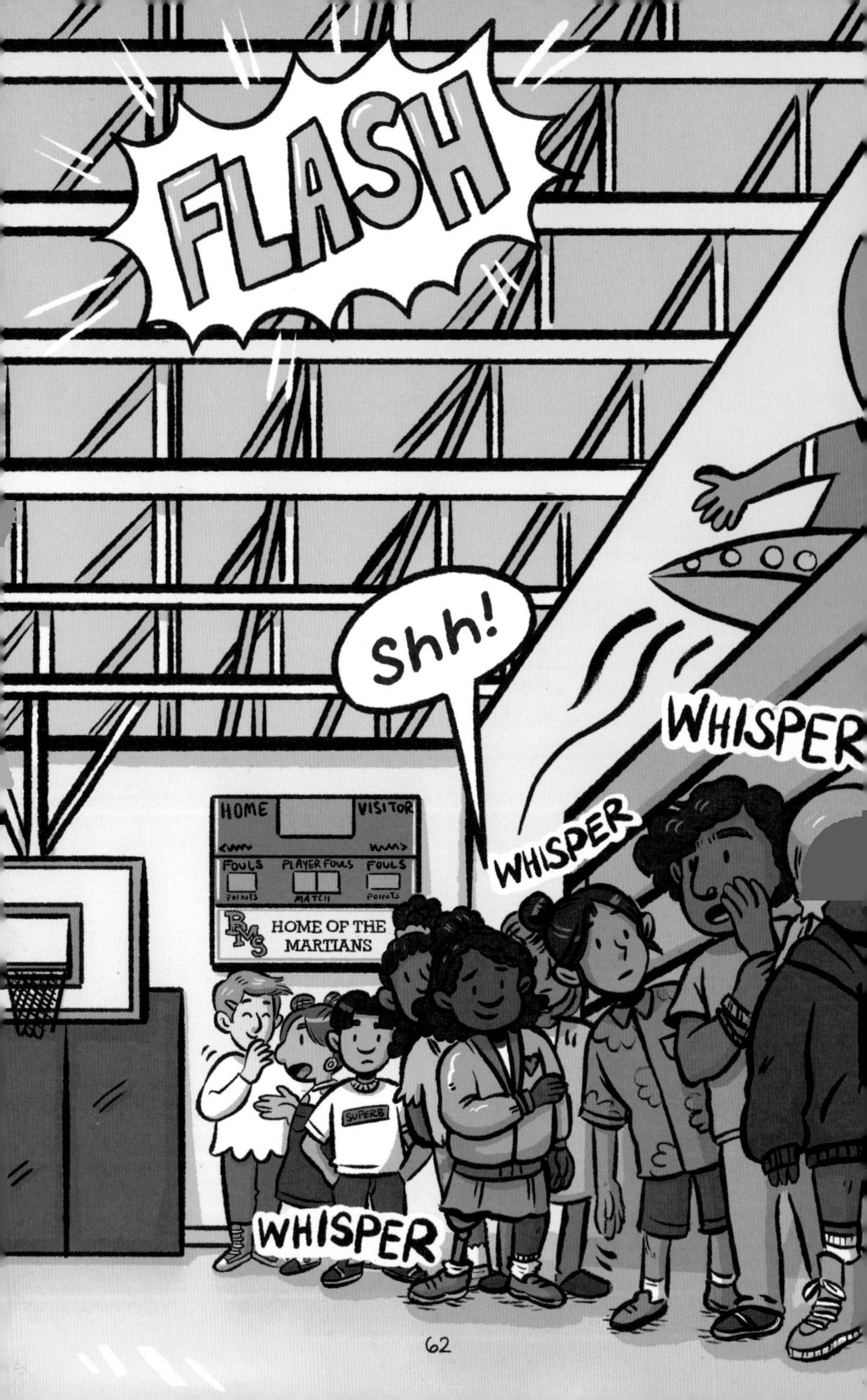
FLASH
Shh!
WHISPER
WHISPER
WHISPER
HOME
VISITOR
FOULS
PLAYER FOULS
FOULS
POINTS
MATCH
POINTS
HOME OF THE MARTIANS
SUPERB

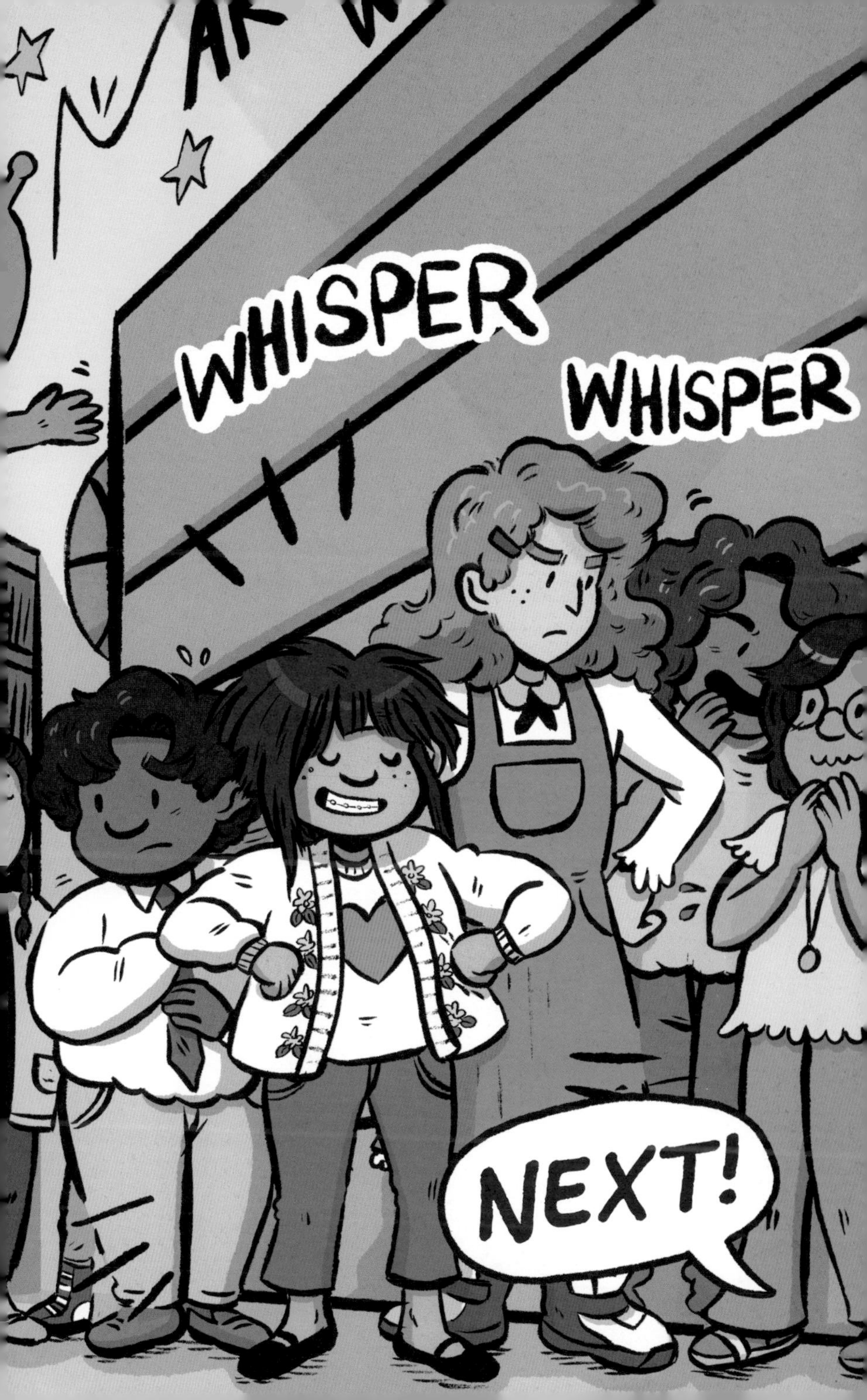
WHISPER
WHISPER
NEXT!

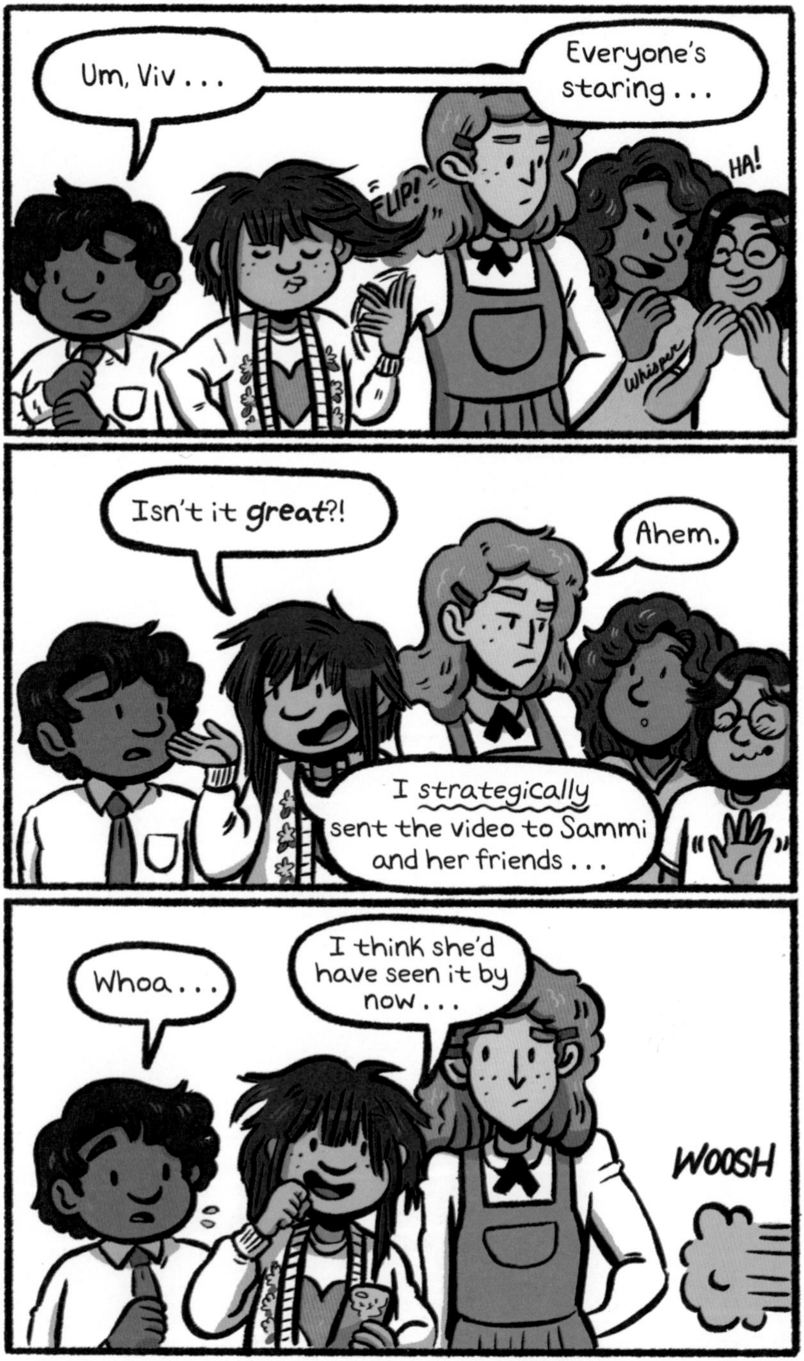
Um, Viv . . .
Everyone's staring . . .
FLIP!
HA!
Whisper
Isn't it **great**?!
Ahem.
I strategically sent the video to Sammi and her friends . . .
Whoa . . .
I think she'd have seen it by now . . .
WOOSH

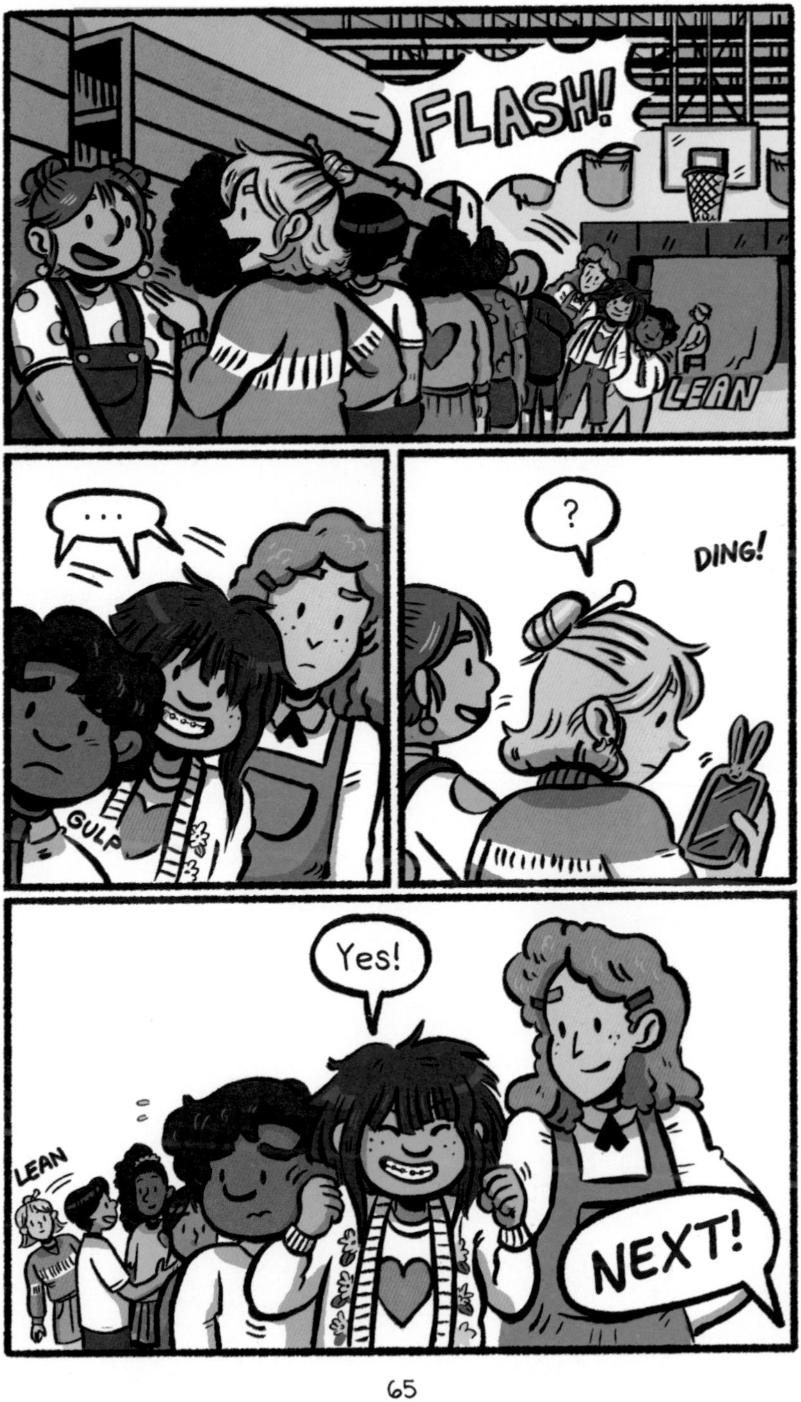
FLASH!
LEAN
...
GULP
?
DING!
Yes!
LEAN
NEXT!

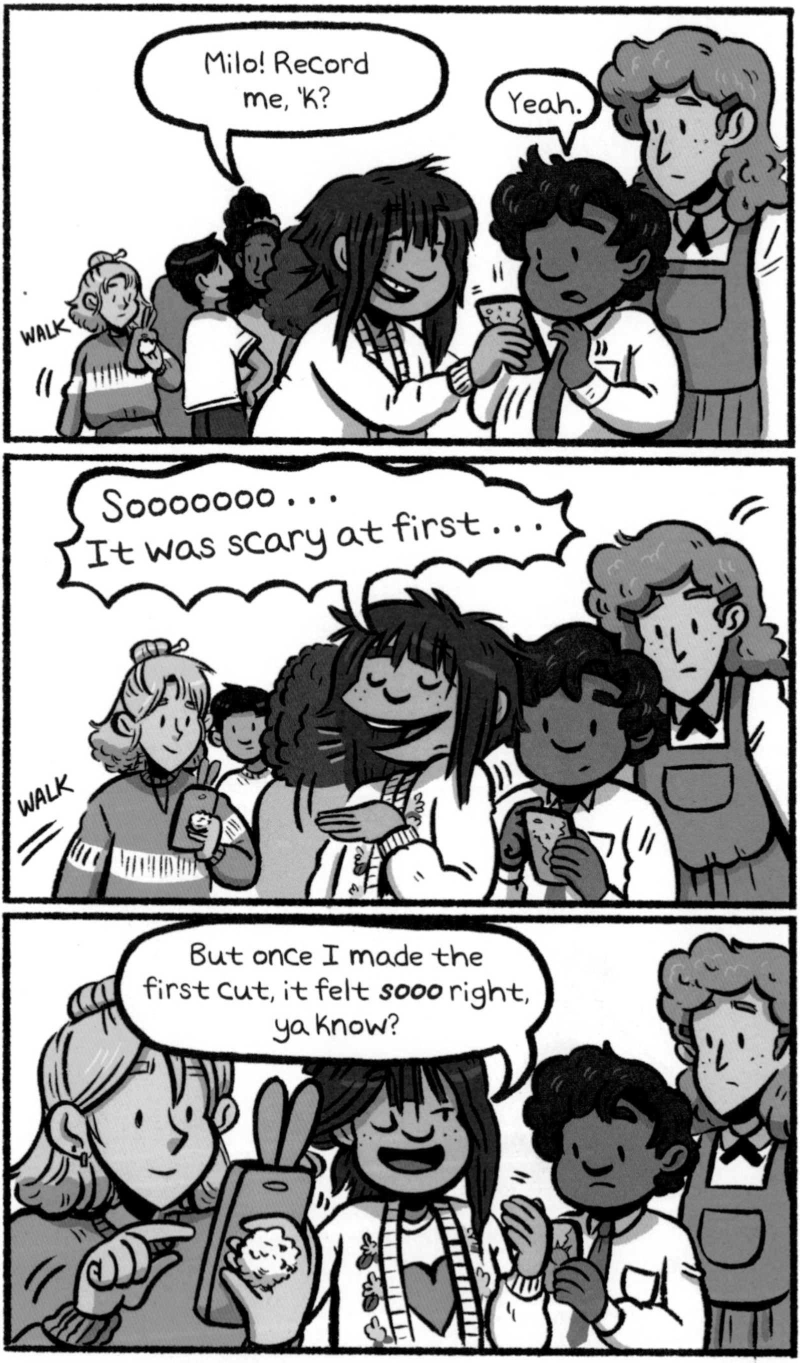
Milo! Record me, 'K?
Yeah.
WALK
Sooooooo . . .
It was scary at first . . .
WALK
But once I made the first cut, it felt ***sooo*** right, ya know?

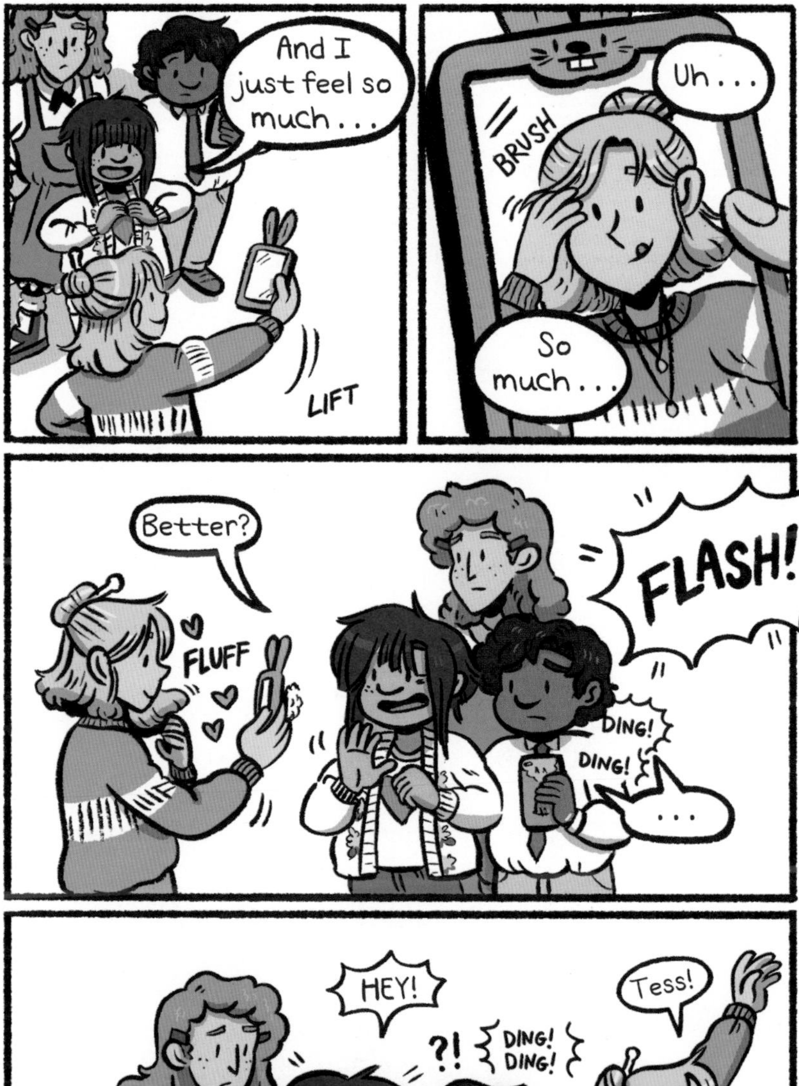
And I just feel so much . . .
LIFT
Uh . . .
BRUSH
So much . . .
Better?
FLUFF
FLASH!
DING!
DING!
. . .
HEY!
?!
DING!
DING!
Tess!
DING!
NEXT!

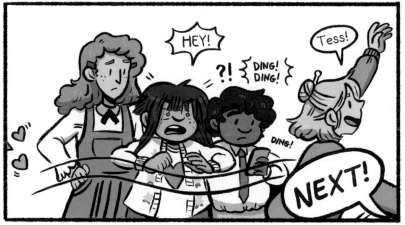

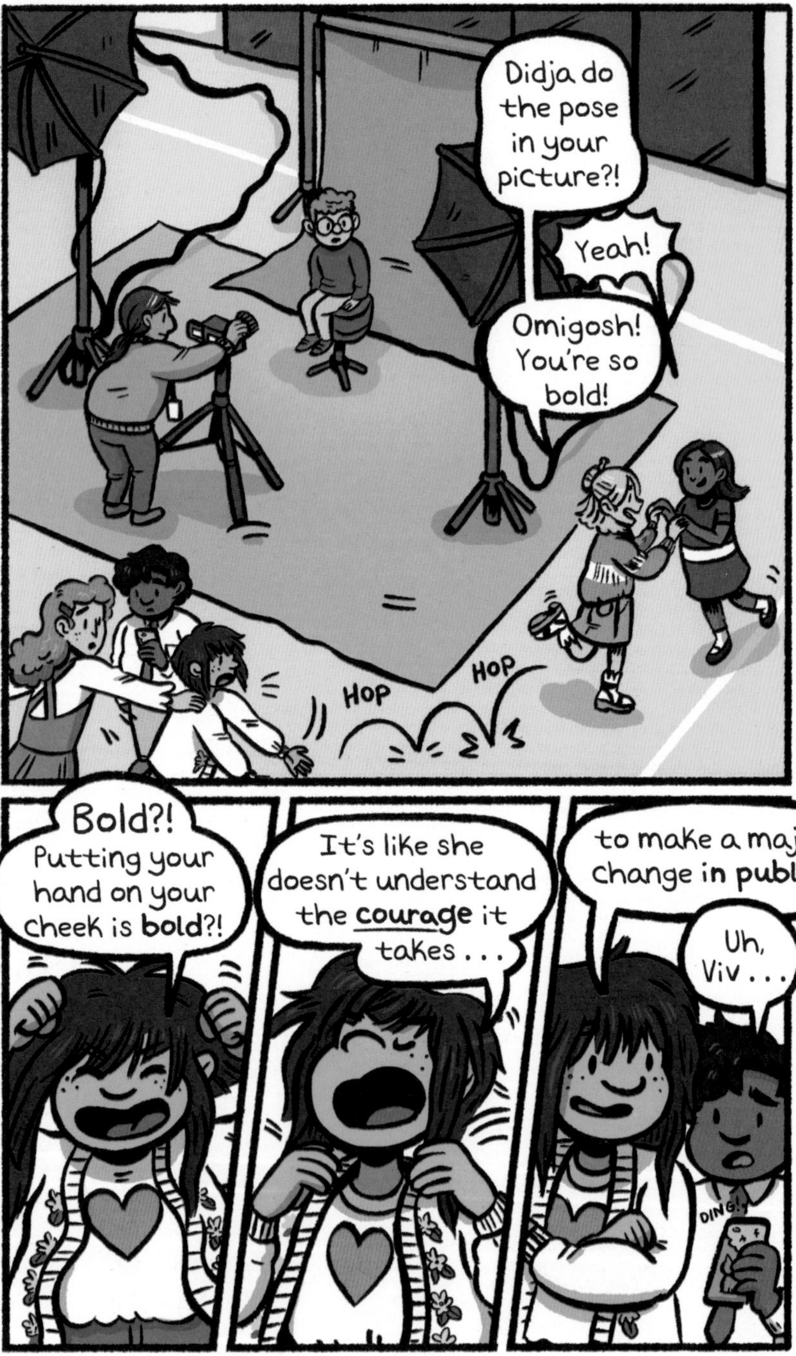
Didja do the pose in your picture?!
Yeah!
Omigosh! You're so bold!
HOP
HOP
Bold?! Putting your hand on your cheek is **bold**?!
It's like she doesn't understand the **courage** it takes . . .
to make a major change **in public**!
Uh, Viv . . .
DING!

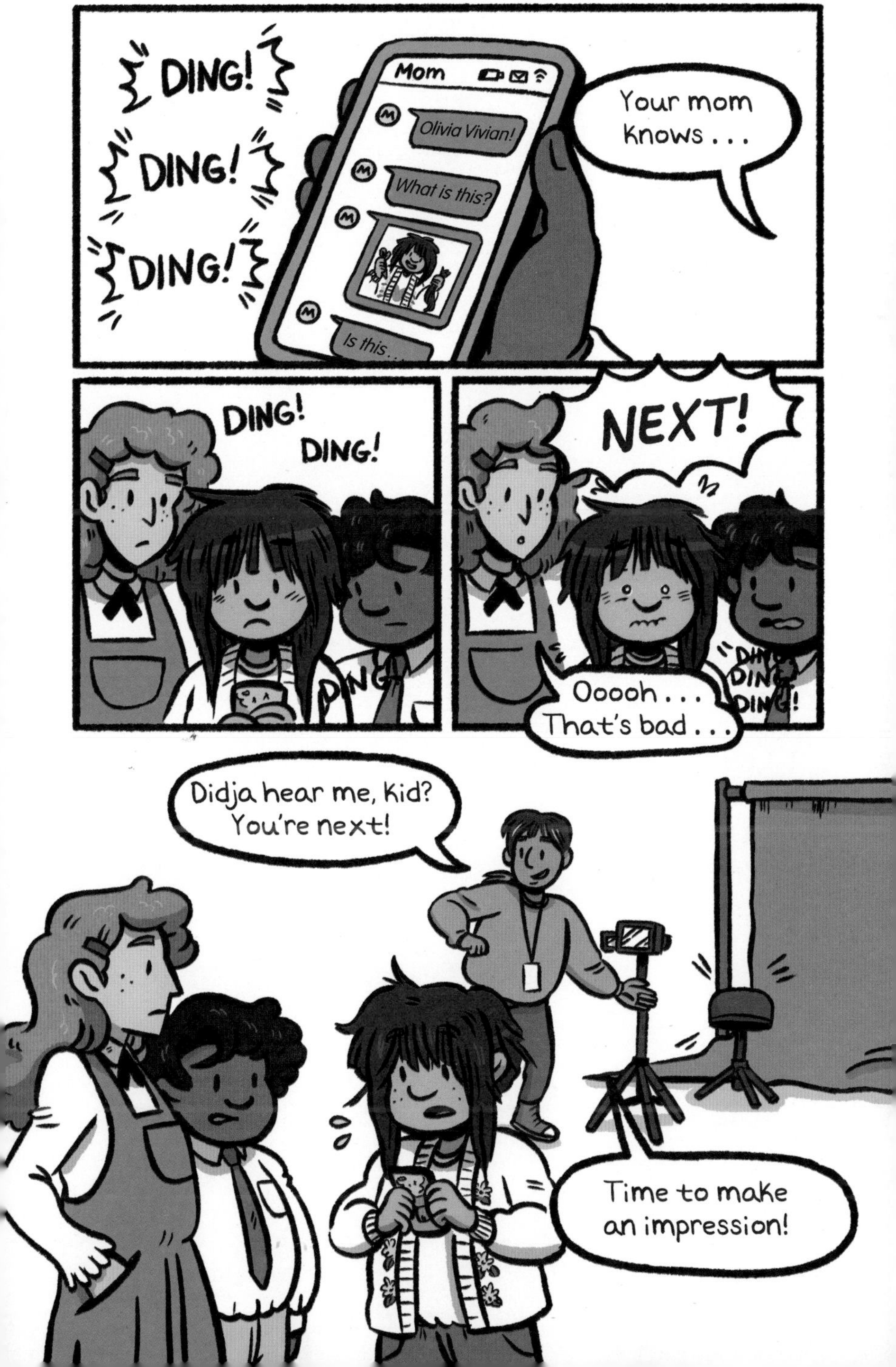
DING!
DING!
DING!
Mom
Olivia Vivian!
What is this?
Is this...
Your mom knows . . .
DING!
DING!
DING!
NEXT!
Ooooh . . .
That's bad . . .
Didja hear me, kid?
You're next!
Time to make an impression!

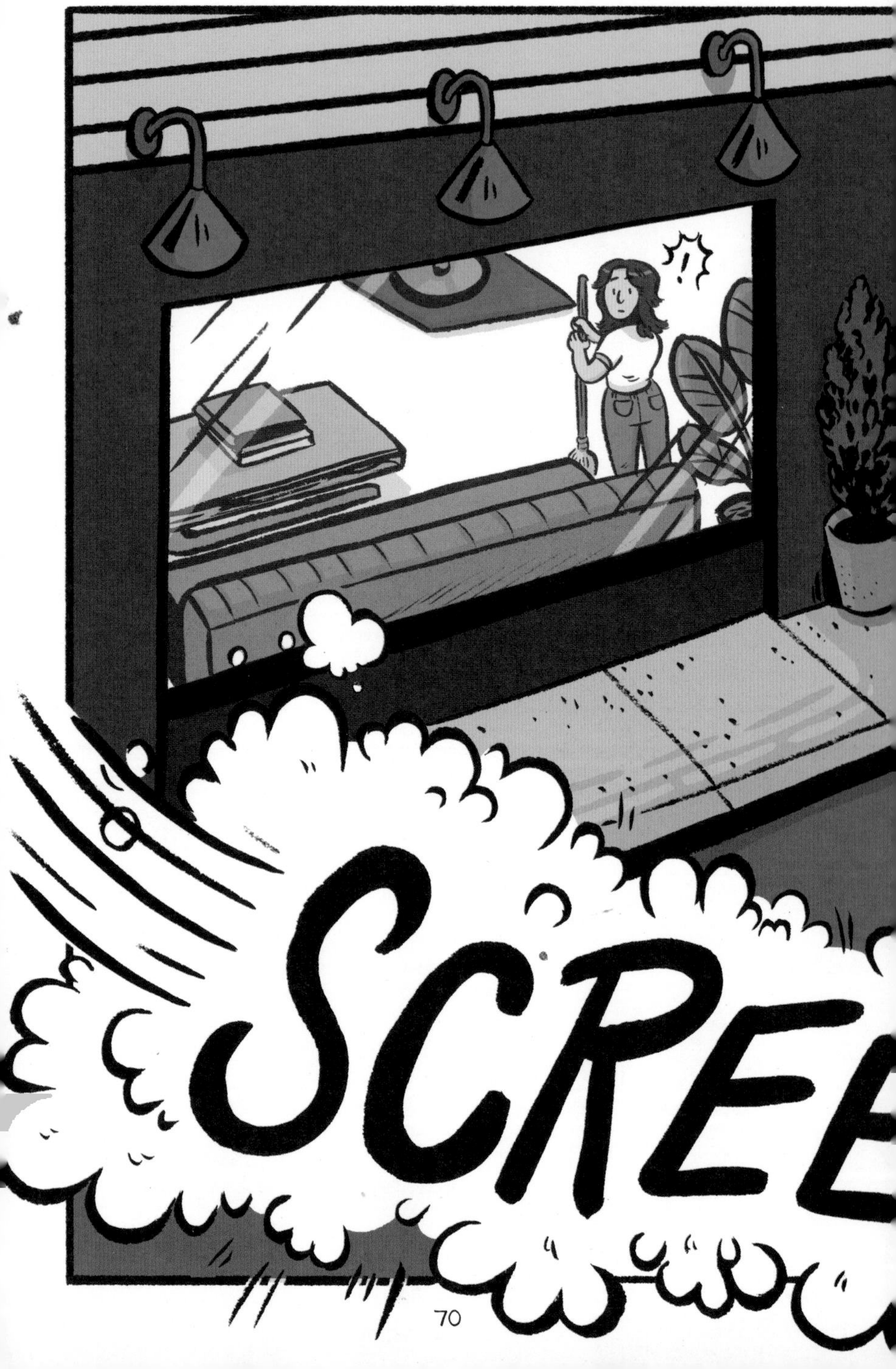

!
SCREE

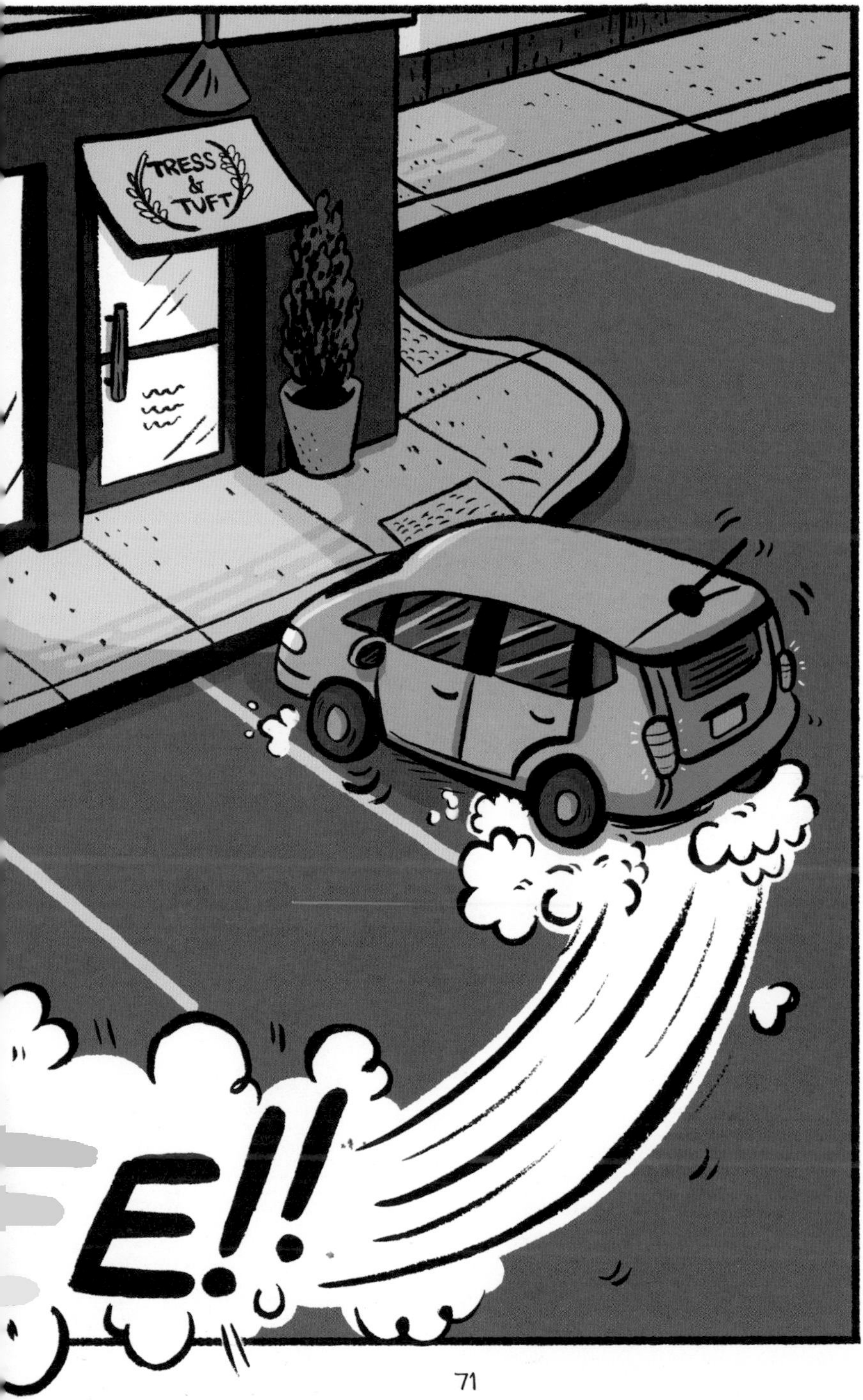
TRESS & TUFT
E!!

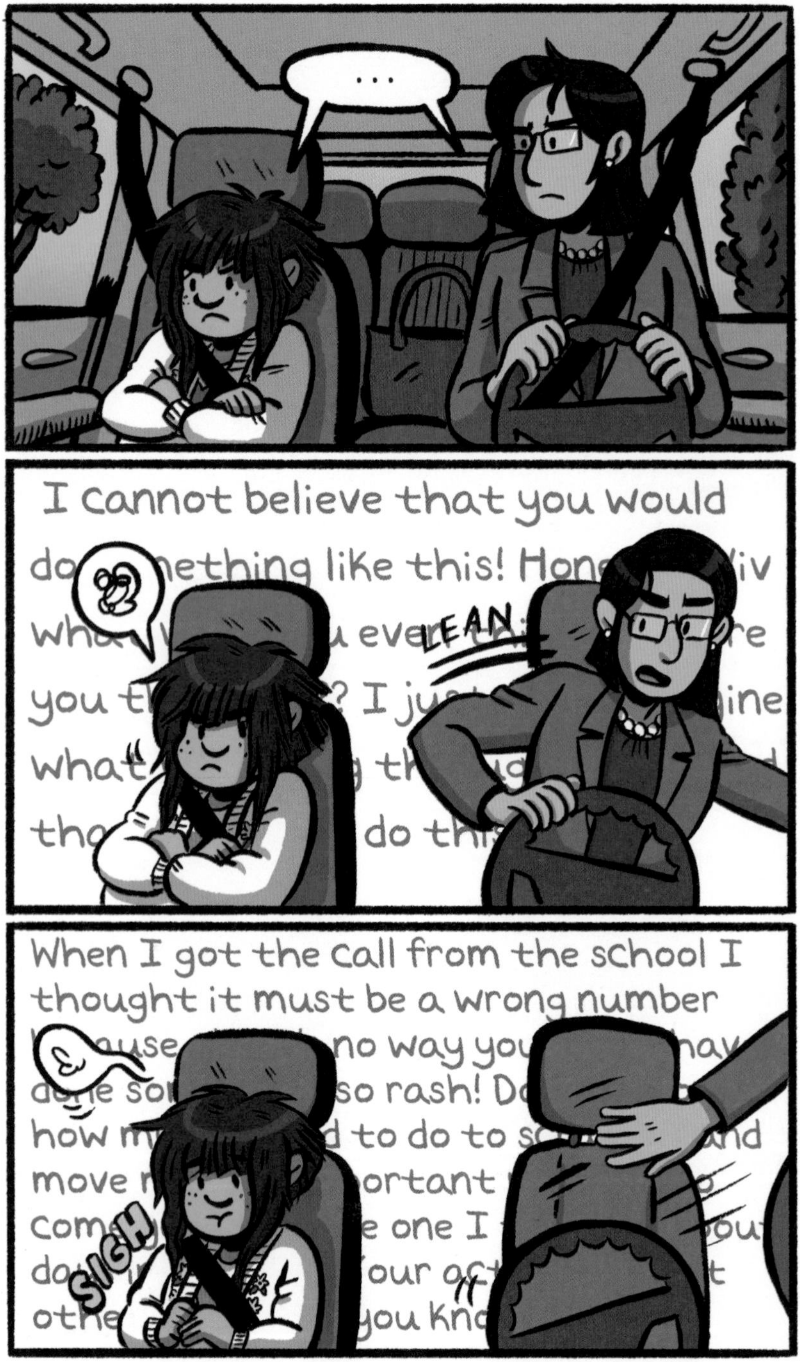
...
I cannot believe that you would
like this!
LEAN
do
When I got the call from the school I
thought it must be a wrong number
no way
so rash!
to do to
move
one
you
SIGH

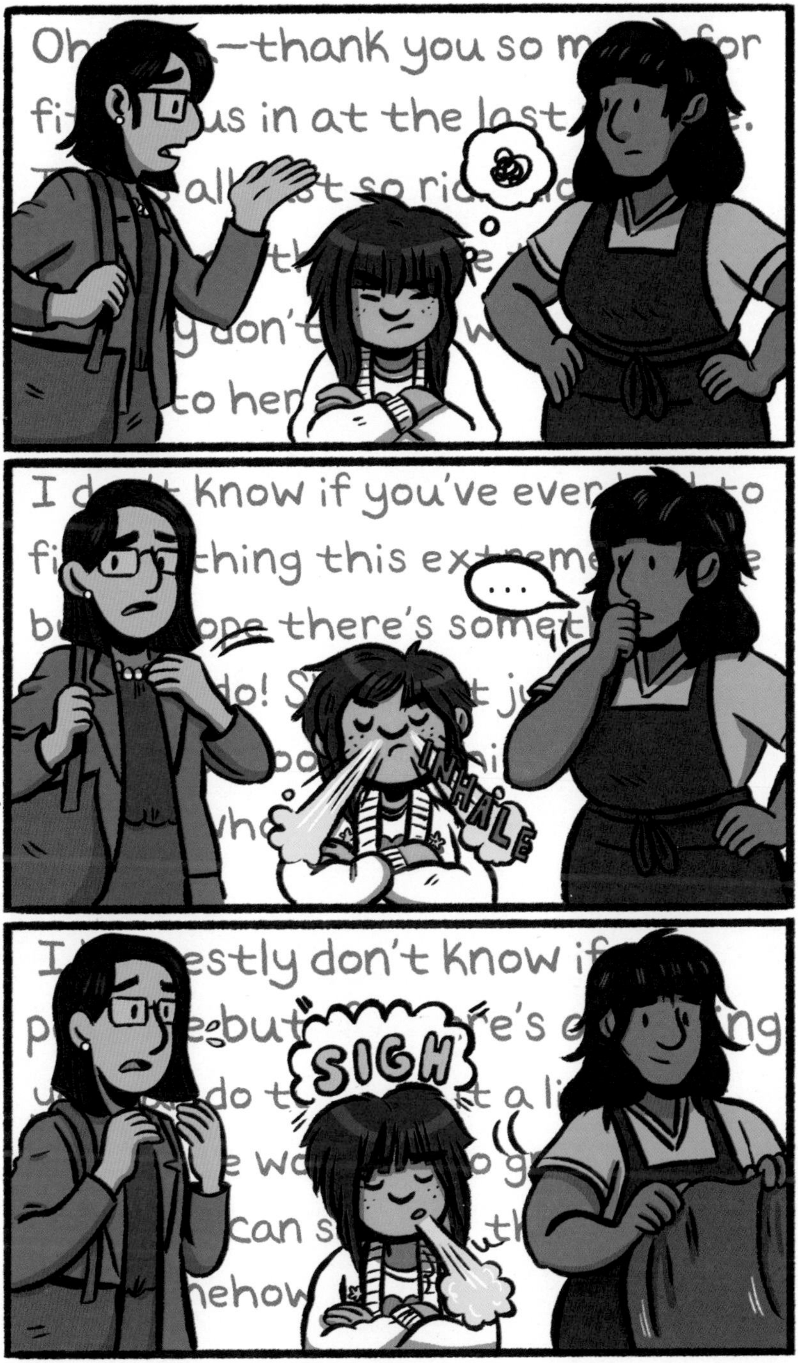
—thank you so m
for
us in at the last
know if you've ever
thing this ex
there's some
INHALE
...
estly don't know if
SIGH
can s

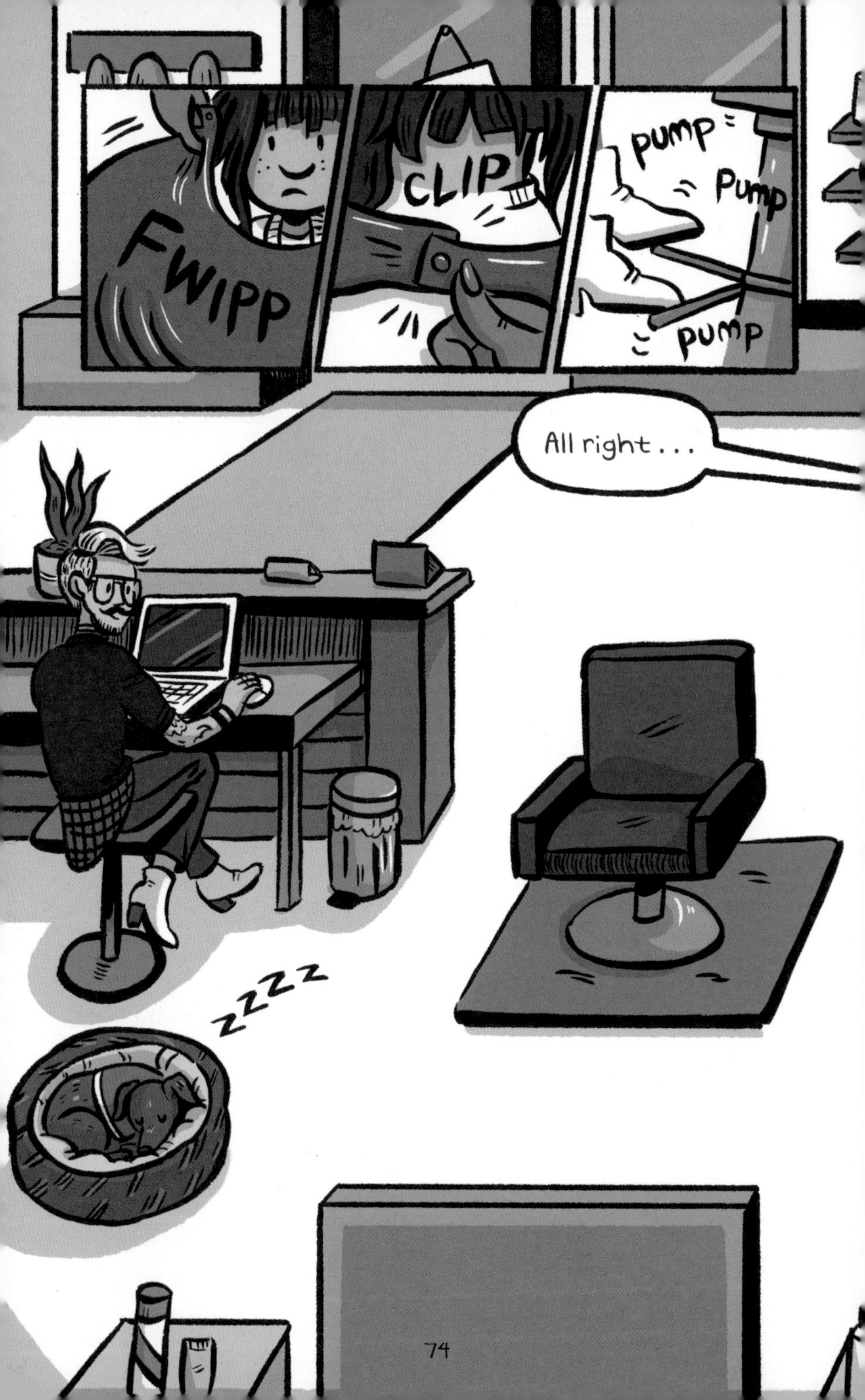
FWIPP
CLIP
PUMP
PUMP
PUMP
All right . . .
ZZZZ

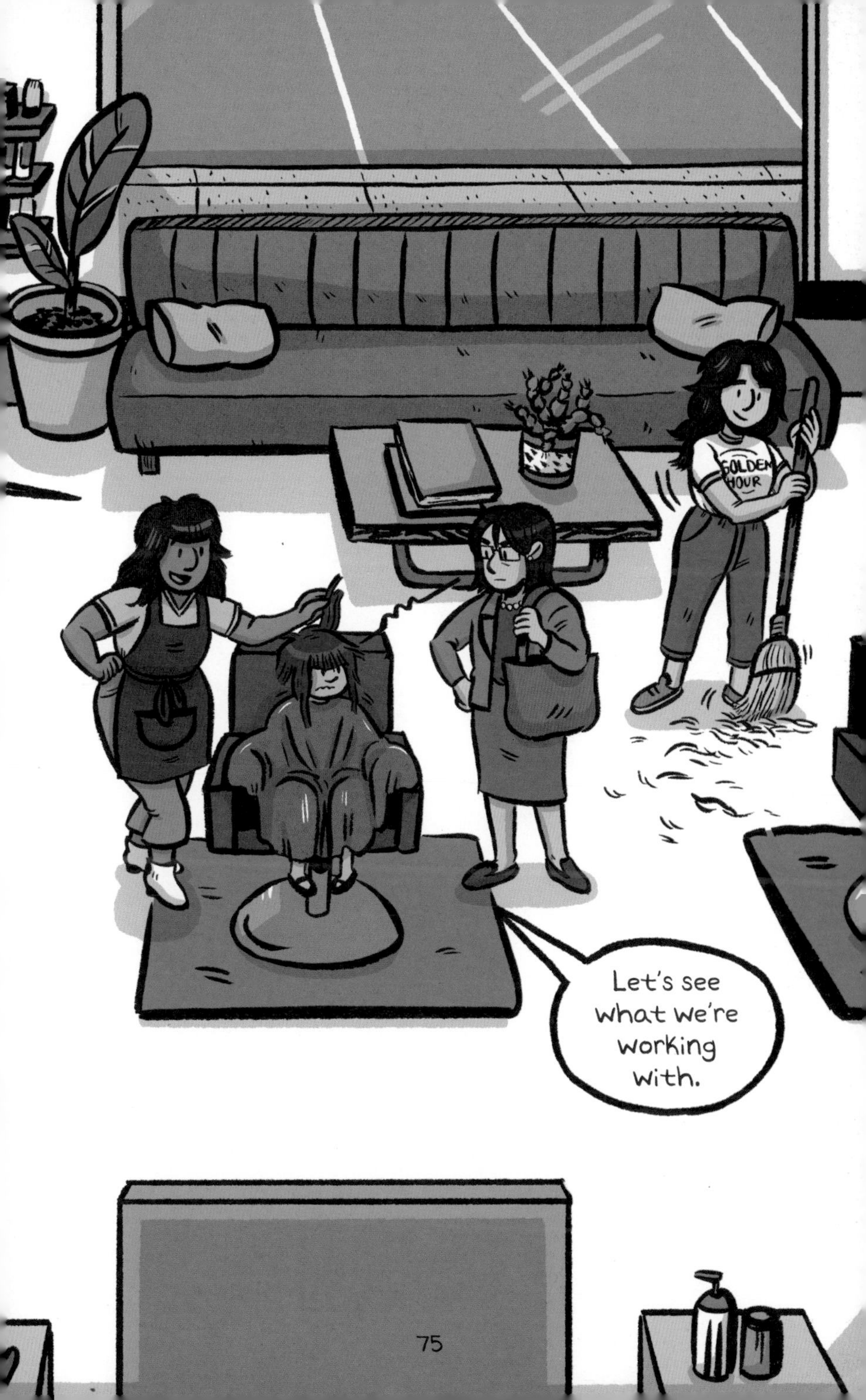
GOLDEN HOUR
Let's see what we're working with.

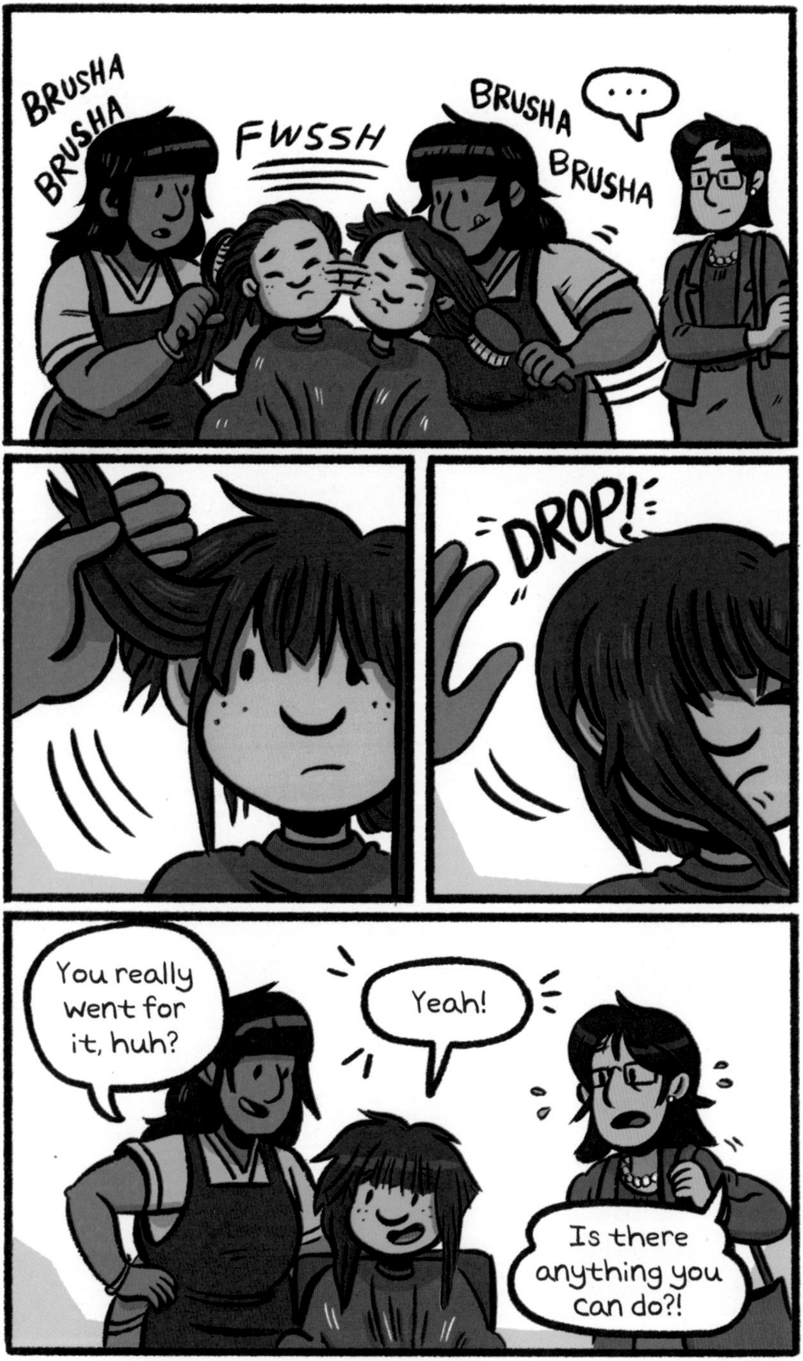
BRUSHA BRUSHA
FWSSH
BRUSHA BRUSHA
...
DROP!
You really went for it, huh?
Yeah!
Is there anything you can do?!

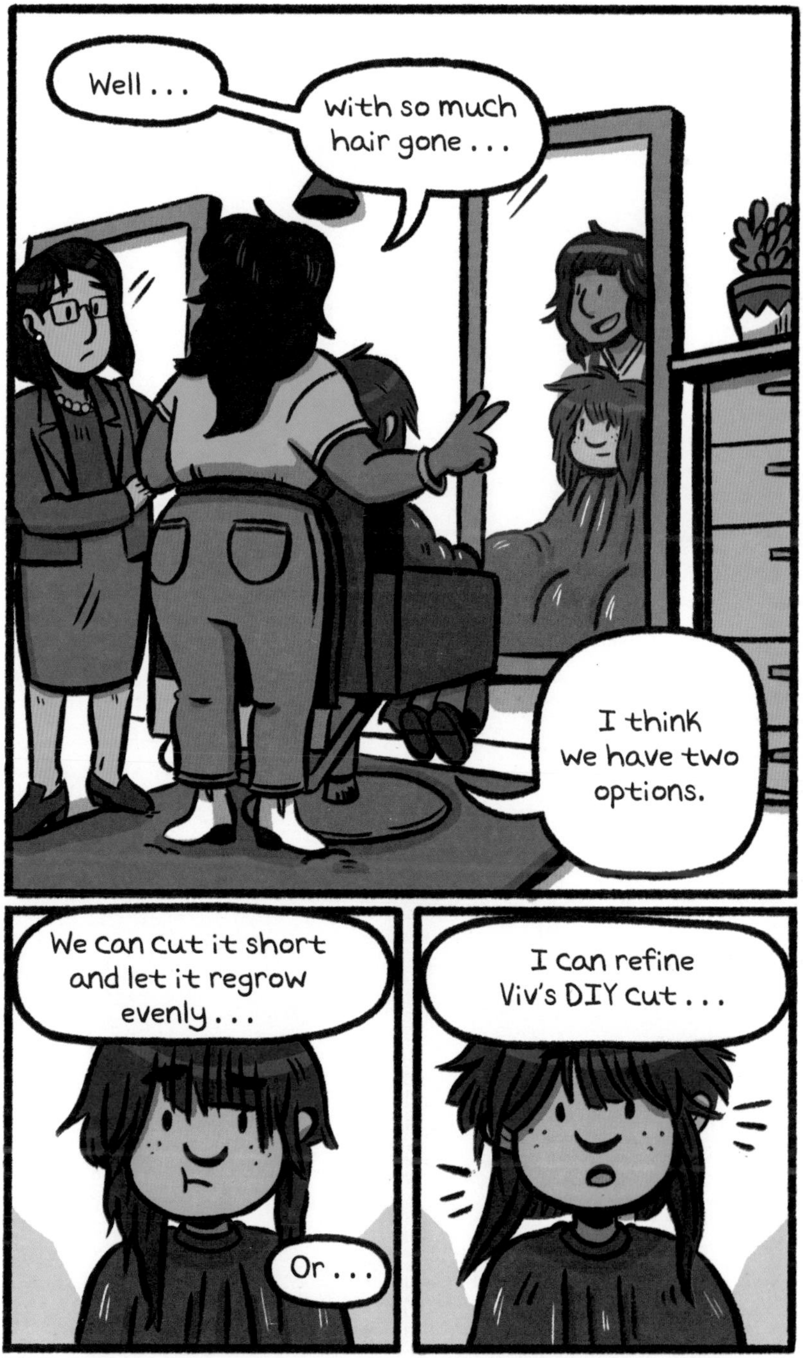
Well . . .
With so much hair gone . . .
I think we have two options.
We can cut it short and let it regrow evenly . . .
Or . . .
I can refine Viv's DIY cut . . .

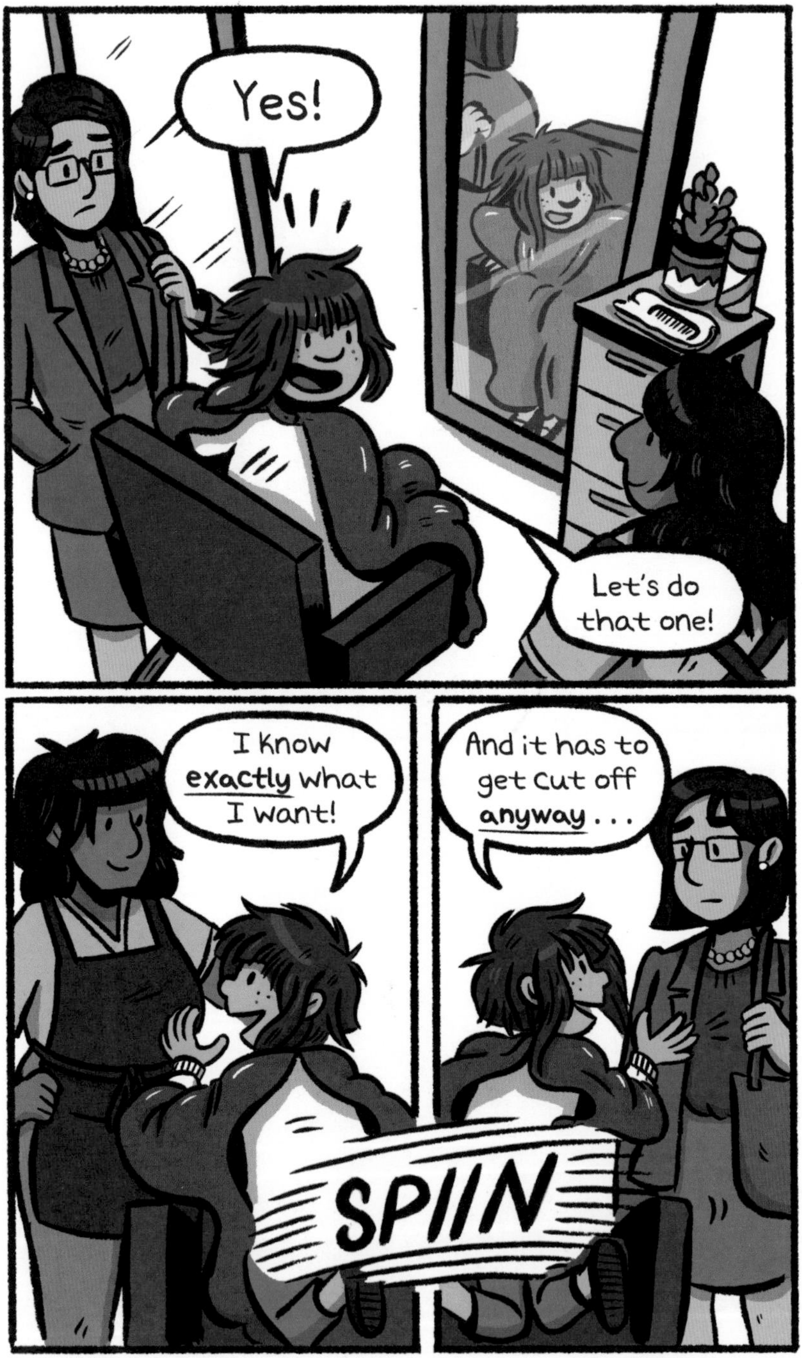
Yes!
Let's do that one!
I know exactly what I want!
And it has to get cut off anyway . . .
SPIIN

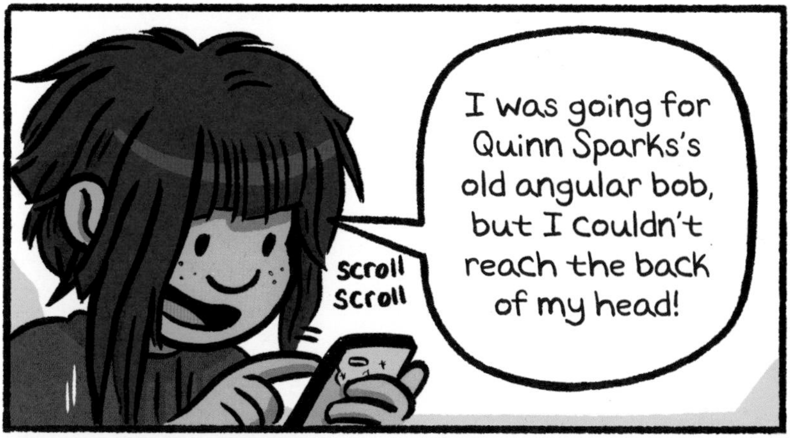
scroll
scroll
I was going for Quinn Sparks's old angular bob, but I couldn't reach the back of my head!

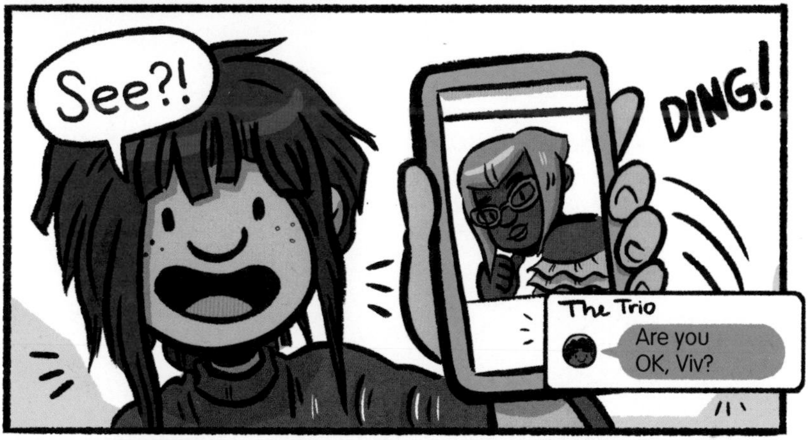
See?!
DING!
The Trio
Are you OK, Viv?

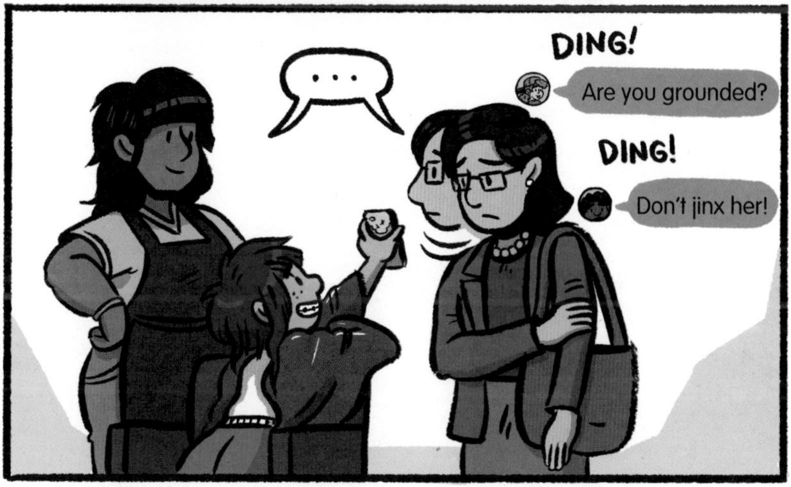
. . .
DING!
Are you grounded?
DING!
Don't jinx her!

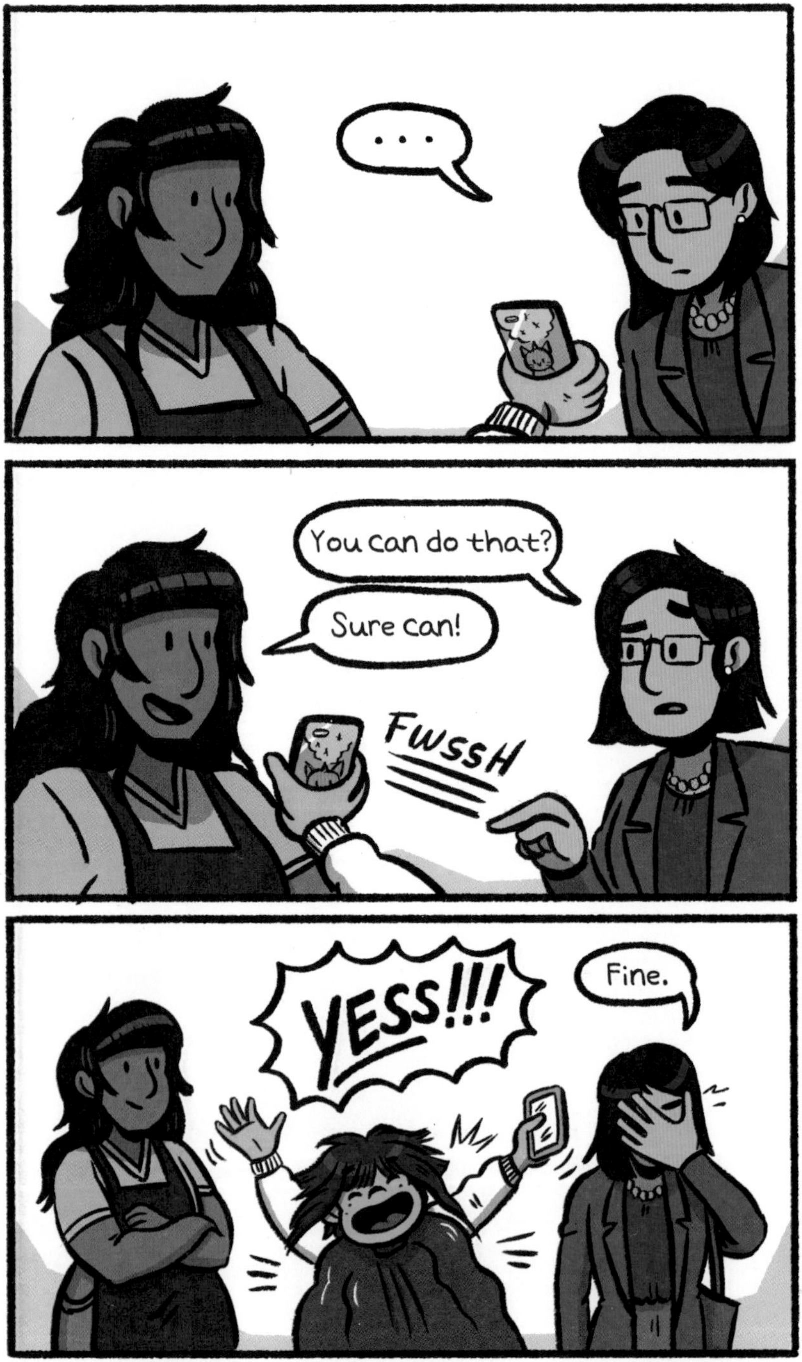
...
You can do that?
Sure can!
FWSSH
YESS!!!
Fine.

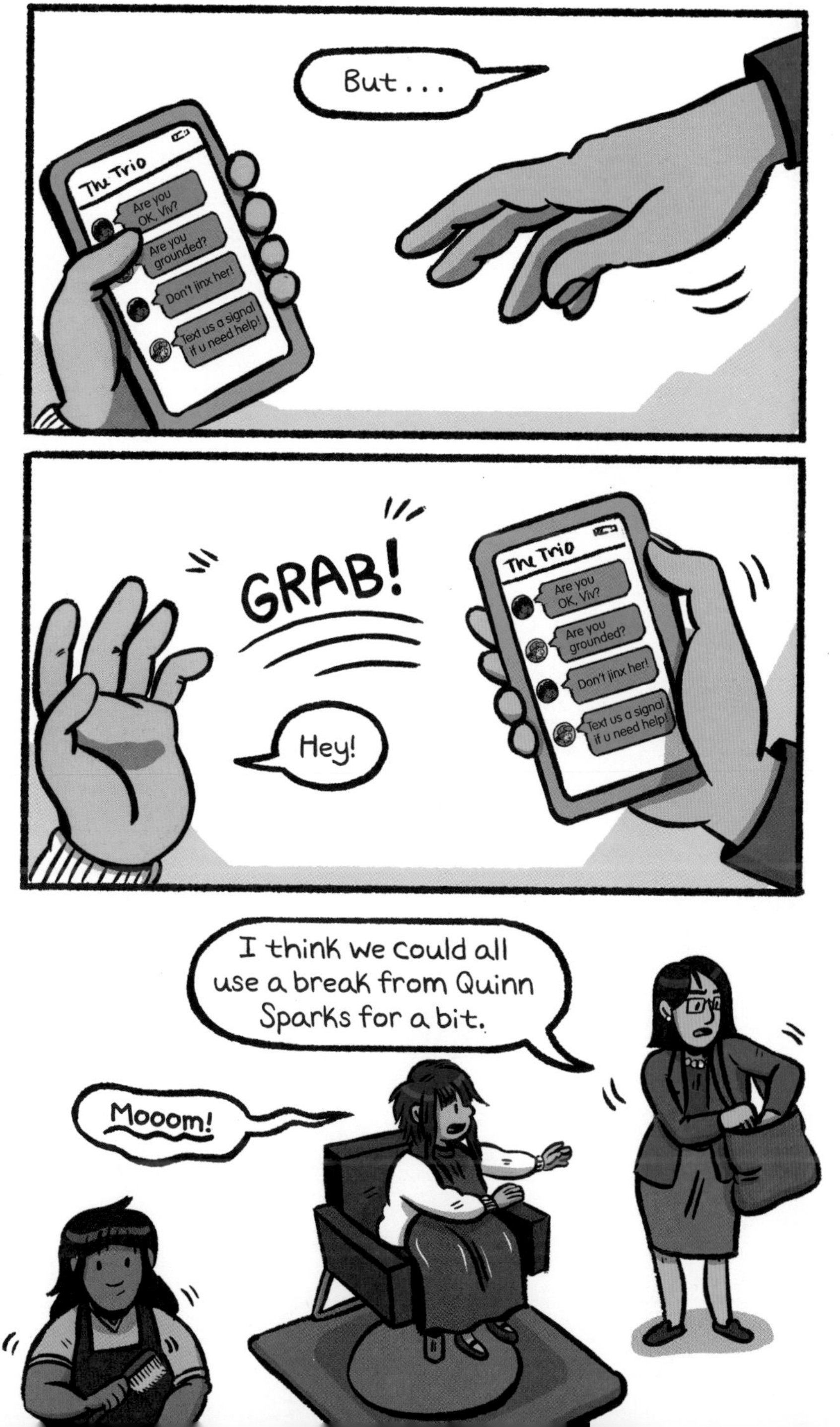

But...
The Trio
Are you OK, Viv?
Are you grounded?
Don't jinx her!
Text us a signal if u need help!
GRAB!
Hey!
The Trio
Are you OK, Viv?
Are you grounded?
Don't jinx her!
Text us a signal if u need help!
I think we could all use a break from Quinn Sparks for a bit.
Mooom!

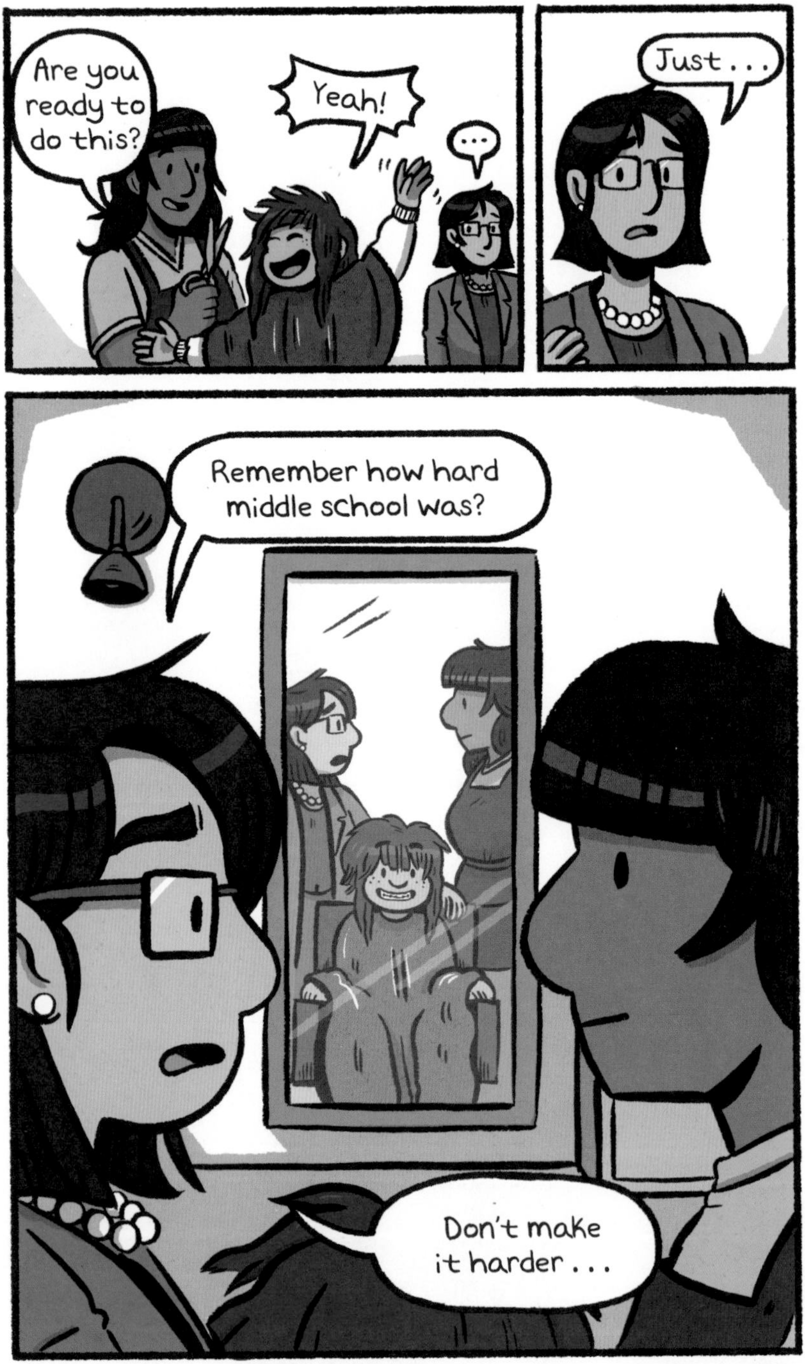
Are you ready to do this?
Yeah!
...
Just...
Remember how hard middle school was?
Don't make it harder...

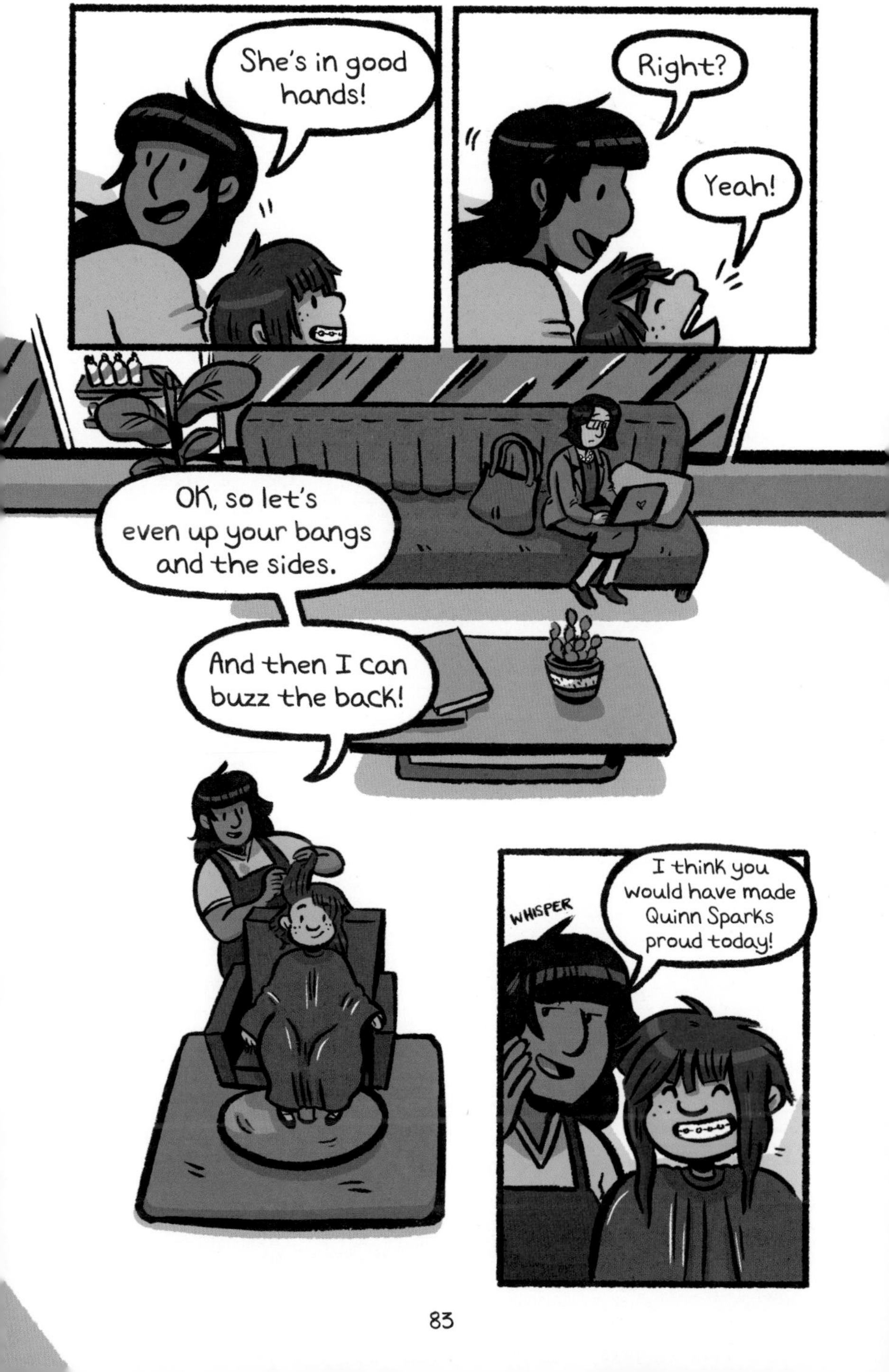
She's in good hands!
Right?
Yeah!
OK, so let's even up your bangs and the sides.
And then I can buzz the back!
WHISPER
I think you would have made Quinn Sparks proud today!

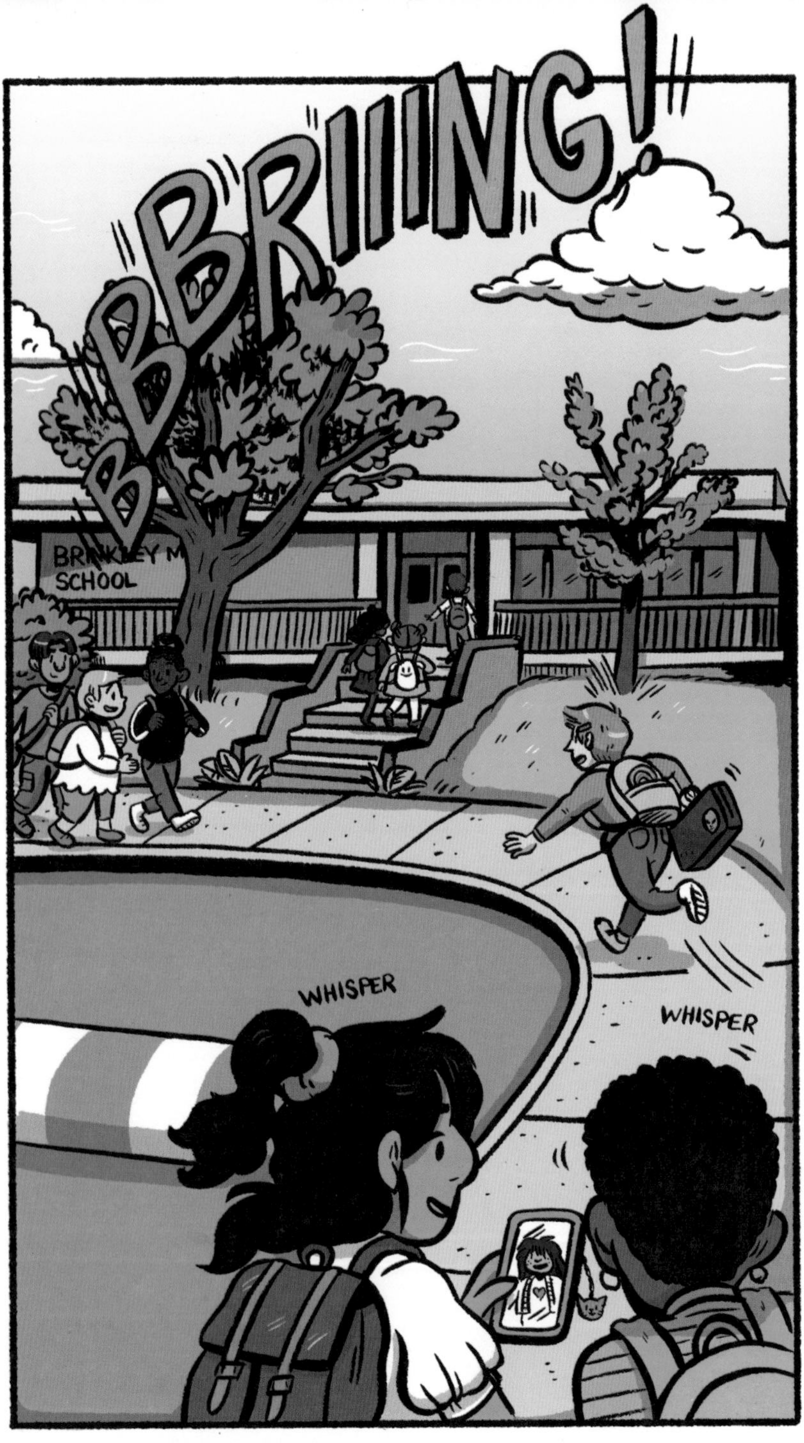
BBBRIIING!
SCHOOL
WHISPER
WHISPER

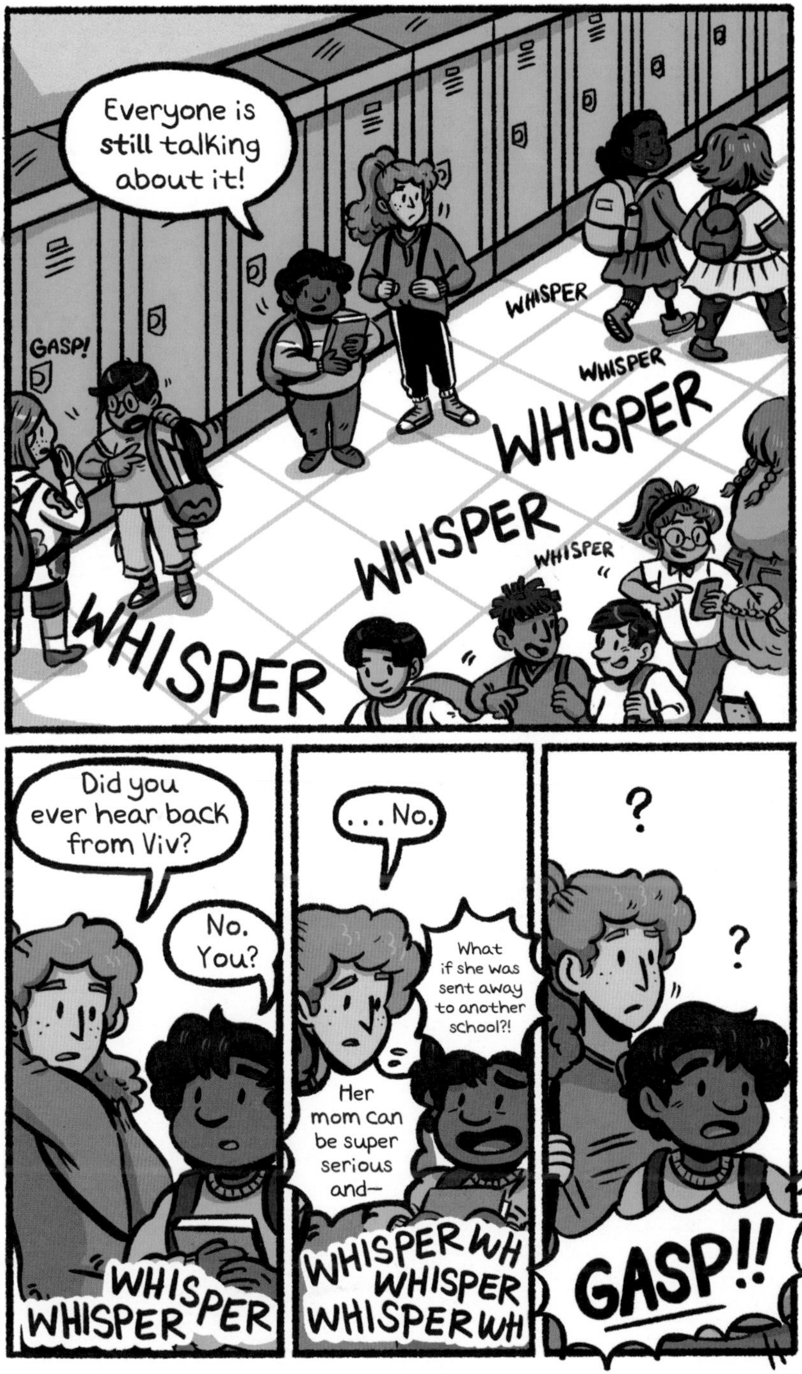
Everyone is still talking about it!
GASP!
WHISPER
WHISPER
WHISPER
WHISPER
WHISPER
WHISPER
Did you ever hear back from Viv?
No. You?
WHISPER
WHISPER WHISPER
...No.
What if she was sent away to another school?!
Her mom can be super serious and—
WHISPERWH
WHISPER
WHISPERWH
?
?
GASP!!

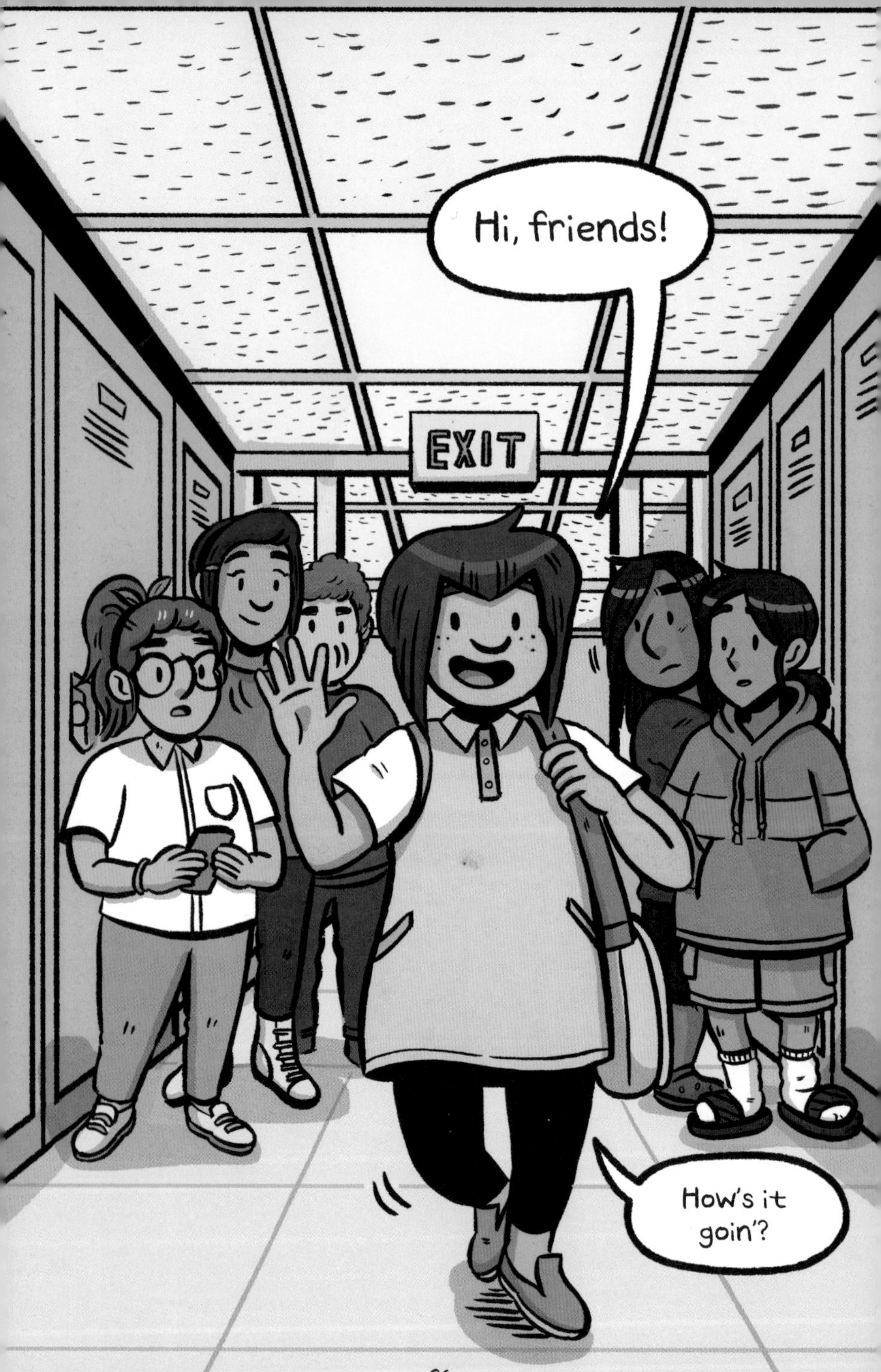
EXIT
Hi, friends!
How's it goin'?

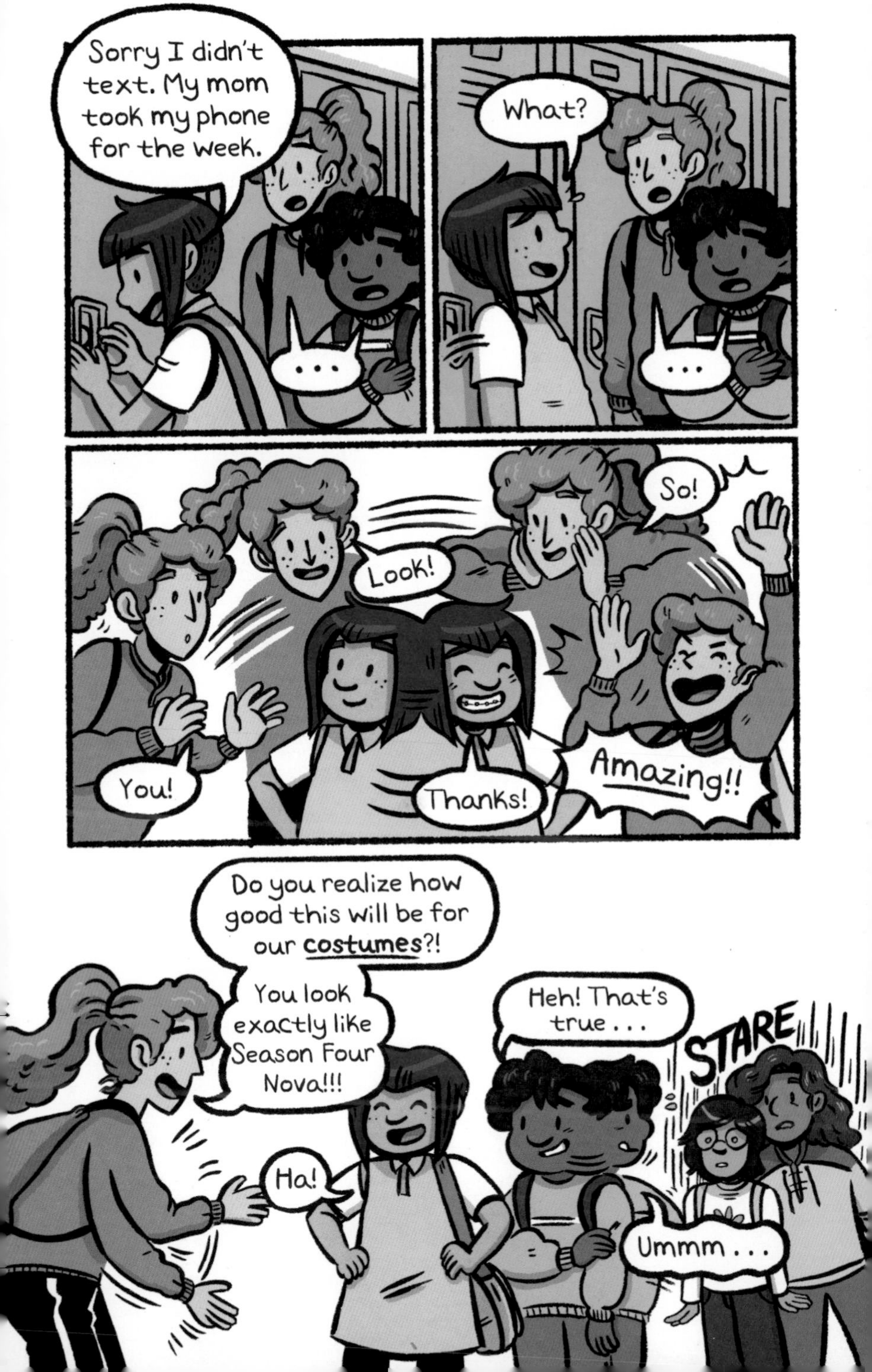
Sorry I didn't text. My mom took my phone for the week.
. . .
What?
. . .
Look!
So!
You!
Thanks!
Amazing!!
Do you realize how good this will be for our costumes?!
You look exactly like Season Four Nova!!!
Heh! That's true . . .
STARE
Ha!
Ummm . . .

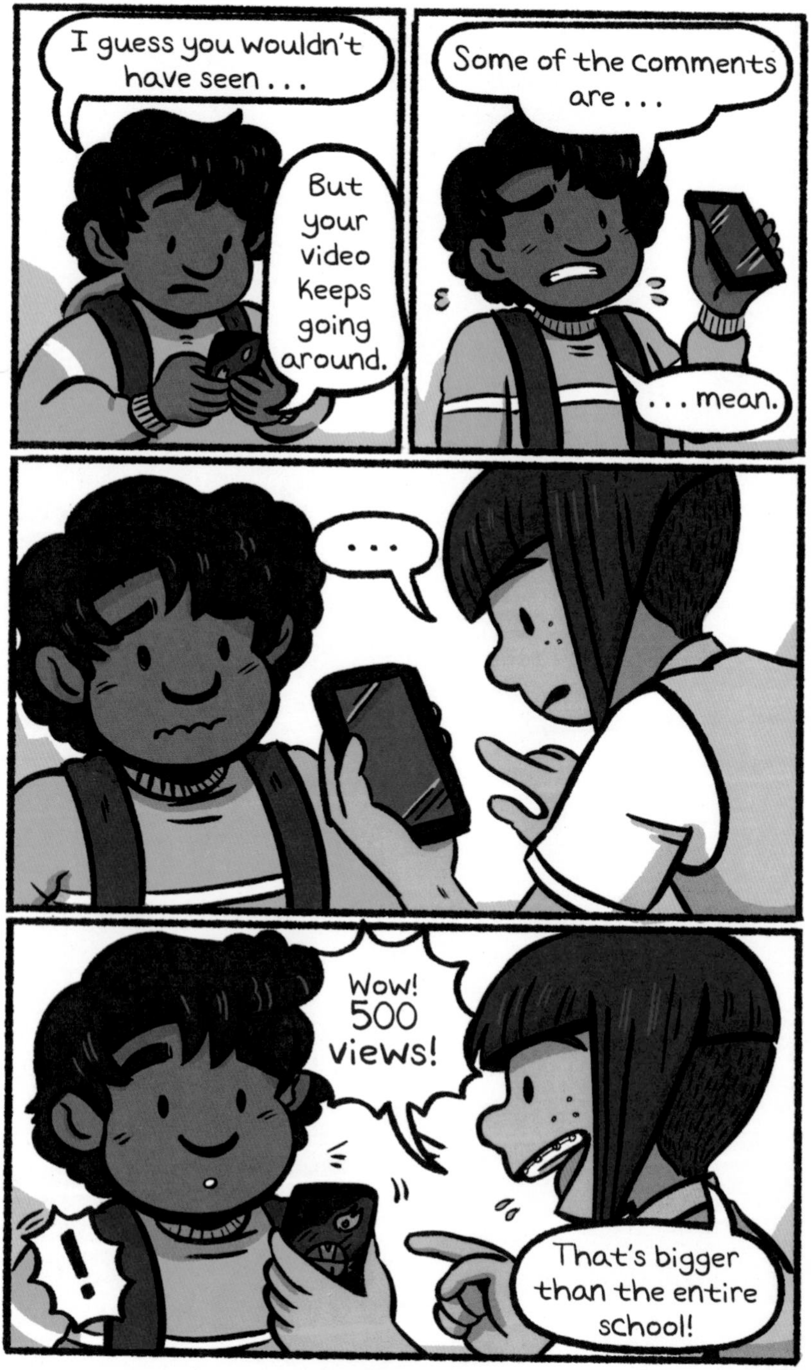
I guess you wouldn't have seen . . .
But your video keeps going around.
Some of the comments are . . .
. . . mean.
. . .
Wow! 500 views!
!
That's bigger than the entire school!

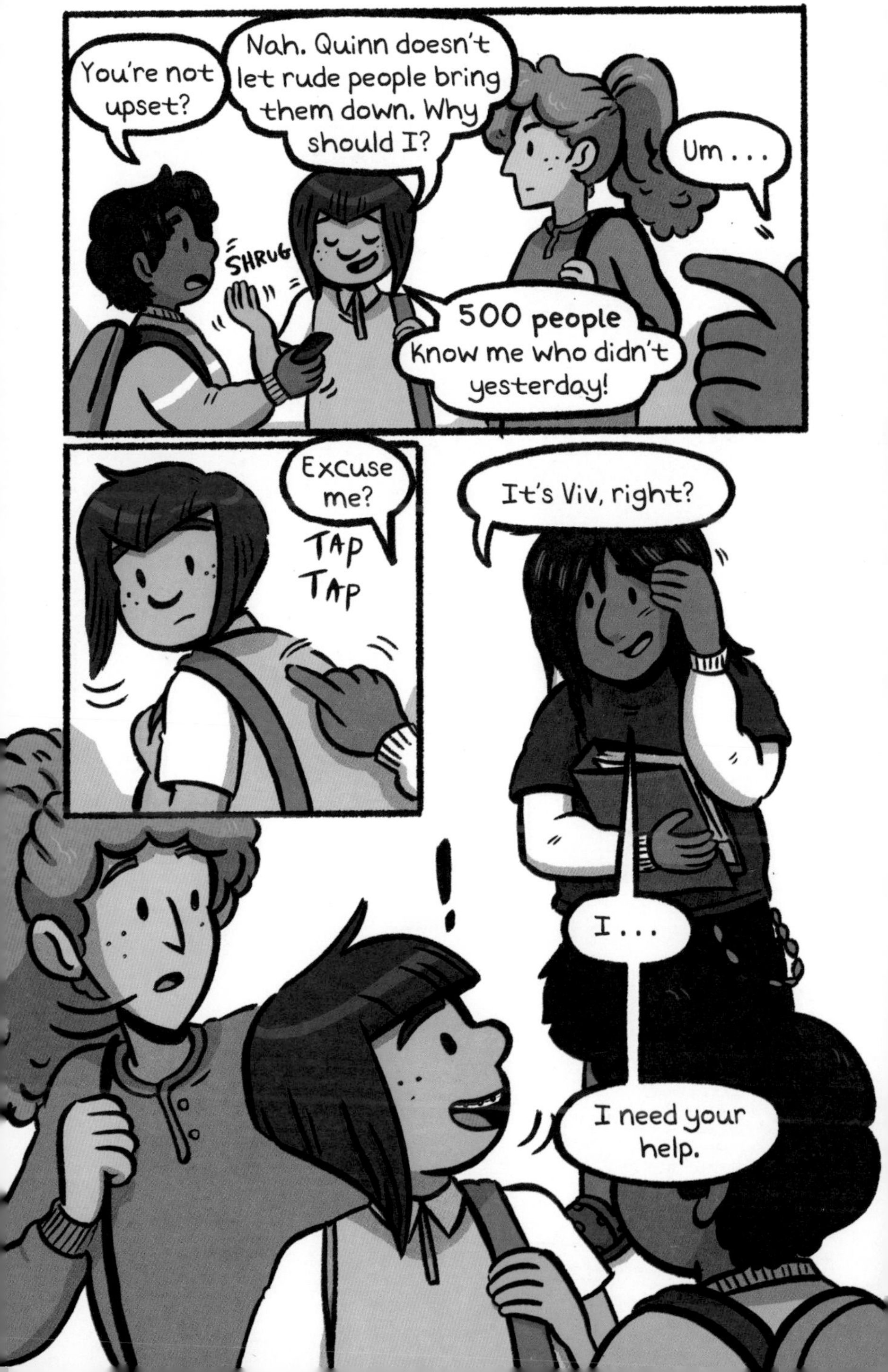
You're not upset?
Nah. Quinn doesn't let rude people bring them down. Why should I?
SHRUG
Um . . .
500 people know me who didn't yesterday!
Excuse me?
TAP
TAP
It's Viv, right?
!
I . . .
I need your help.

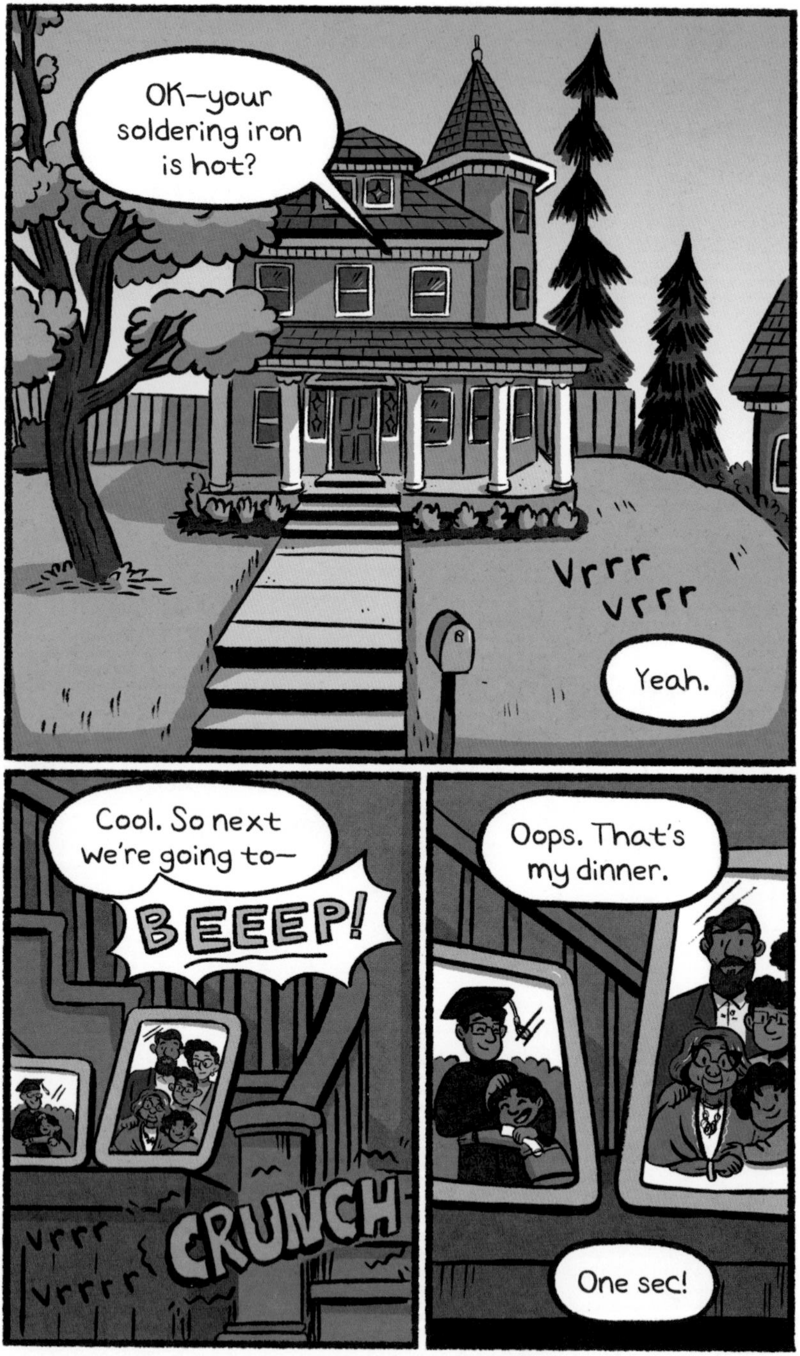
OK—your soldering iron is hot?
Vrrr vrrr
Yeah.
Cool. So next we're going to—
BEEEP!
vrrr vrrrr
CRUNCH
Oops. That's my dinner.
One sec!

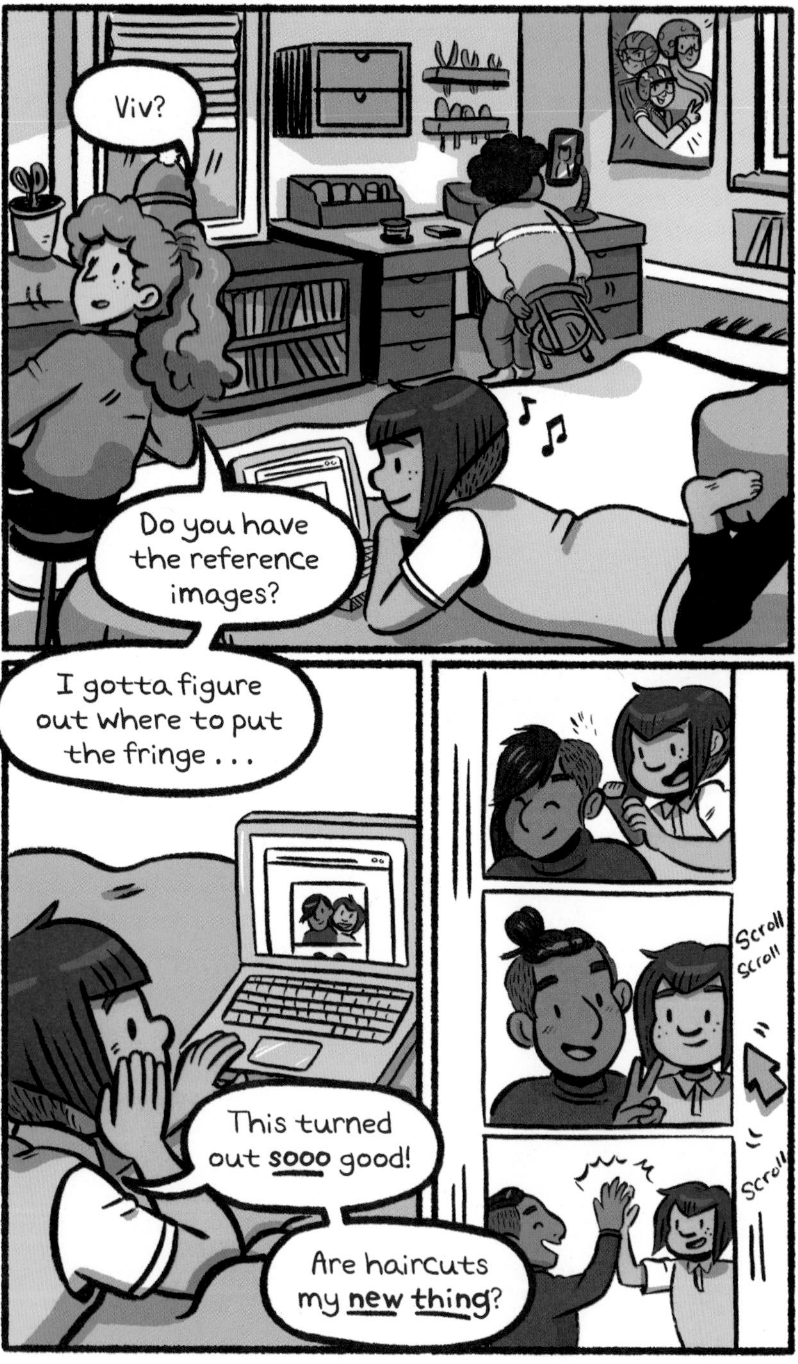
Viv?
Do you have the reference images?
I gotta figure out where to put the fringe . . .
This turned out sooo good!
Are haircuts my new thing?
Scroll scroll
Scroll

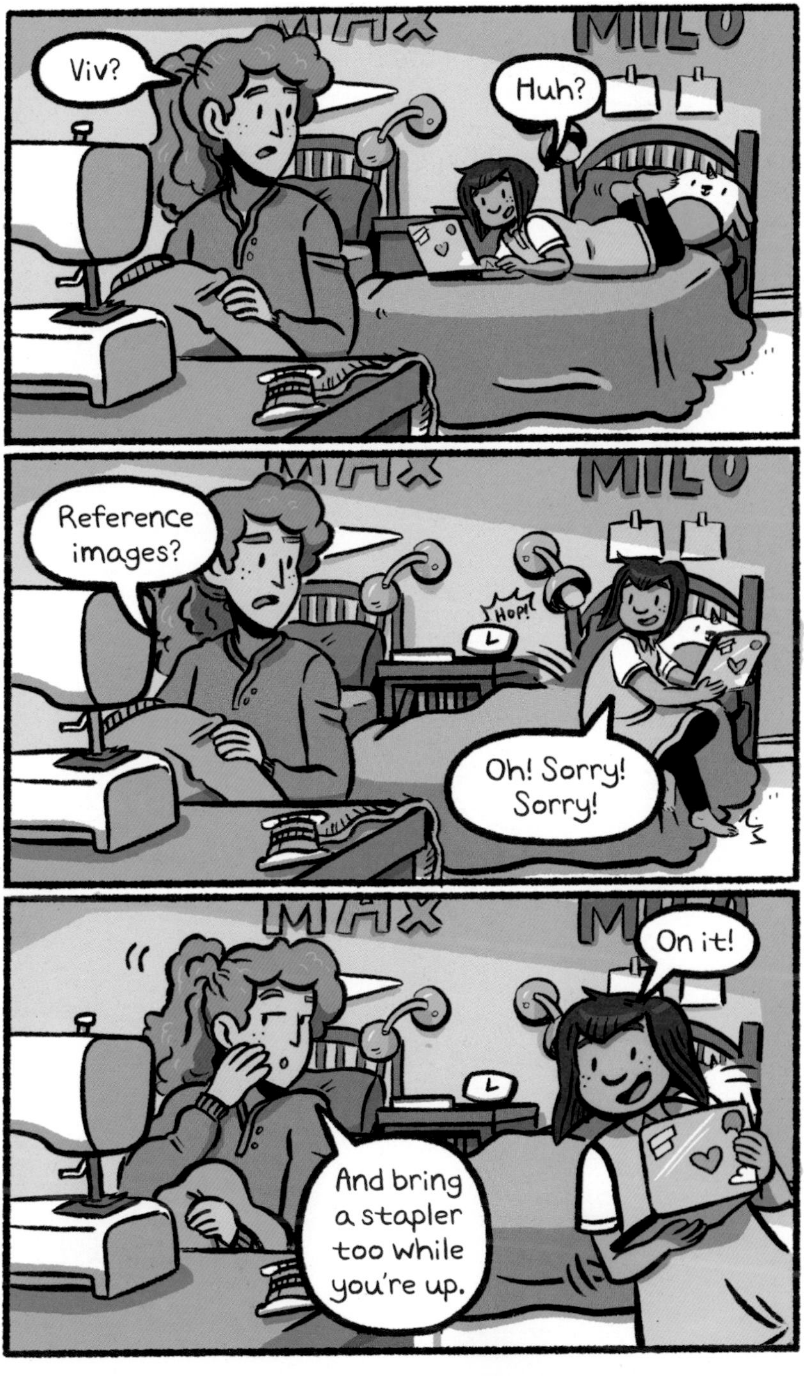
Viv?
Huh?
Reference images?
HOP!
Oh! Sorry! Sorry!
On it!
And bring a stapler too while you're up.

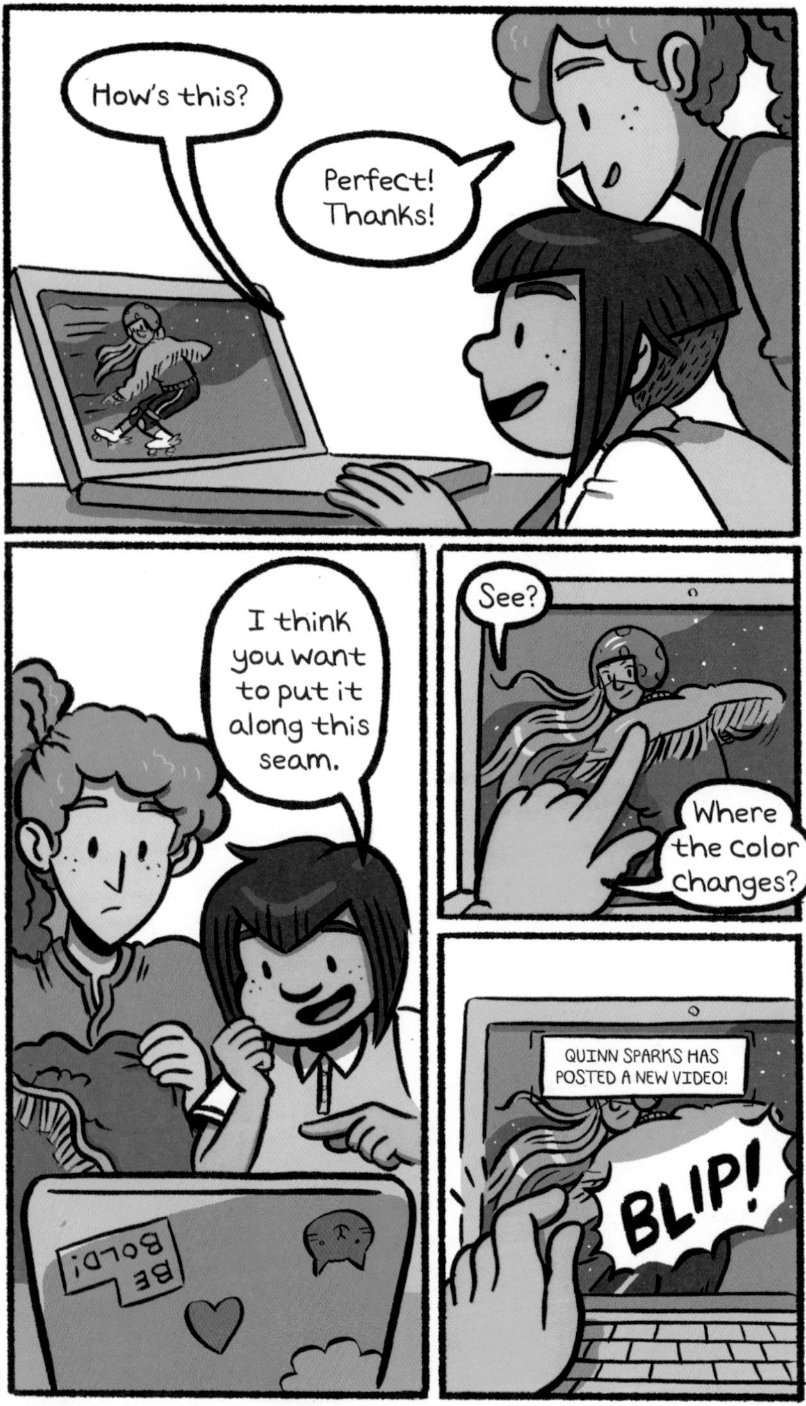
How's this?
Perfect! Thanks!
I think you want to put it along this seam.
See?
Where the color changes?
QUINN SPARKS HAS POSTED A NEW VIDEO!
BLIP!
BE BOLD!

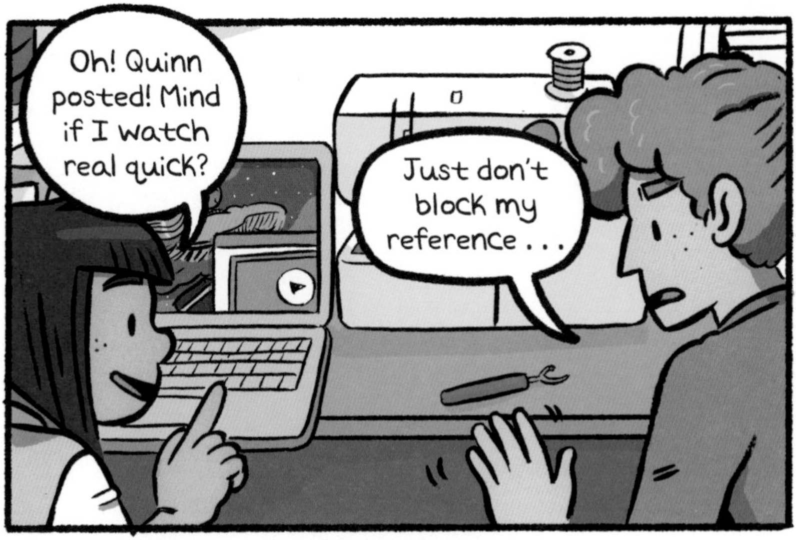
Oh! Quinn posted! Mind if I watch real quick?
Just don't block my reference . . .

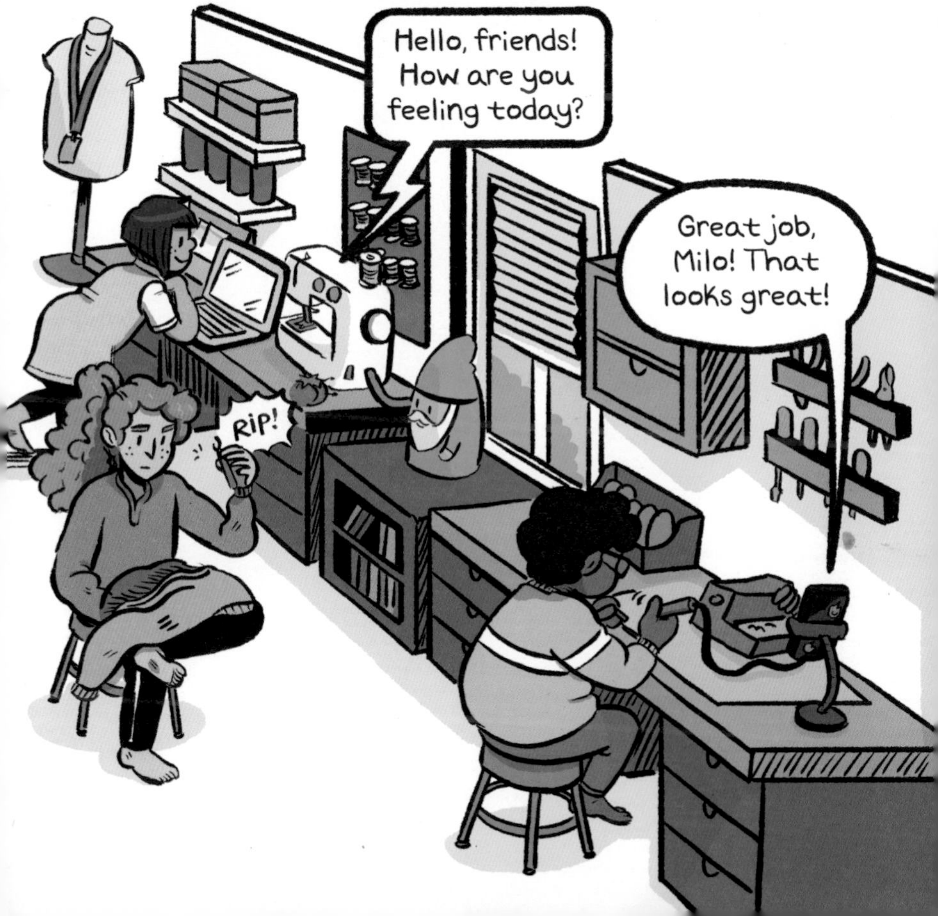
Hello, friends! How are you feeling today?
Great job, Milo! That looks great!
RIP!

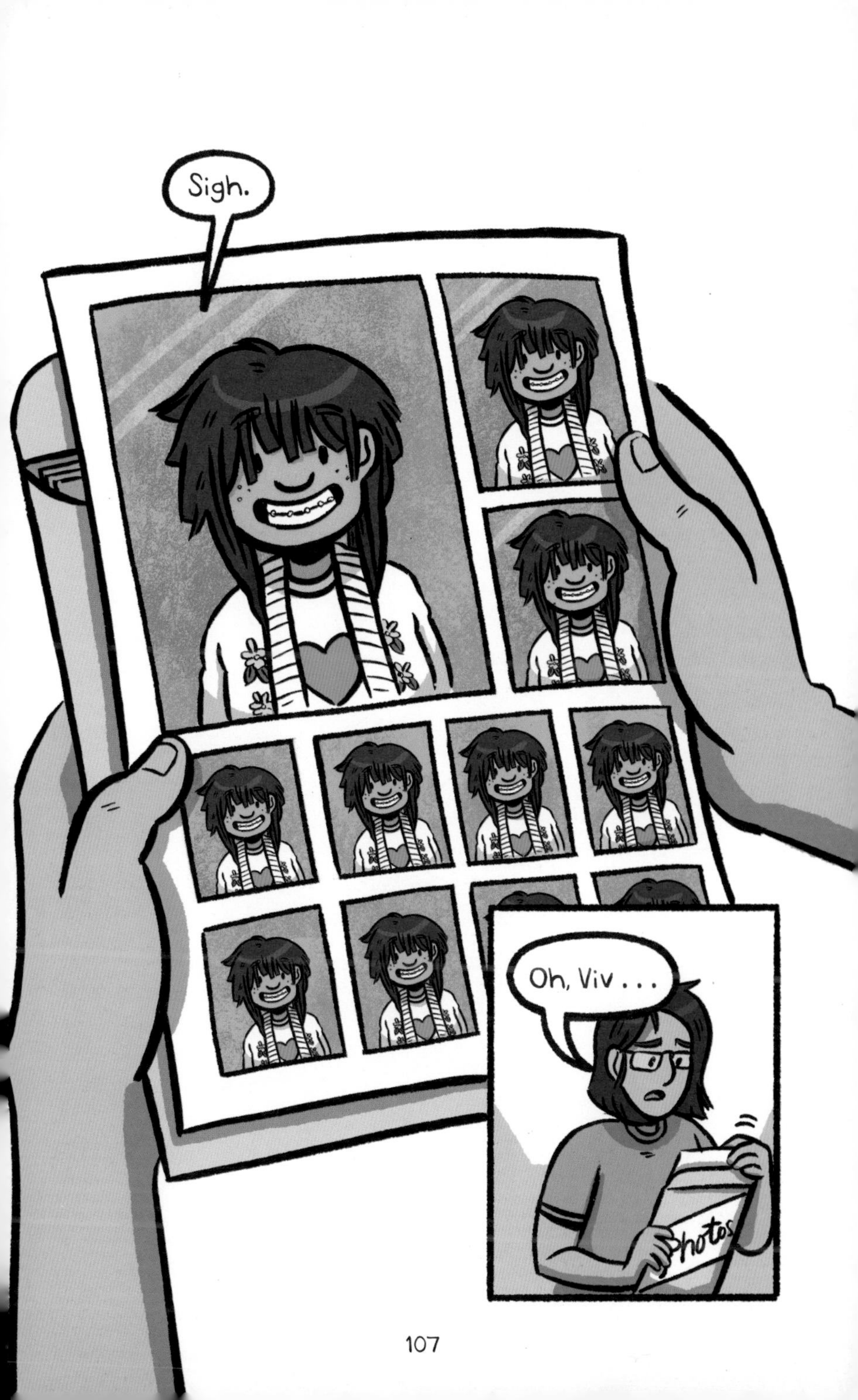
Sigh.
Oh, Viv . . .
Photos

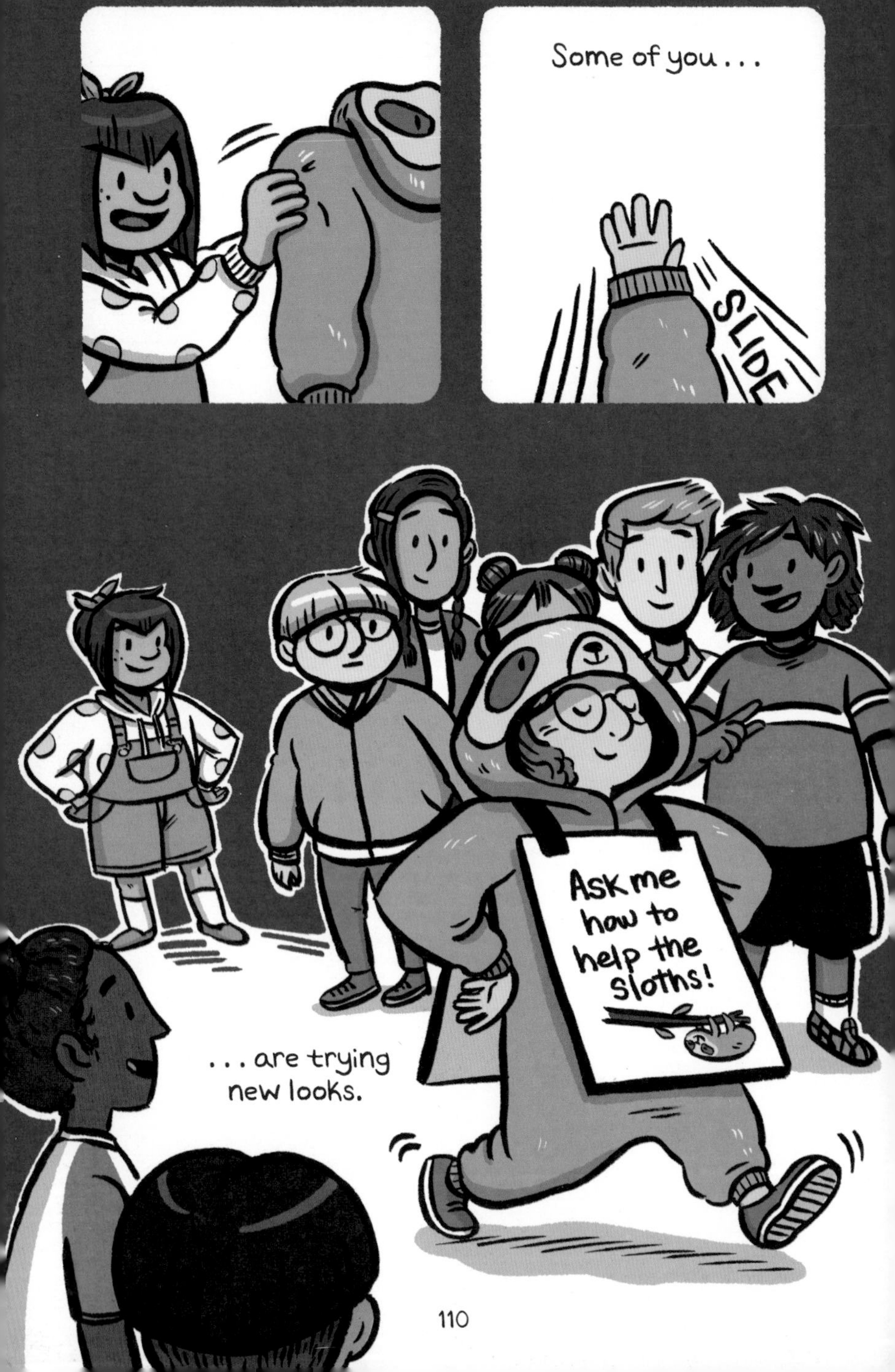
Some of you . . .
SLIDE
. . . are trying new looks.
Ask me how to help the sloths!

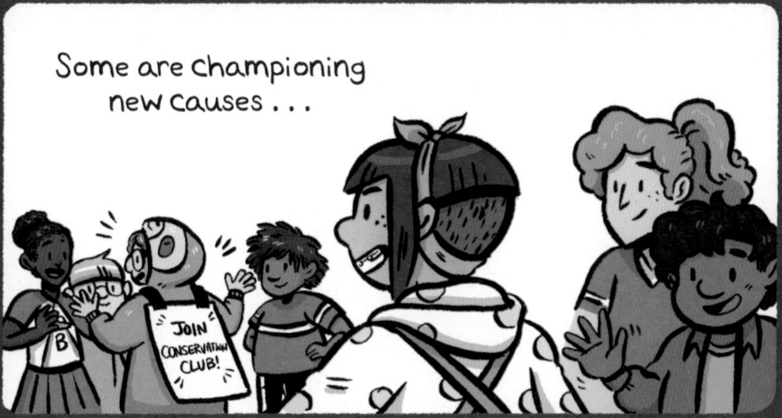
Some are championing new causes . . .
B
JOIN CONSERVATION CLUB!

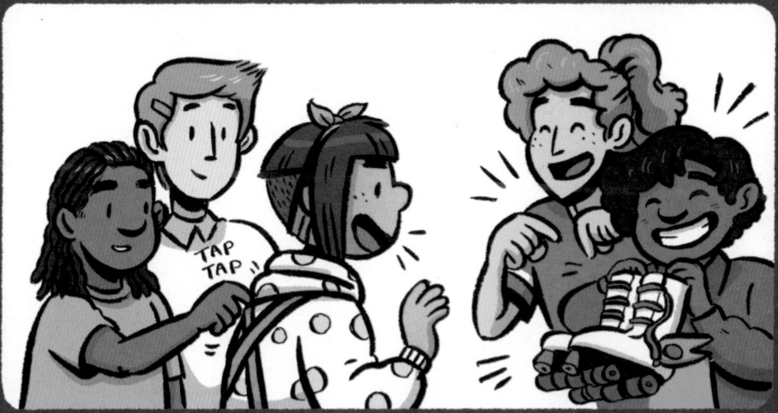
TAP TAP

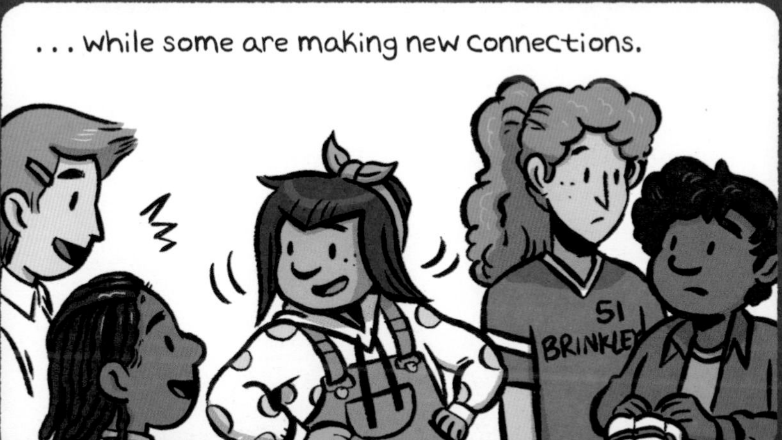
. . . while some are making new connections.
51 BRINKLEY

The trend in my comments is clear:

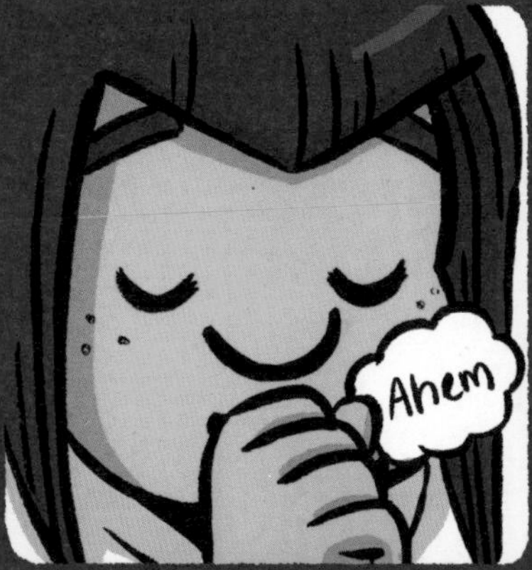
Ahem

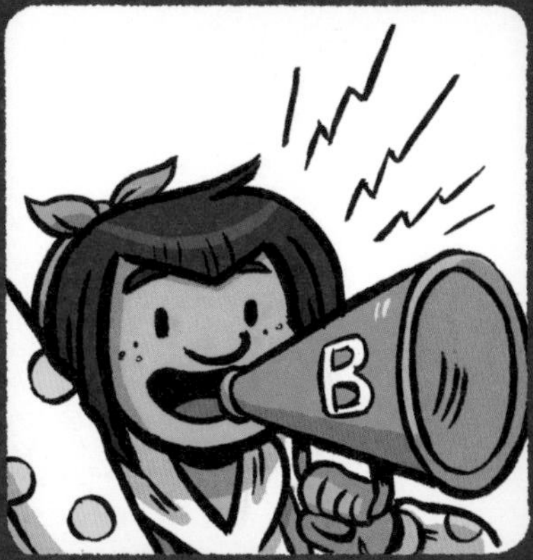
B

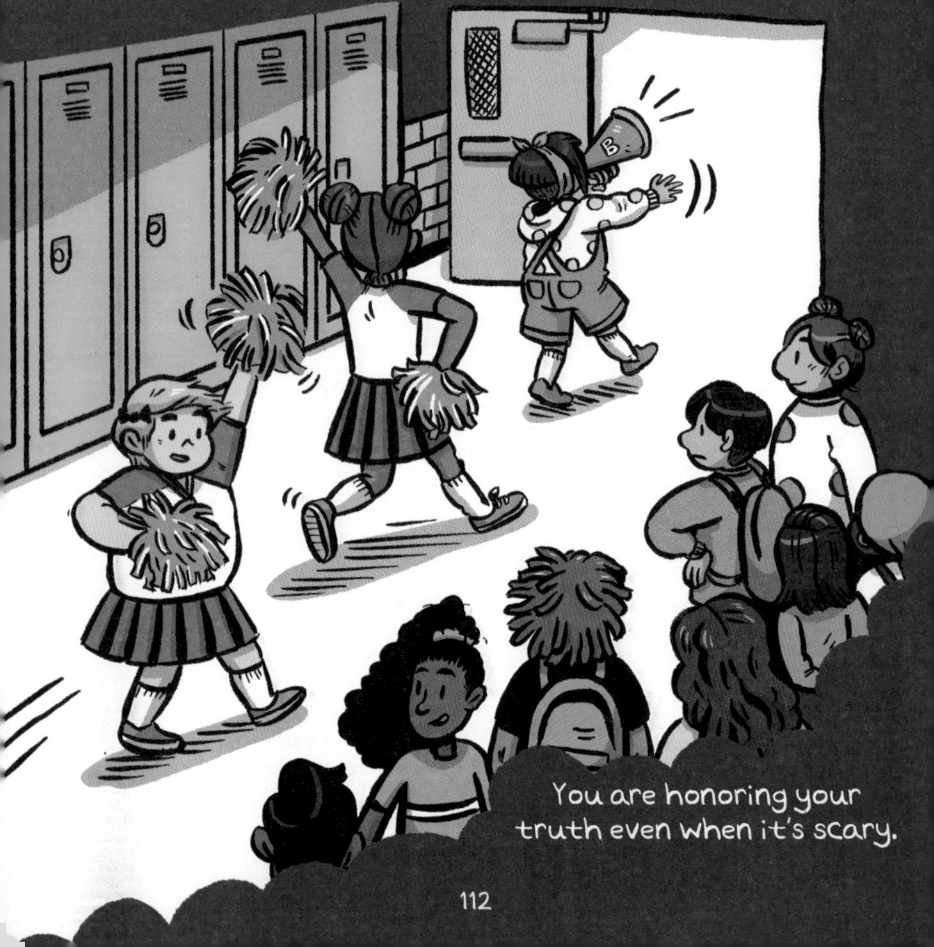
B
You are honoring your truth even when it's scary.

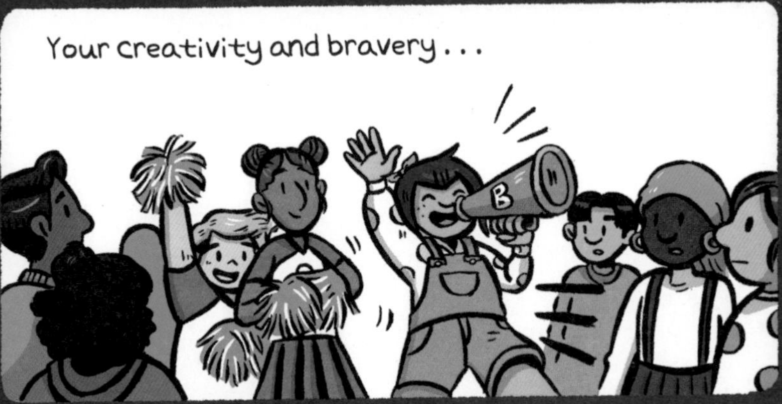
Your creativity and bravery . . .
B

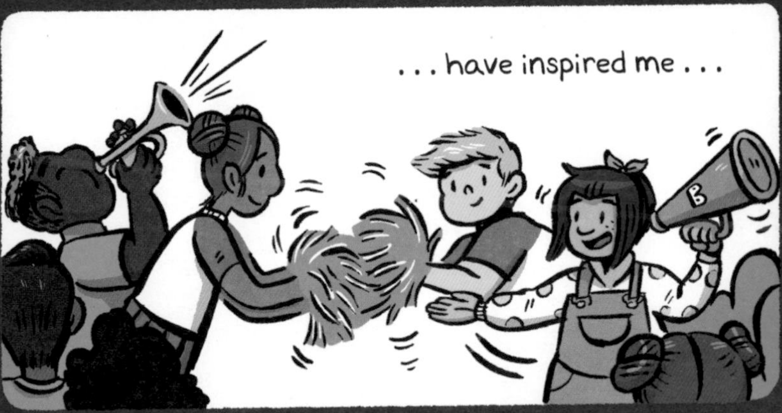
. . . have inspired me . . .
B

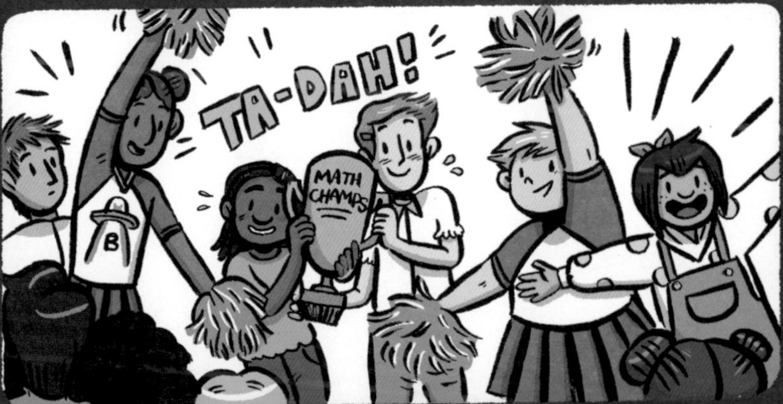
TA-DAH!
MATH CHAMPS
B

. . . to push even farther outside my comfort zone.

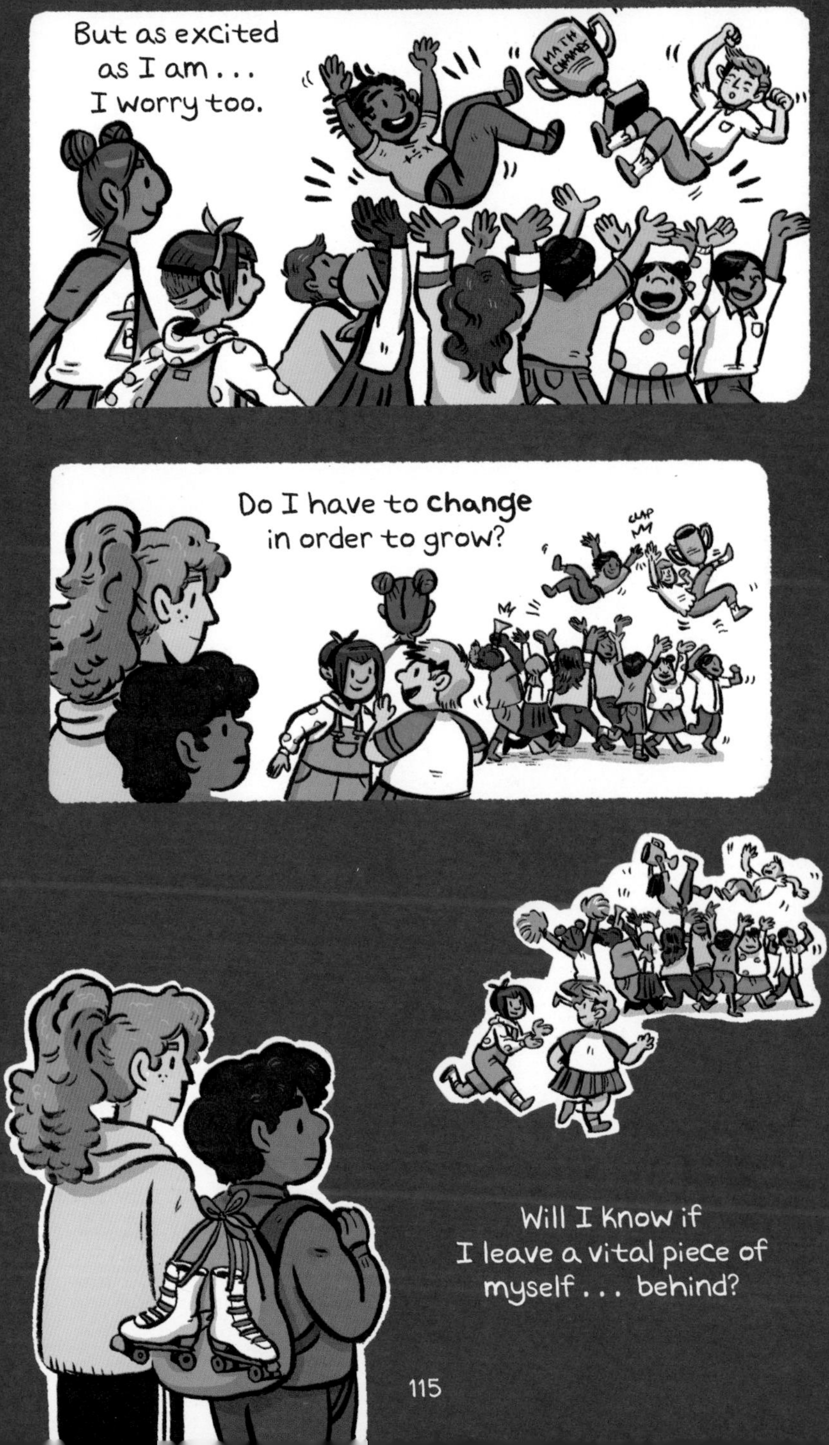
But as excited as I am . . . I worry too.
Do I have to **change** in order to grow?
Will I know if I leave a vital piece of myself . . . behind?

From total makeovers to **big celebrations** for under-the-radar victories . . .

TURN

the winds of **change** are blowing at Brinkley Middle School!

But what prompted this change?

Something in the cafeteria food?

I don't know the answer **yet** . . .

LIVE

But I'll be there to bring you the next **big thing!**

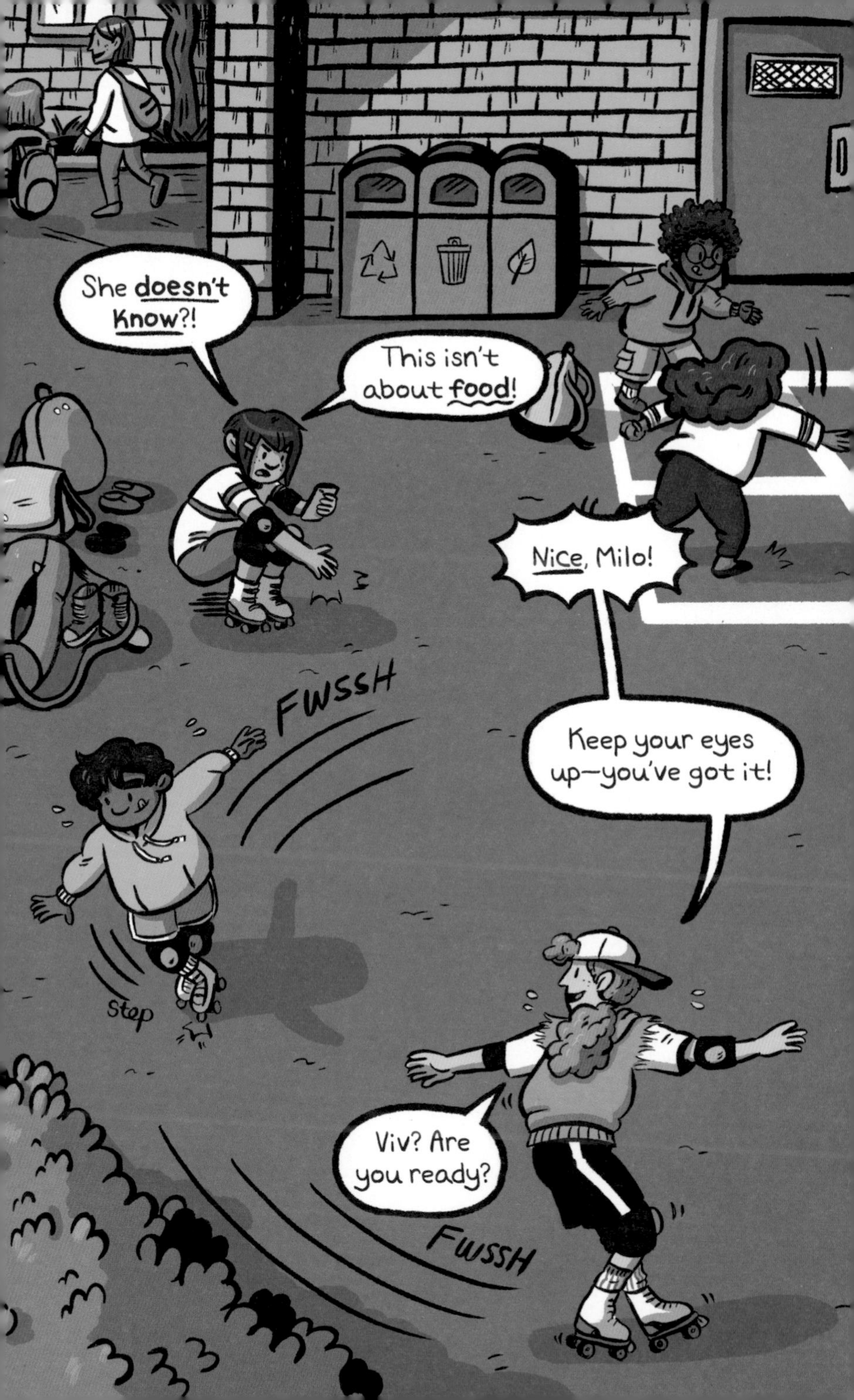

She doesn't know?!
This isn't about food!
Nice, Milo!
Keep your eyes up—you've got it!
FWSSH
step
Viv? Are you ready?
FWSSH

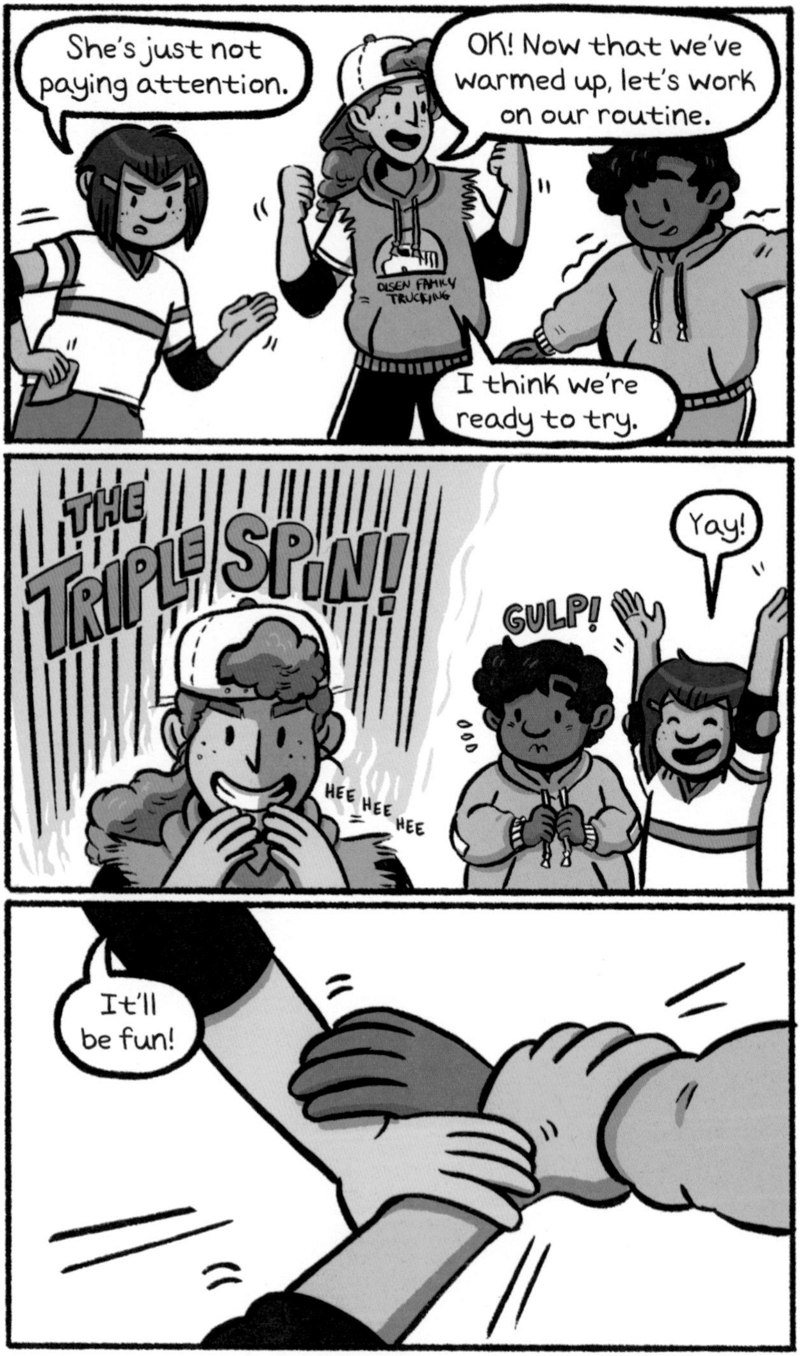
She's just not paying attention.
OK! Now that we've warmed up, let's work on our routine.
OLSEN FAMILY TRUCKING
I think we're ready to try.
THE TRIPLE SPIN!
Yay!
GULP!
HEE HEE HEE
It'll be fun!

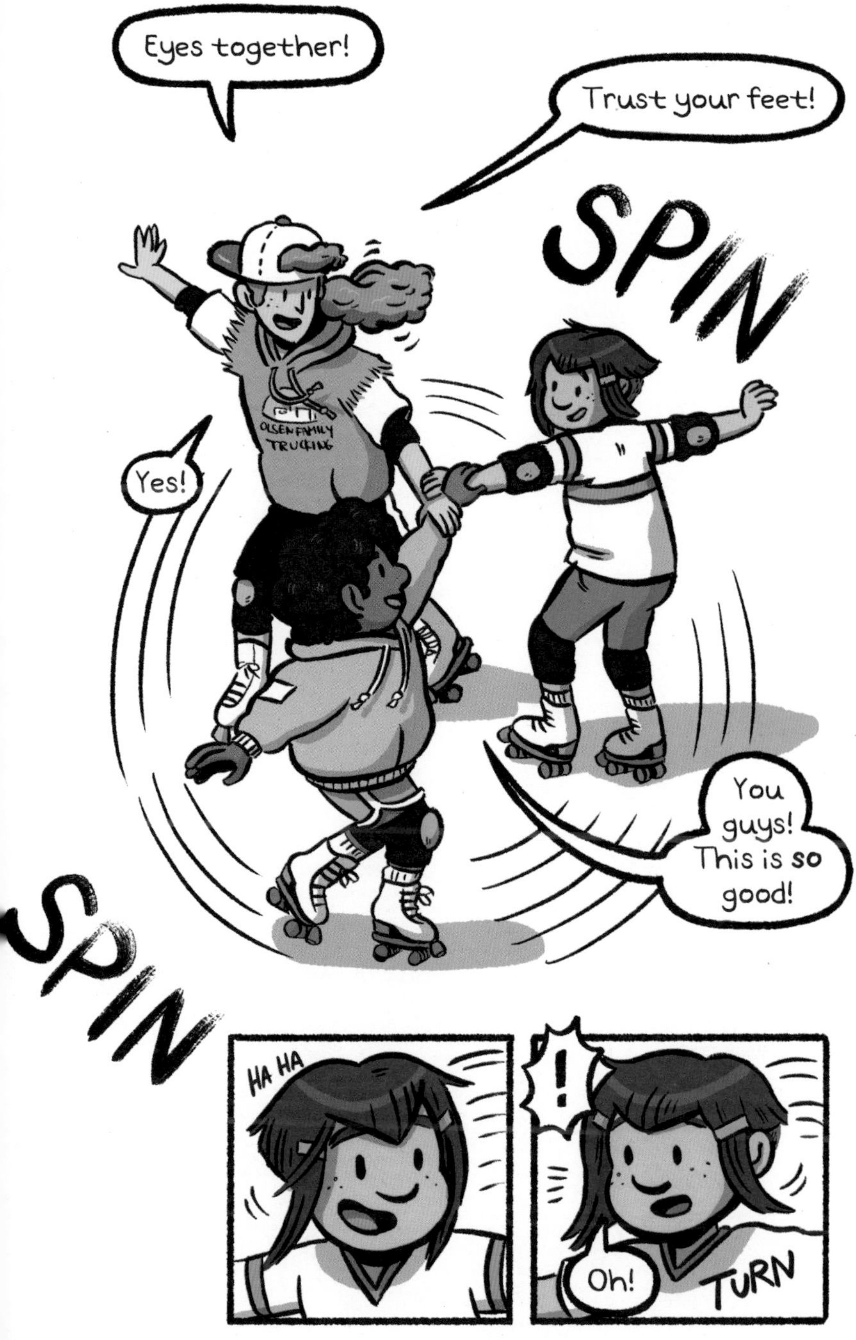
Eyes together!
Trust your feet!
SPIN
Yes!
You guys! This is so good!
SPIN
HA HA
!
Oh!
TURN

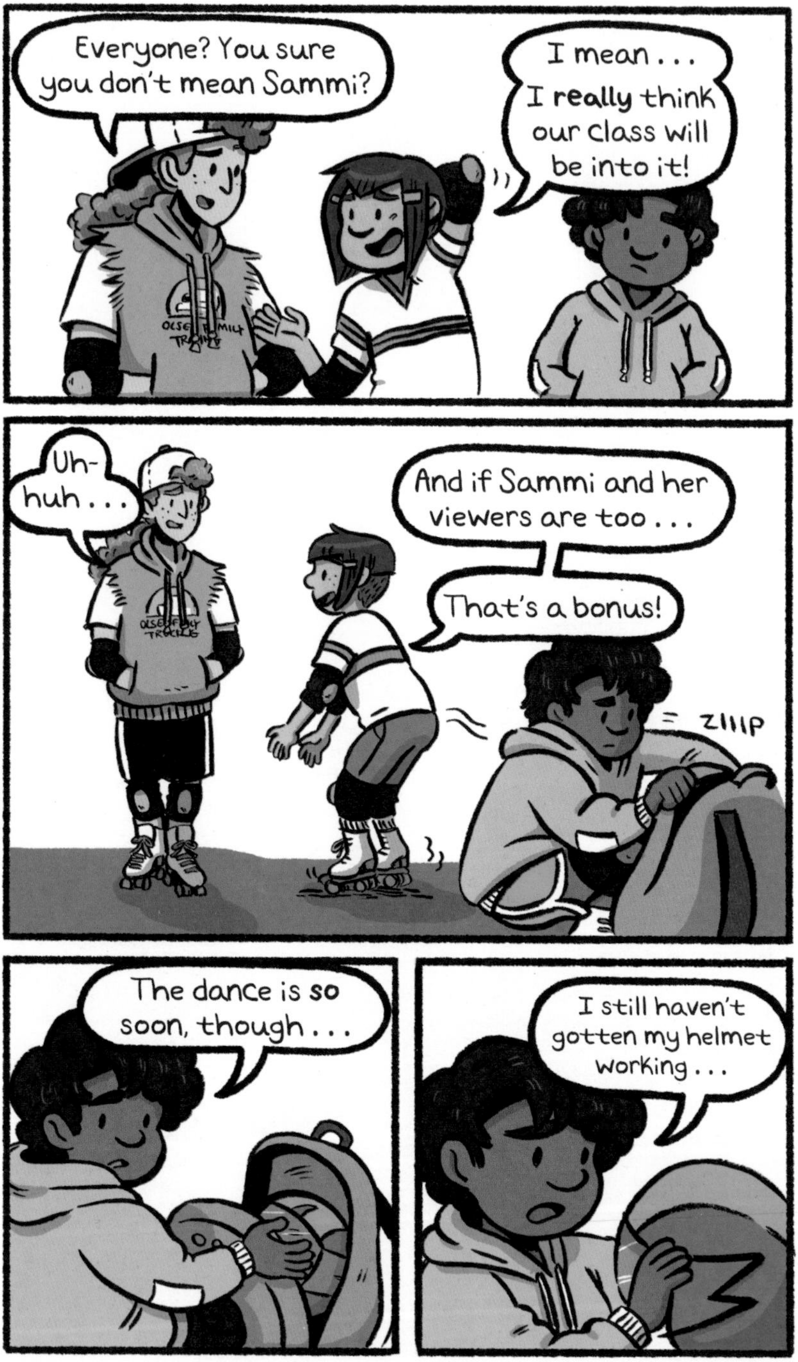

Everyone? You sure you don't mean Sammi?
I mean . . .
I **really** think our class will be into it!
OLSEN FAMILY TRAINING
Uh-huh . . .
And if Sammi and her viewers are too . . .
That's a bonus!
ZIIIP
The dance is **so** soon, though . . .
I still haven't gotten my helmet working . . .

It doesn't have to be perfect.

It'll be like a practice for the Con!

I dunno . . .

WOBBLE WOBBLE

TRIP

We need a practice for our practice . . .

Our crossovers are a mess.

TAP

We don't have an end sequence.

We need **time** to focus and refine **together**.

I want us to be a **perfect** team.

NOD NOD

OLSE... TRU...

But right now we're just . . .

SIGH

not ready.

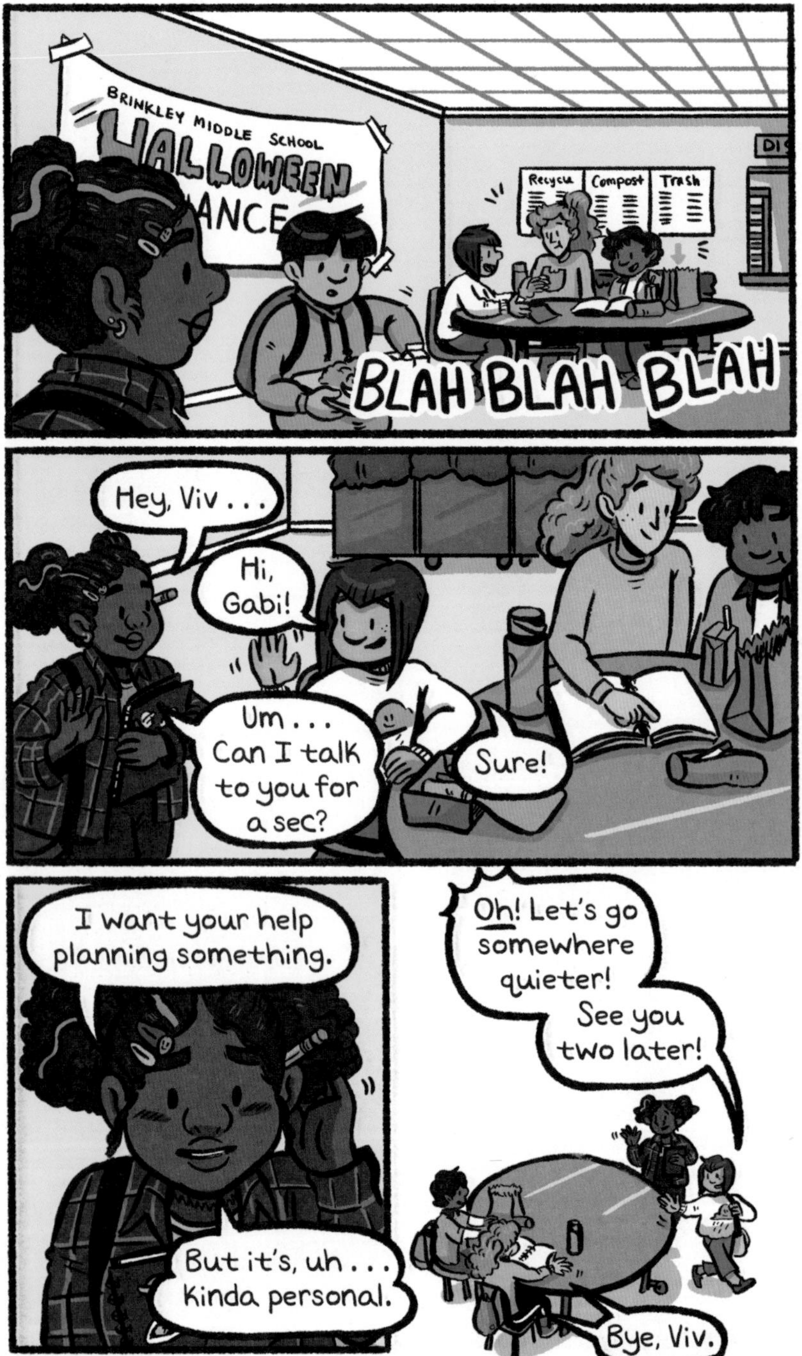
BRINKLEY MIDDLE SCHOOL
HALLOWEEN
ANCE
Recycle
Compost
Trash
DIS
BLAH BLAH BLAH
Hey, Viv . . .
Hi, Gabi!
Um . . . Can I talk to you for a sec?
Sure!
I want your help planning something.
But it's, uh . . . kinda personal.
Oh! Let's go somewhere quieter!
See you two later!
Bye, Viv.

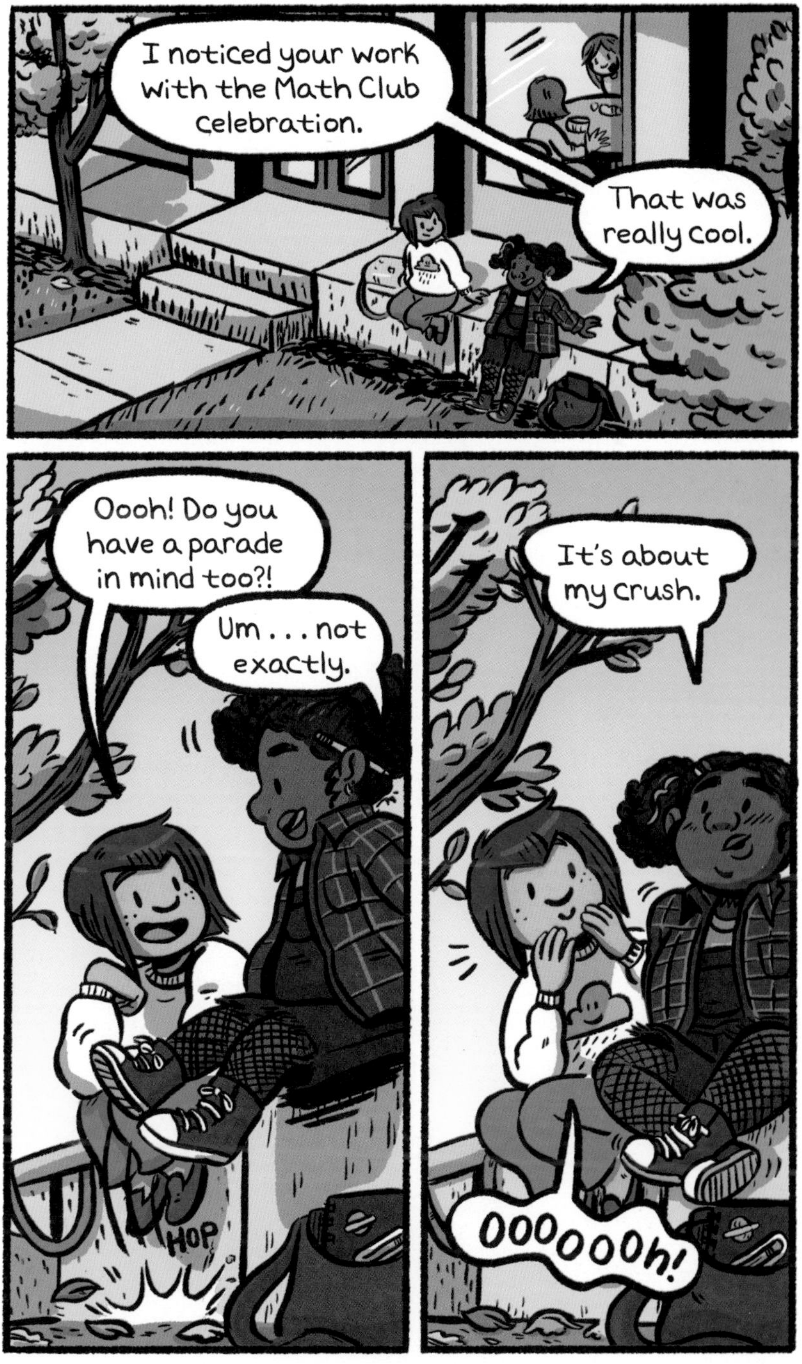
I noticed your work with the Math Club celebration.
That was really cool.
Oooh! Do you have a parade in mind too?!
Um . . . not exactly.
HOP
It's about my crush.
OOOOOOh!

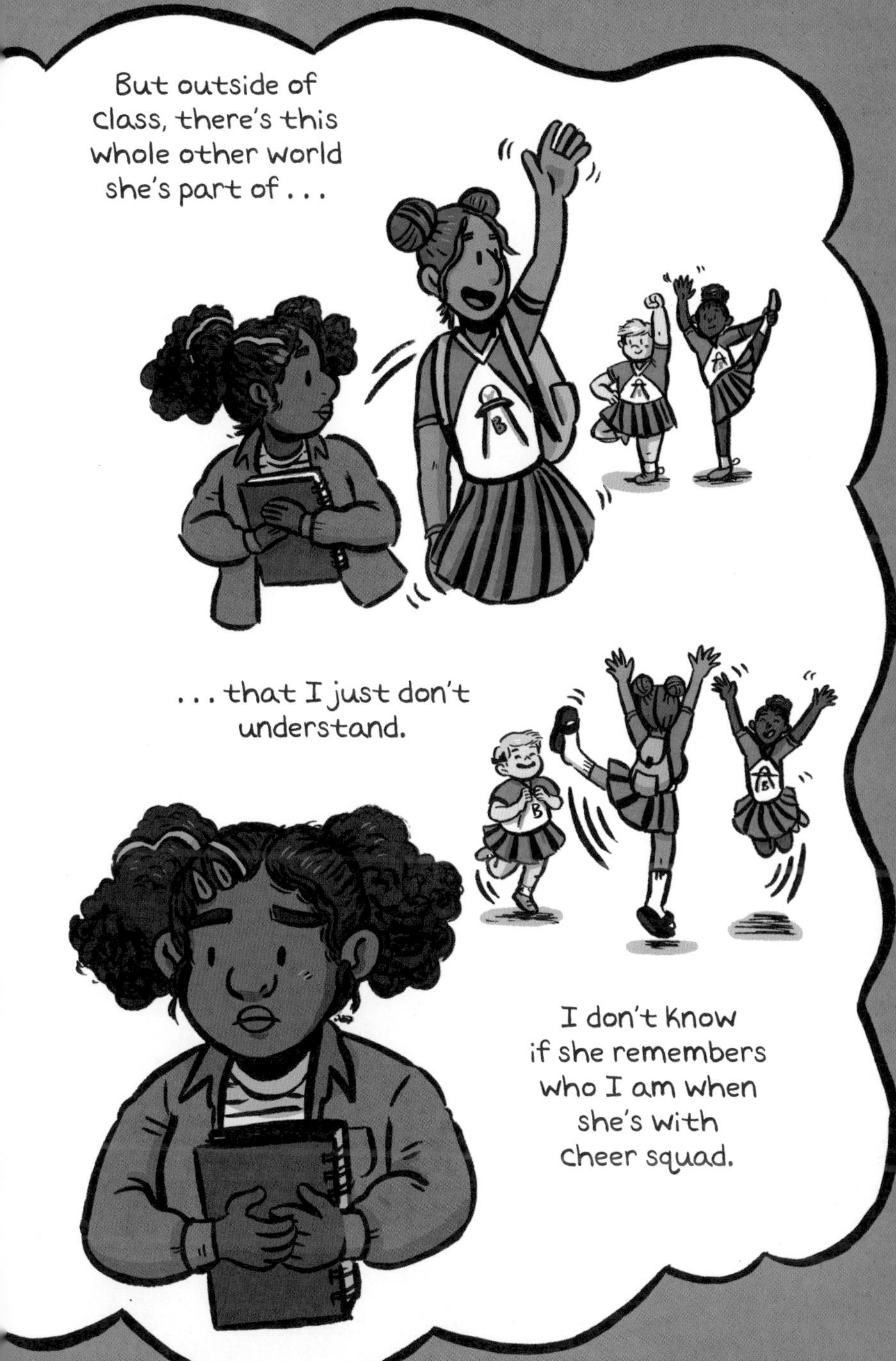
But outside of class, there's this whole other world she's part of . . .
. . . that I just don't understand.
I don't know if she remembers who I am when she's with cheer squad.

130

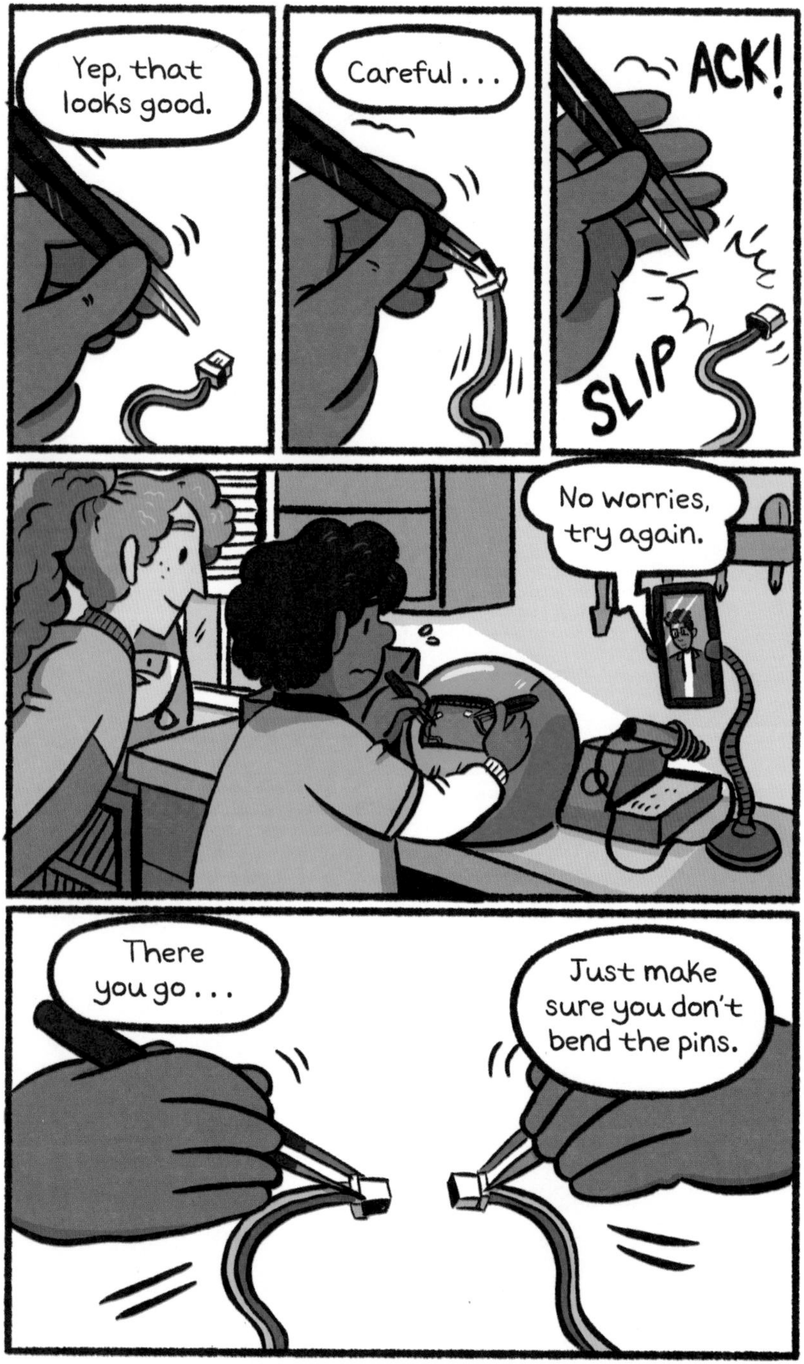
Yep, that looks good.
Careful . . .
ACK!
SLIP
No worries, try again.
There you go . . .
Just make sure you don't bend the pins.

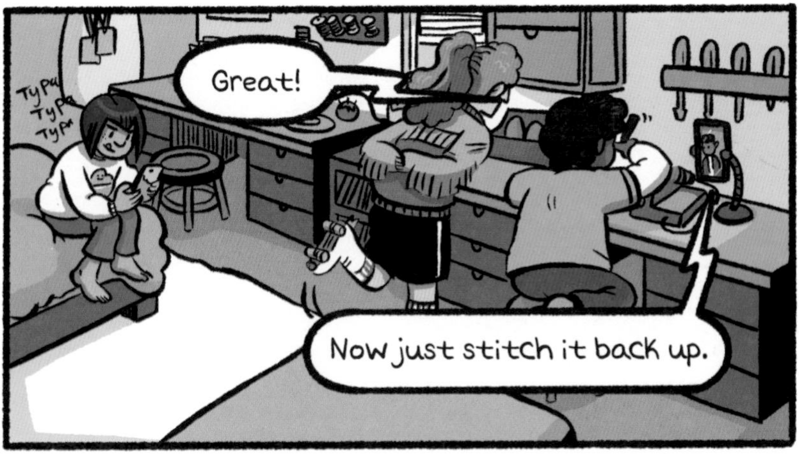
Typa Typa Typa
Great!
Now just stitch it back up.

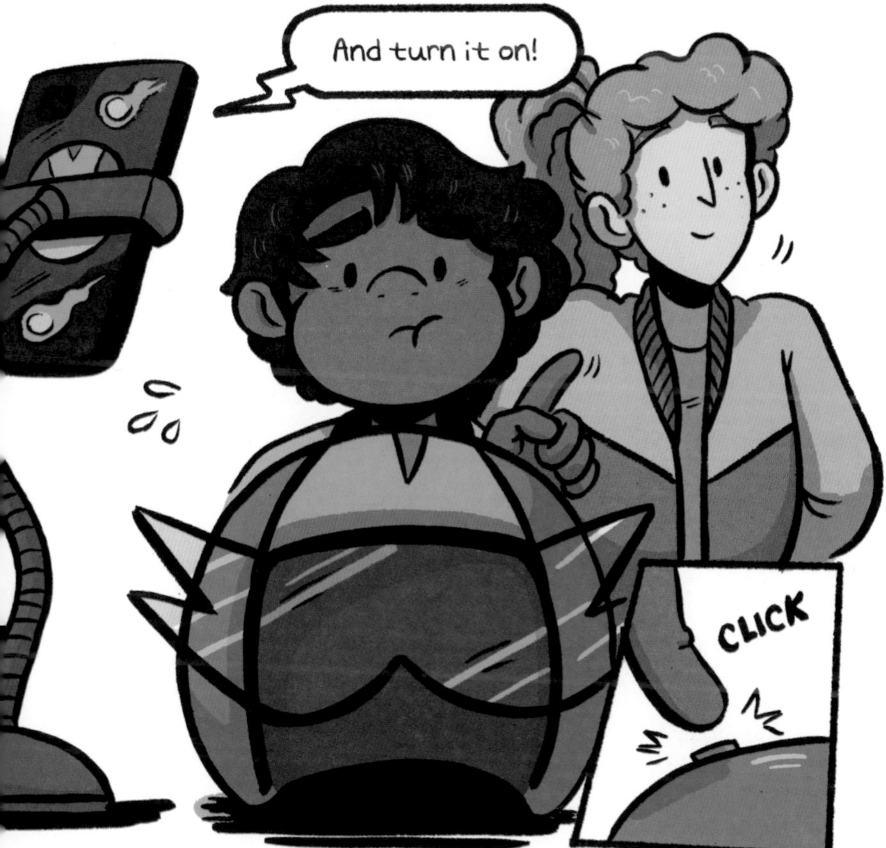
And turn it on!
CLICK

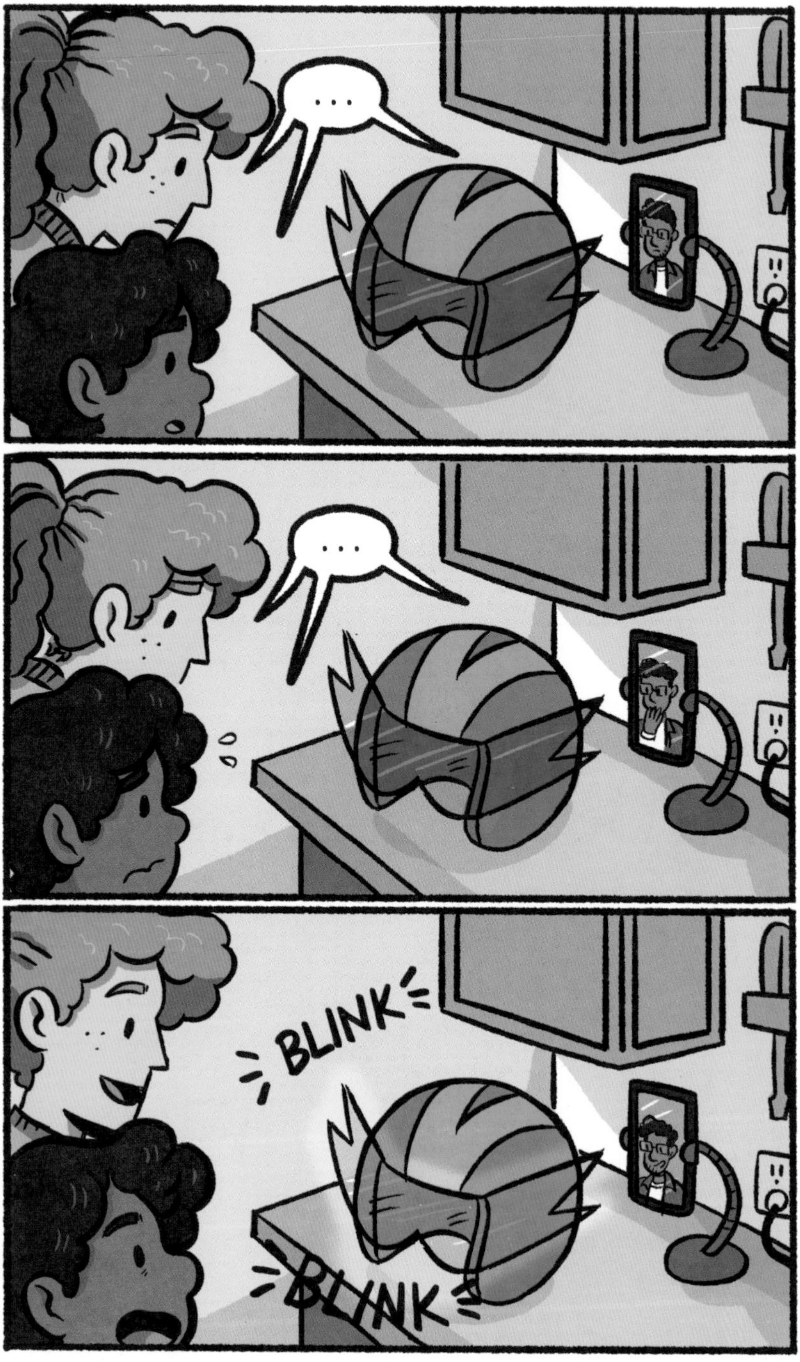
...
...
BLINK
BLINK

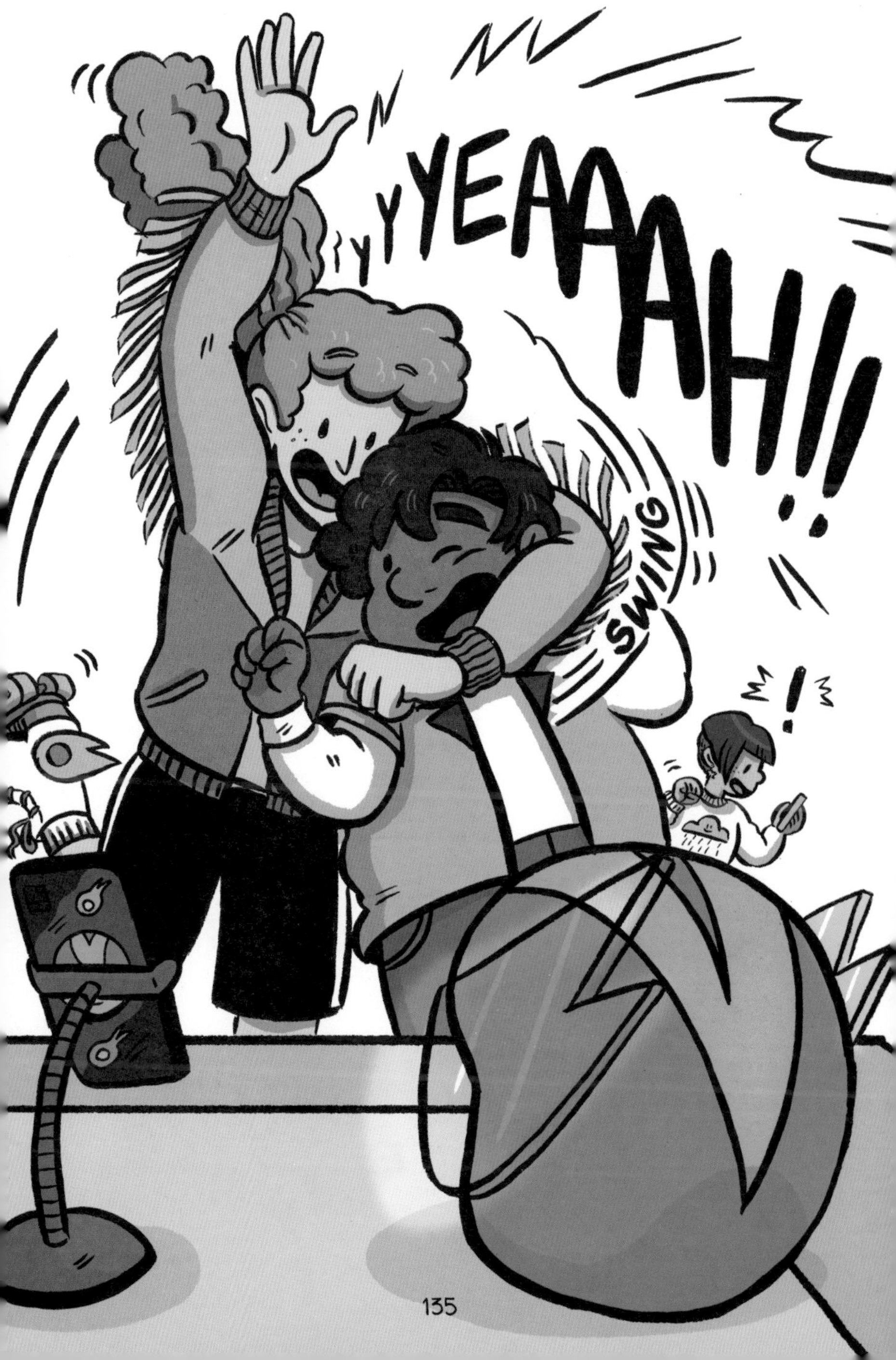
yYYEAAAAH!!!
SWING
!

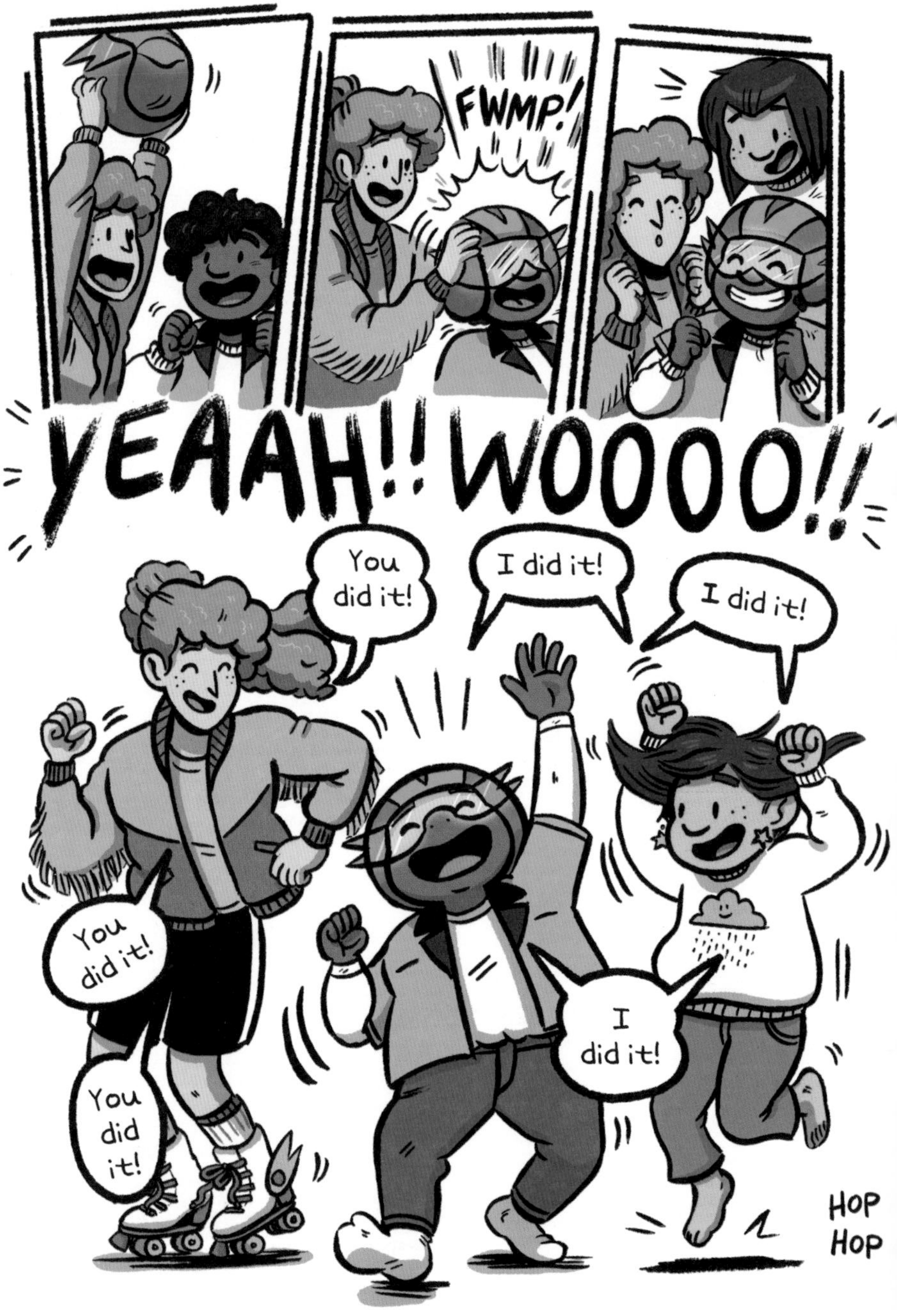
FWMP!
YEAAH!! WOOOO!!
You did it!
I did it!
I did it!
You did it!
You did it!
I did it!
HOP HOP

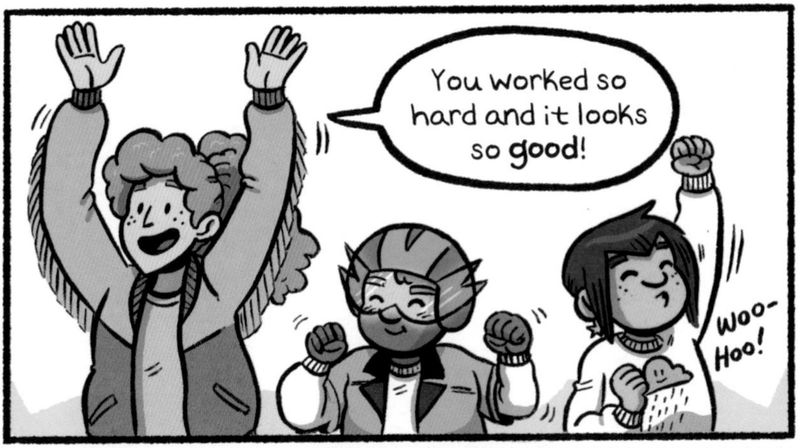
You worked so hard and it looks so good!
WOO-HOO!
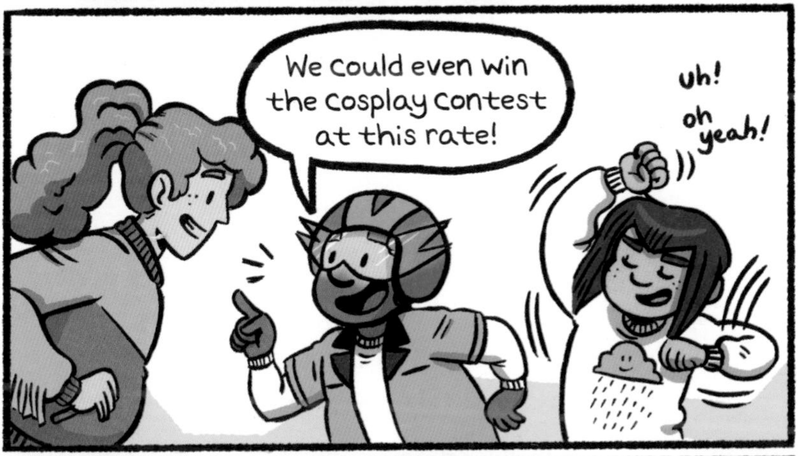
We could even win the cosplay contest at this rate!
Uh! oh yeah!
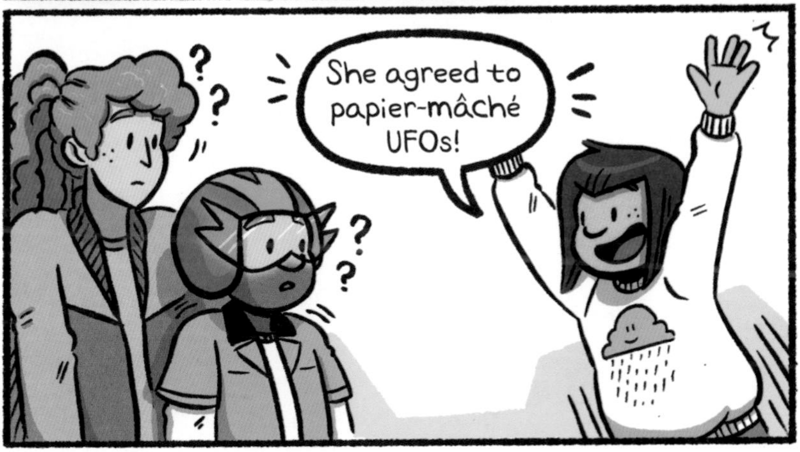
She agreed to papier-mâché UFOs!

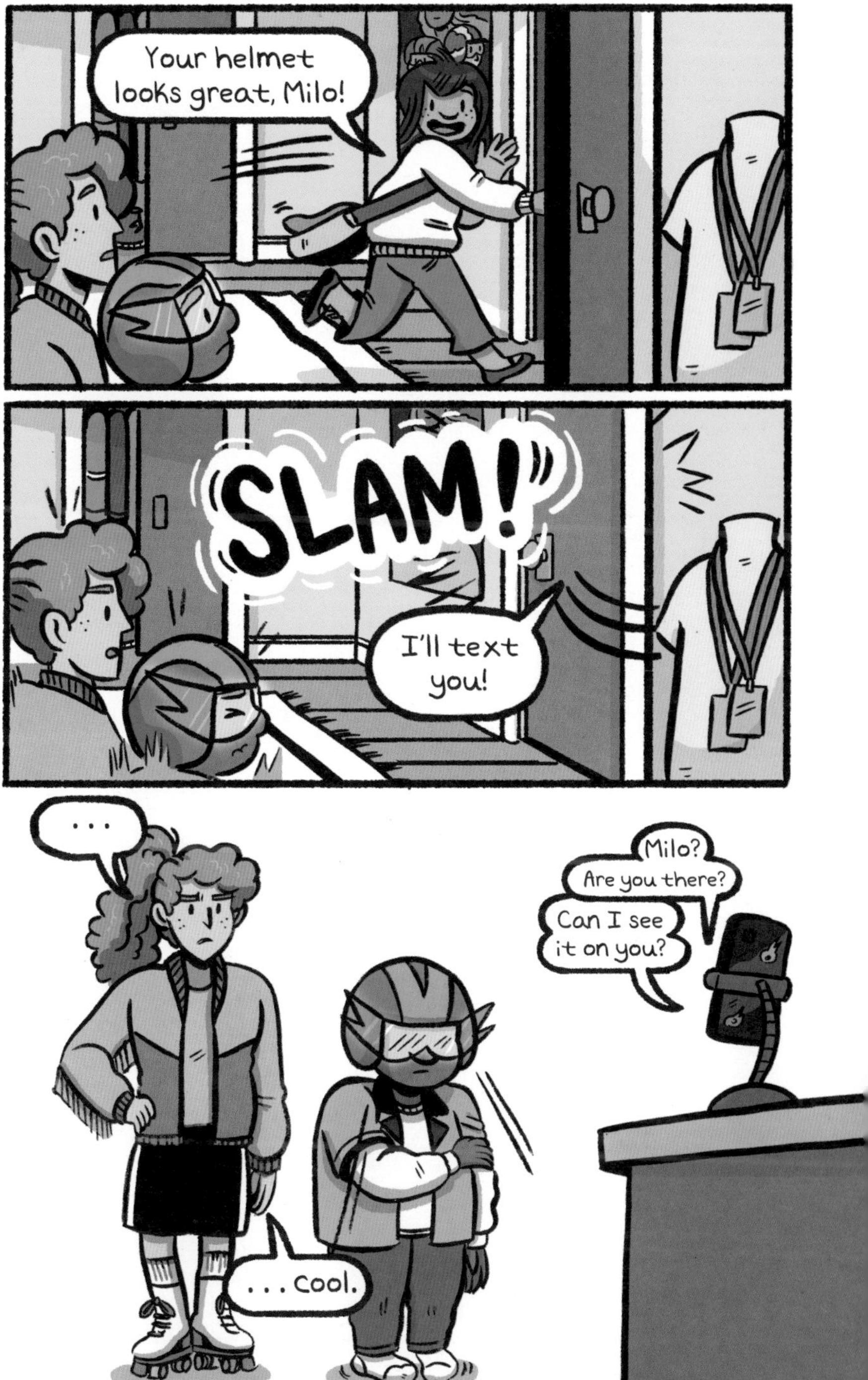
Your helmet looks great, Milo!
SLAM!
I'll text you!
. . .
Milo?
Are you there?
Can I see it on you?
. . . cool.

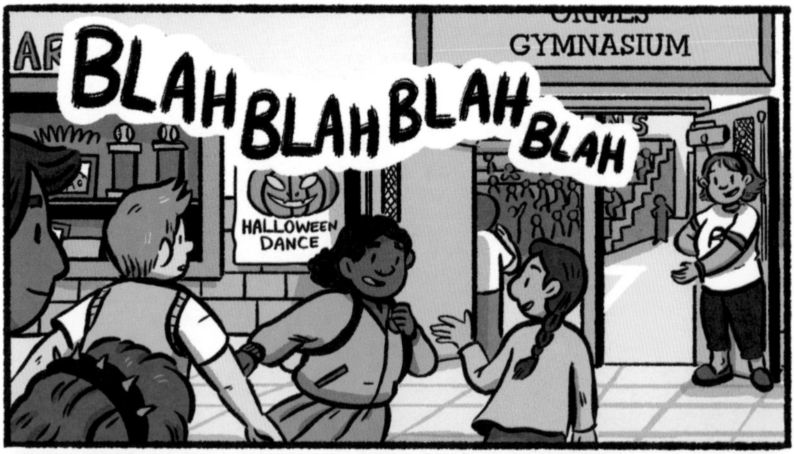
ARMES
GYMNASIUM
BLAH BLAH BLAH BLAH
HALLOWEEN DANCE

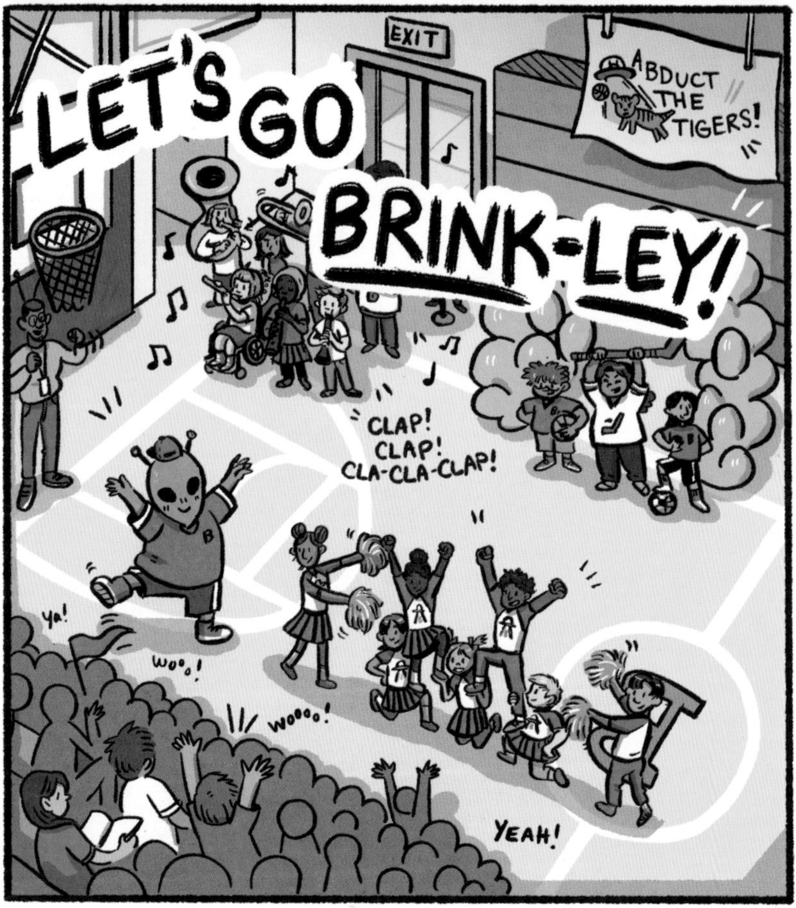
EXIT
ABDUCT THE TIGERS!
LET'S GO BRINK-LEY!
CLAP! CLAP! CLA-CLA-CLAP!
ya!
wooo!
woooo!
YEAH!

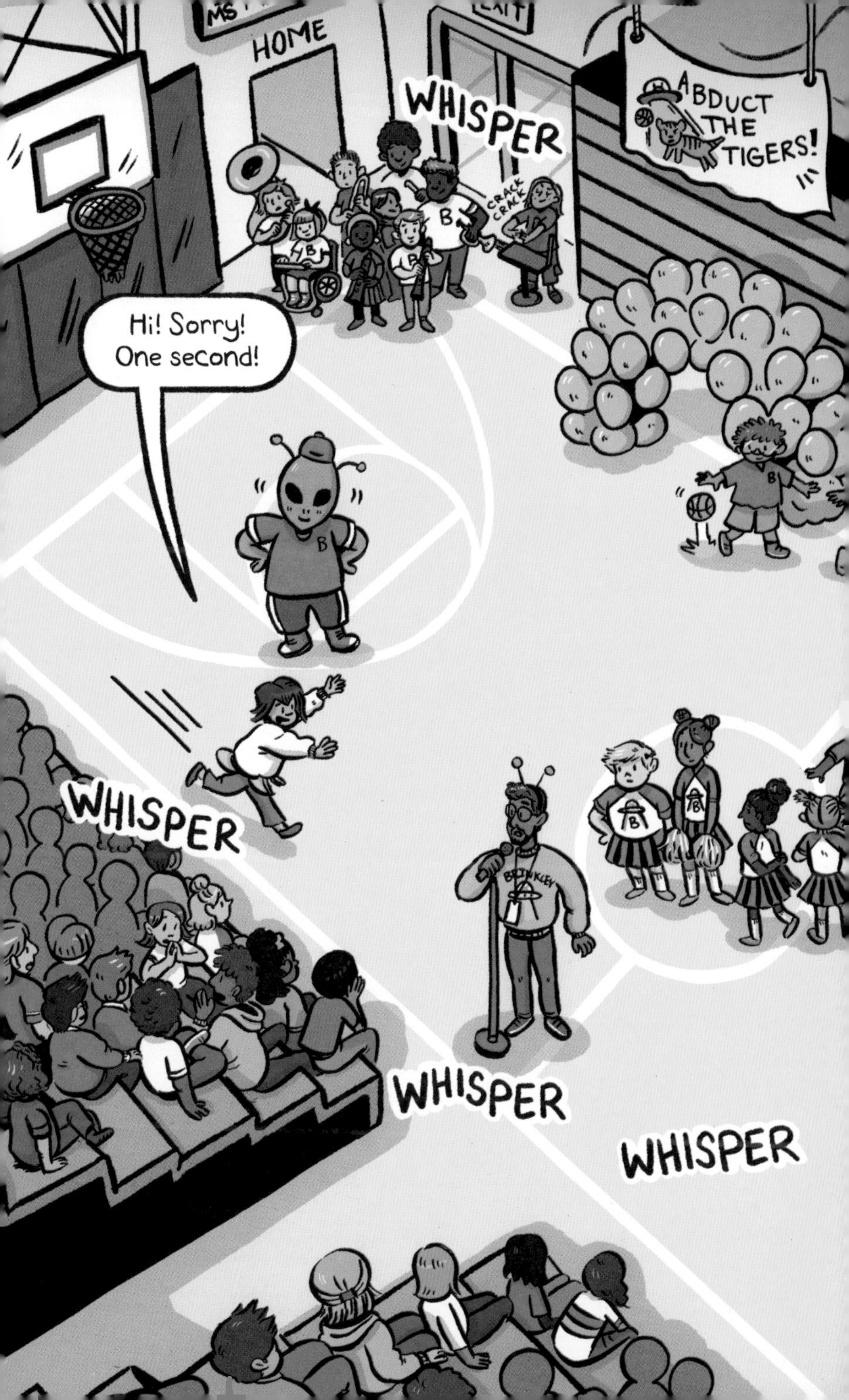
HOME
WHISPER
ABDUCT THE TIGERS!
CRACK CRACK
Hi! Sorry! One second!
WHISPER
WHISPER
WHISPER

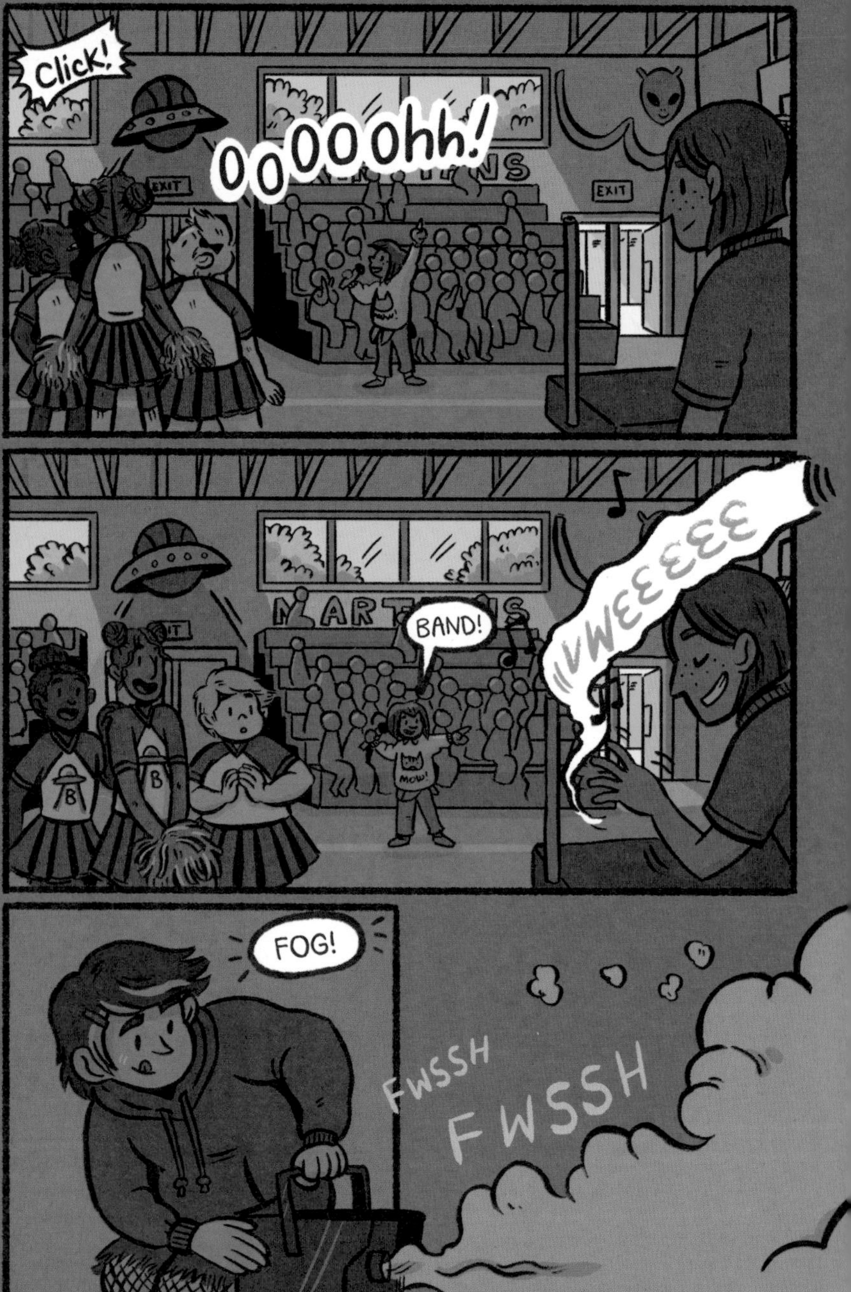
Click!
OOOOOhh!
EXIT
EXIT
BAND!
VWEEEEE
MOW!
FOG!
FWSSH
FWSSH

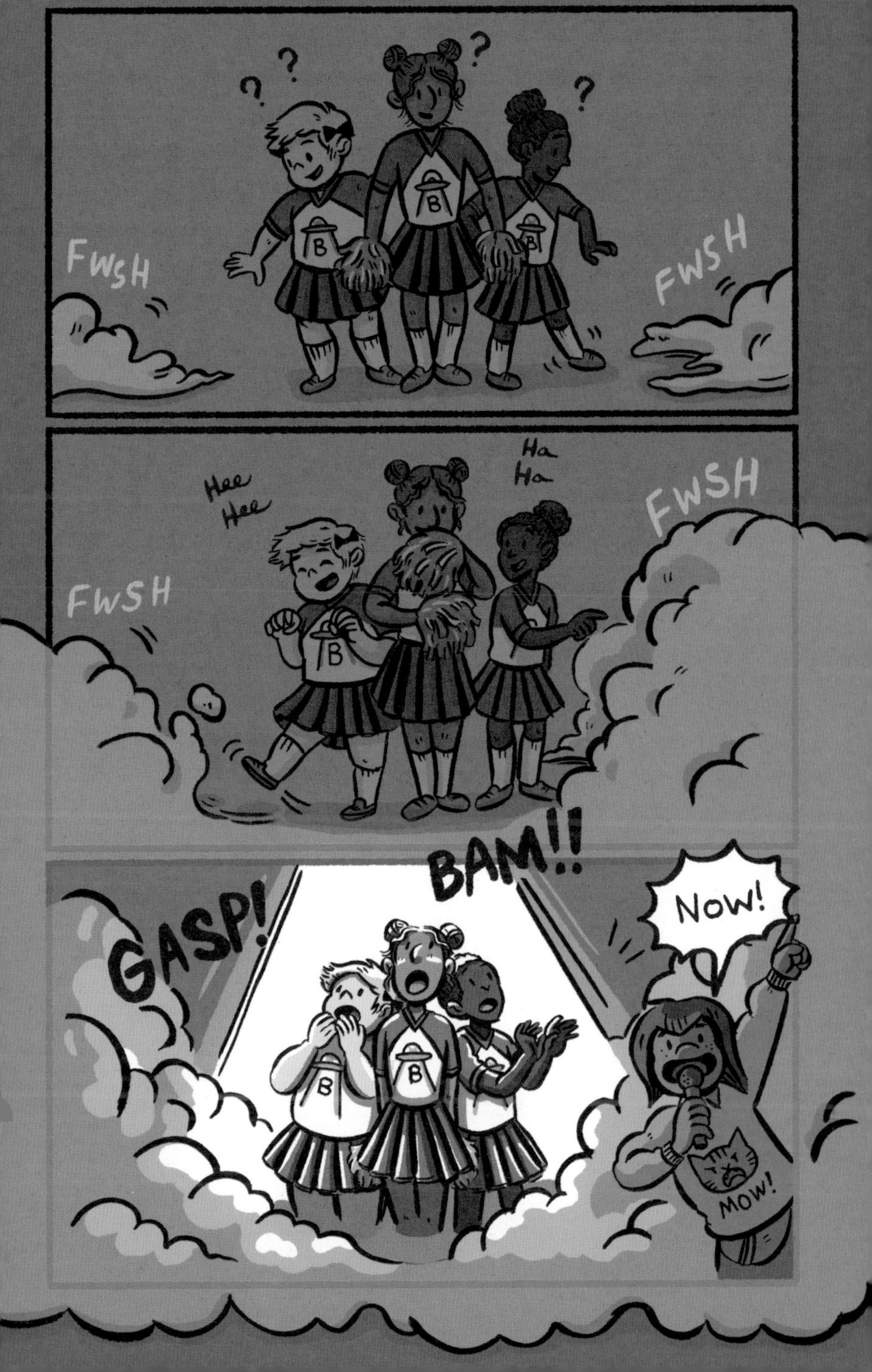
? ?
?
?
FWSH
FWSH
Hee Hee
Ha Ha
FWSH
FWSH
GASP!
BAM!!
Now!
MOW!

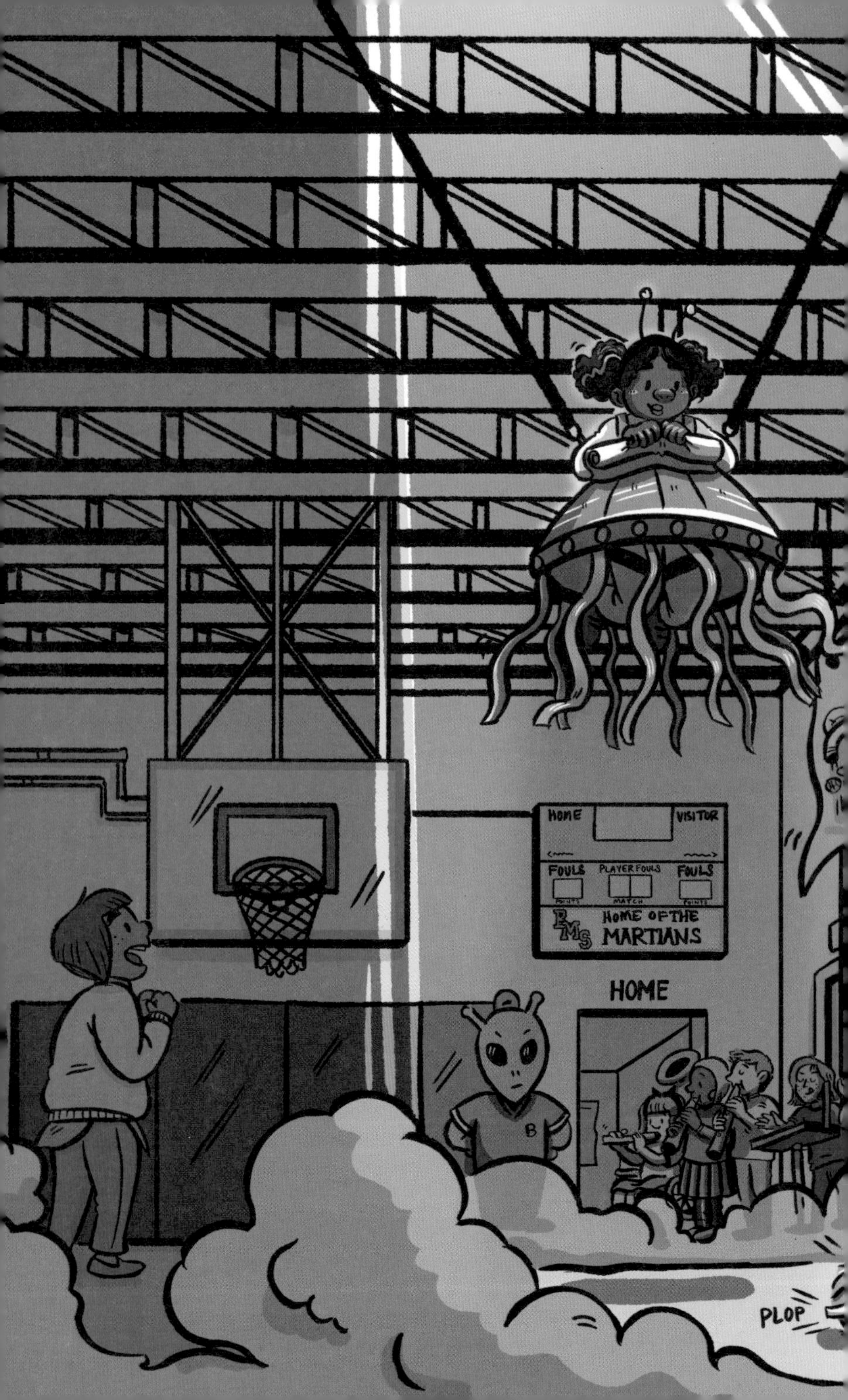
HOME
VISITOR
FOULS
PLAYER FOULS
FOULS
BMS
HOME OF THE MARTIANS
HOME
PLOP

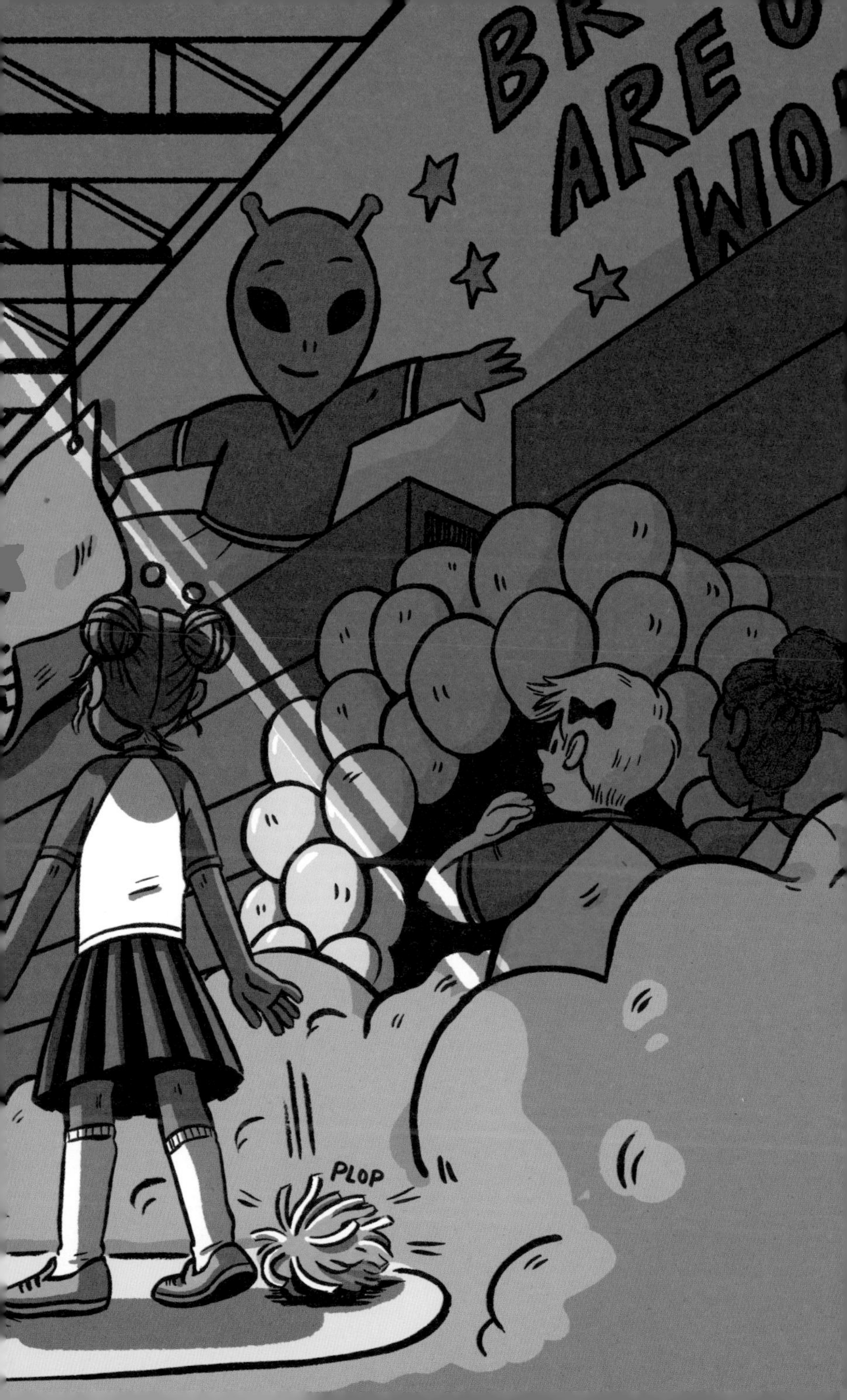
PLOP

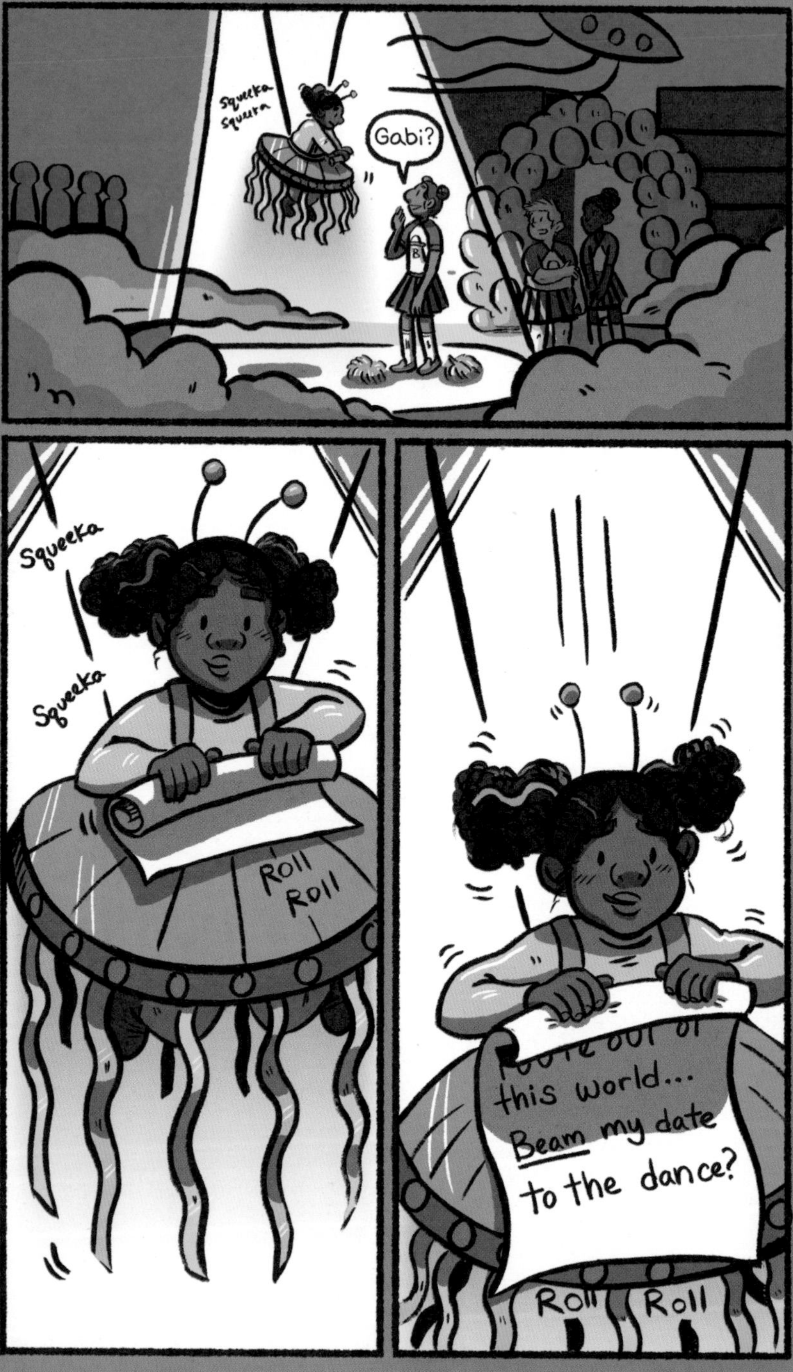
Squeeka
squeeka
Gabi?
Squeeka
Squeeka
Roll
Roll
this world...
Beam my date
to the dance?
Roll Roll

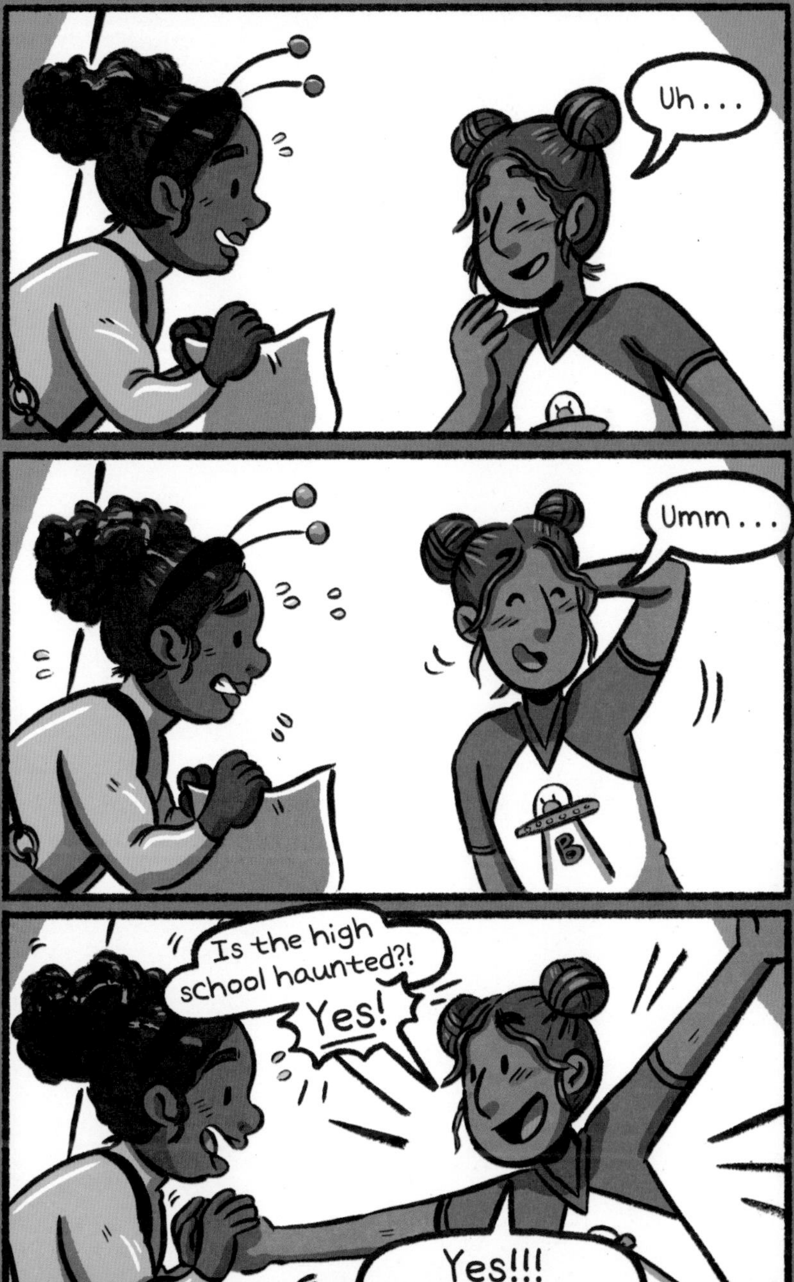
Uh...
Umm...
Is the high school haunted?!
Yes!
Yes!!!
Of course I will!

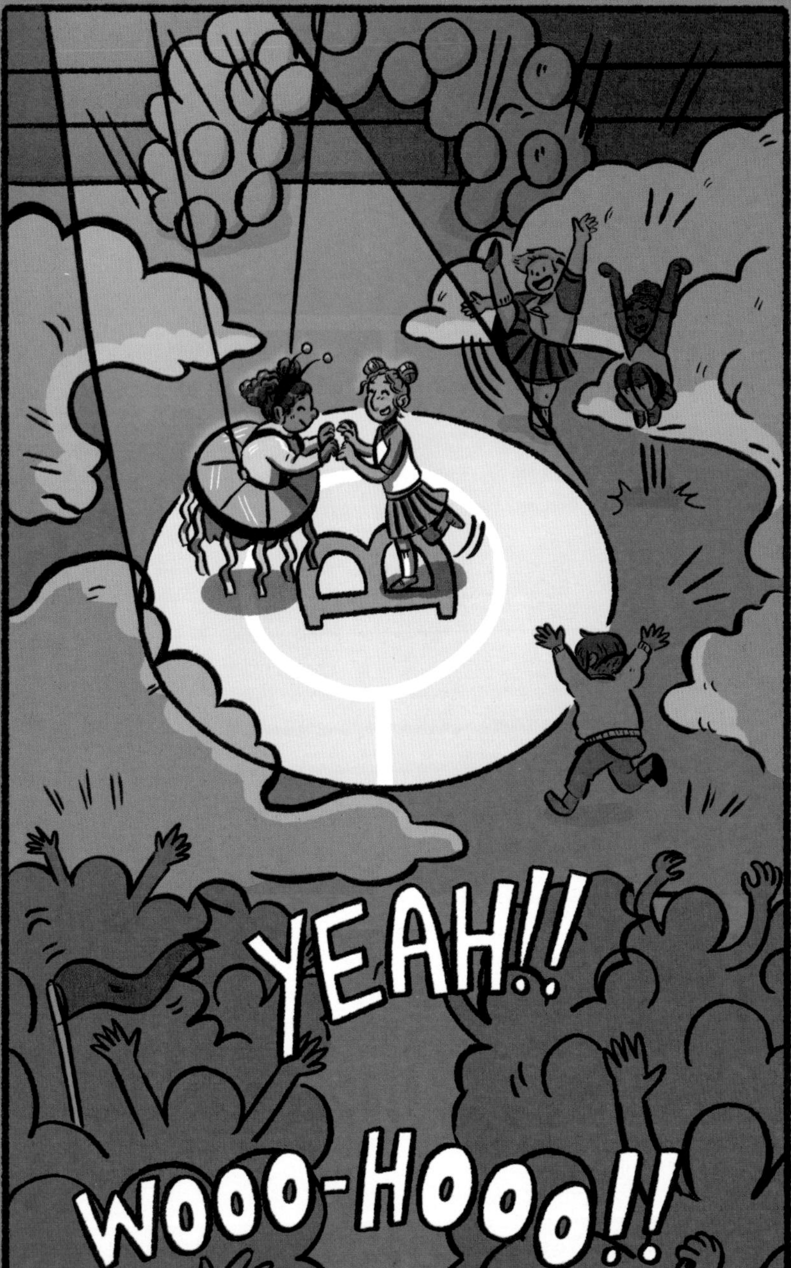
YEAH!!
WOOO-HOOOO!!

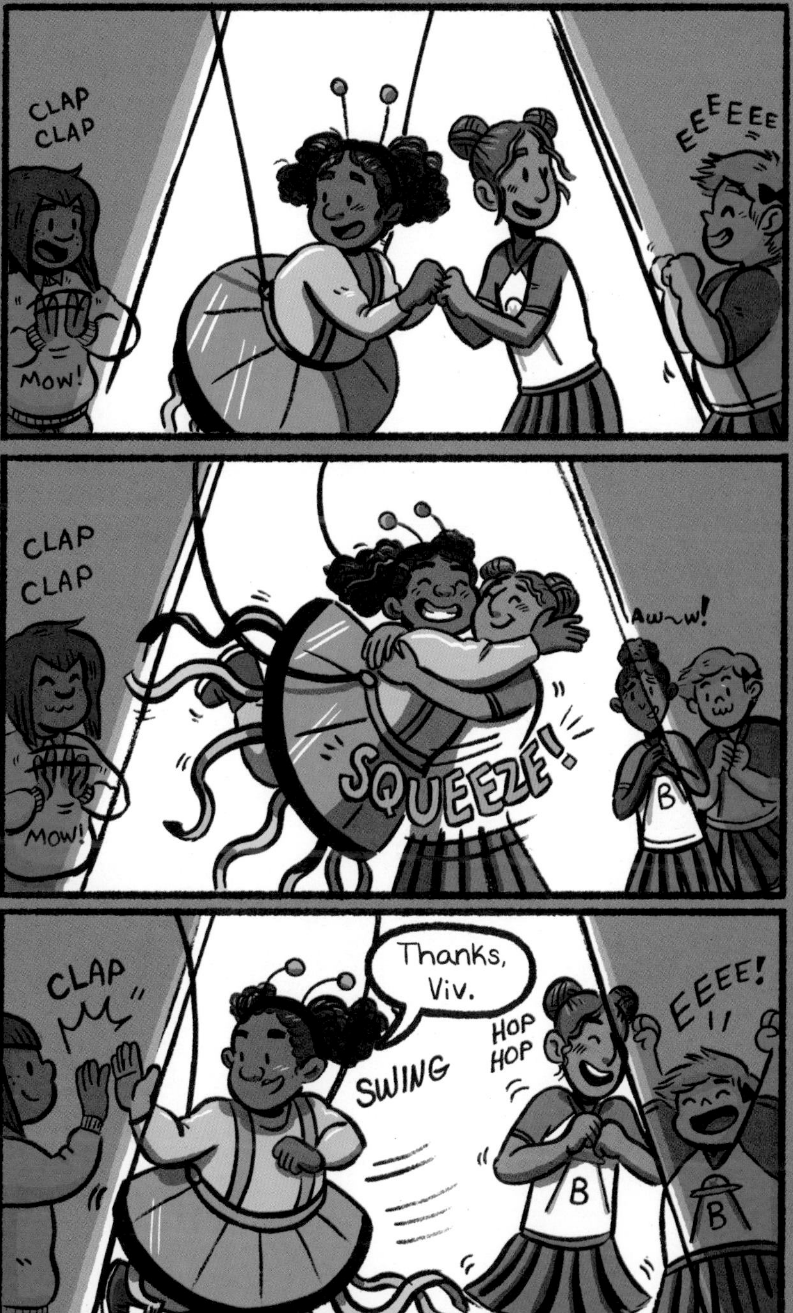
CLAP
CLAP
MOW!
EEEEEE
CLAP
CLAP
MOW!
SQUEEZE!
AW~W!
CLAP
Thanks, Viv.
SWING
HOP
HOP
EEEE!

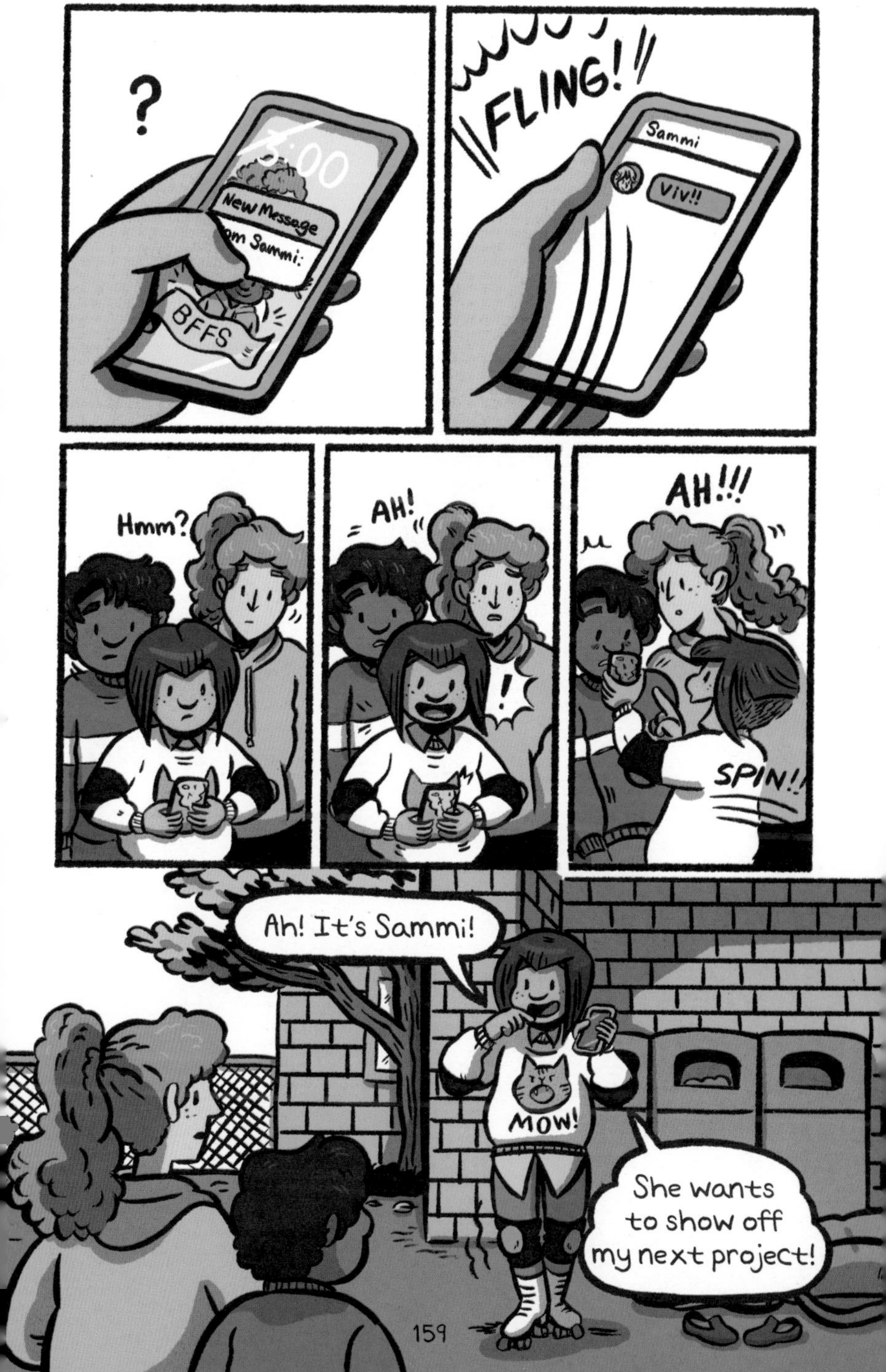
?
3:00
New Message
om Sammi:
BFFS
FLING!
Sammi
Viv!!
Hmm?
AH!
!
AH!!!
SPIN!!
Ah! It's Sammi!
MOW!
She wants to show off my next project!

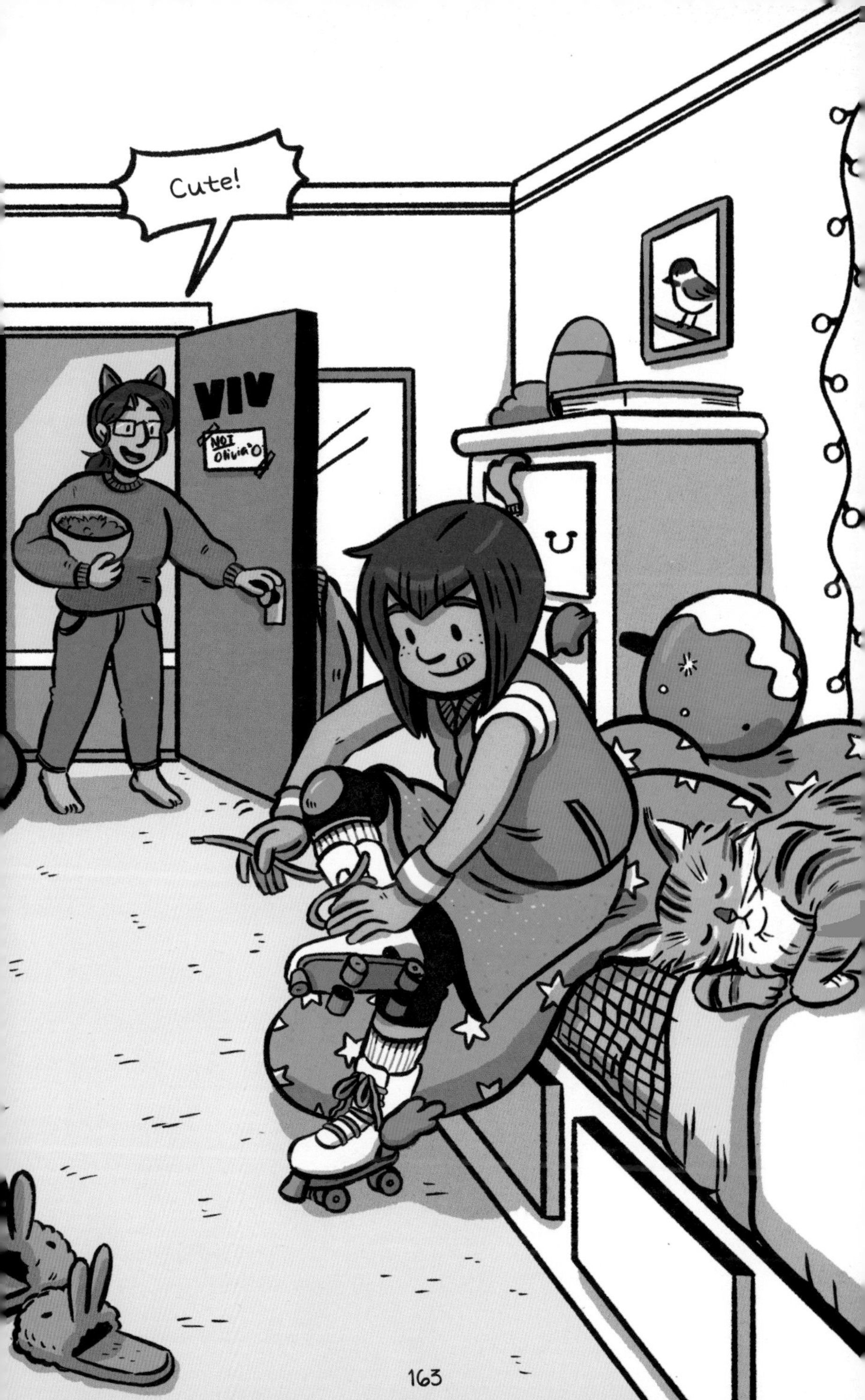
Cute!
VIV
NO! Olivia

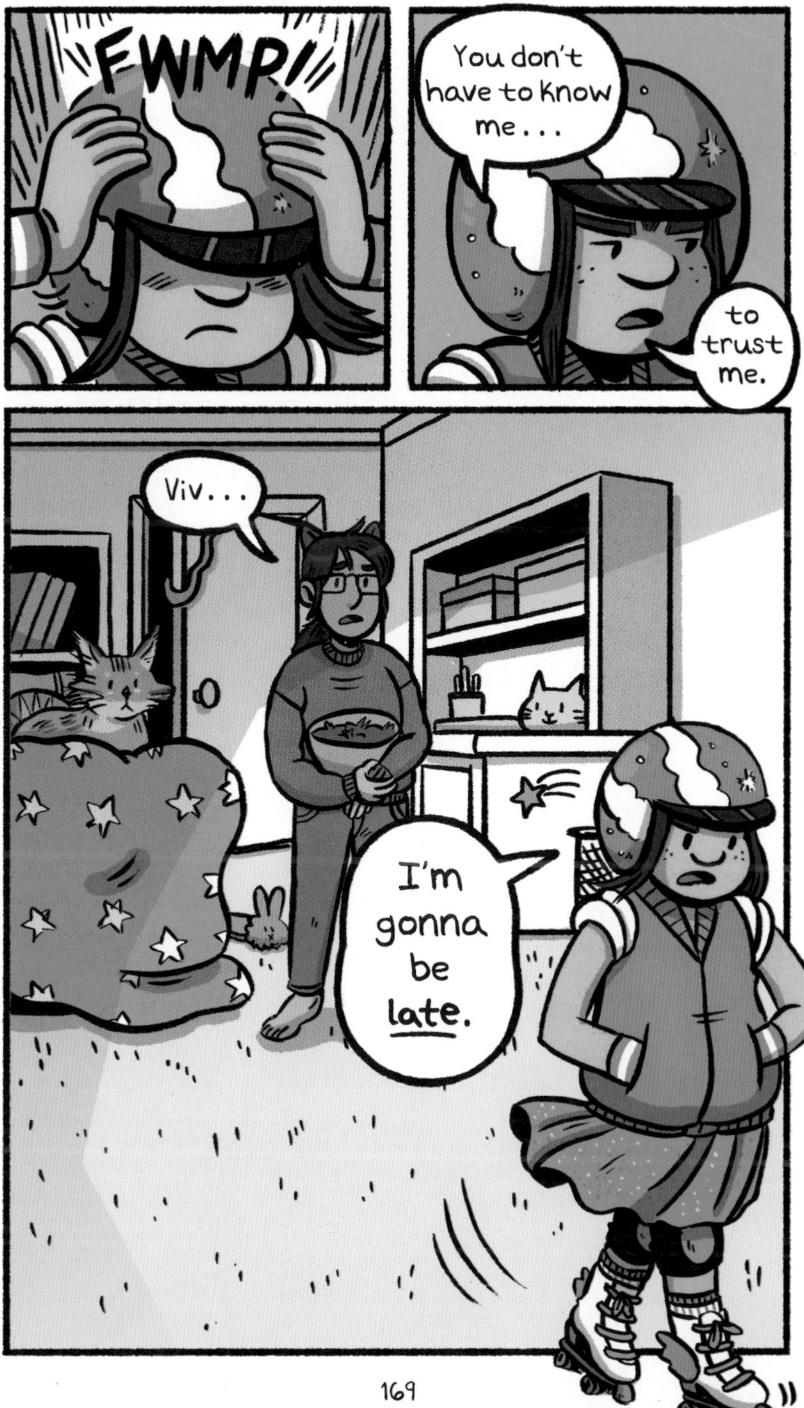
FWMP!
You don't have to know me...
to trust me.
Viv...
I'm gonna be late.

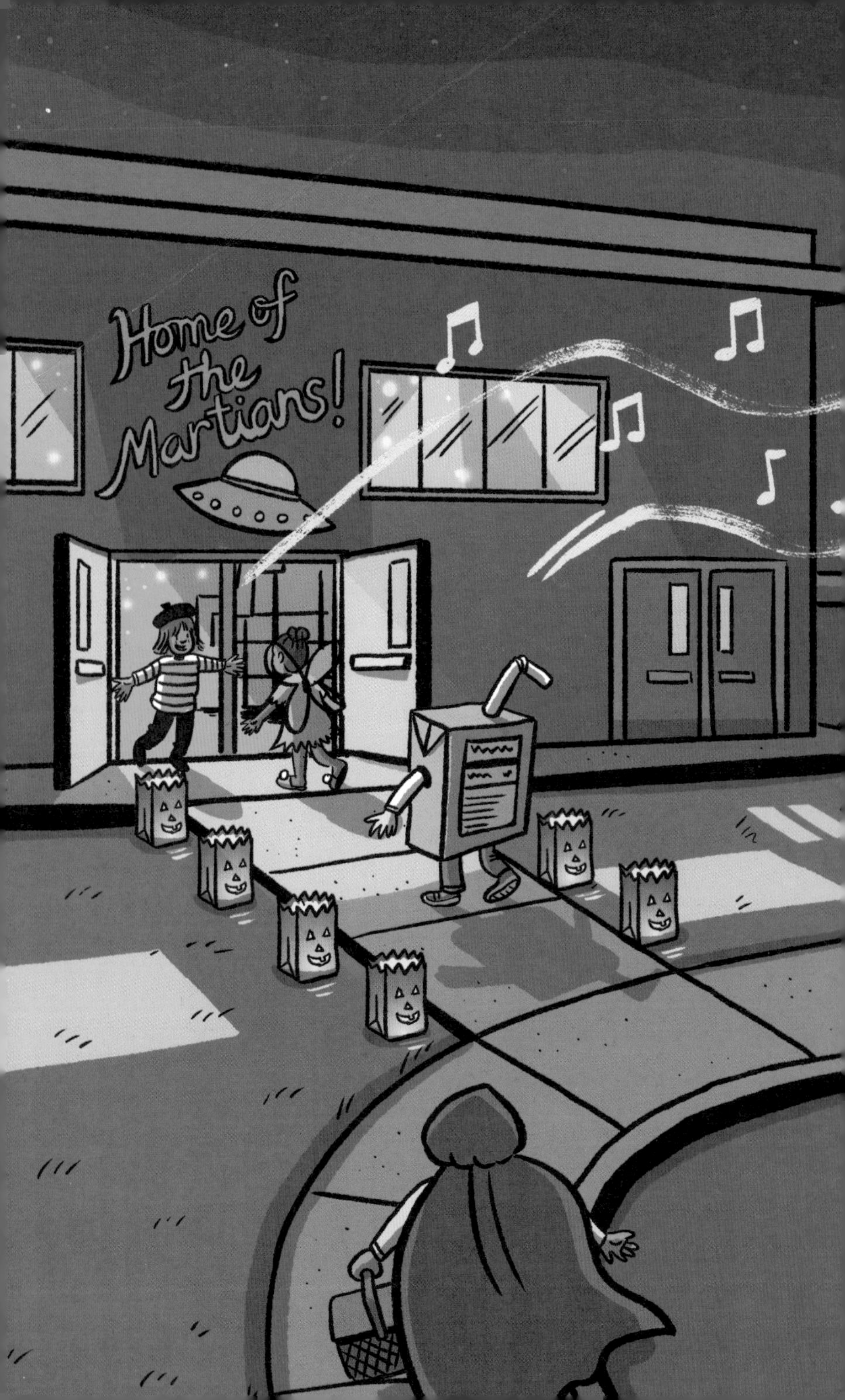
Home of the Martians!

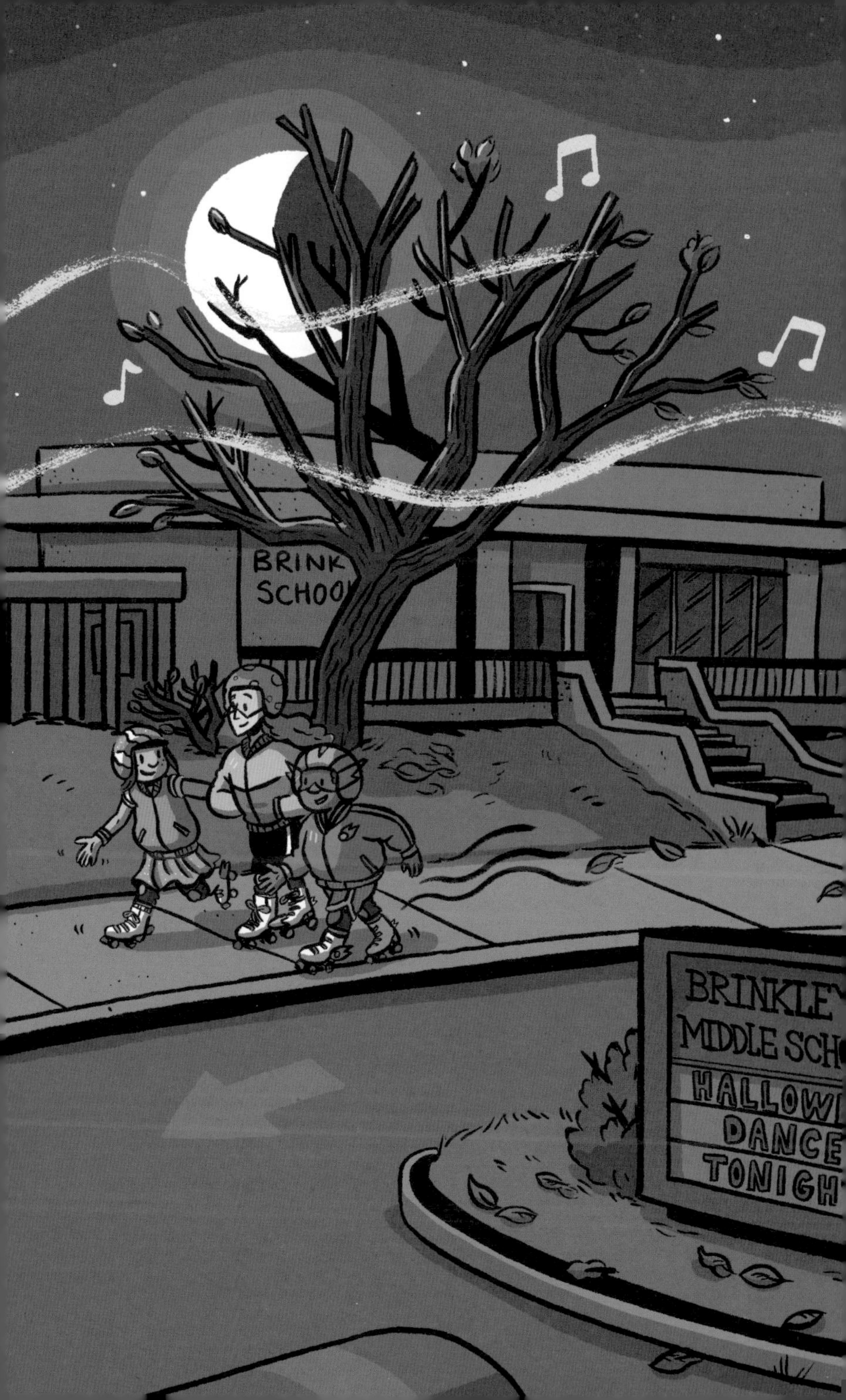
BRINK
SCHOO
BRINKLE
MIDDLE SCHO
HALLOW
DANCE
TONIGH

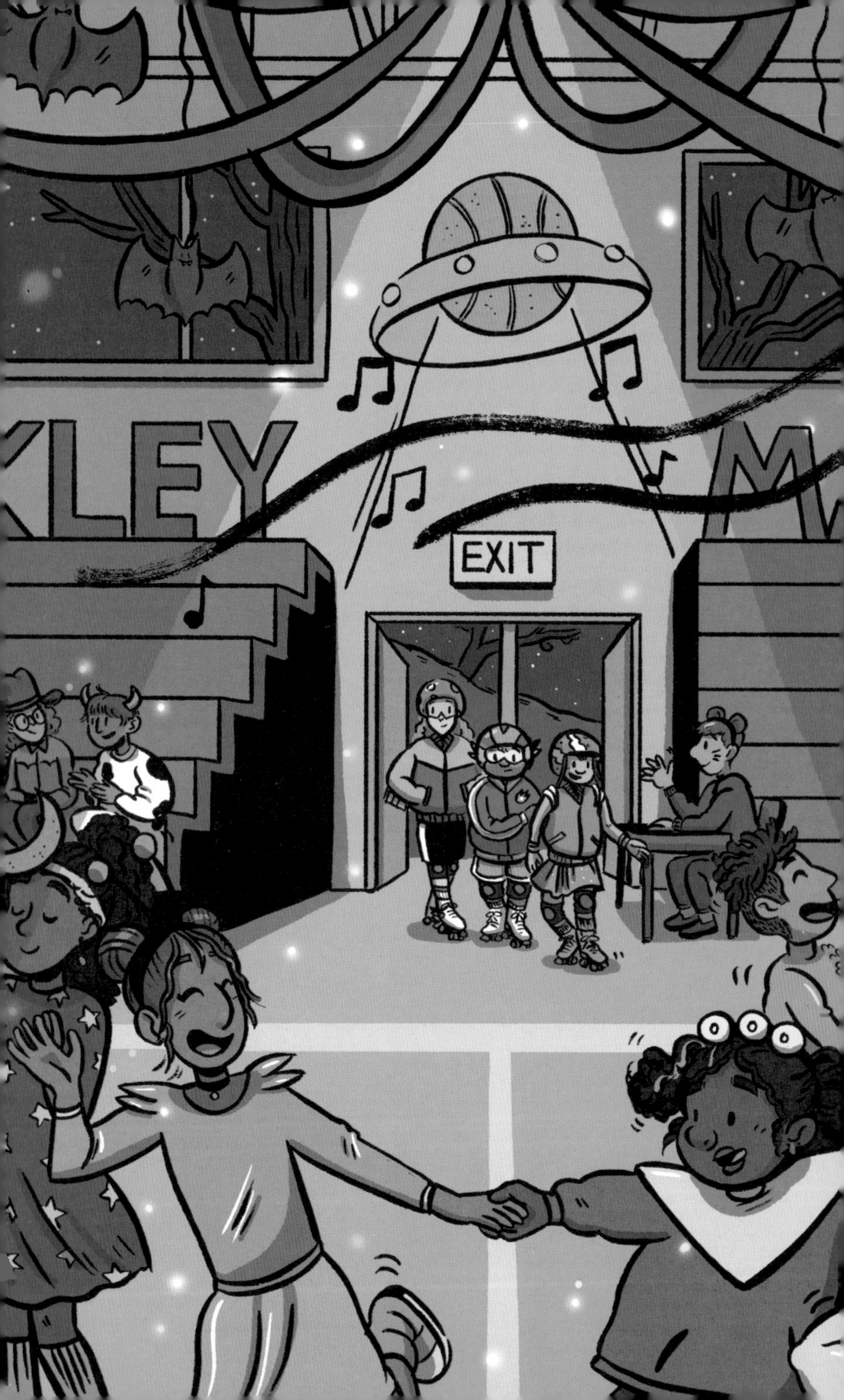
EXIT

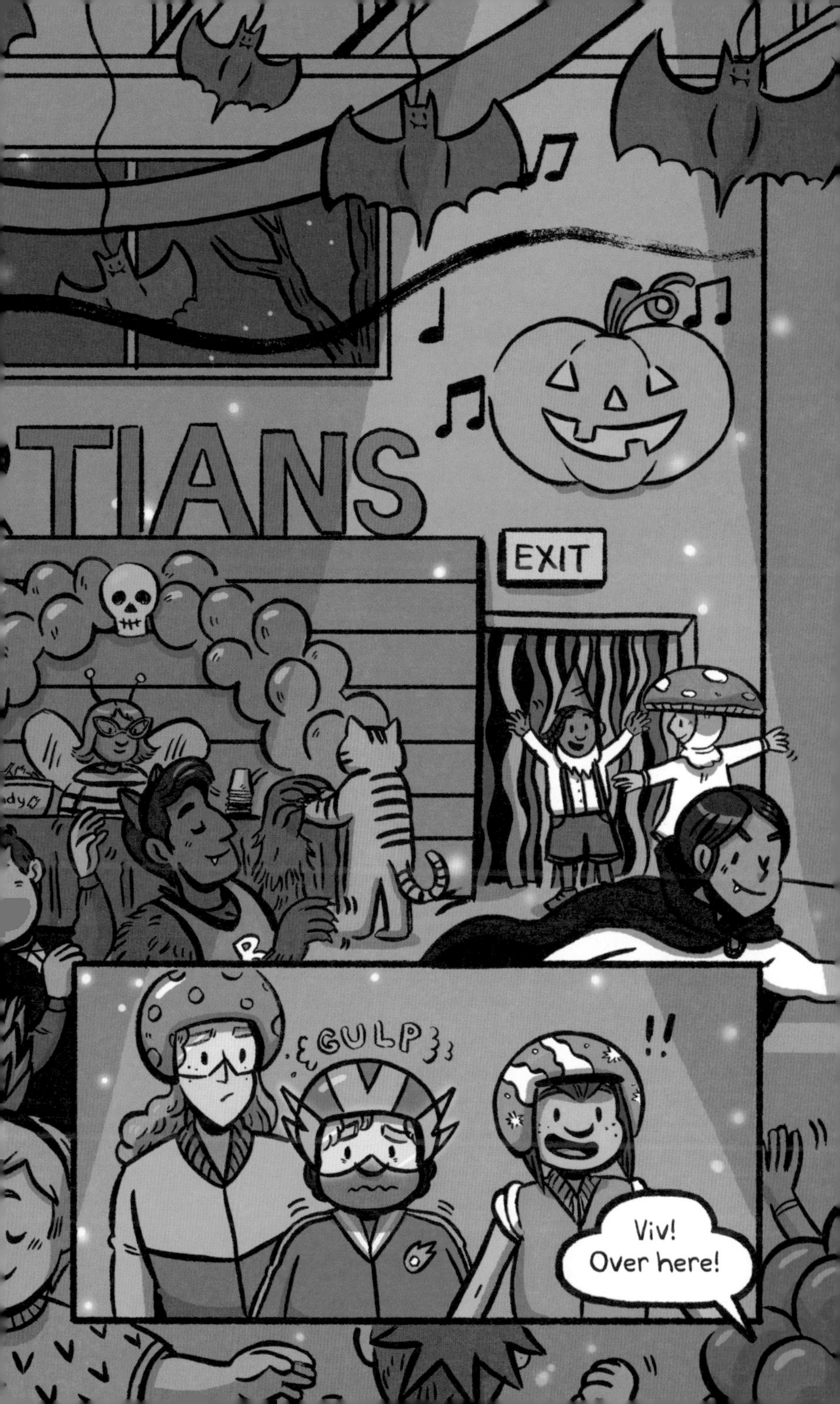
TIANS
EXIT
GULP
!!
Viv!
Over here!

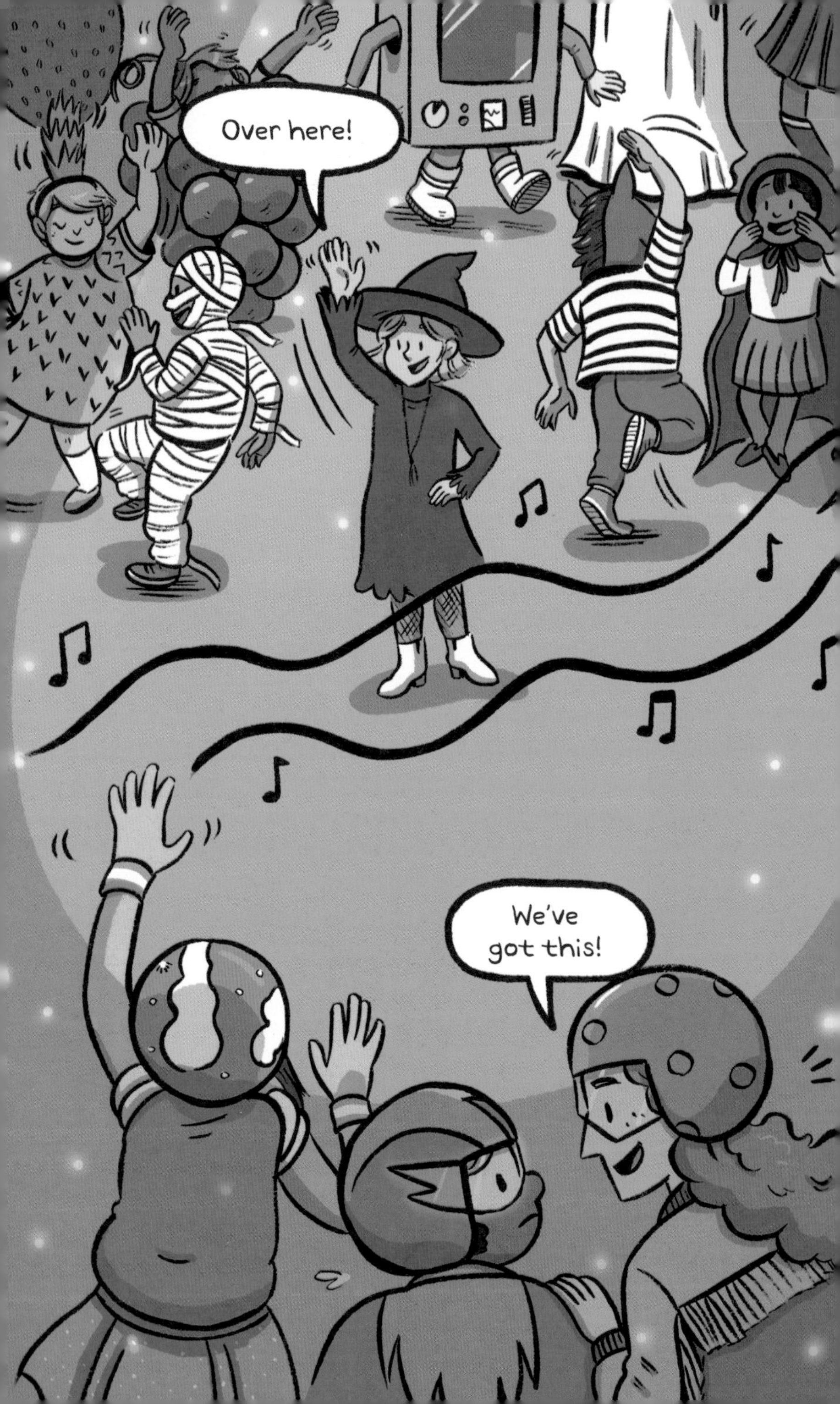
Over here!
We've got this!

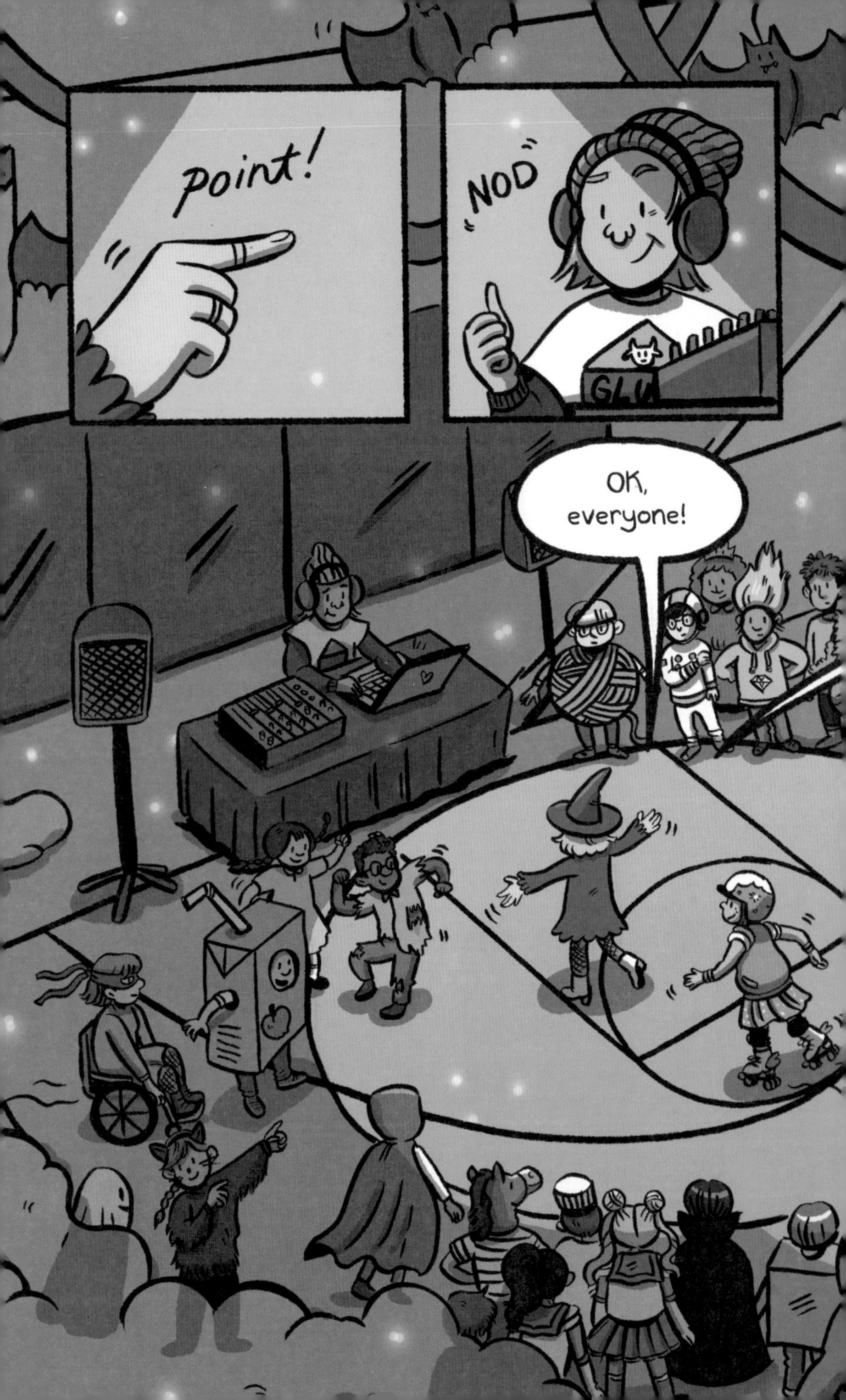
point!
NOD
GLU
OK, everyone!

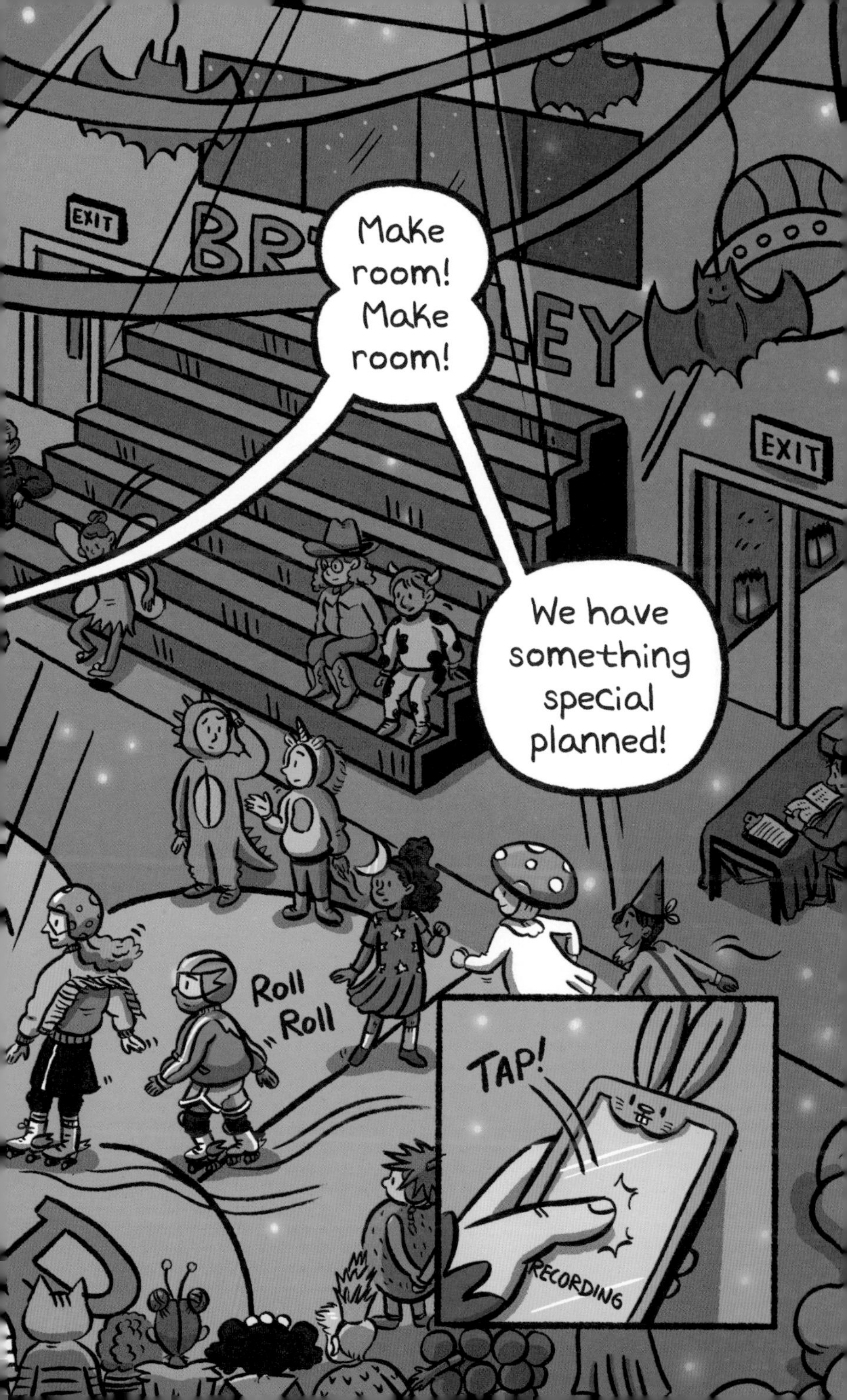
EXIT
BRADLEY
Make room! Make room!
We have something special planned!
EXIT
Roll Roll
TAP!
RECORDING

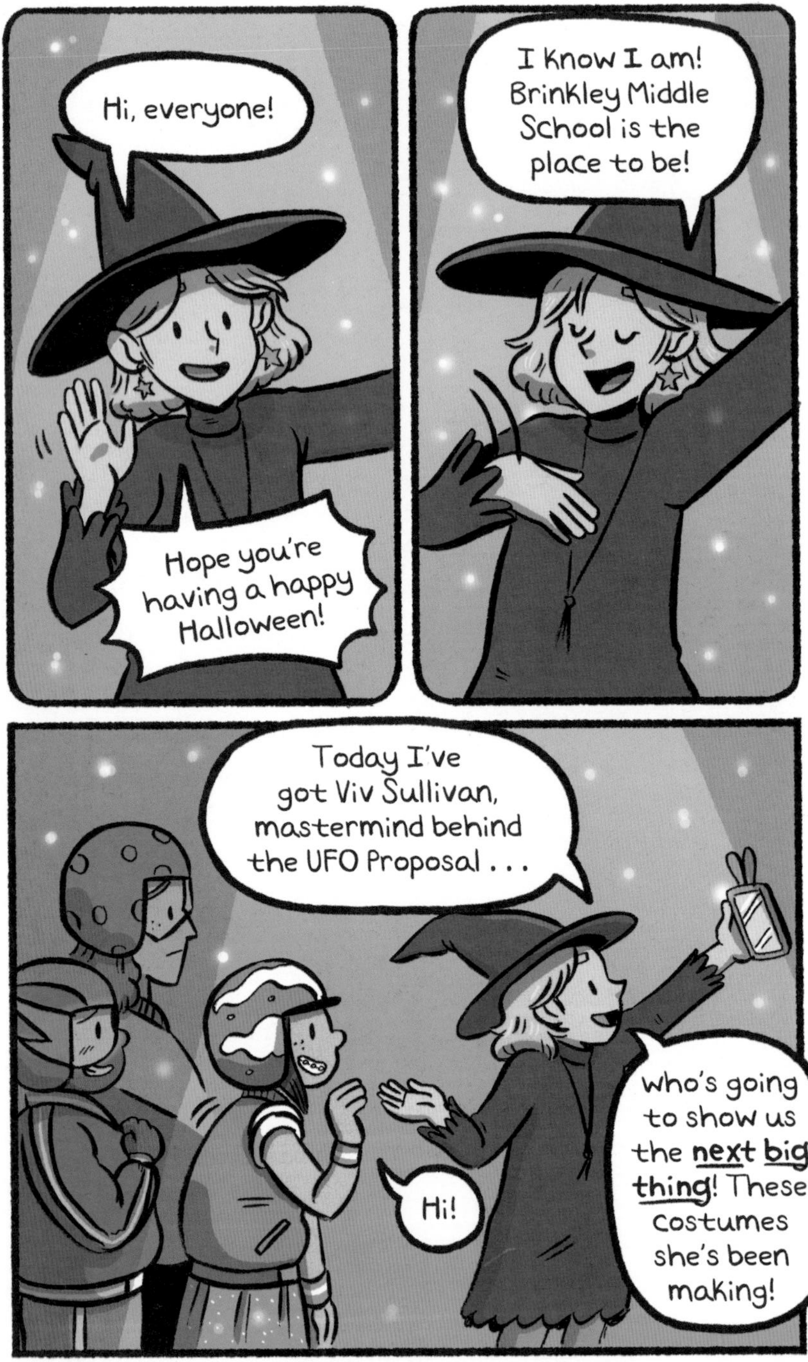
Hi, everyone!
Hope you're having a happy Halloween!
I know I am! Brinkley Middle School is the place to be!
Today I've got Viv Sullivan, mastermind behind the UFO Proposal . . .
Hi!
Who's going to show us the next big thing! These costumes she's been making!

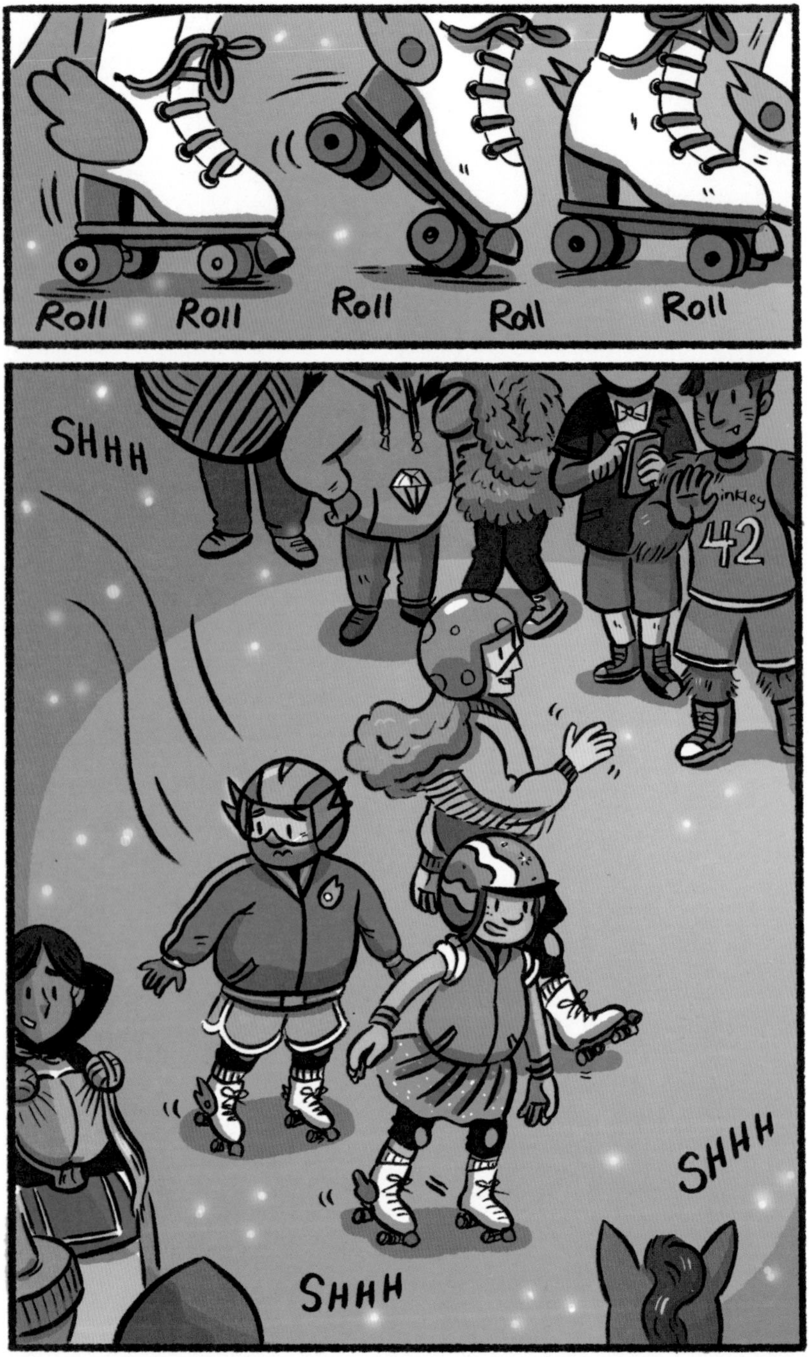
Roll
Roll
Roll
Roll
Roll
SHHH
SHHH
SHHH

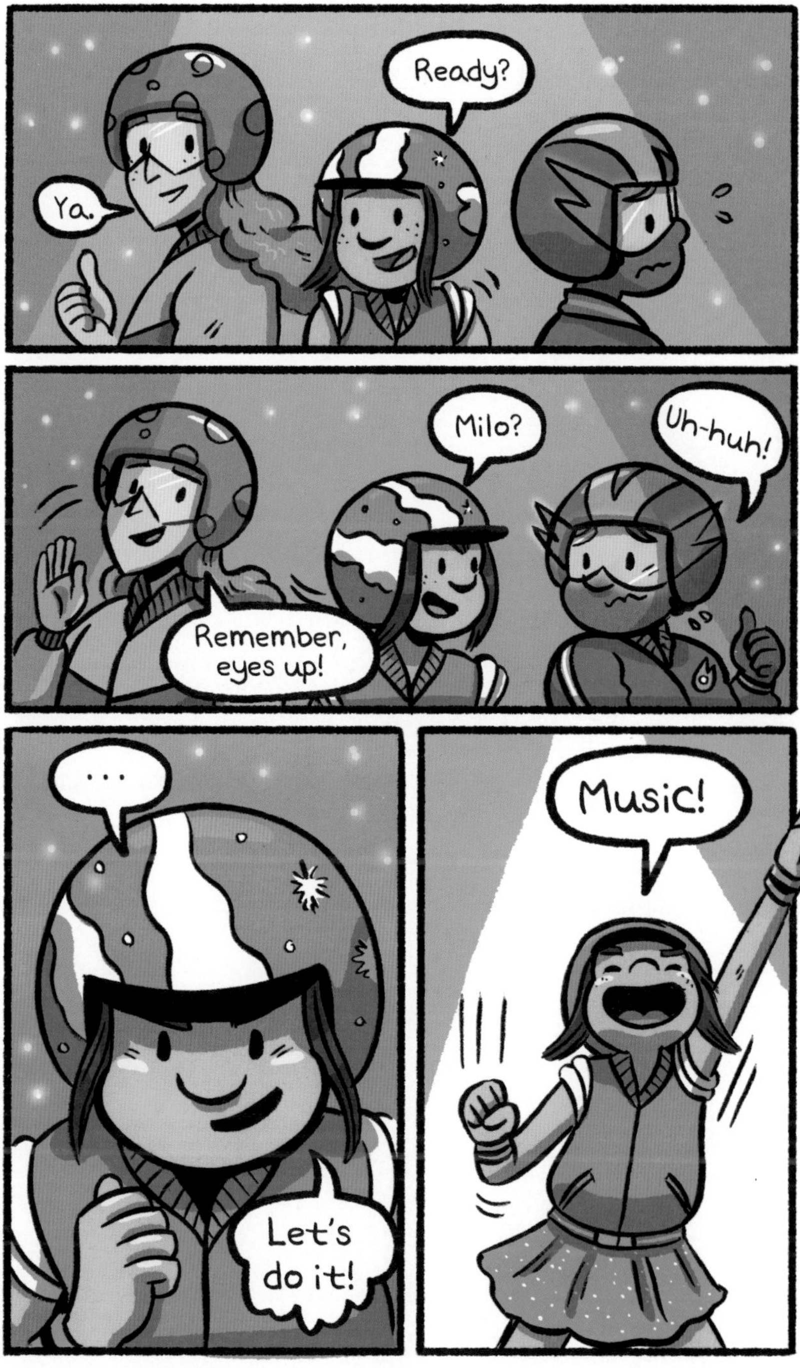
Ready?
Ya.
Milo?
Uh-huh!
Remember, eyes up!
...
Let's do it!
Music!

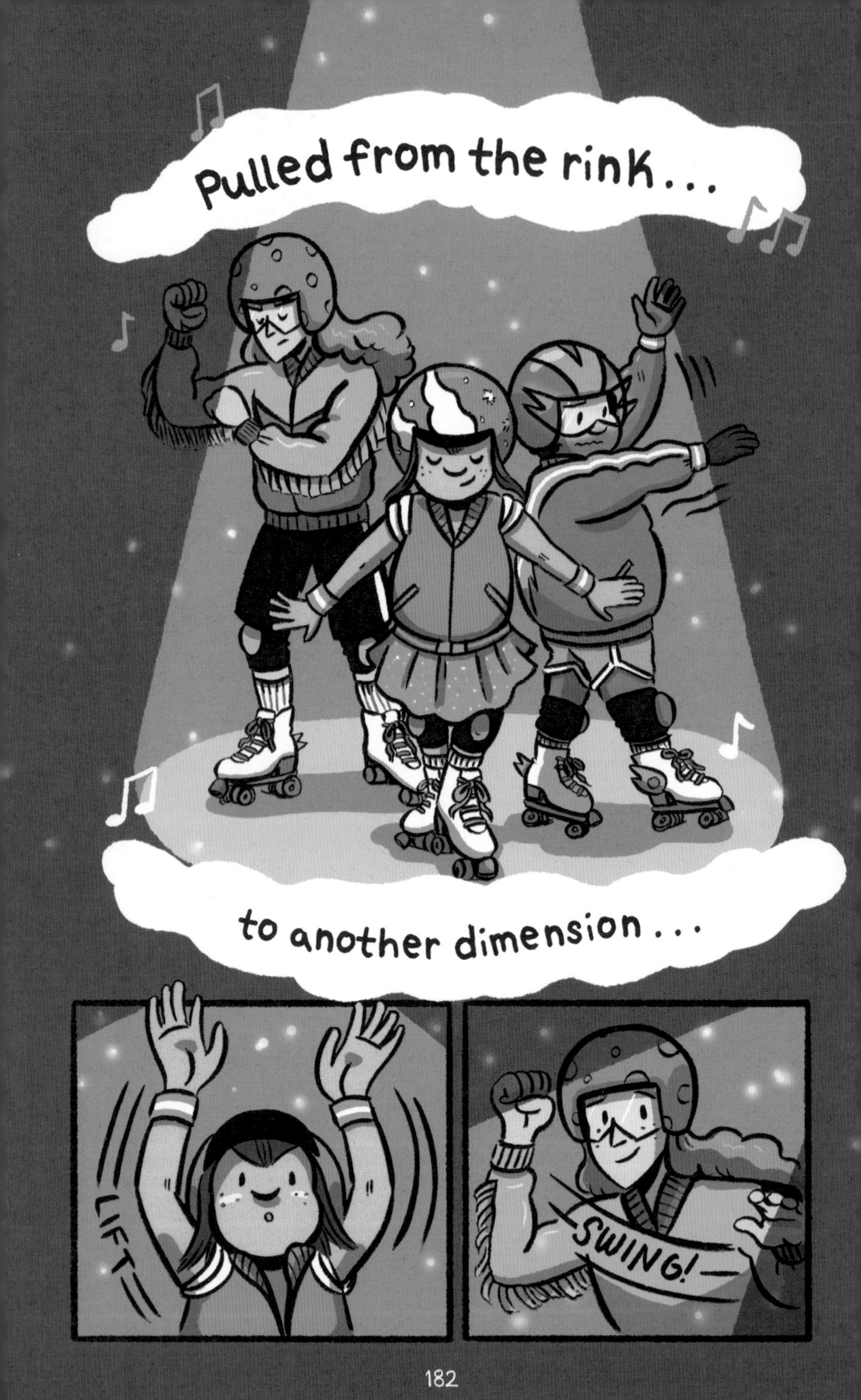
Pulled from the rink...
to another dimension...
LIFT
SWING!

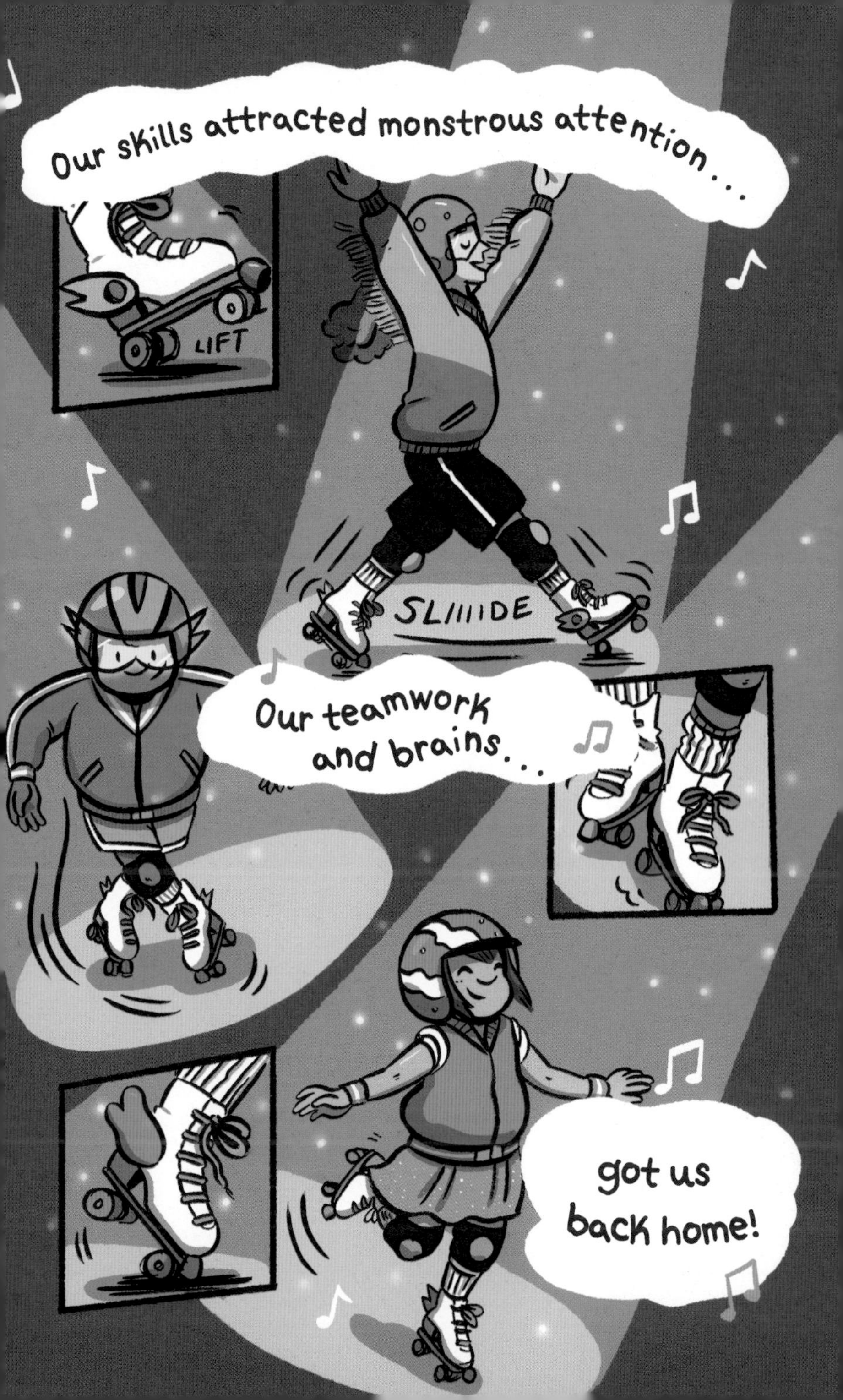
Our skills attracted monstrous attention...
LIFT
SLIIIIDE
Our teamwork and brains...
got us back home!

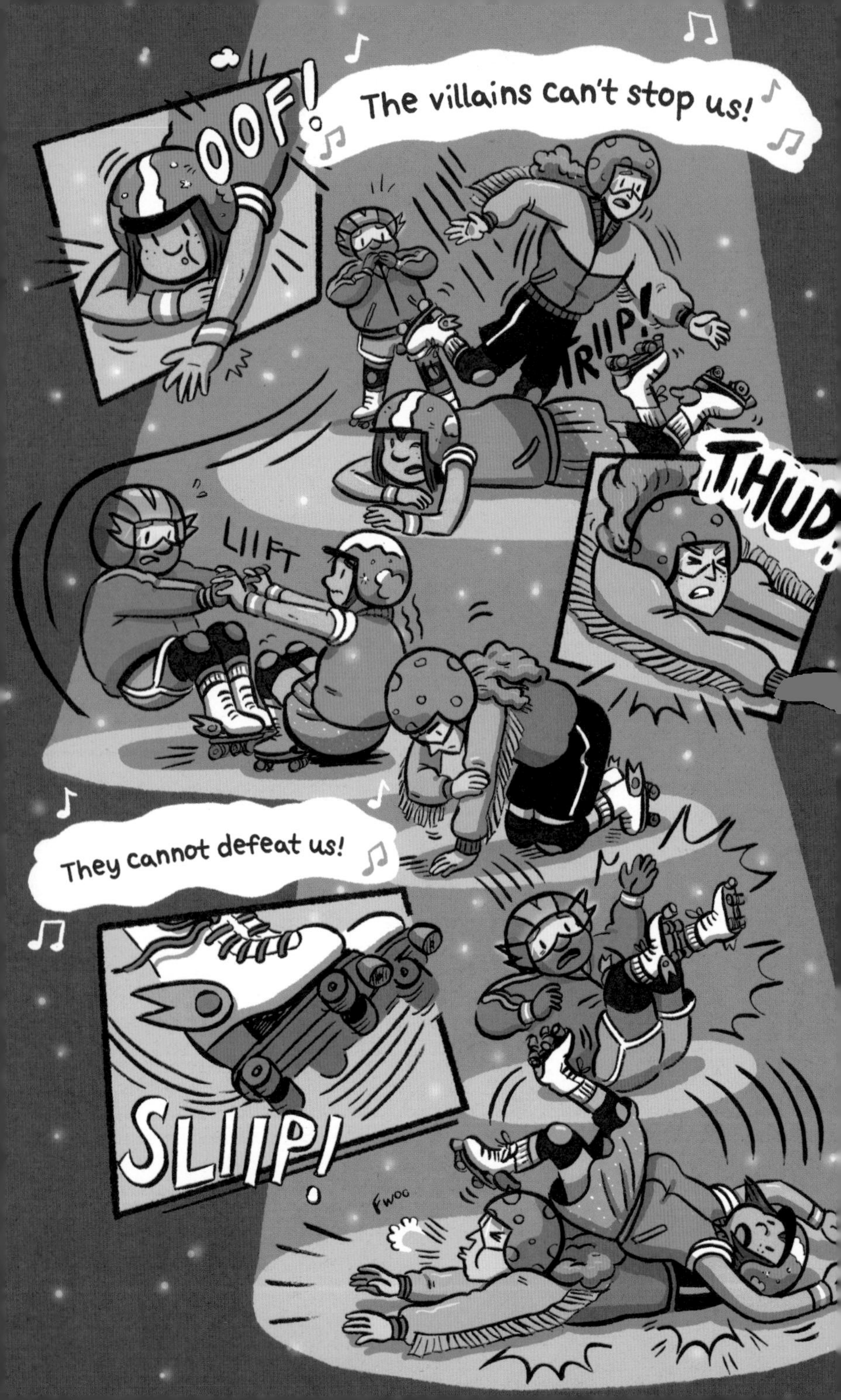

OOF!
The villains can't stop us!
RIIP!
THUD!
LIIFT
They cannot defeat us!
SLIIP!
FWOO

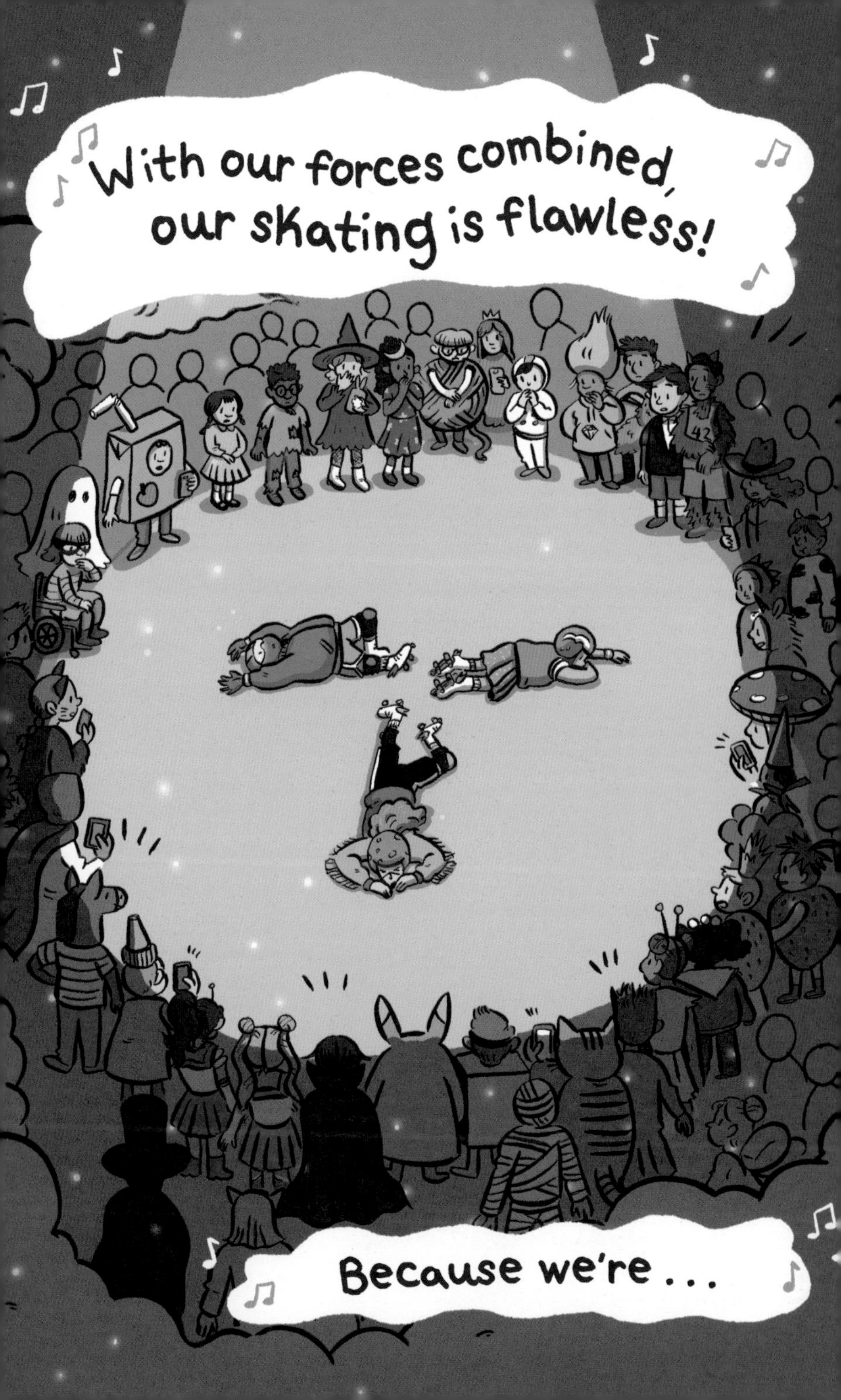
With our forces combined, our skating is flawless!
Because we're . . .

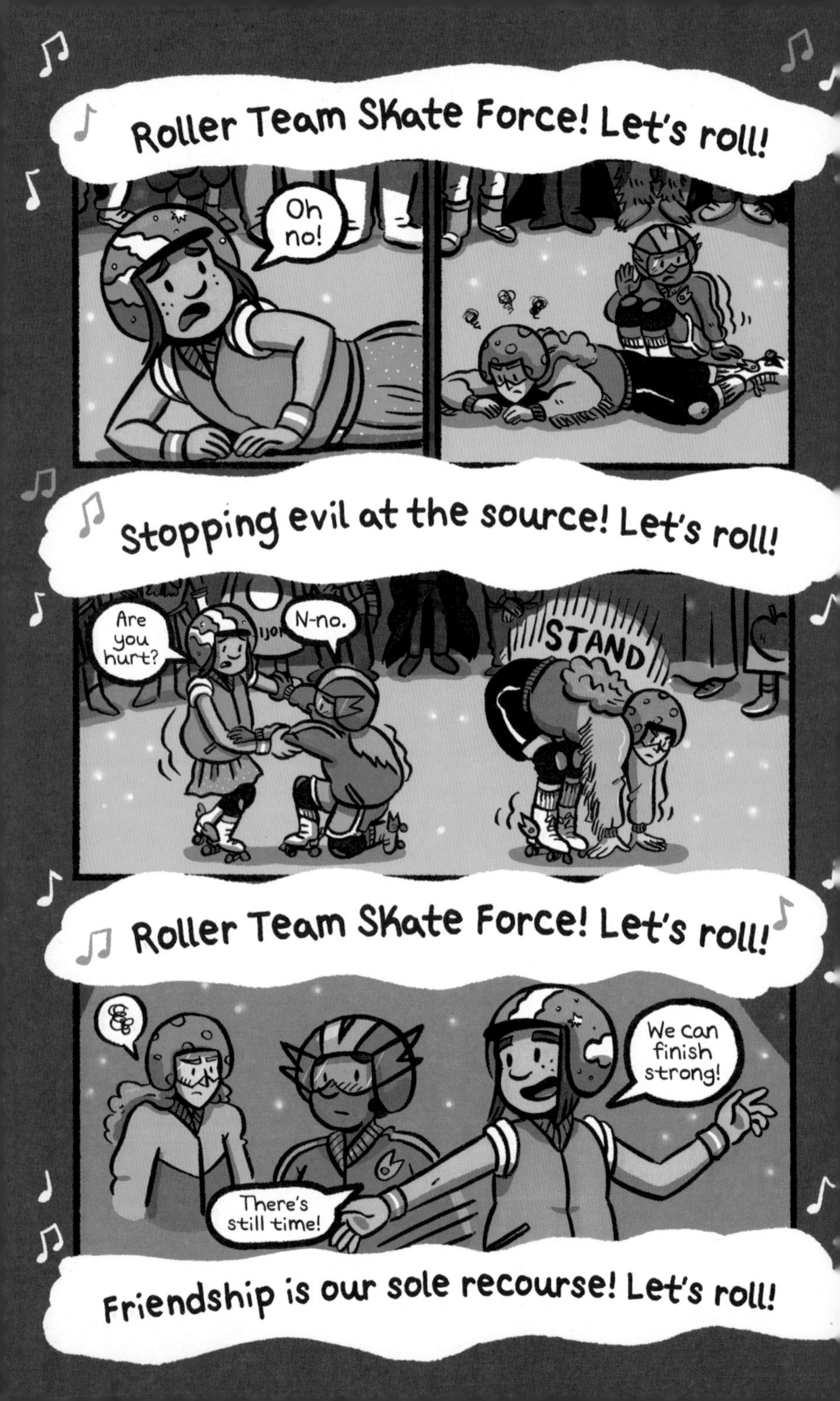

Roller Team Skate Force! Let's roll!
Oh no!
Stopping evil at the source! Let's roll!
Are you hurt?
N-no.
STAND
Roller Team Skate Force! Let's roll!
We can finish strong!
There's still time!
Friendship is our sole recourse! Let's roll!

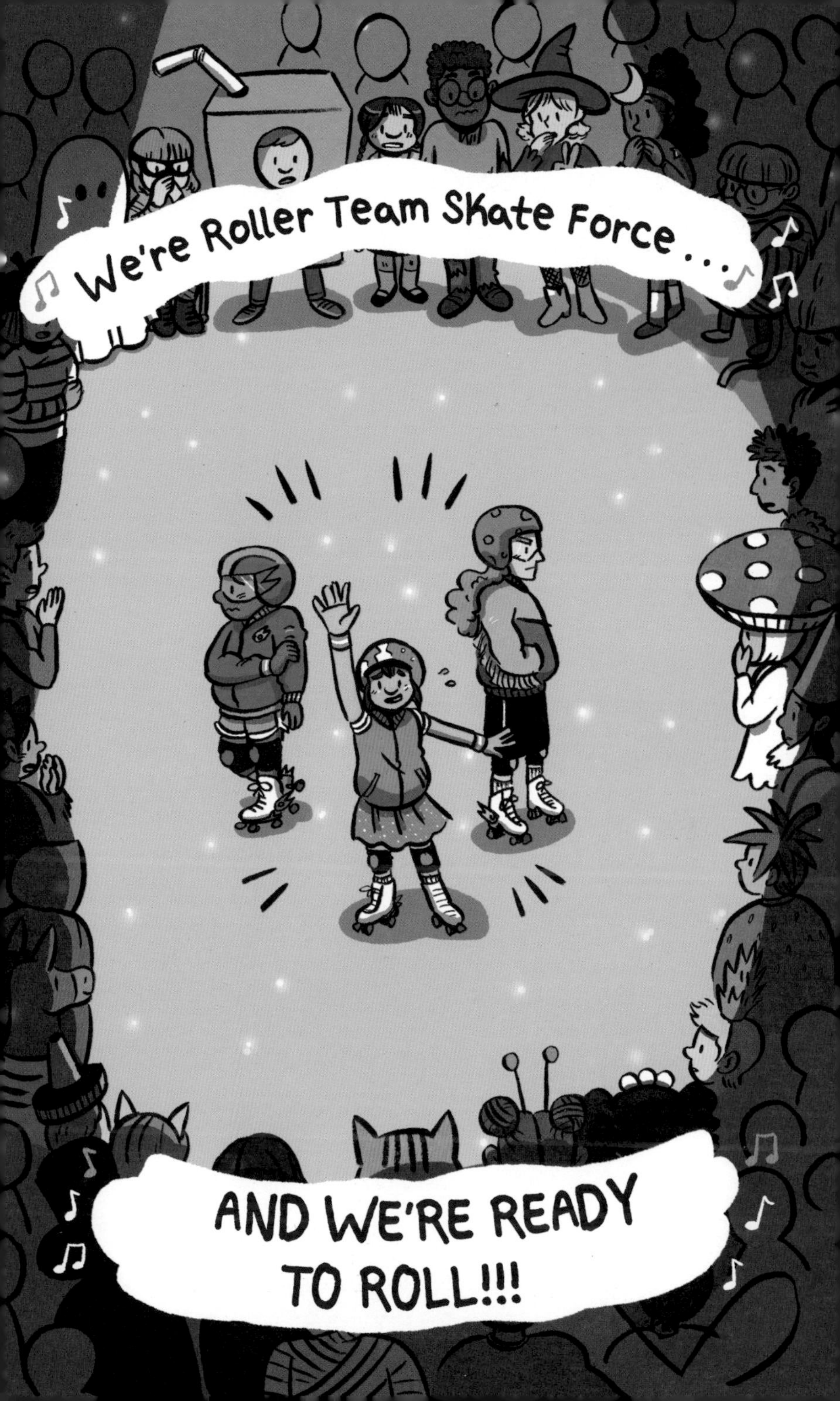
We're Roller Team Skate Force . . .
AND WE'RE READY TO ROLL!!!

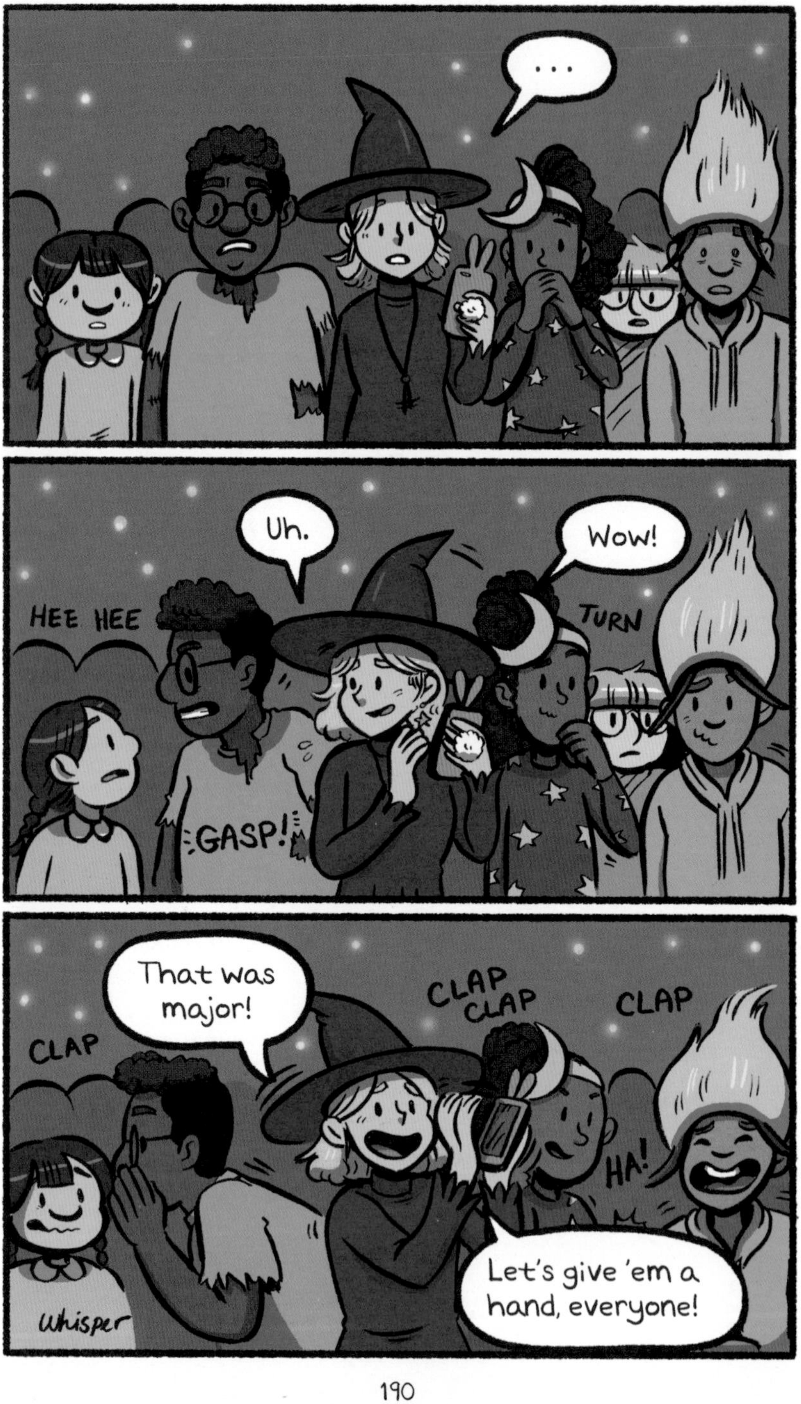
...
Uh.
Wow!
HEE HEE
TURN
GASP!
That was major!
CLAP
CLAP CLAP
CLAP
HA!
Let's give 'em a hand, everyone!
whisper

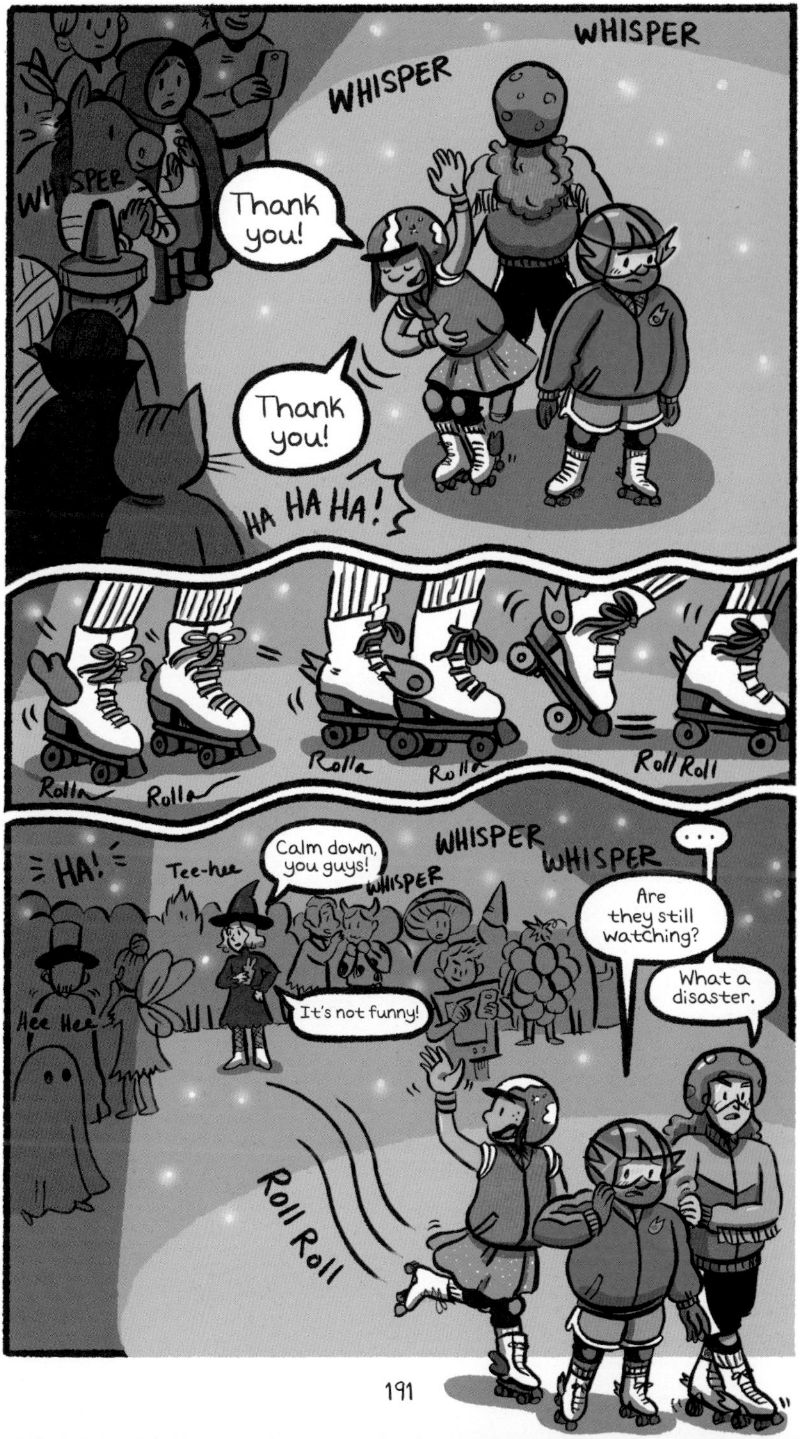
WHISPER
WHISPER
WHISPER
Thank you!
Thank you!
HA HA HA!
Rolla
Rolla
Rolla
Rolla
Roll Roll
HA!
Tee-hee
Calm down, you guys!
WHISPER
WHISPER
WHISPER
...
Are they still watching?
What a disaster.
It's not funny!
Hee Hee
Roll Roll

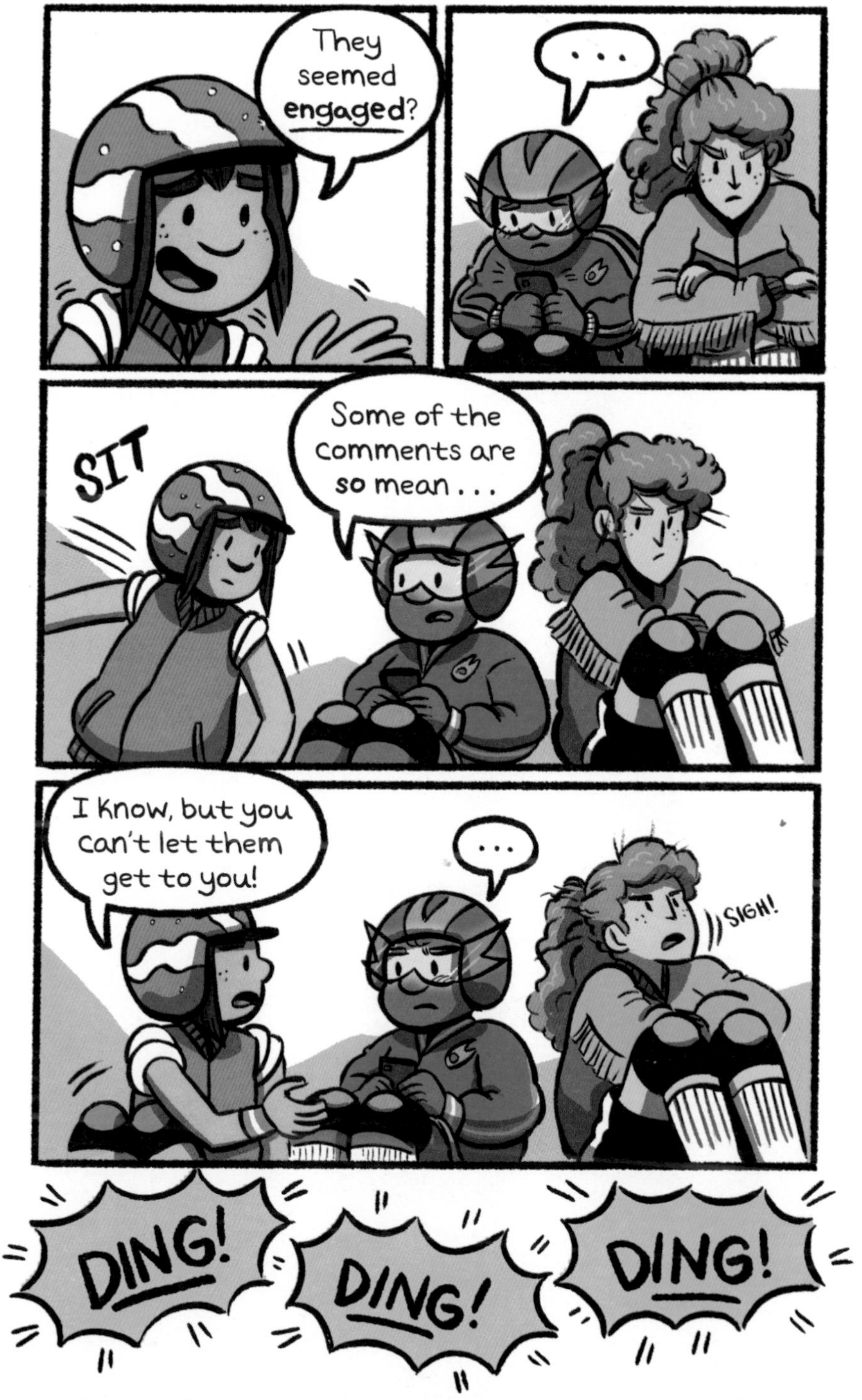
They seemed engaged?
...
SIT
Some of the comments are so mean...
I know, but you can't let them get to you!
...
SIGH!
DING!
DING!
DING!

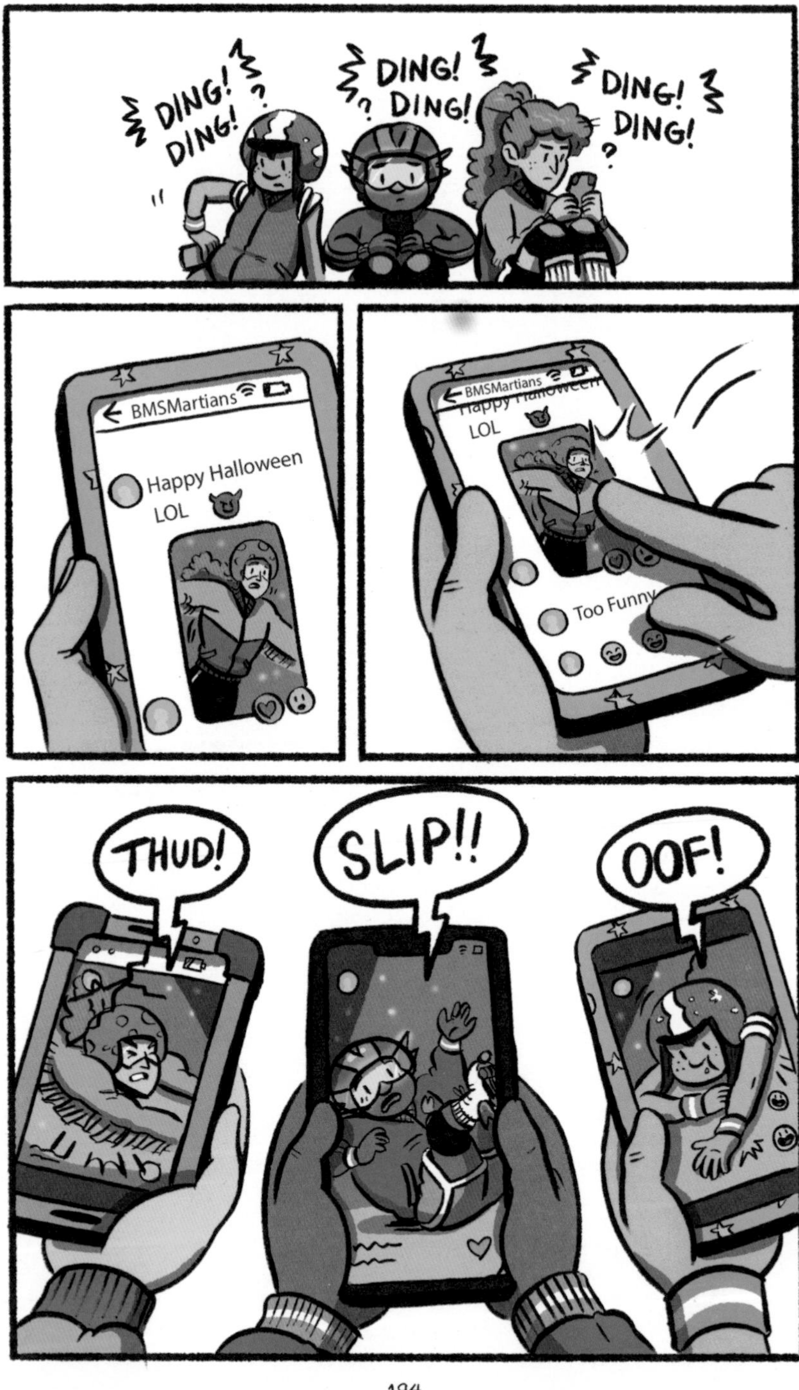
DING! DING!
DING! DING!
DING! DING!
BMSMartians
Happy Halloween
LOL
BMSMartians
LOL
Too Funny
THUD!
SLIP!!
OOF!

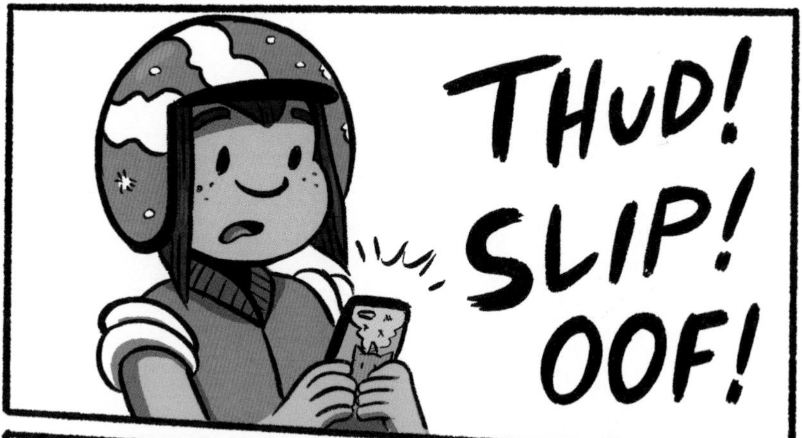
THUD!
SLIP!
OOF!

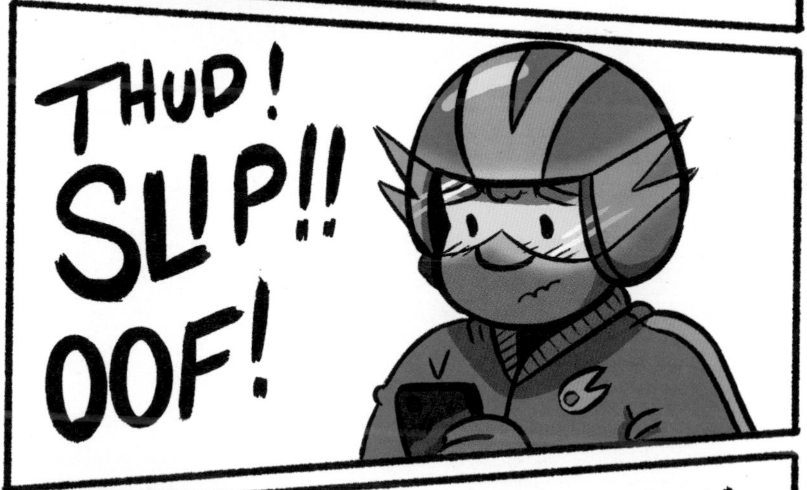
THUD!
SLIP!!
OOF!

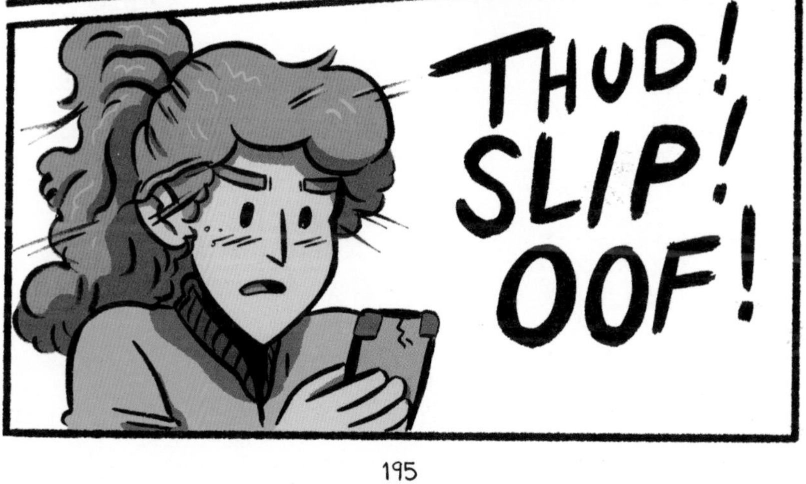
THUD!
SLIP!
OOF!

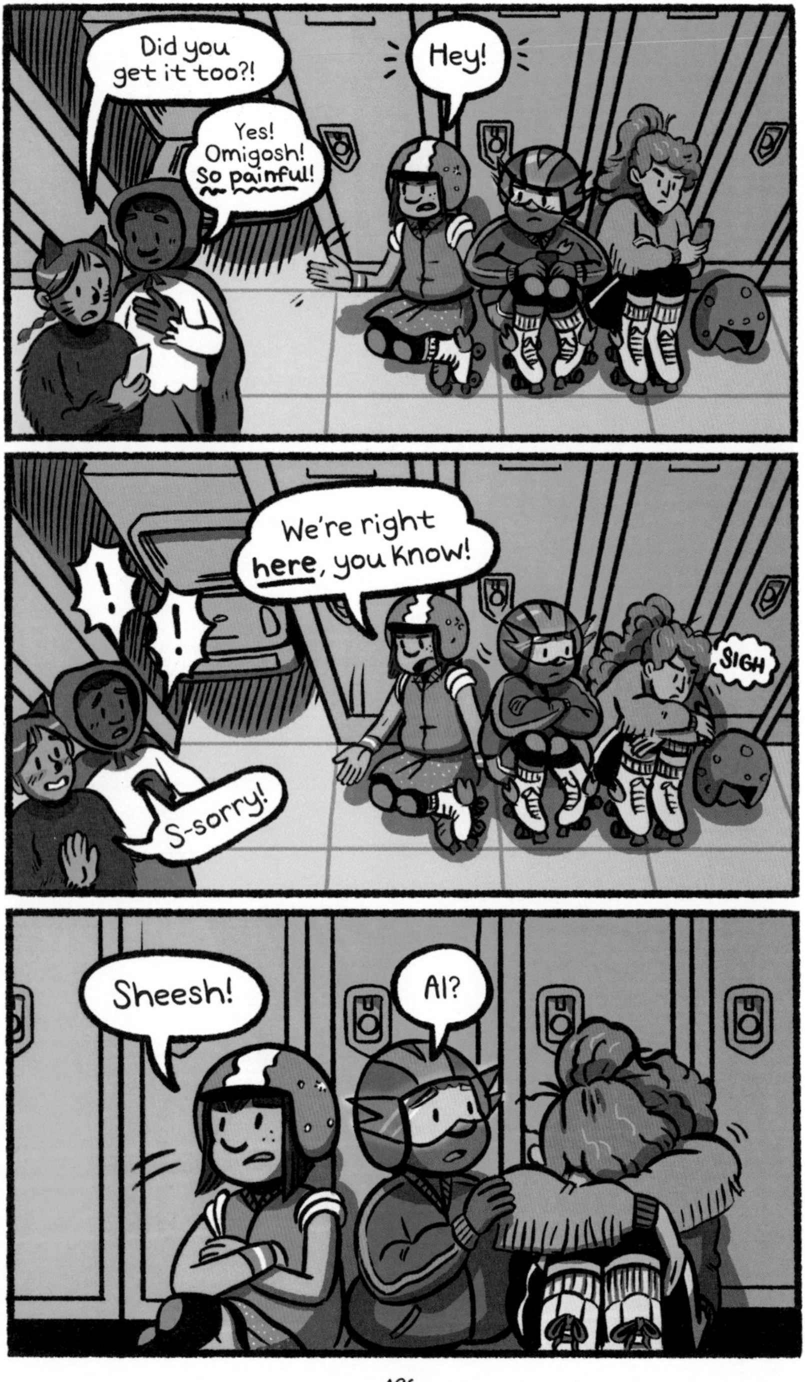
Did you get it too?!
Yes! Omigosh! So painful!
Hey!
We're right here, you know!
S-sorry!
SIGH
Sheesh!
Al?

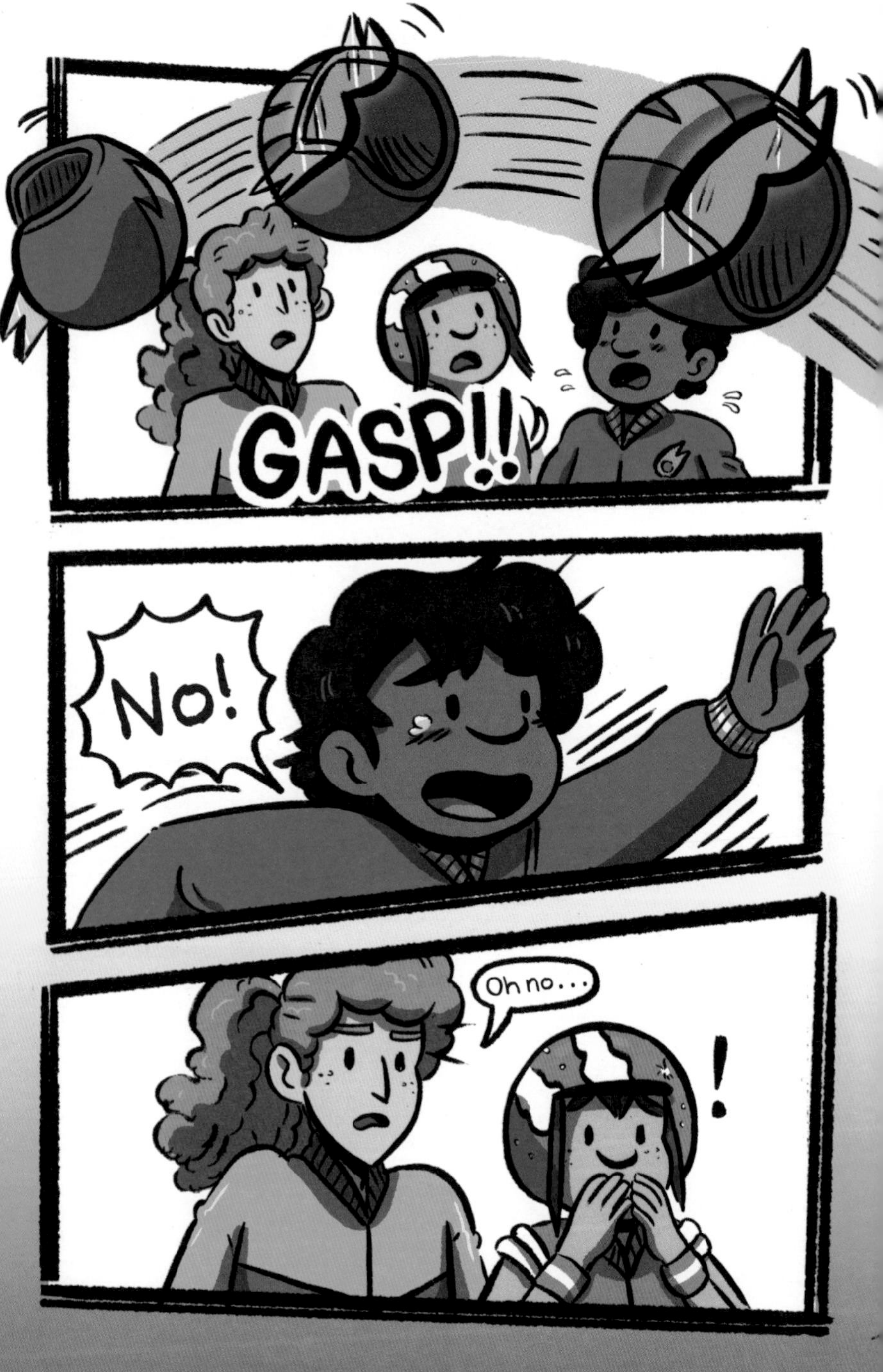
GASP!!
No!
Oh no...
!

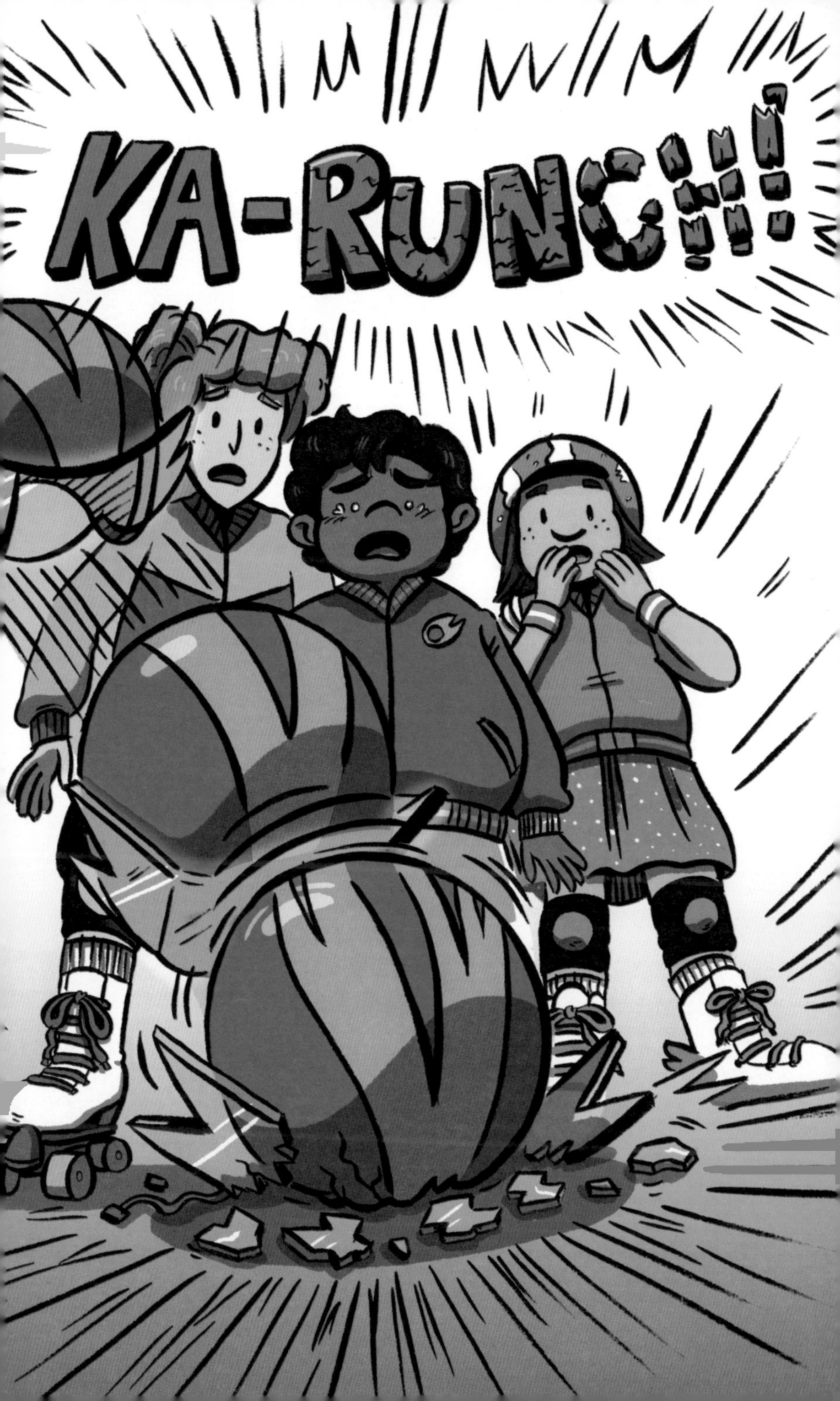
KA-RUNCH!!!

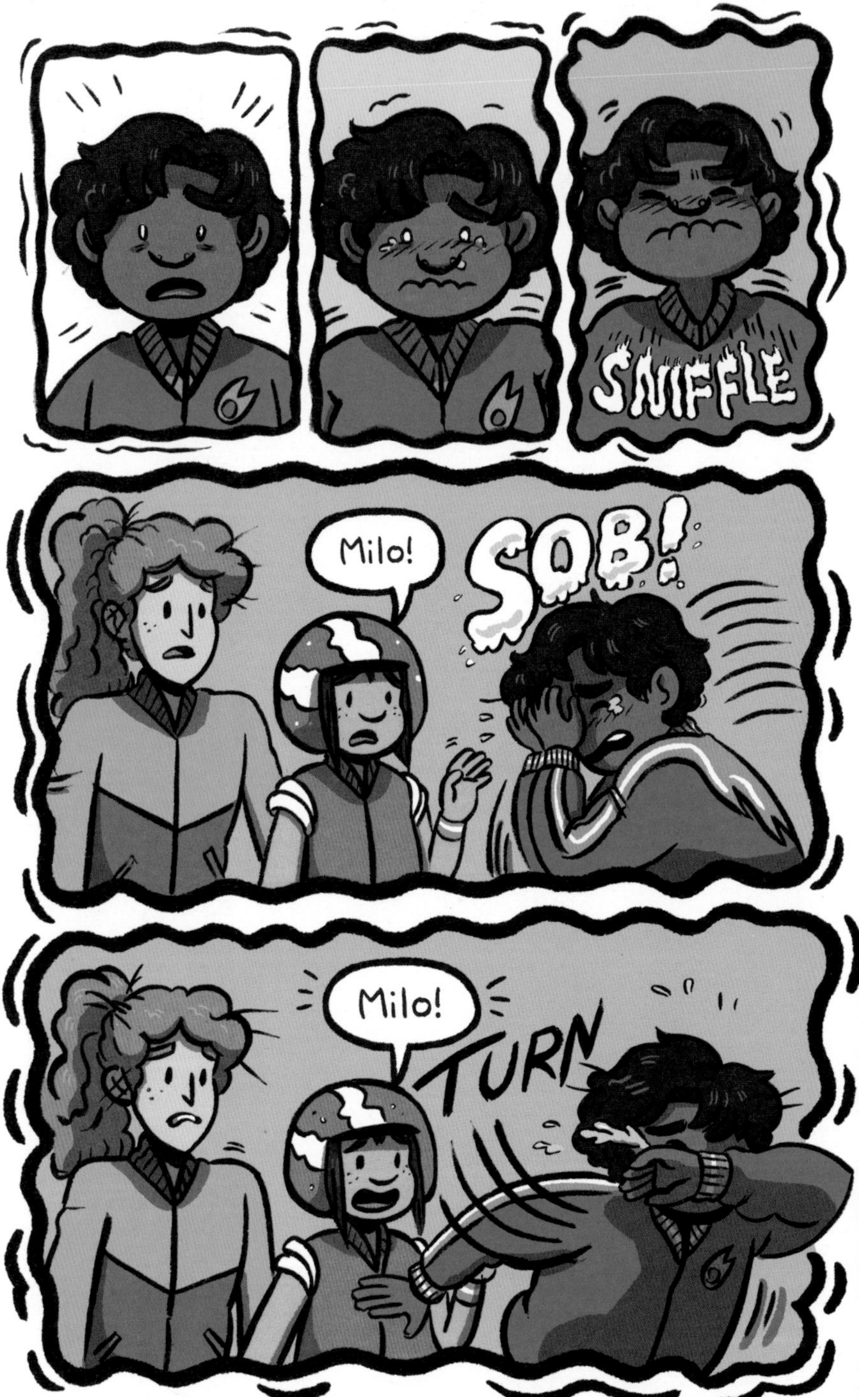
SNIFFLE
Milo!
SOB!
Milo!
TURN

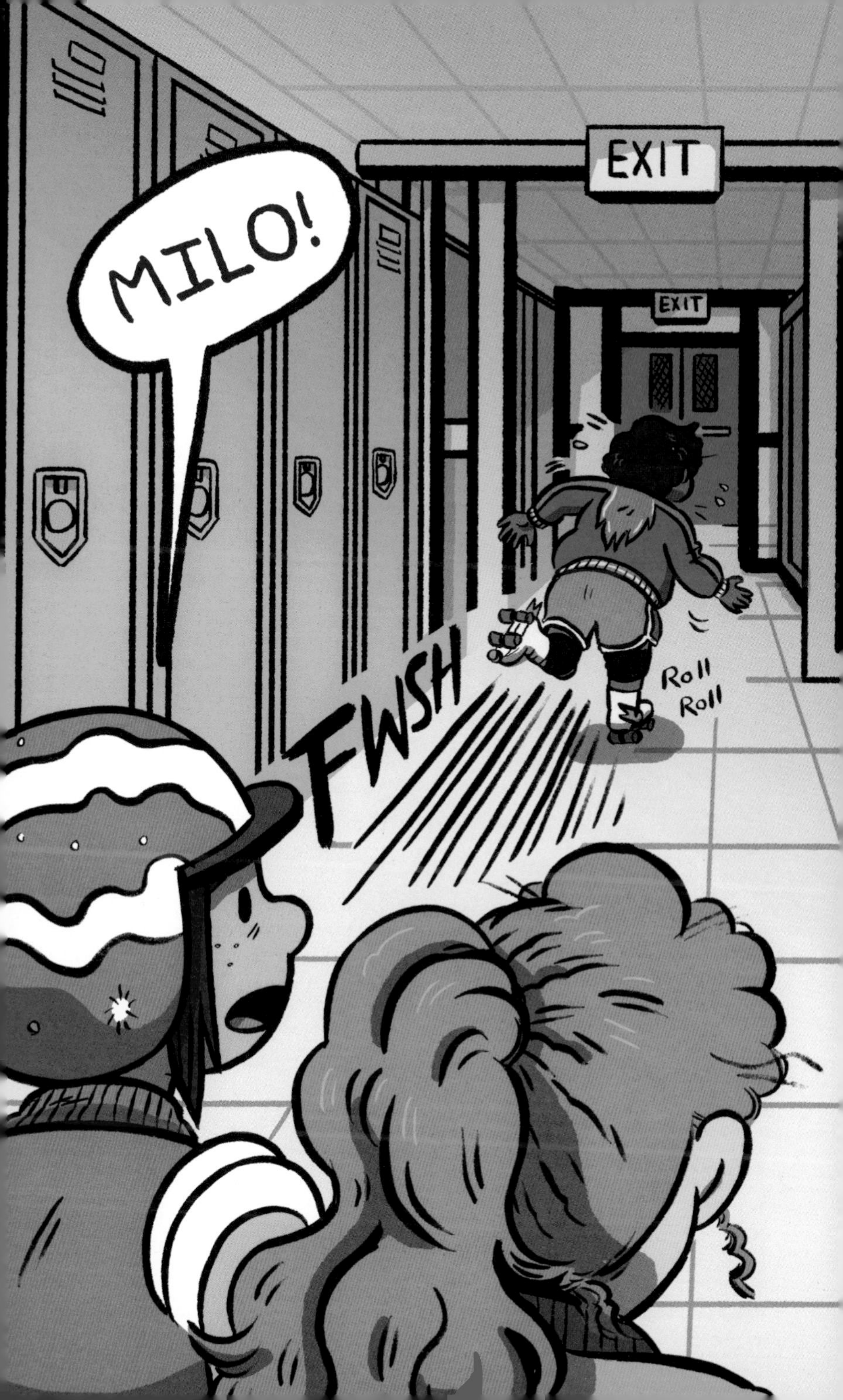
MILO!
EXIT
EXIT
FWSH
Roll
Roll

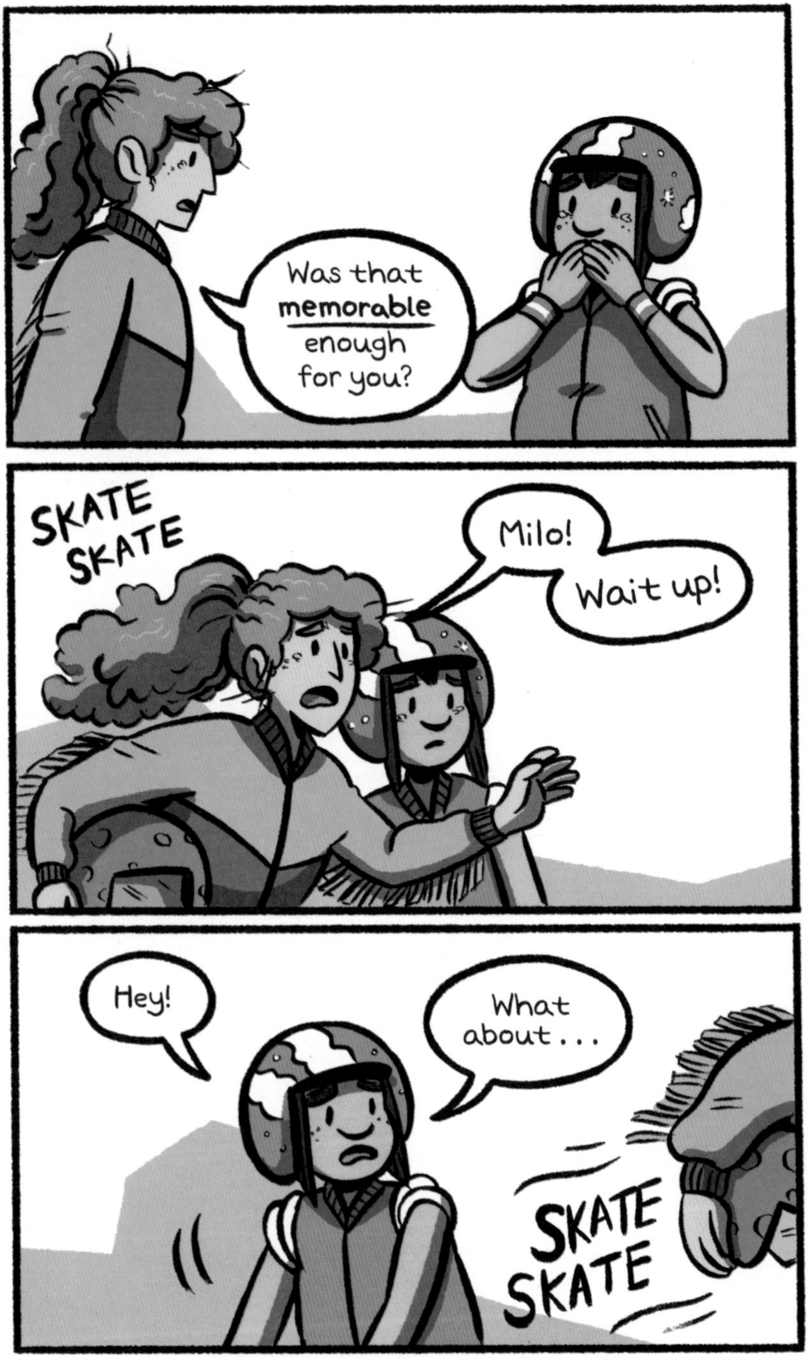
Was that **memorable** enough for you?
SKATE SKATE
Milo!
Wait up!
Hey!
What about...
SKATE SKATE

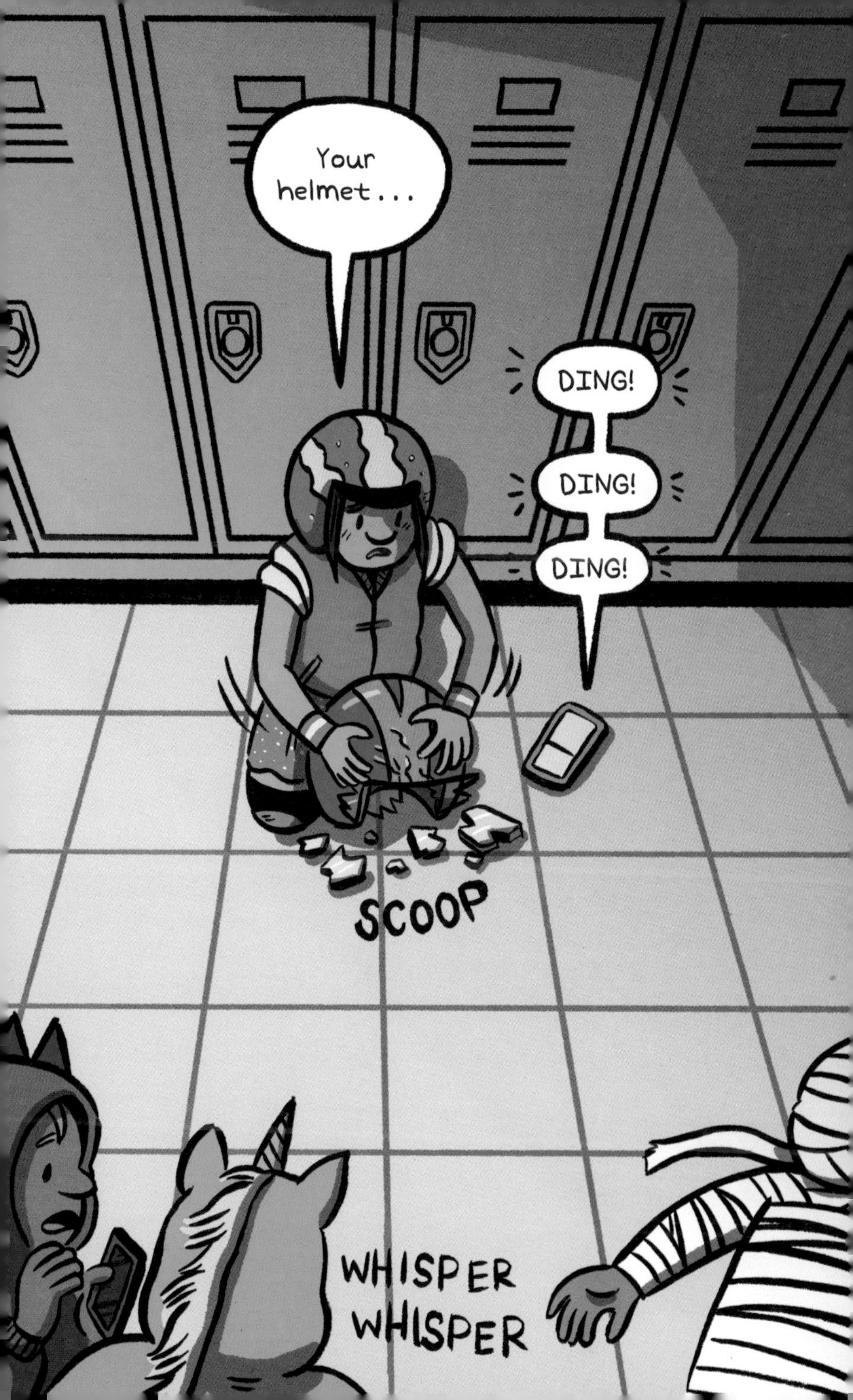
Your helmet...
DING!
DING!
DING!
SCOOP
WHISPER
WHISPER

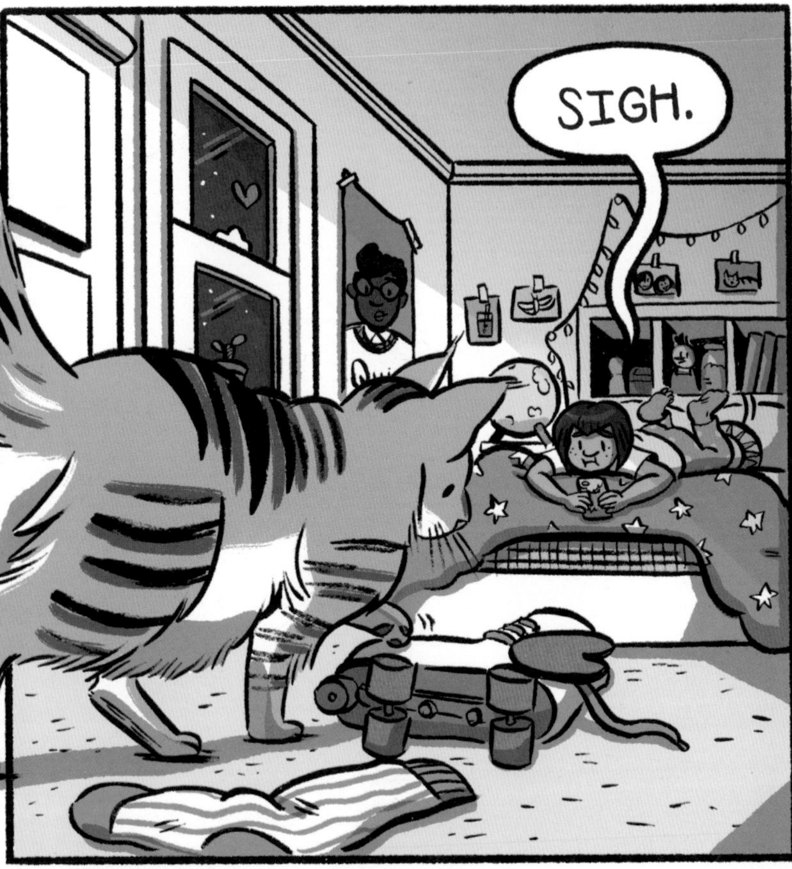
SIGH.

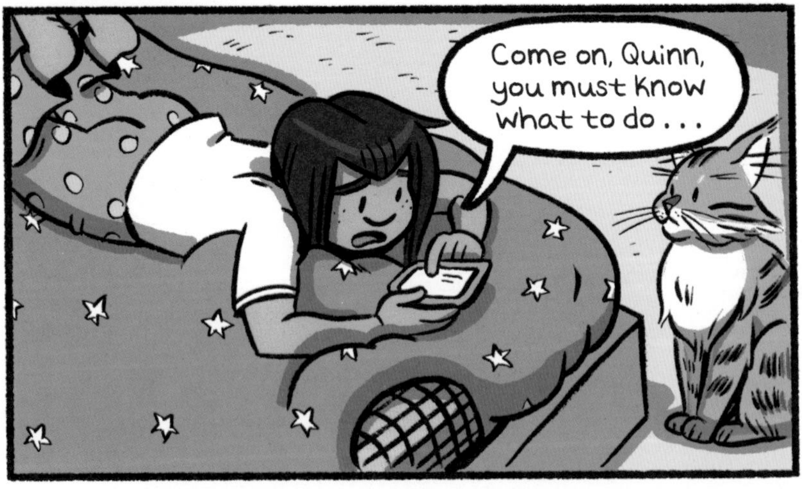
Come on, Quinn, you must know what to do . . .

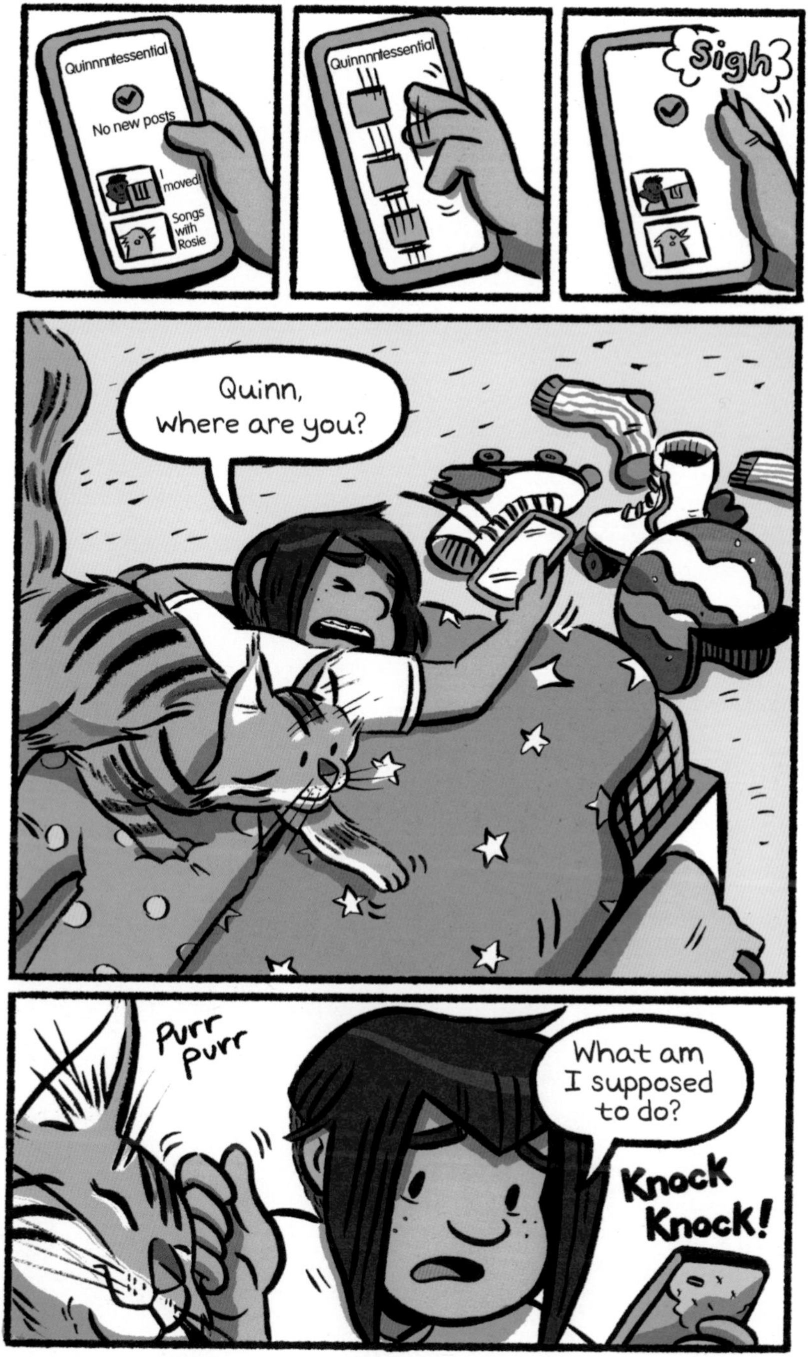
Quinnnntessential
No new posts
I moved!
Songs with Rosie
Quinnnntessential
Sigh
Quinn, where are you?
Purr purr
What am I supposed to do?
Knock Knock!

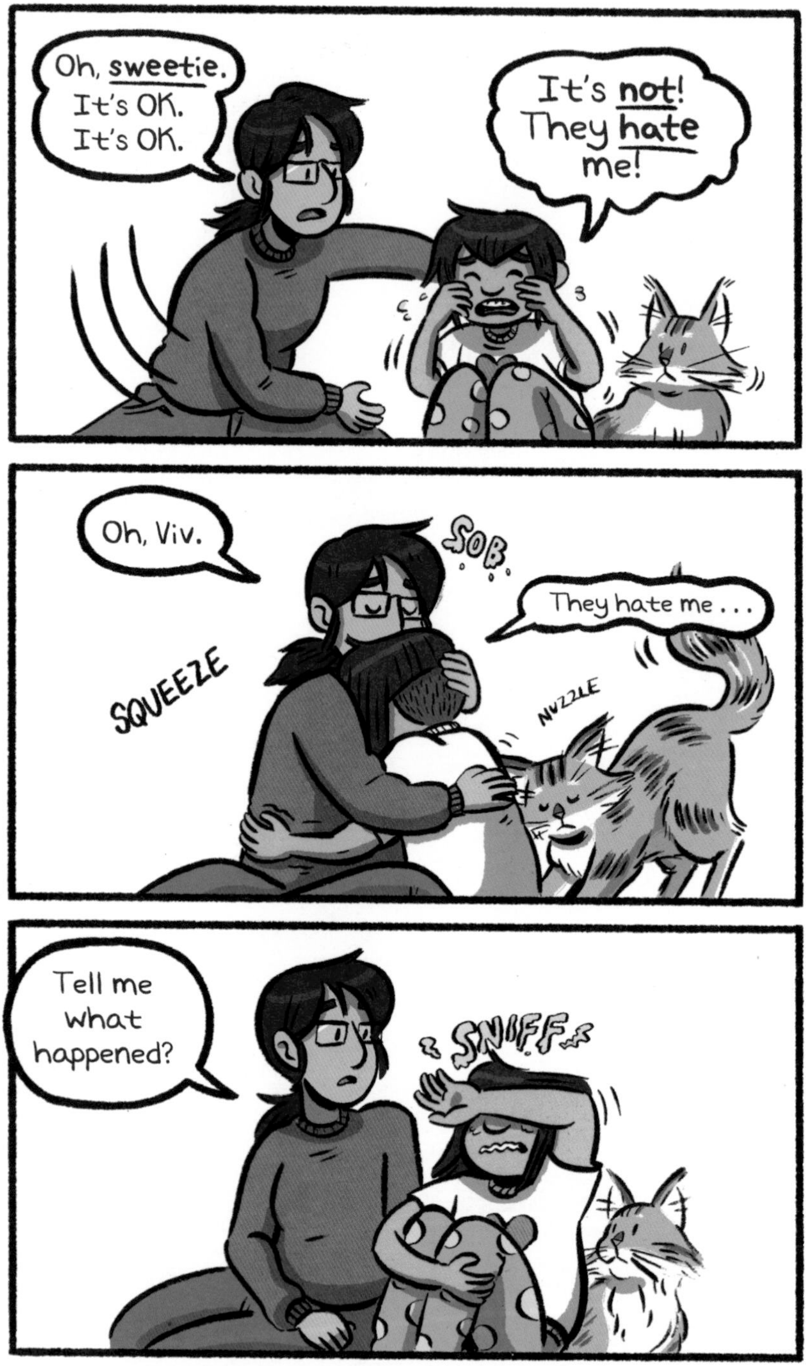
Oh, sweetie.
It's OK.
It's OK.
It's not! They hate me!
Oh, Viv.
SOB
They hate me . . .
SQUEEZE
NUZZLE
Tell me what happened?
SNIFF

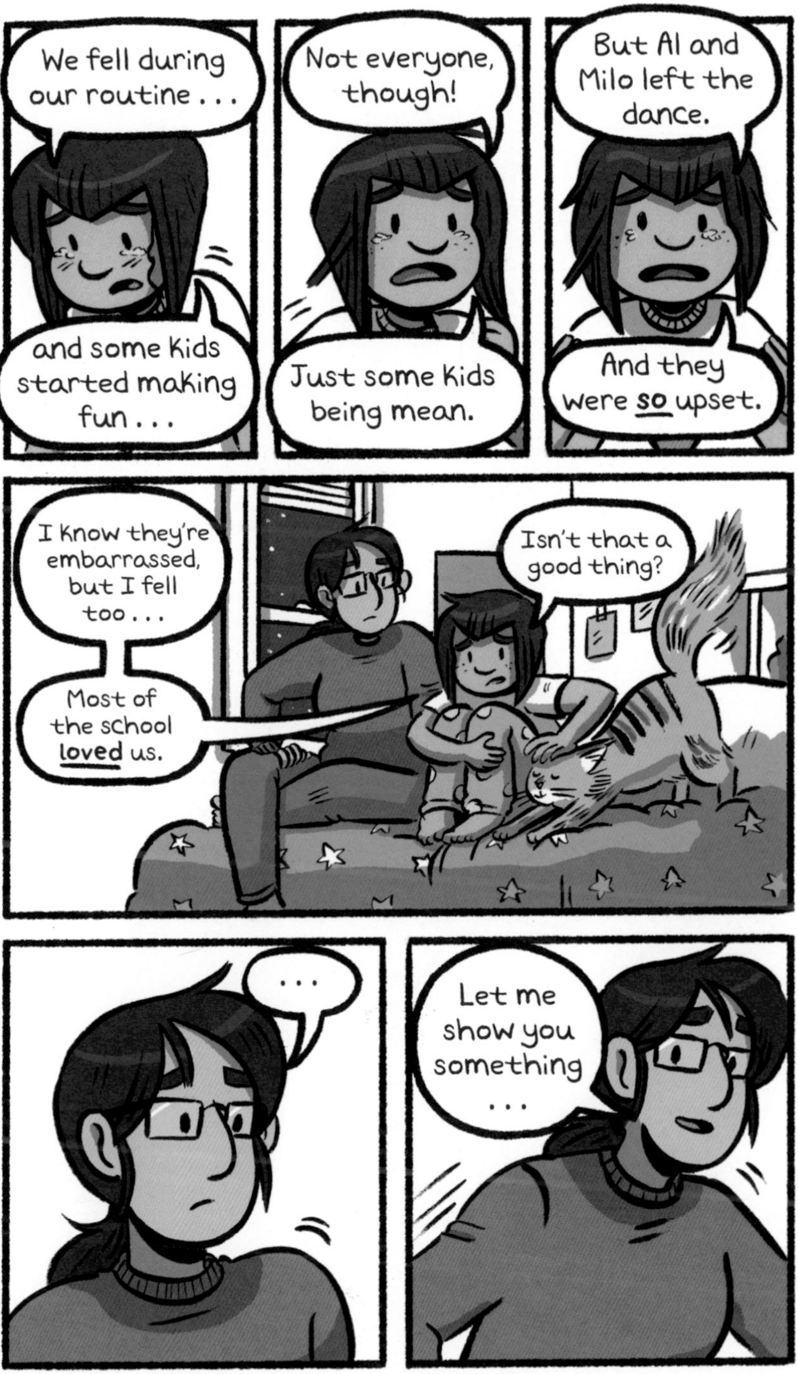
We fell during our routine . . .
and some kids started making fun . . .
Not everyone, though!
Just some kids being mean.
But Al and Milo left the dance.
And they were so upset.
I know they're embarrassed, but I fell too . . .
Most of the school loved us.
Isn't that a good thing?
. . .
Let me show you something . . .

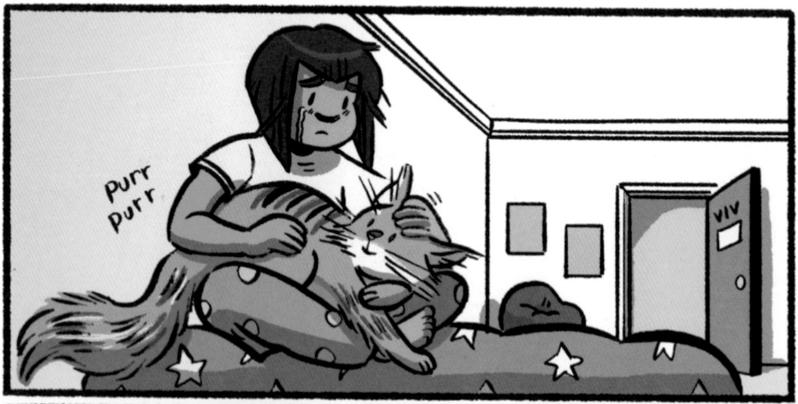
purr
purr
VIV

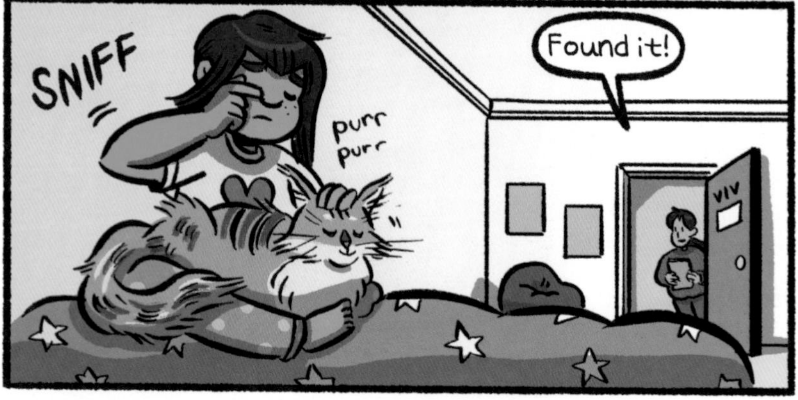
SNIFF
purr
purr
Found it!
VIV

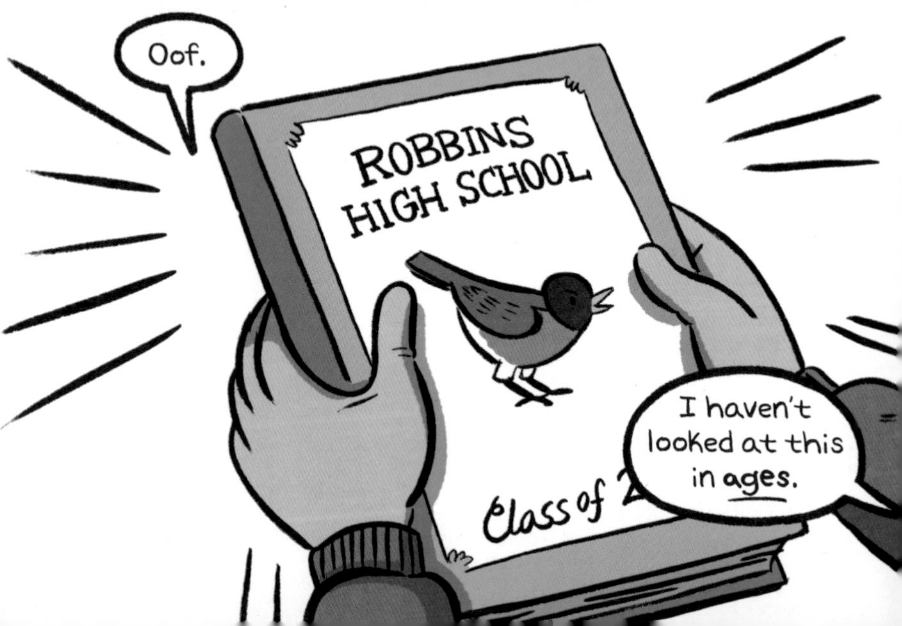
Oof.
ROBBINS
HIGH SCHOOL
Class of
I haven't looked at this in ages.

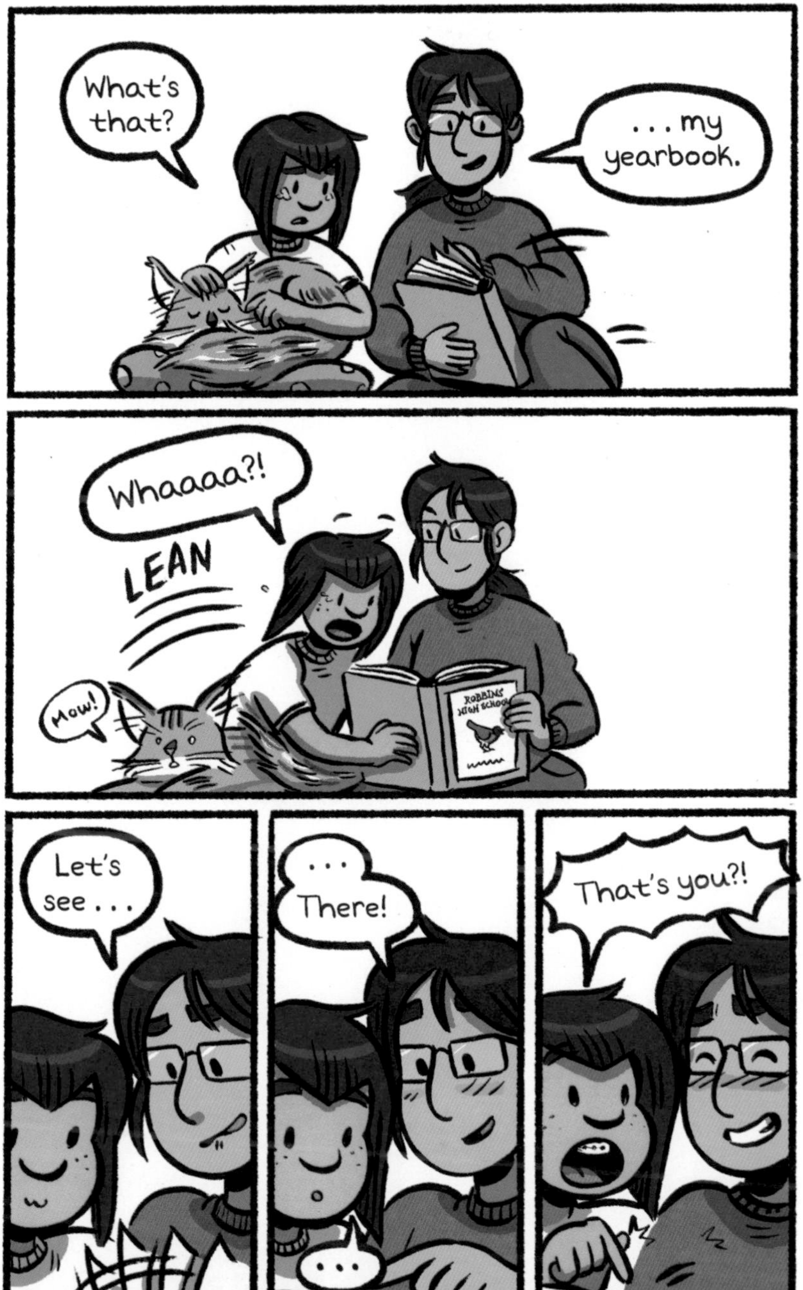
What's that?
. . . my yearbook.
Whaaaa?!
LEAN
Mow!
ROBBINS HIGH SCHOOL
Let's see . . .
FLIP FLIP
. . . There!
. . .
That's you?!

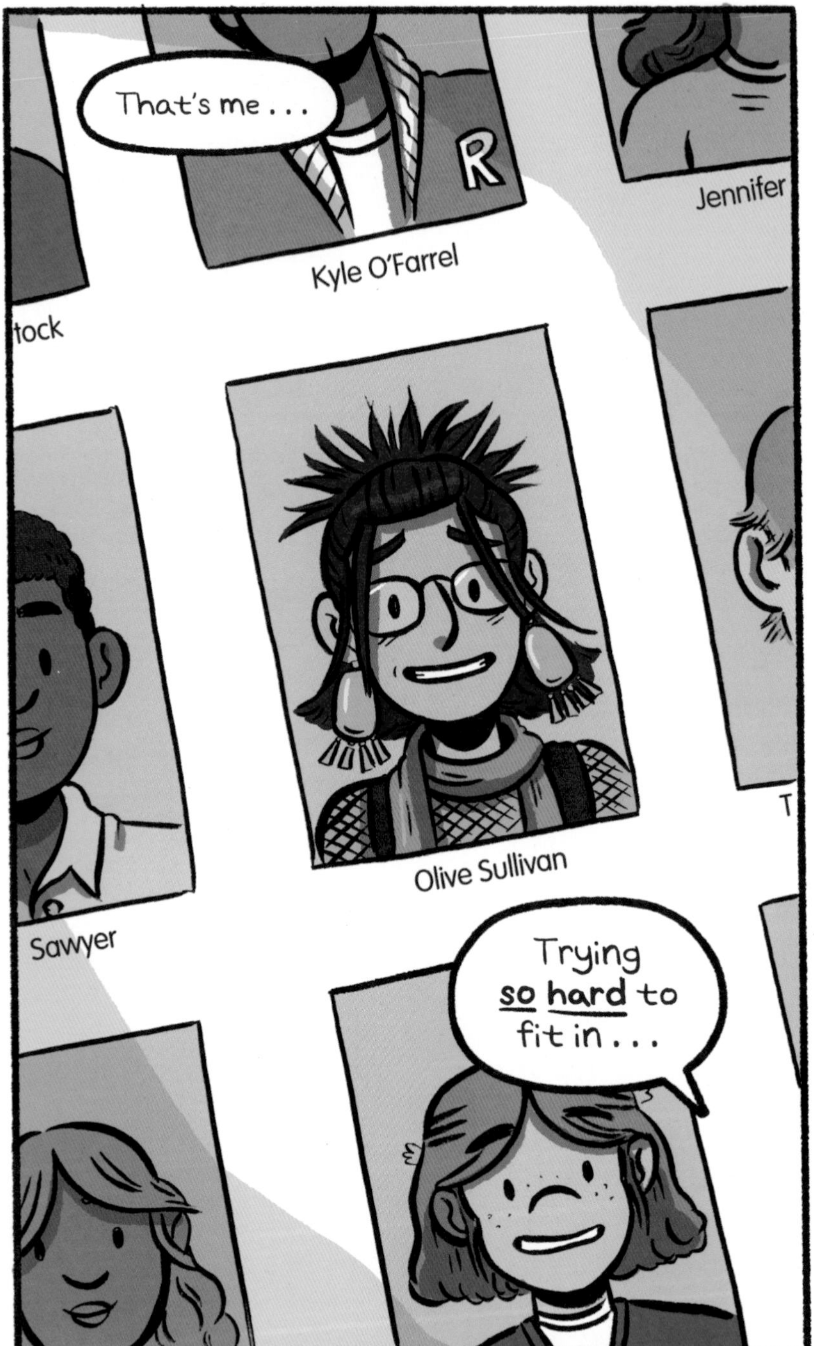
That's me...
Kyle O'Farrel
Jennifer
tock
Olive Sullivan
T
Sawyer
Trying so hard to fit in...

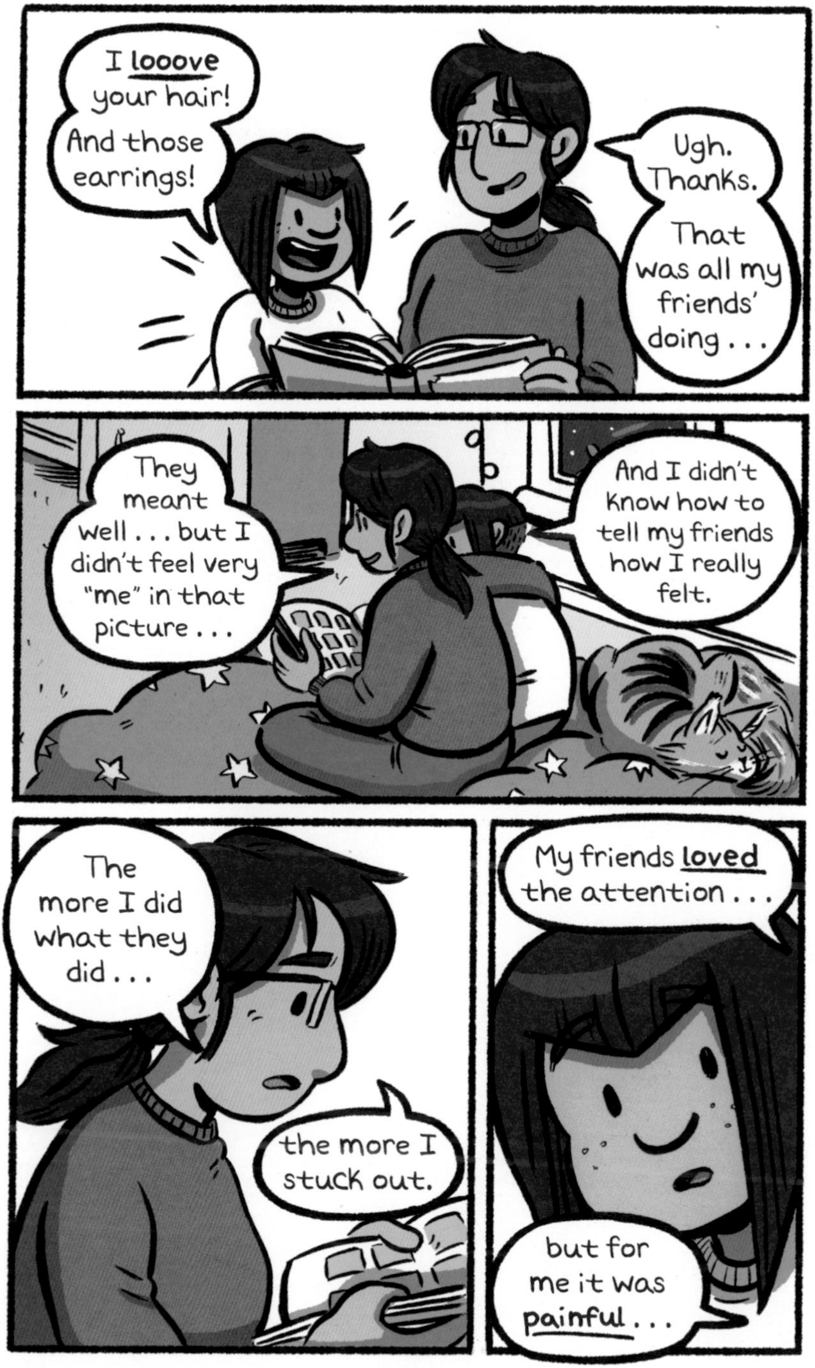
I looove your hair!
And those earrings!
Ugh. Thanks.
That was all my friends' doing . . .
They meant well . . . but I didn't feel very "me" in that picture . . .
And I didn't know how to tell my friends how I really felt.
The more I did what they did . . .
the more I stuck out.
My friends loved the attention . . .
but for me it was painful . . .

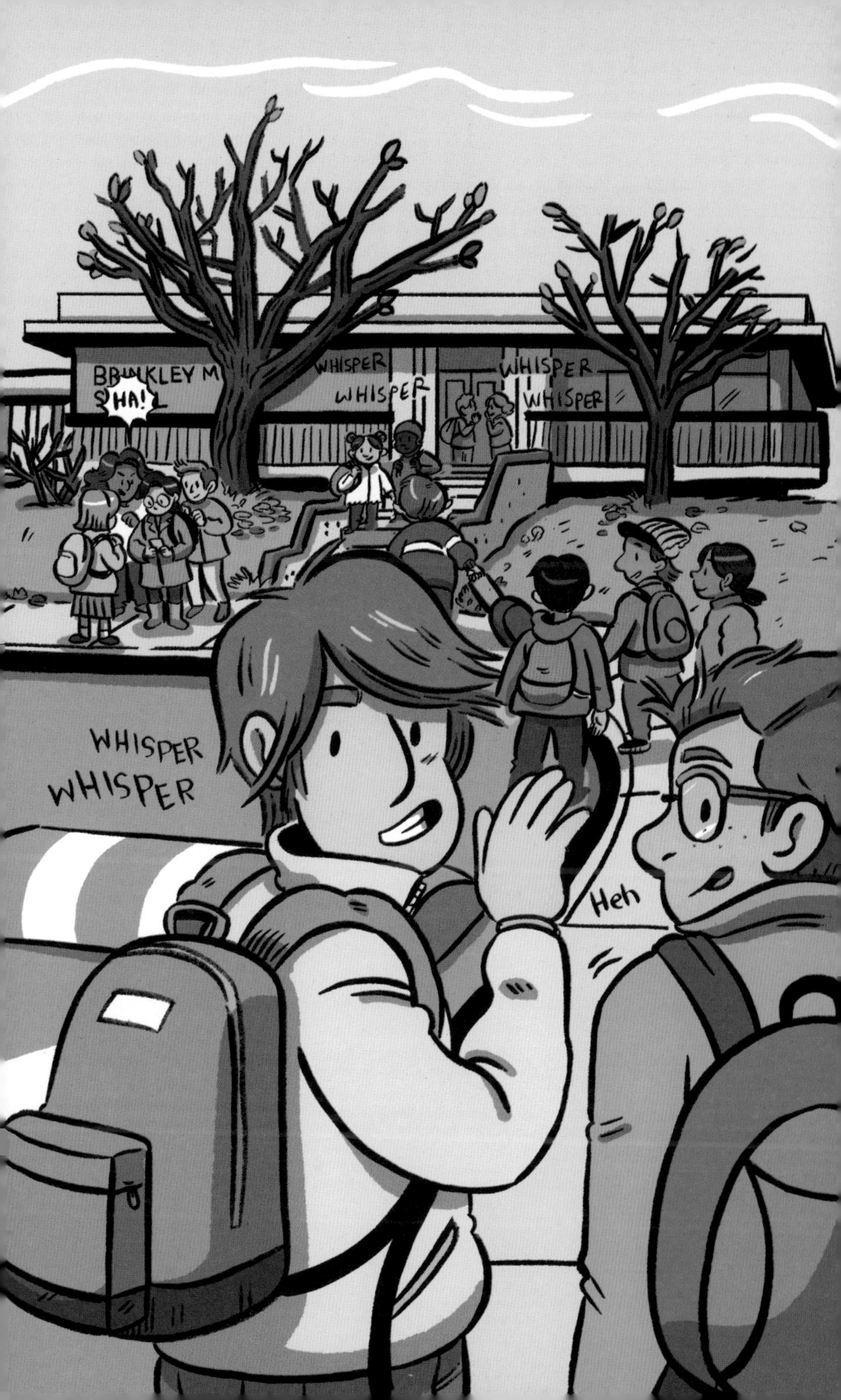
BRINKLEY M
HA!
WHISPER
WHISPER
WHISPER
WHISPER
WHISPER
WHISPER
Heh

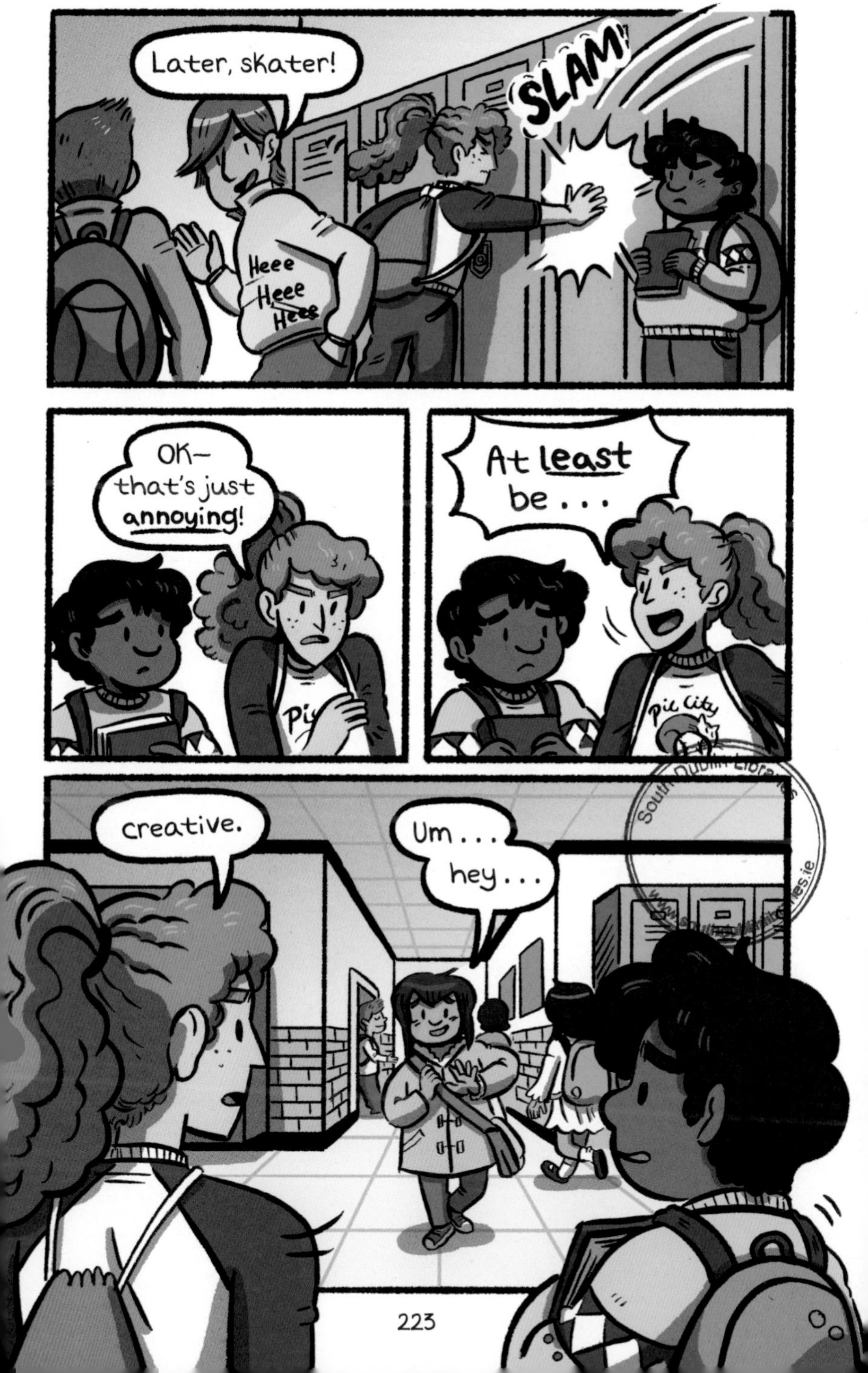
Later, skater!
SLAM
Heee
Heee
Hee
OK—
that's just
annoying!
At least
be . . .
creative.
Um . . .
hey . . .

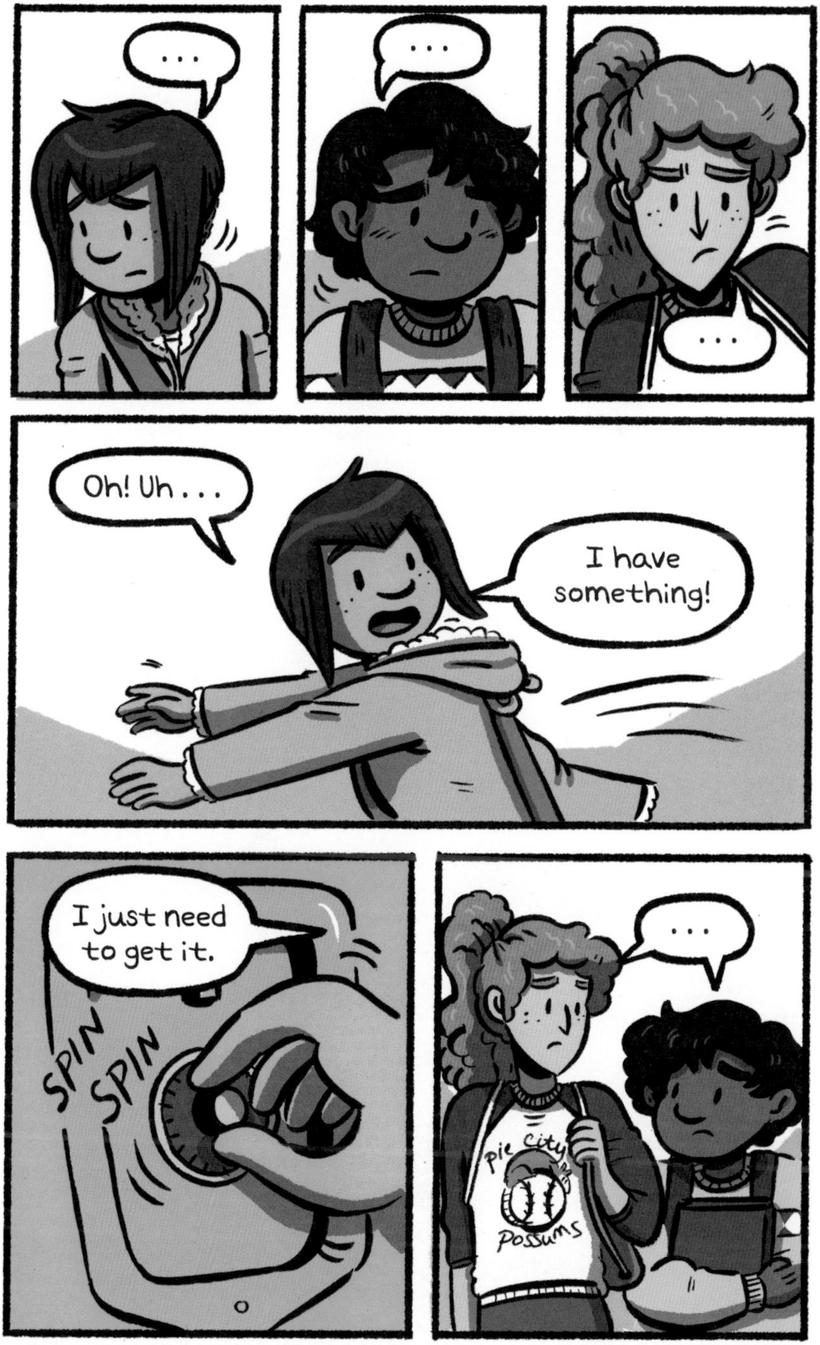
...
...
...
Oh! Uh...
I have something!
I just need to get it.
SPIN
SPIN
...
pie city possums

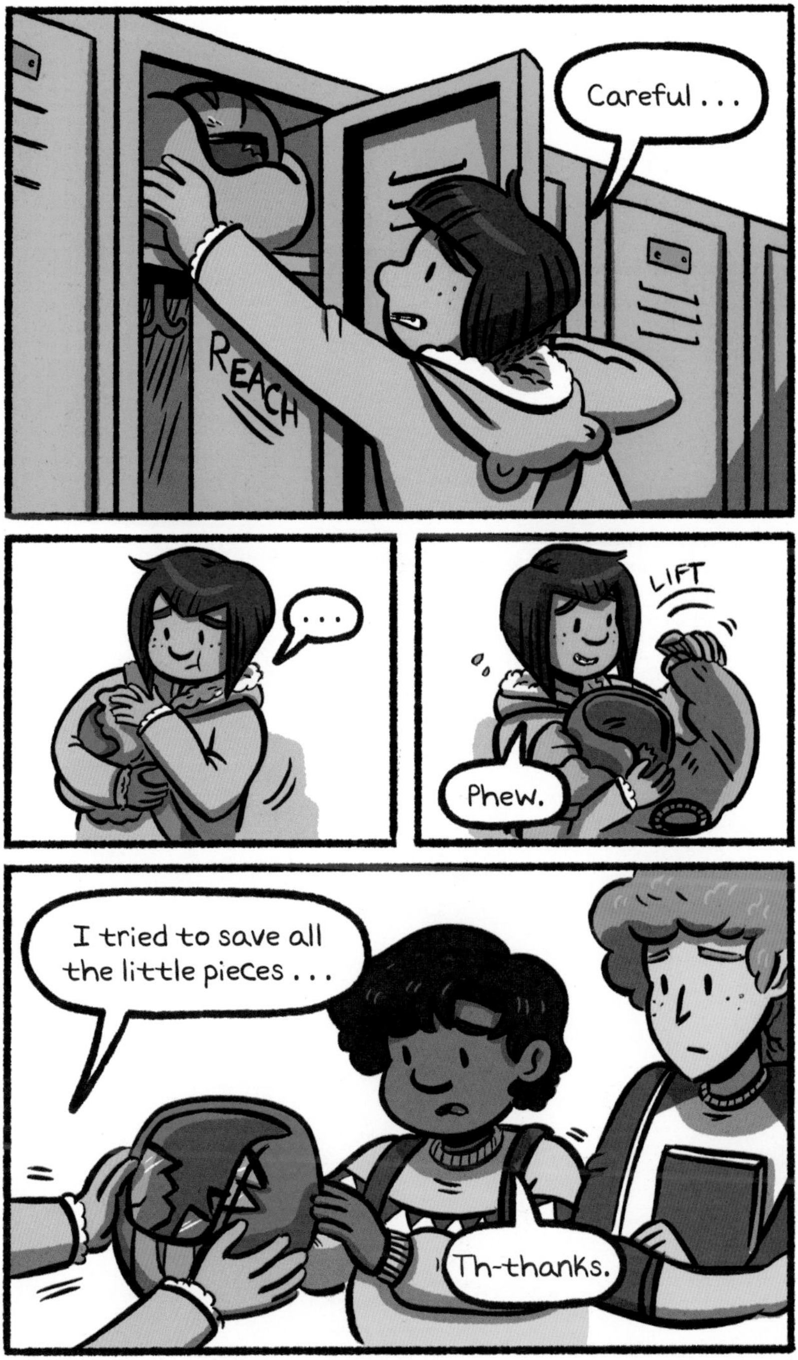
Careful . . .
REACH
. . .
LIFT
Phew.
I tried to save all the little pieces . . .
Th-thanks.

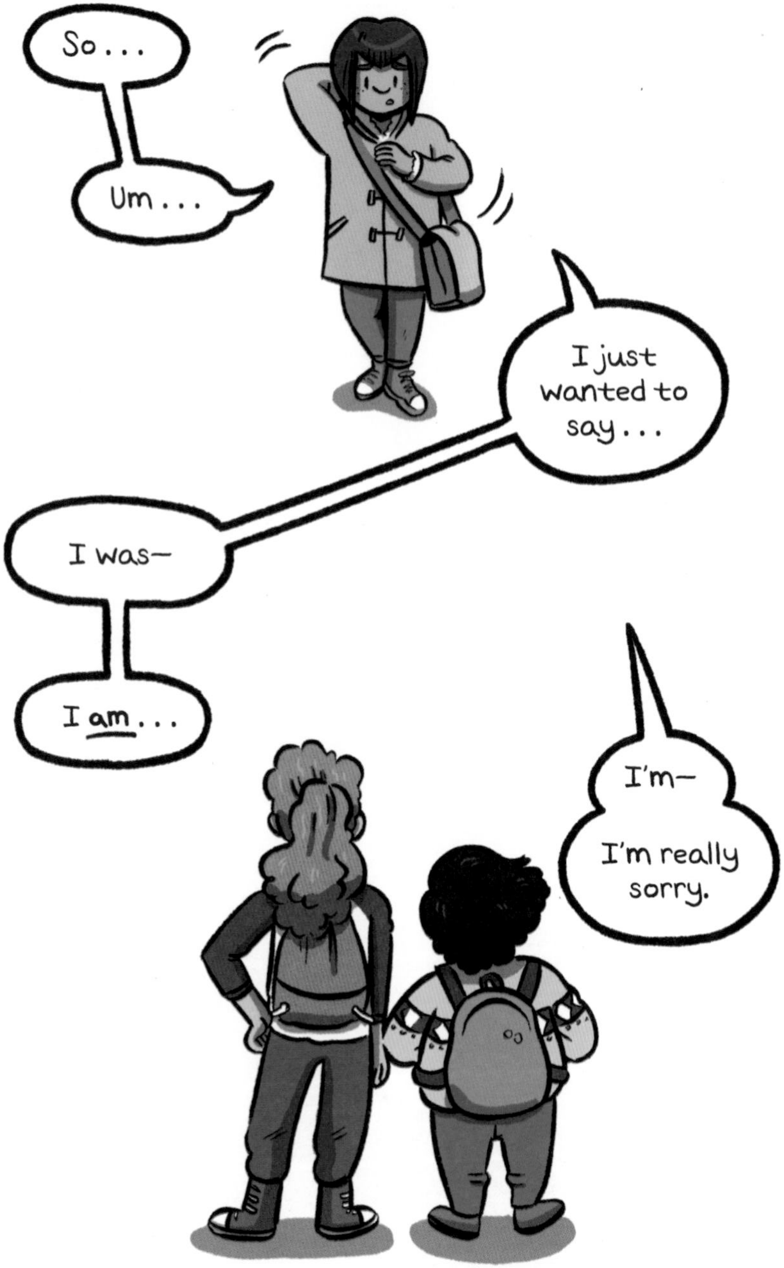
So....
Um...
I just wanted to say...
I was–
I am...
I'm–
I'm really sorry.

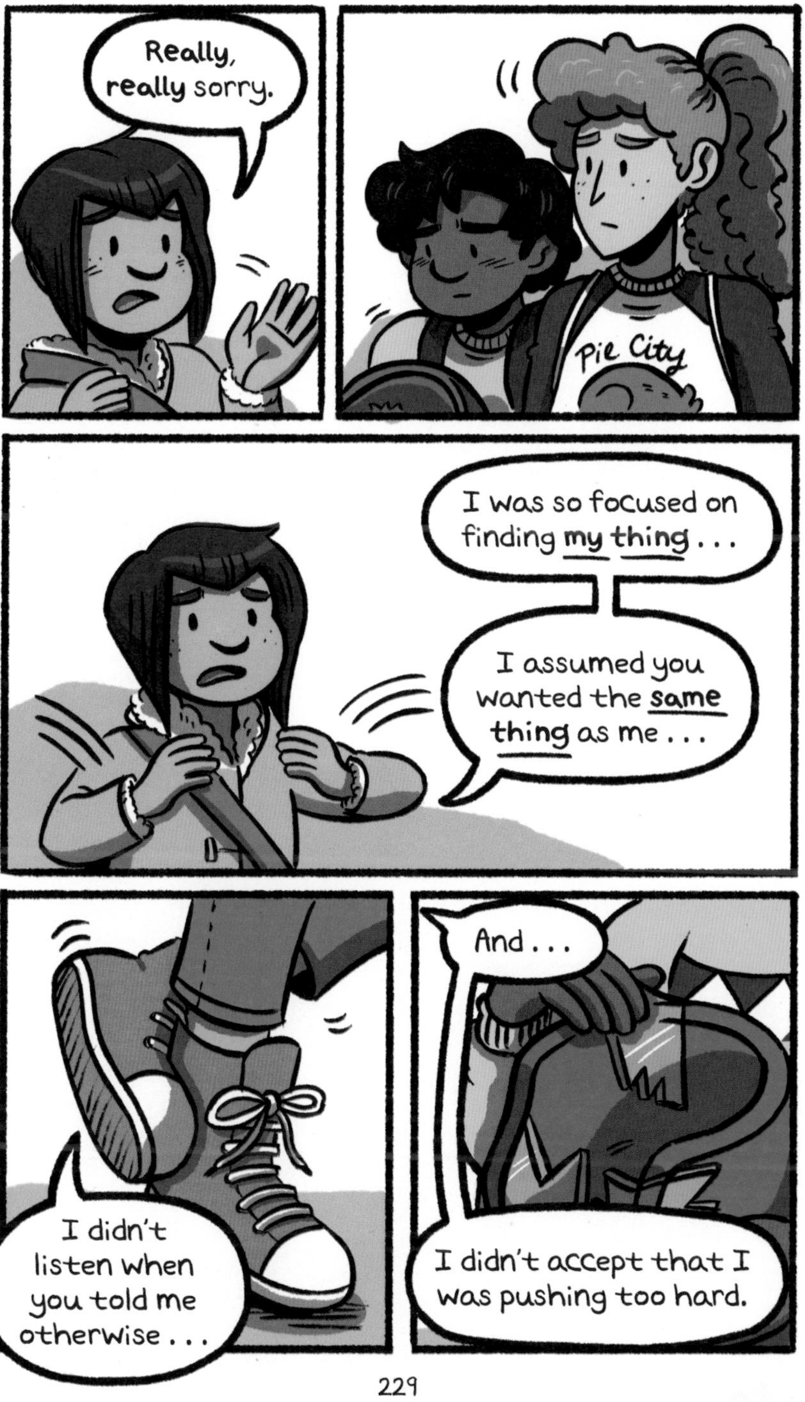
Really, really sorry.
I was so focused on finding my thing . . .
I assumed you wanted the same thing as me . . .
I didn't listen when you told me otherwise . . .
And . . .
I didn't accept that I was pushing too hard.

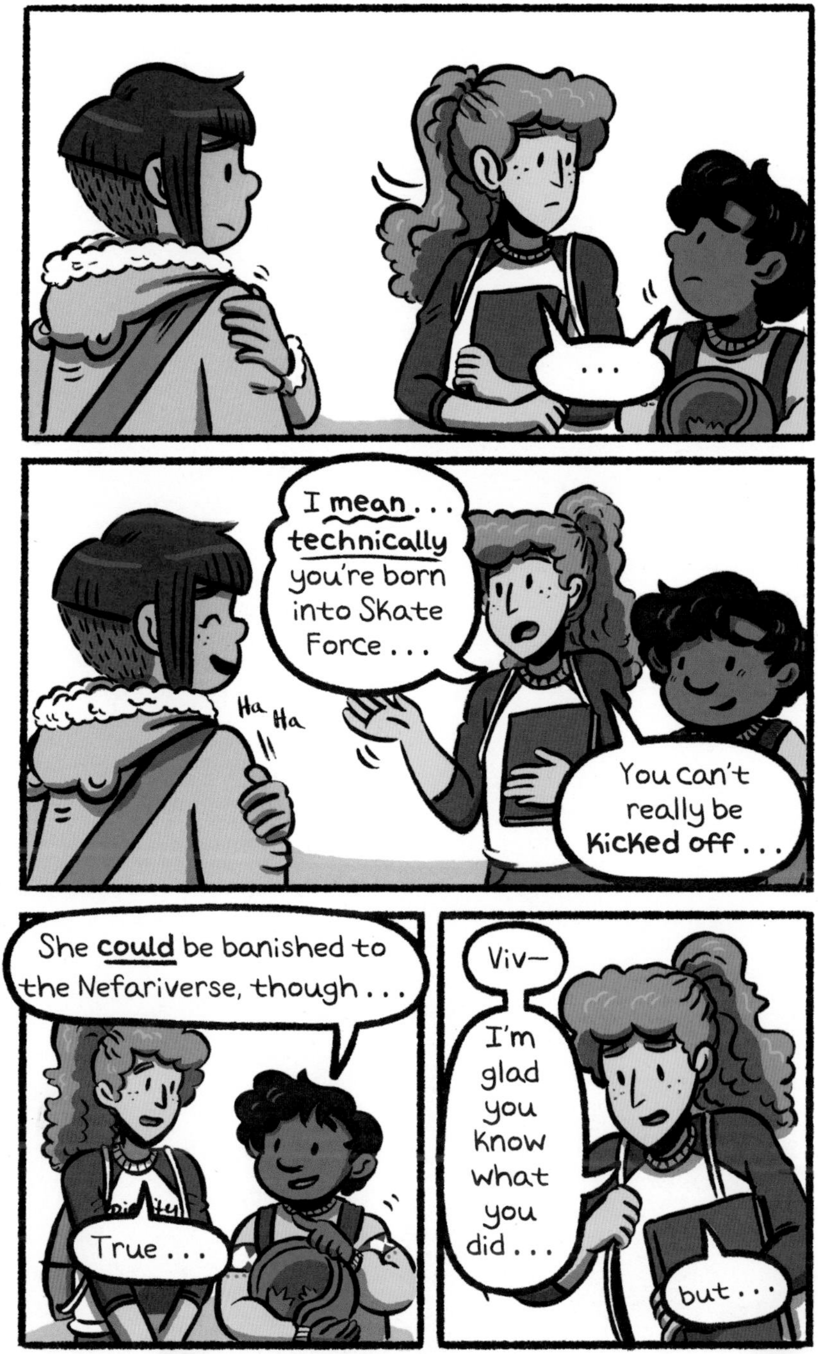
...
I mean . . . technically you're born into Skate Force . . .
Ha Ha
You can't really be Kicked off . . .
She could be banished to the Nefariverse, though . . .
True . . .
Viv—
I'm glad you know what you did . . .
but . . .

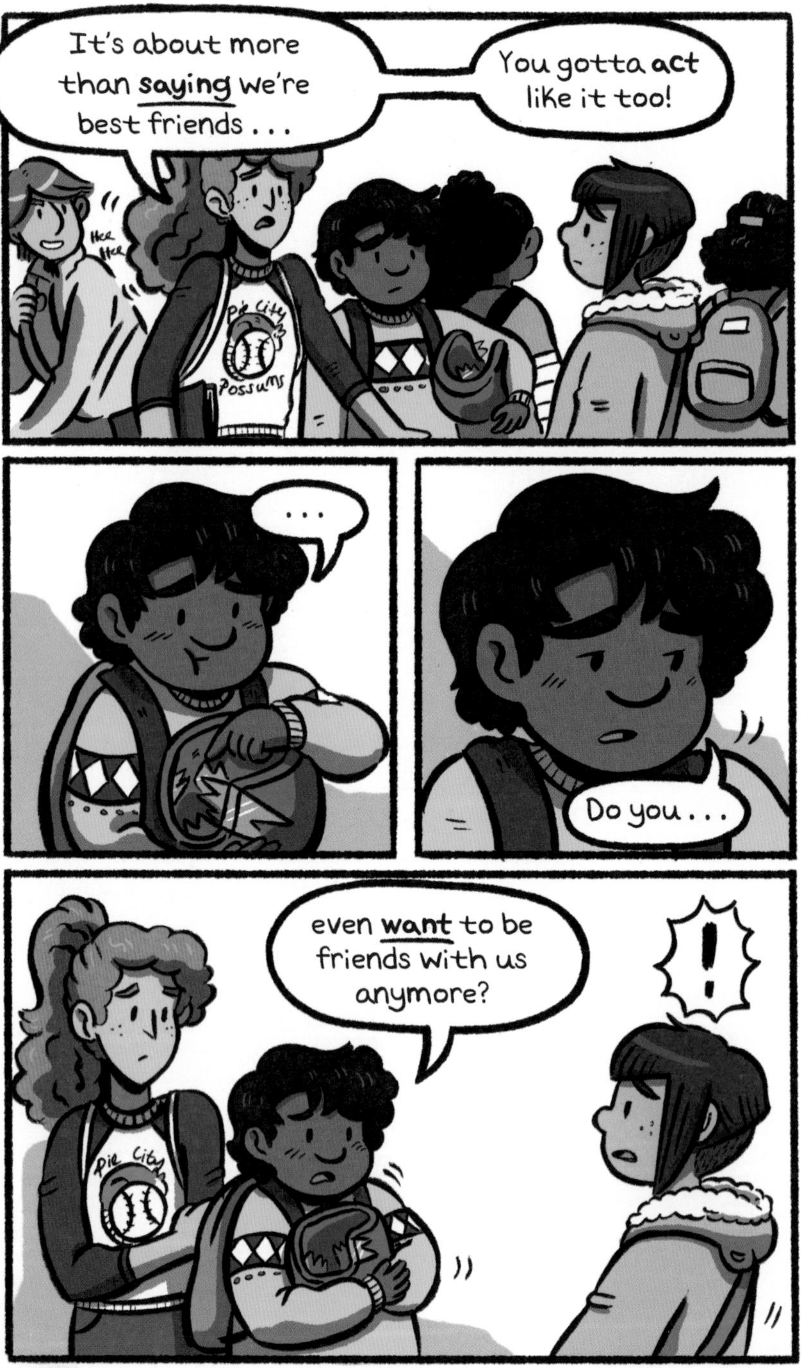
It's about more than saying we're best friends . . .
You gotta act like it too!
Hee Hee
Pie City Possums
. . .
Do you . . .
even want to be friends with us anymore?
!
Pie City

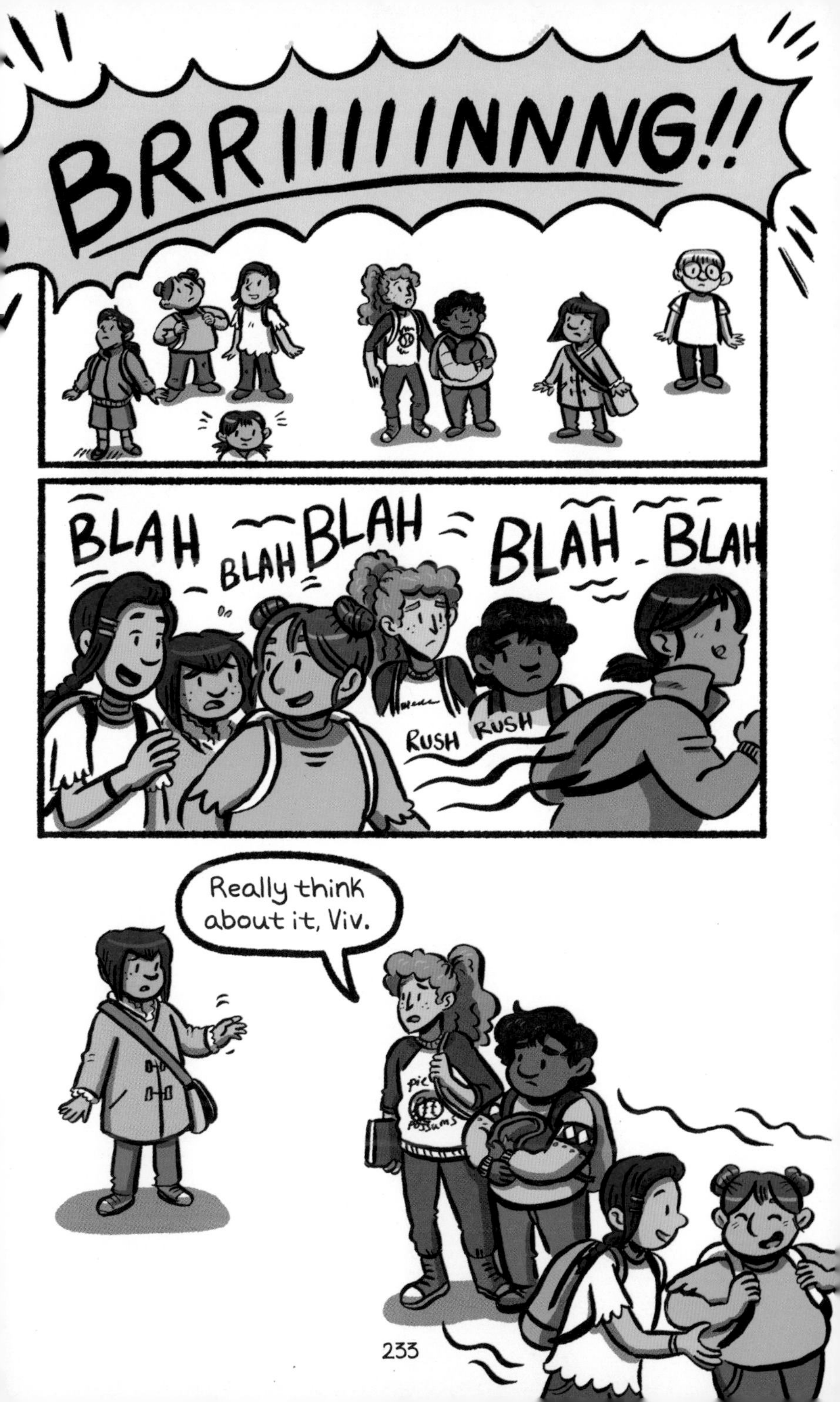

BRRIIIIINNNG!!
BLAH
BLAH
BLAH
BLAH
BLAH
RUSH
RUSH
Really think about it, Viv.
pic
possums

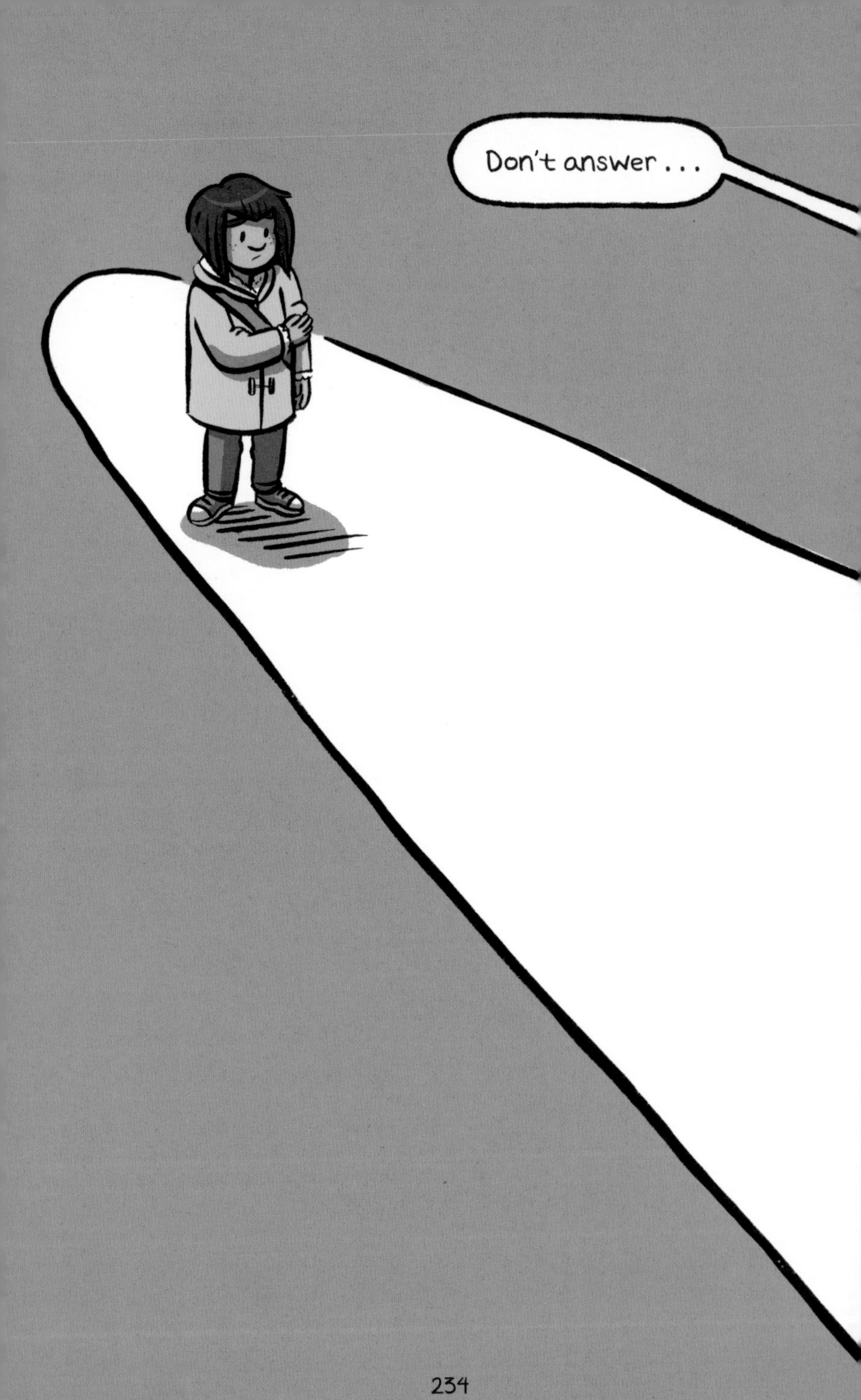
Don't answer . . .

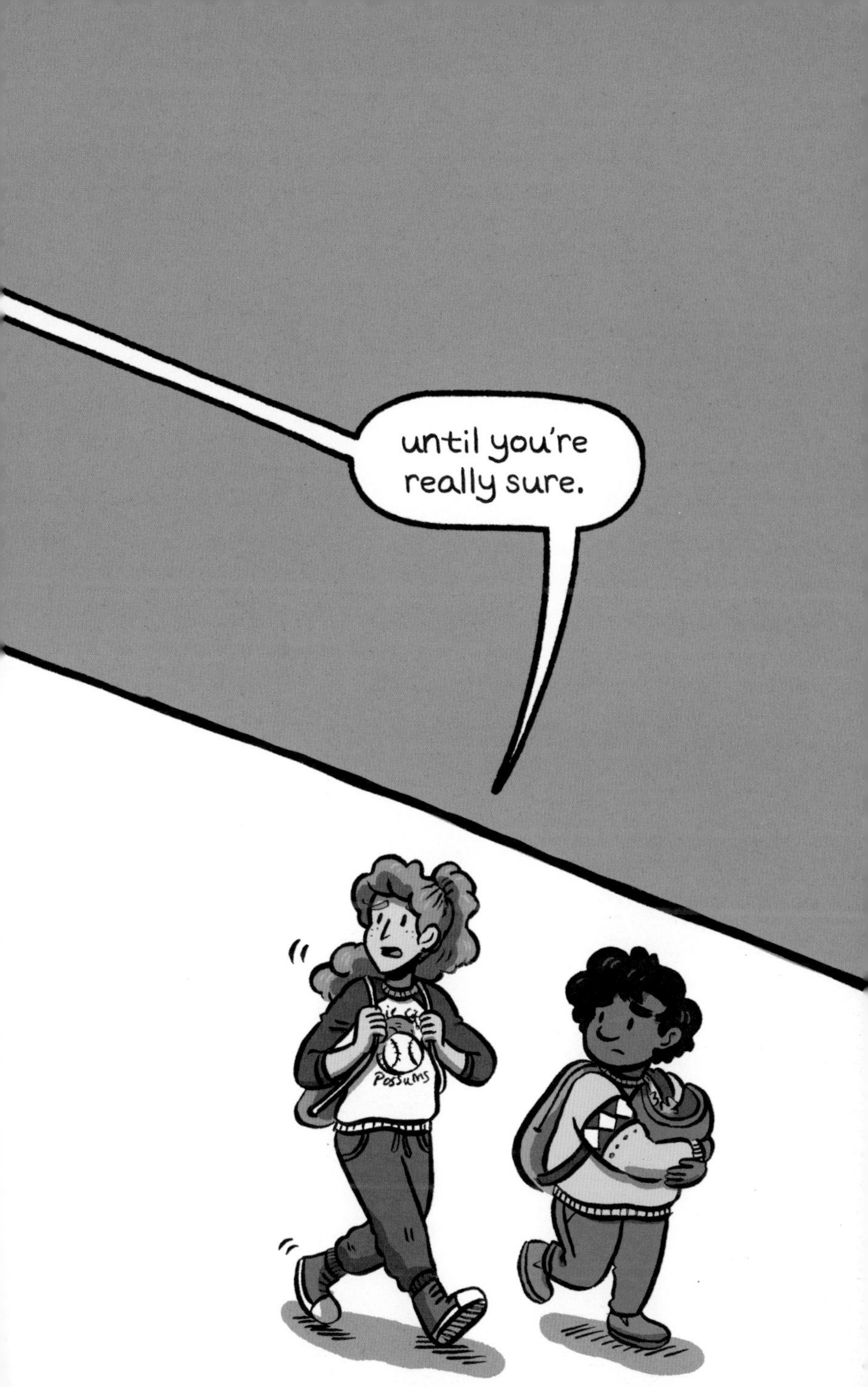

until you're really sure.
POSSUMS

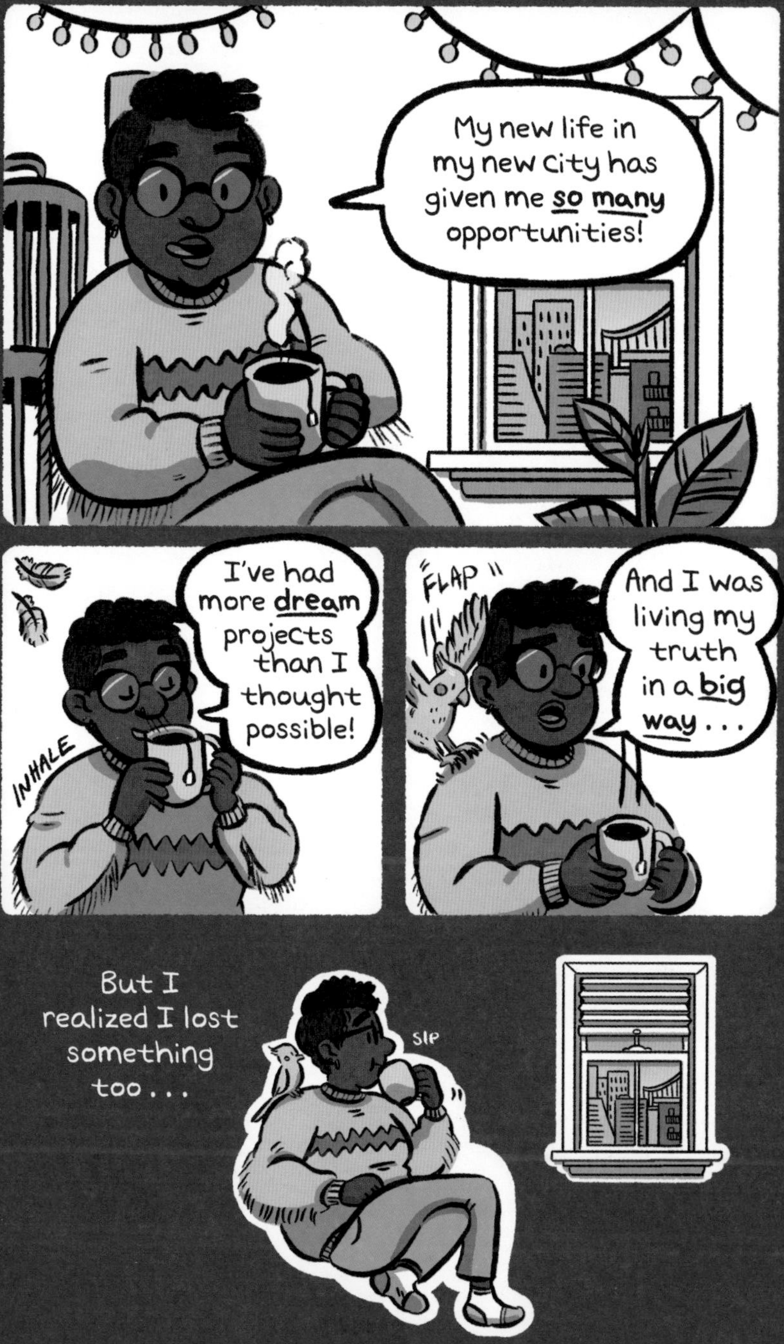
My new life in my new city has given me so many opportunities!
I've had more dream projects than I thought possible!
INHALE
FLAP
And I was living my truth in a big way . . .
But I realized I lost something too . . .
SIP

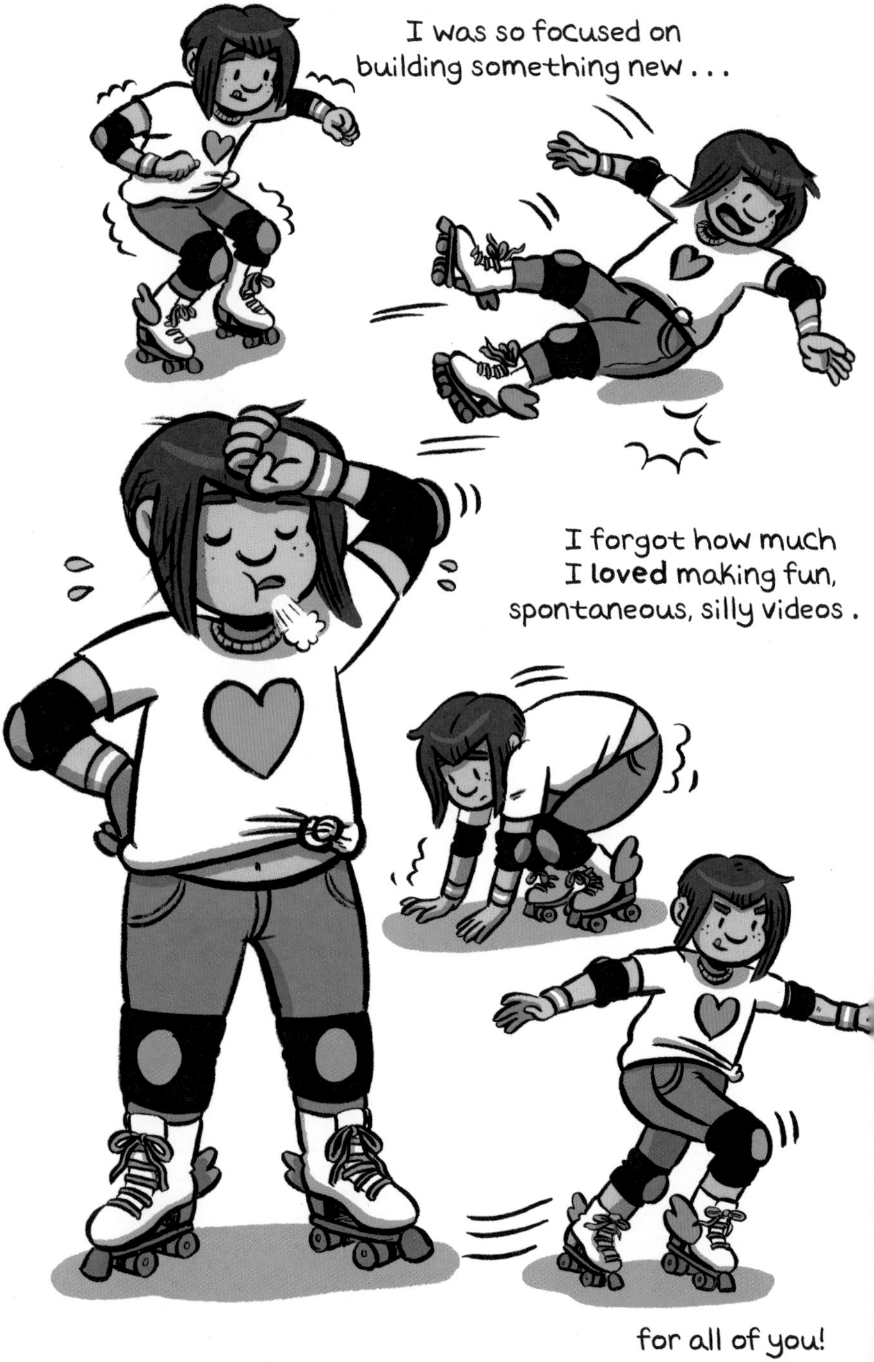
I was so focused on building something new . . .
I forgot how much I **loved** making fun, spontaneous, silly videos .
for all of you!

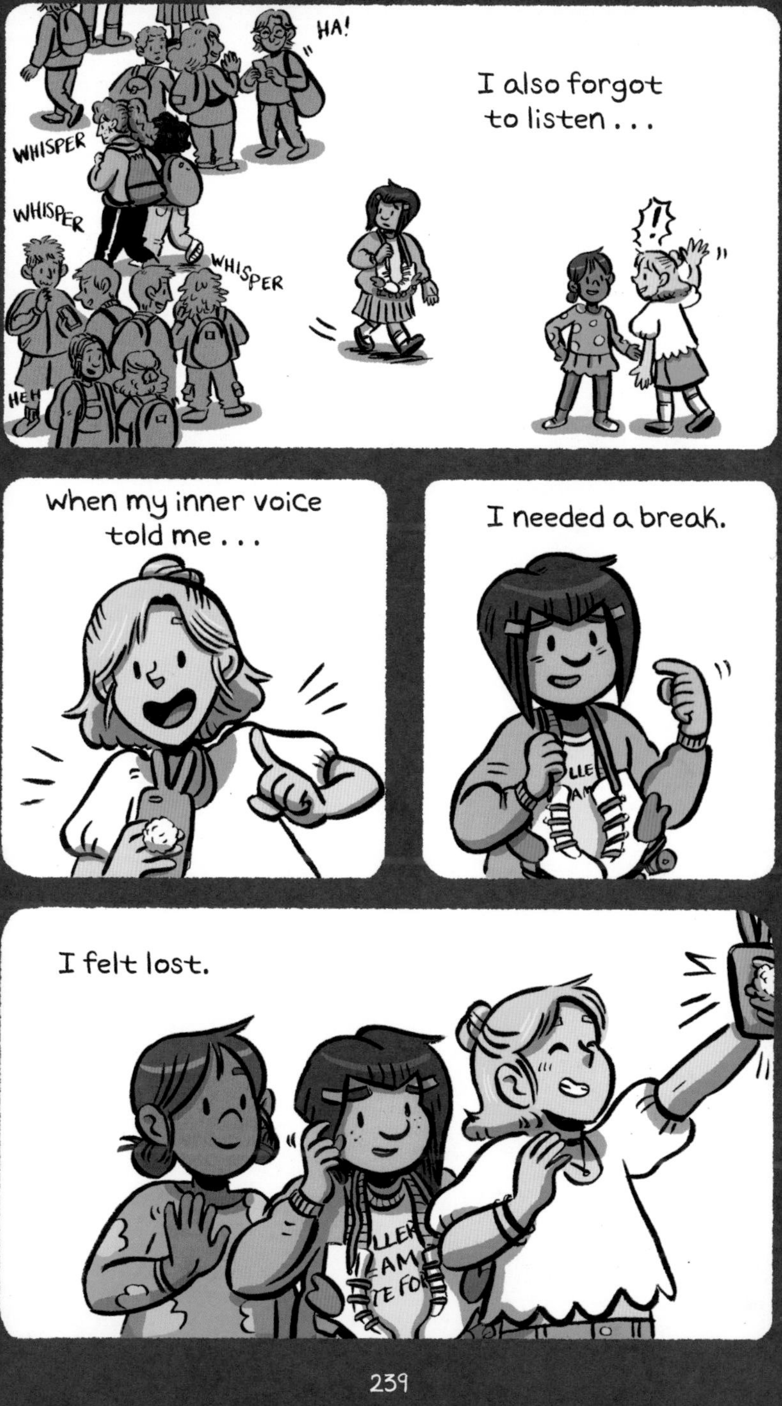
HA!
I also forgot to listen . . .
WHISPER
WHISPER
WHISPER
HEH
!
When my inner voice told me . . .
I needed a break.
I felt lost.

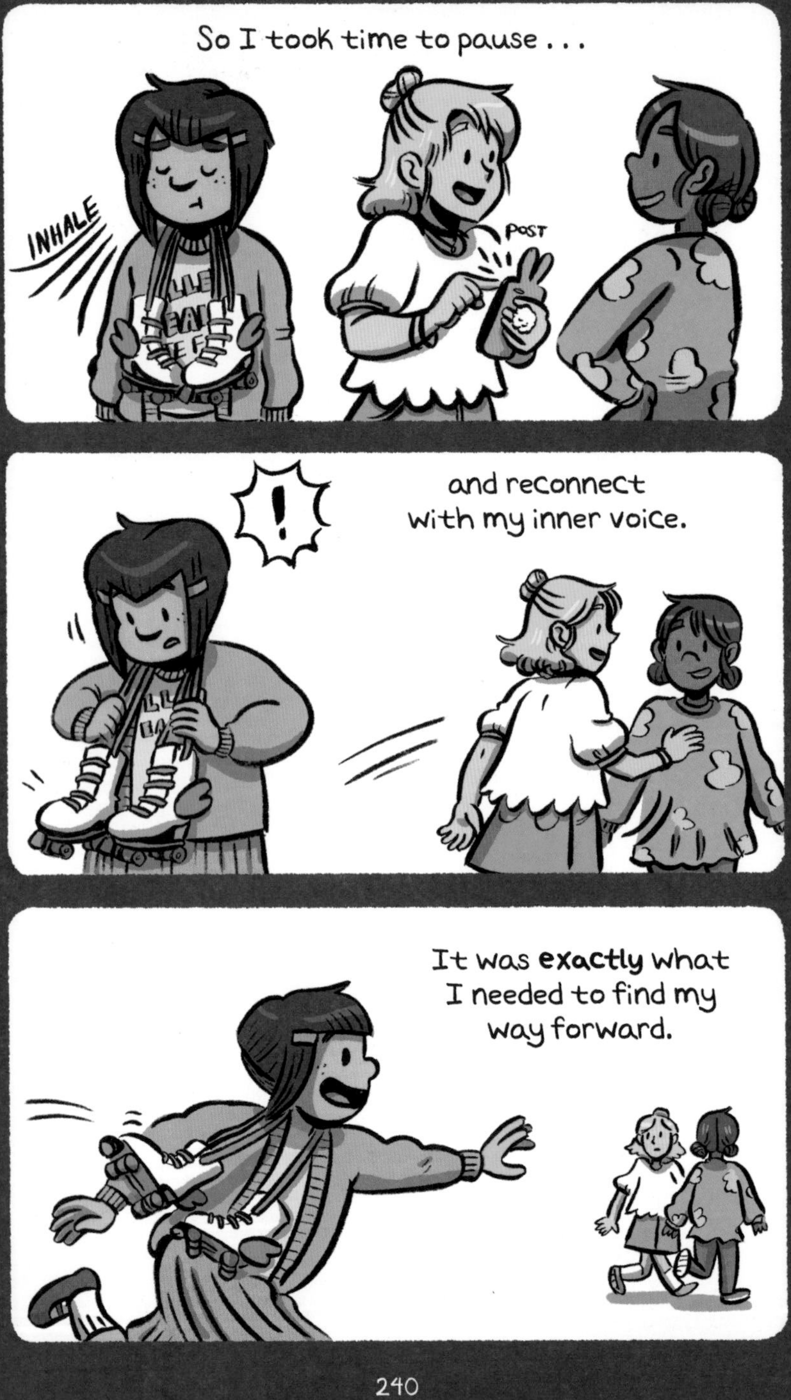

So I took time to pause . . .
INHALE
POST
and reconnect with my inner voice.
!
It was **exactly** what I needed to find my way forward.

I still have lots of plans . . .

for projects and collaborations that I hope you'll **love.**

But I'm also going to post . . . just for fun!

I'm <u>**so**</u> <u>**excited**</u> to grow and change and embrace new versions of myself . . .

while honoring the parts . . .

that have always been there.

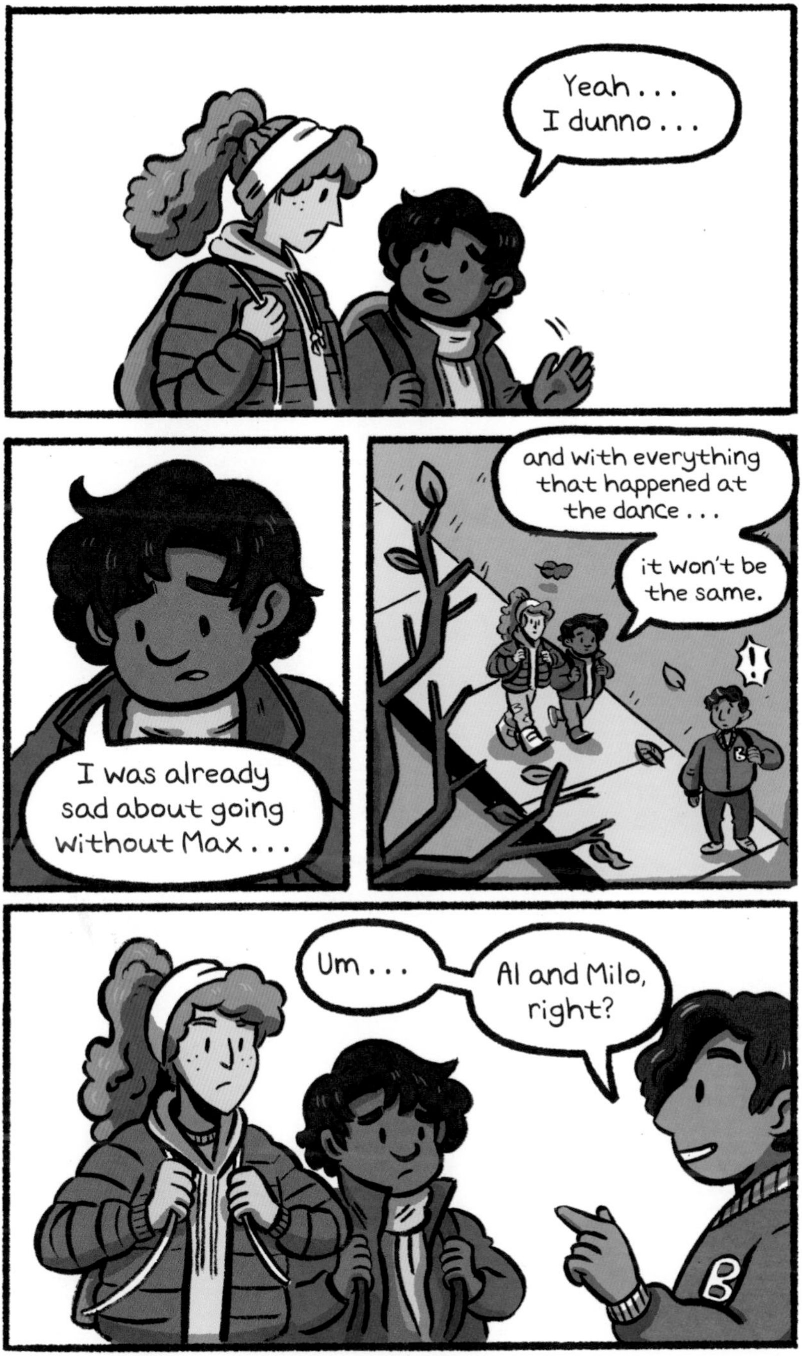
Yeah . . .
I dunno . . .
I was already sad about going without Max . . .
and with everything that happened at the dance . . .
it won't be the same.
!
Um . . .
Al and Milo, right?
B

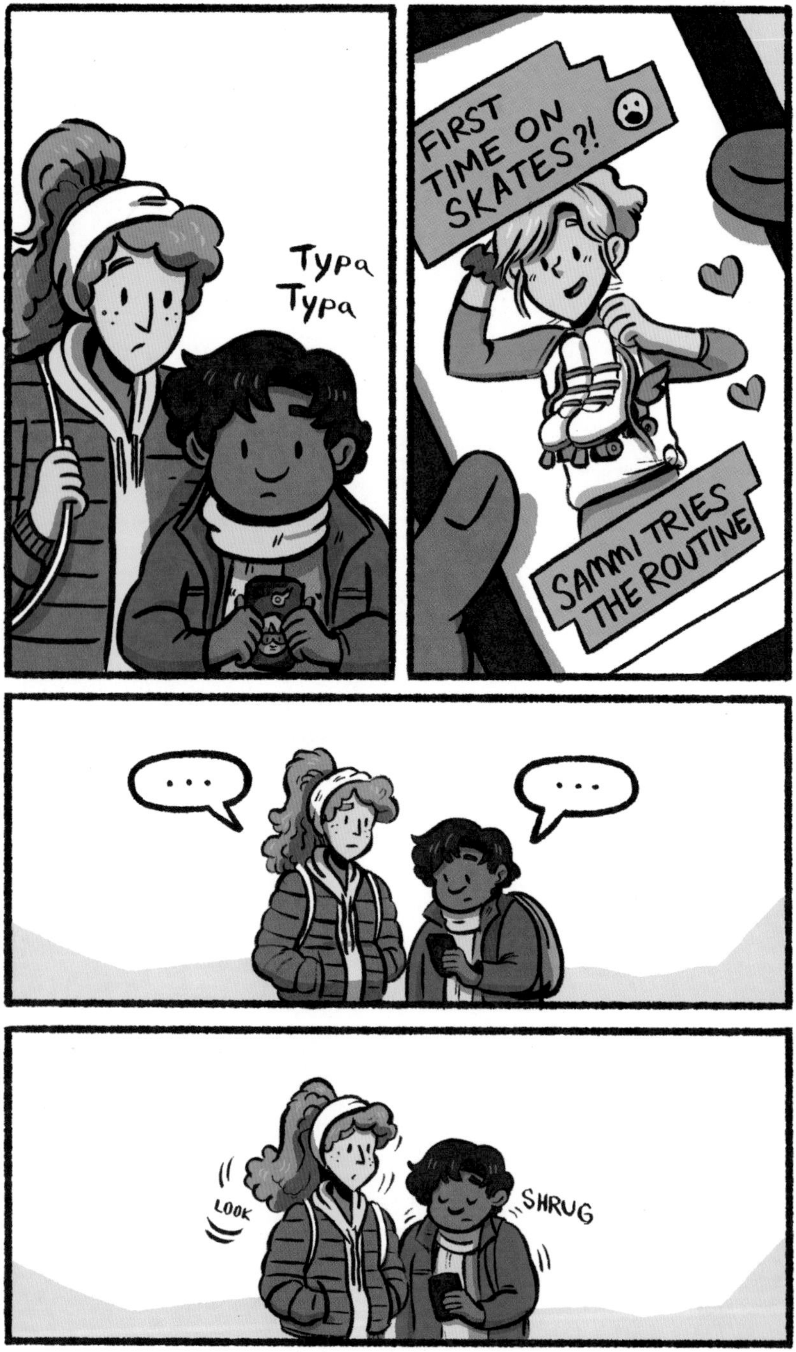
Typa
Typa
FIRST TIME ON SKATES?!
SAMMI TRIES THE ROUTINE
...
...
LOOK
SHRUG

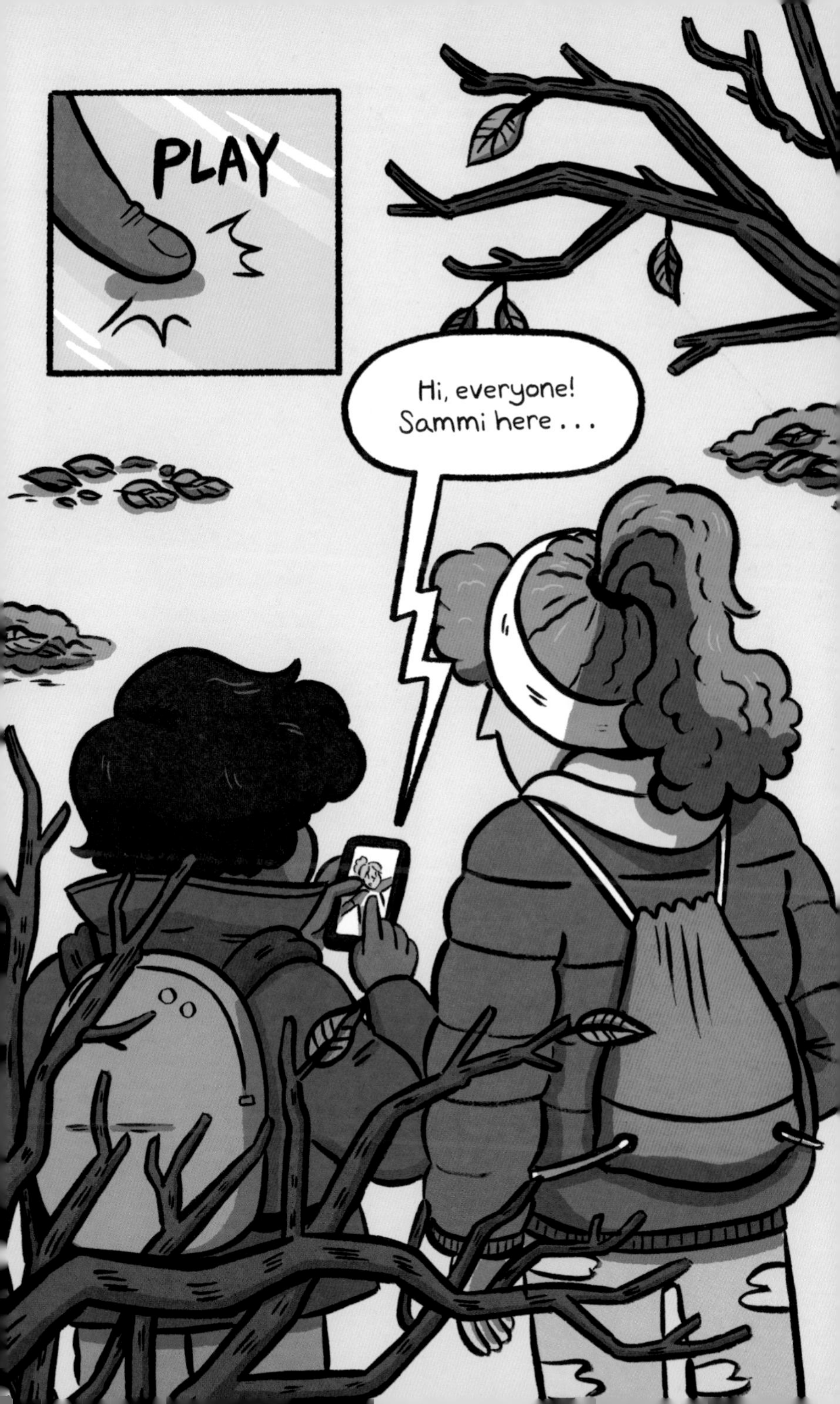
PLAY
Hi, everyone! Sammi here . . .

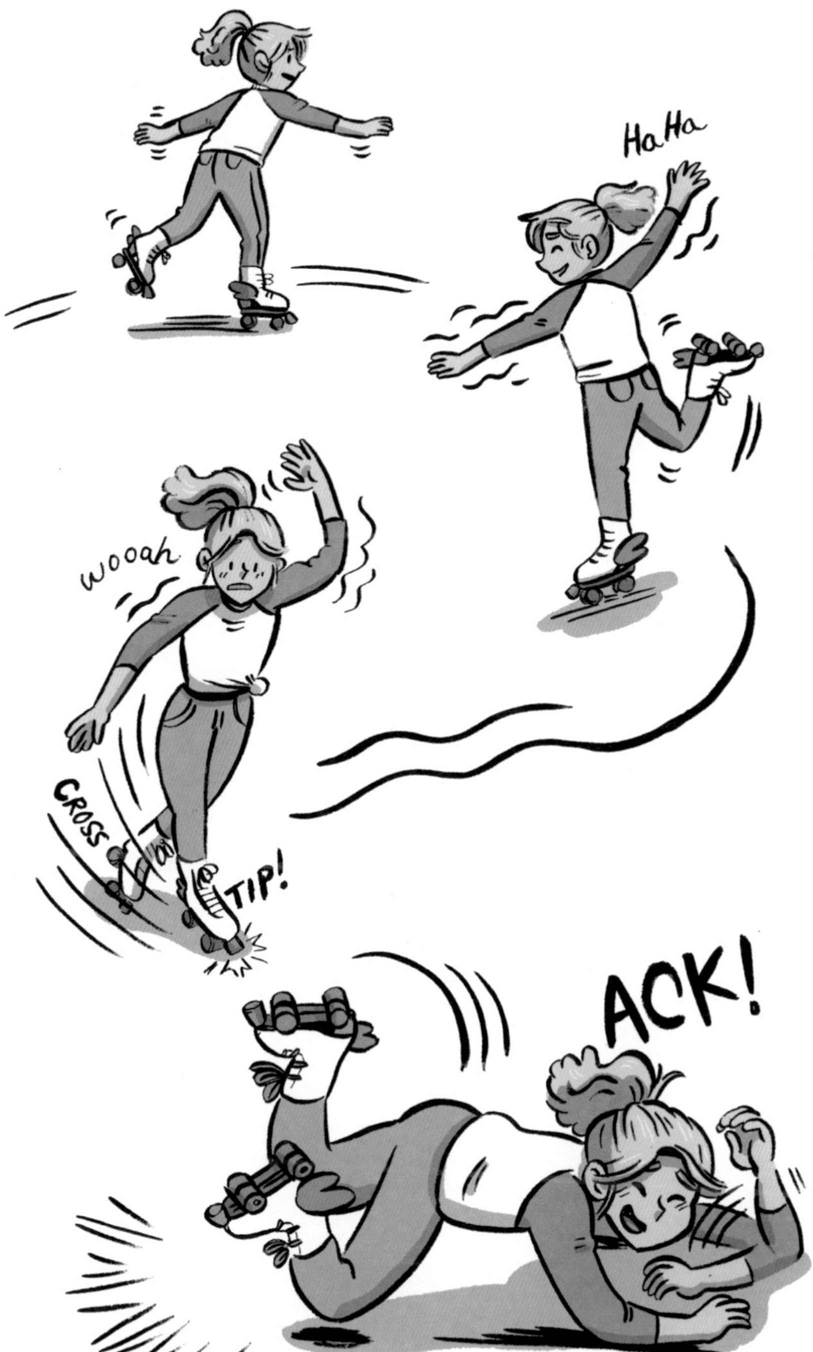
HaHa
wooah
CROSS
TIP!
ACK!

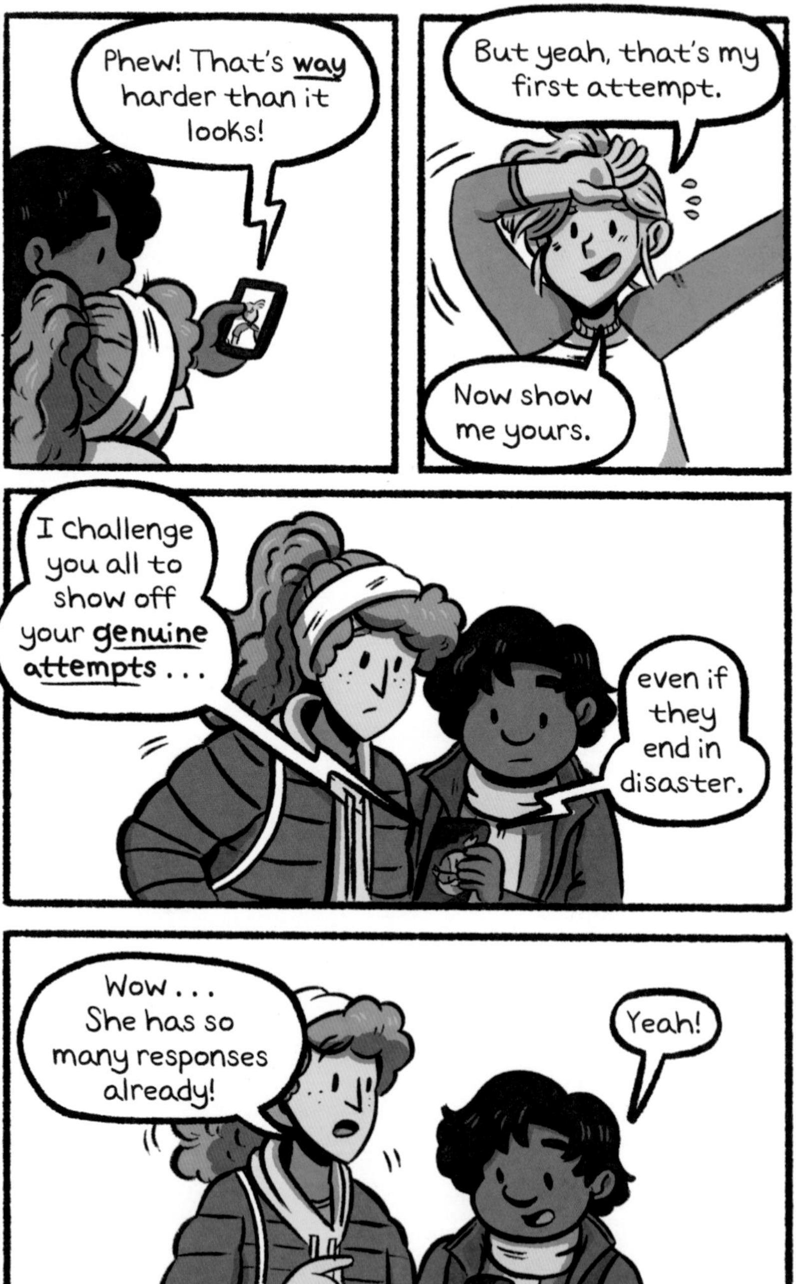
Phew! That's way harder than it looks!
But yeah, that's my first attempt.
Now show me yours.
I challenge you all to show off your genuine attempts . . .
even if they end in disaster.
Wow . . . She has so many responses already!
Yeah!

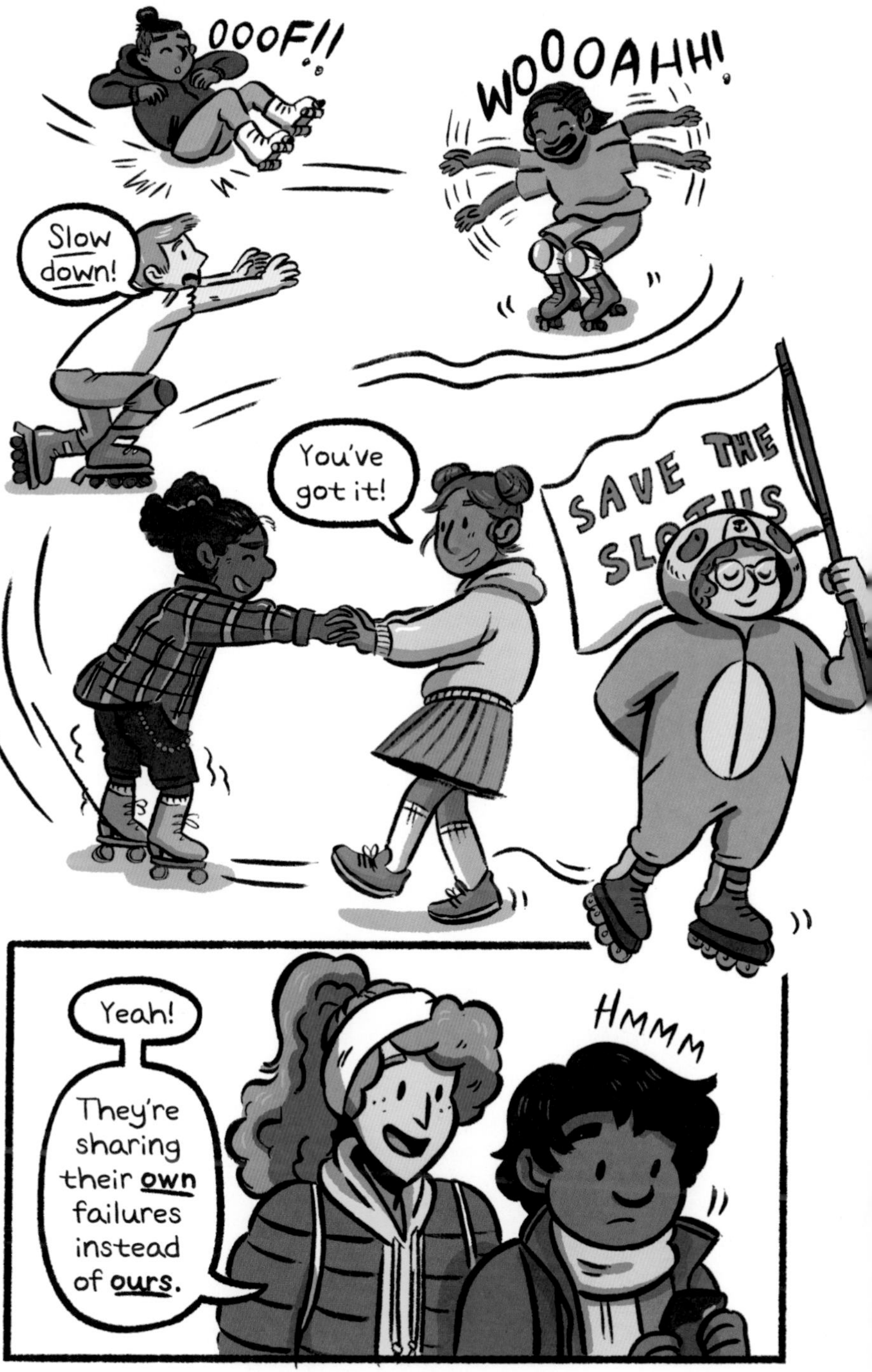

OOOF!!
WOOOAHH!
Slow down!
You've got it!
SAVE THE SLOTHS
Yeah!
They're sharing their **own** failures instead of **ours**.
HMMM

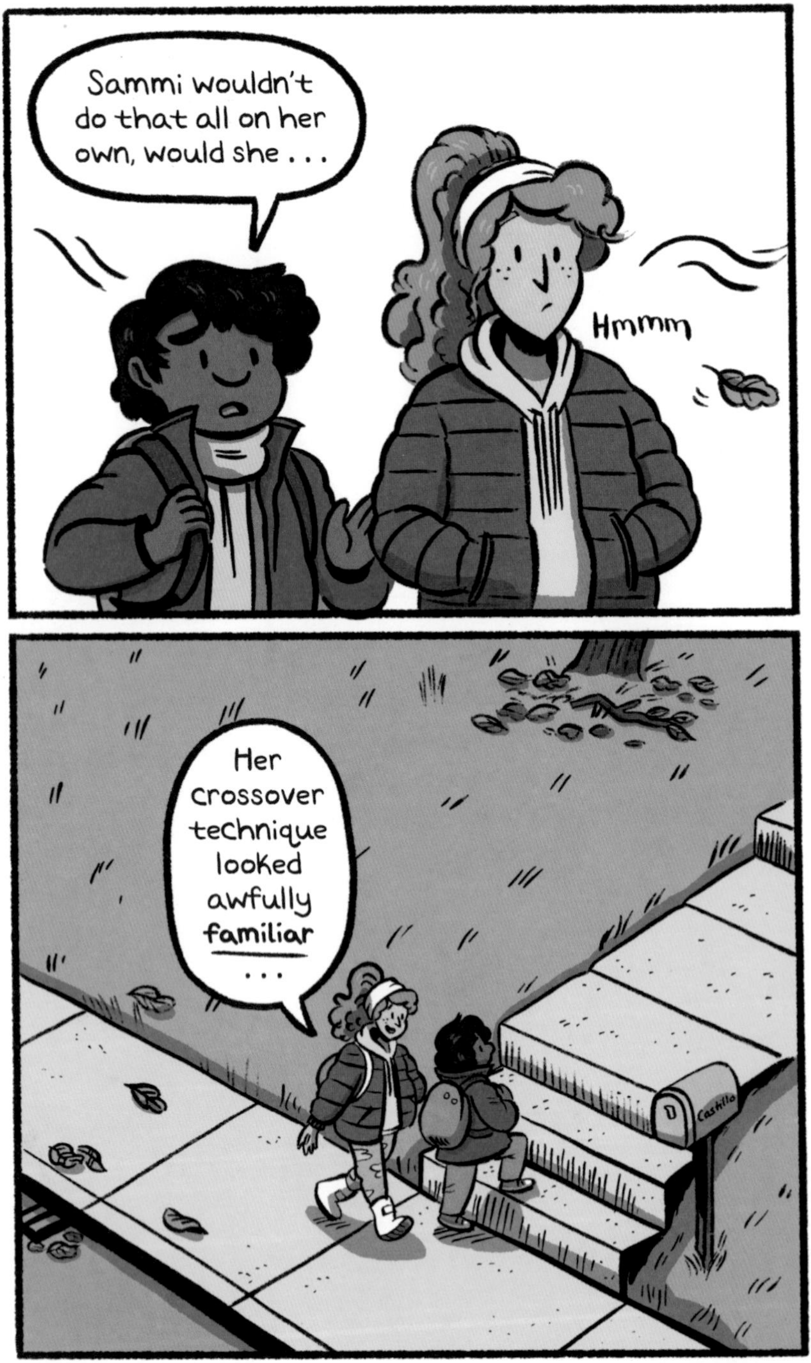
Sammi wouldn't do that all on her own, would she . . .
Hmmm
Her crossover technique looked awfully familiar . . .

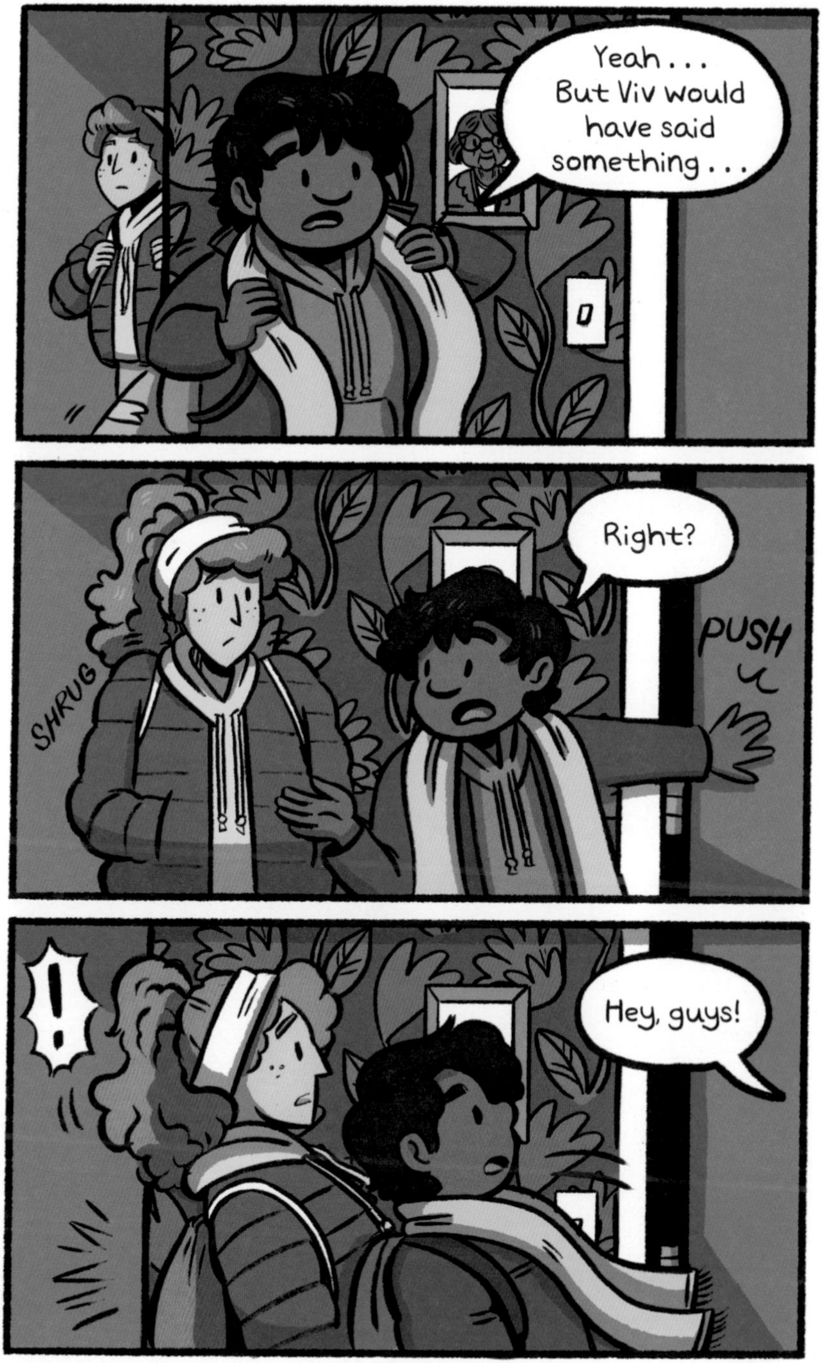
Yeah . . .
But Viv would have said something . . .
Right?
SHRUG
PUSH
!
Hey, guys!

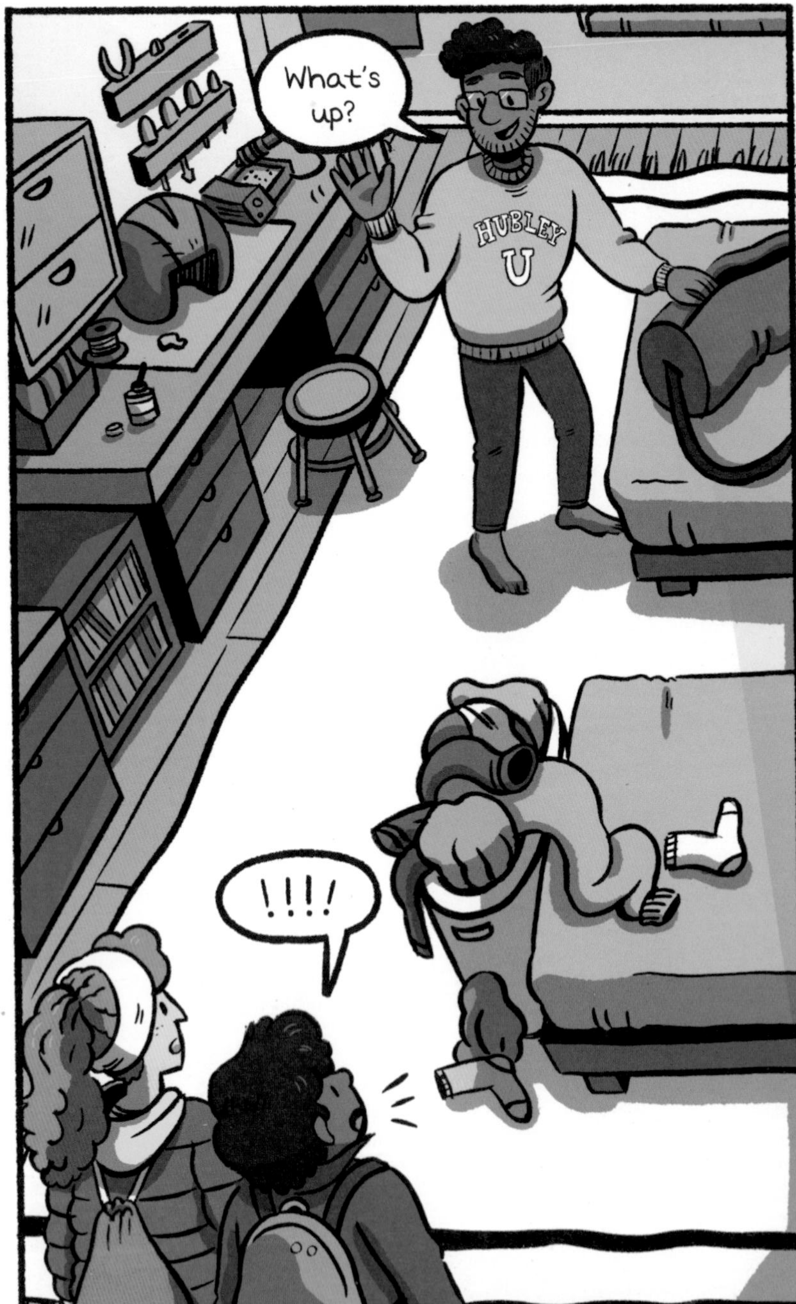
What's up?
HUBLEY U
!!!!

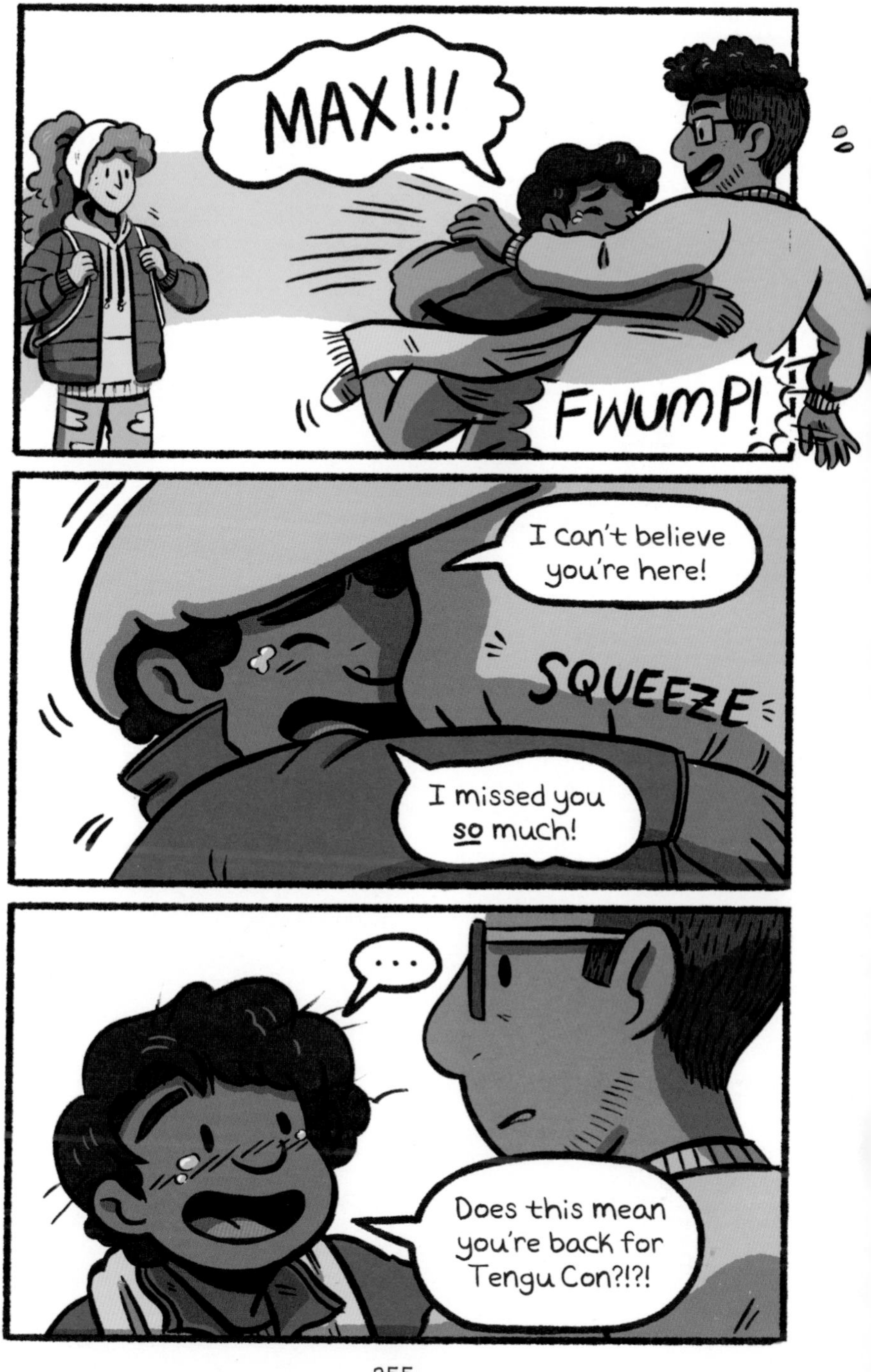
MAX!!!
FWUMP!
I can't believe you're here!
SQUEEZE
I missed you so much!
...
Does this mean you're back for Tengu Con?!?!

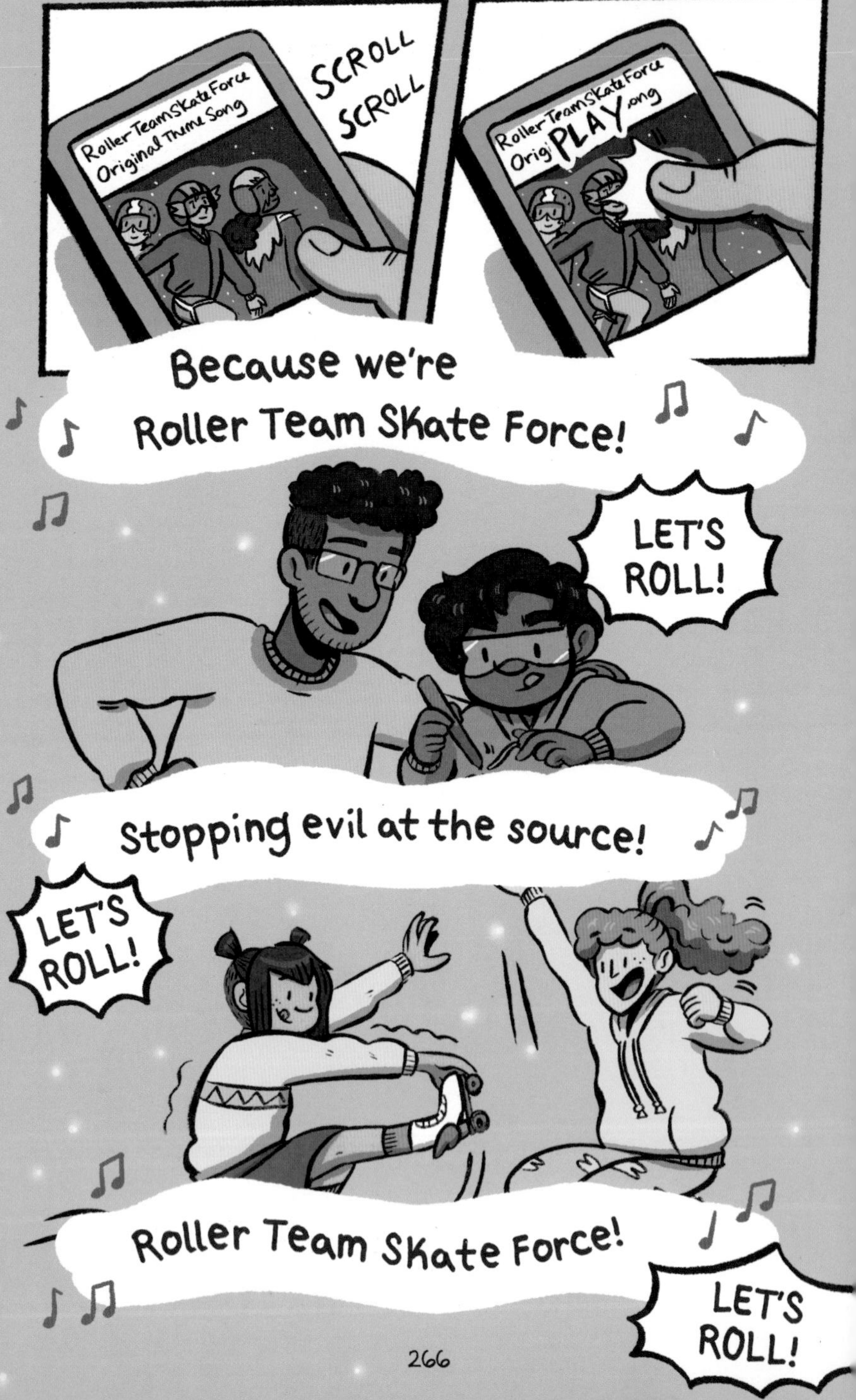

Roller Team Skate Force
Original Theme Song
SCROLL
SCROLL
PLAY
Because we're
Roller Team Skate Force!
LET'S ROLL!
Stopping evil at the source!
LET'S ROLL!
Roller Team Skate Force!
LET'S ROLL!

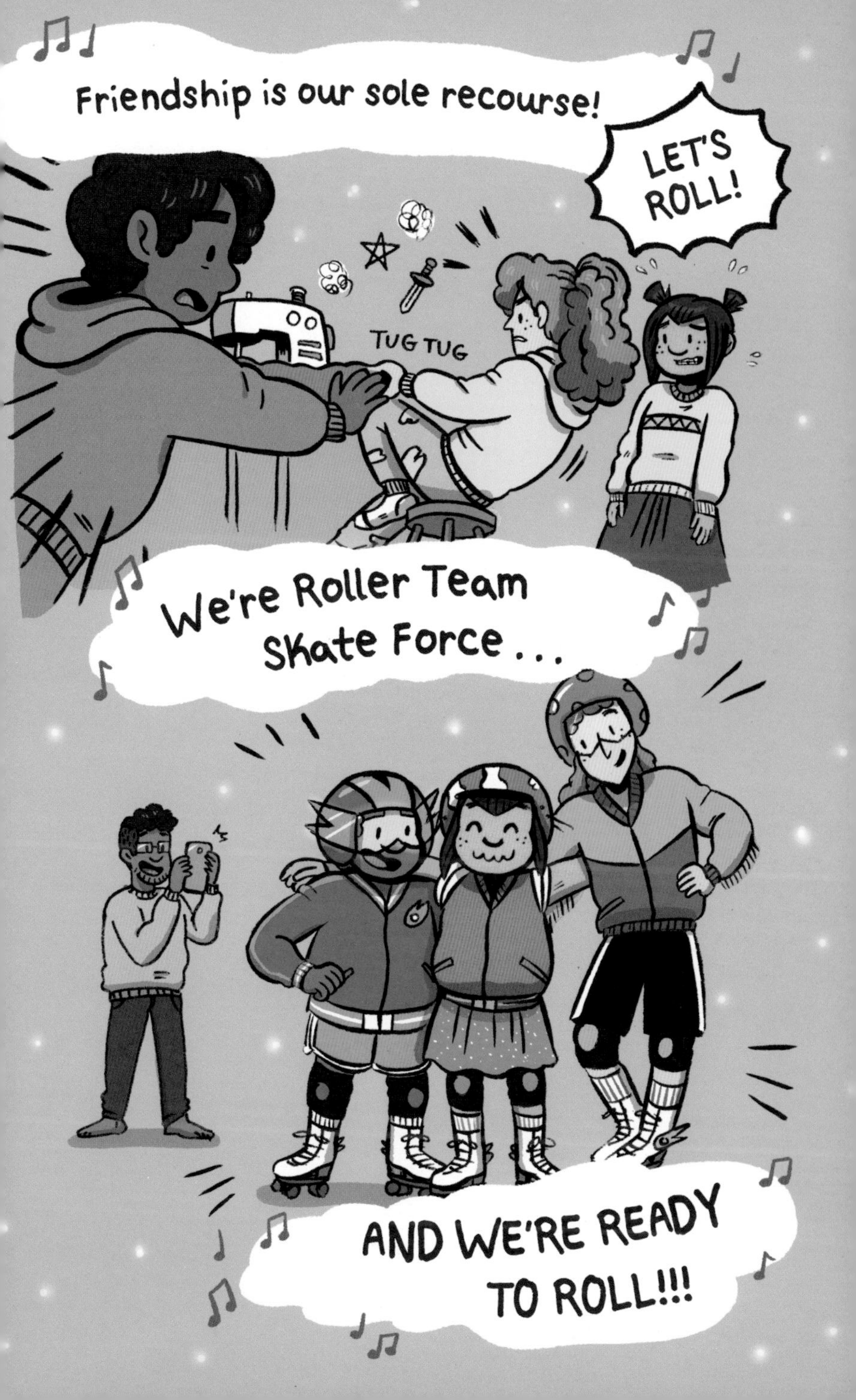
Friendship is our sole recourse!
LET'S ROLL!
TUG TUG
We're Roller Team Skate Force...
AND WE'RE READY TO ROLL!!!

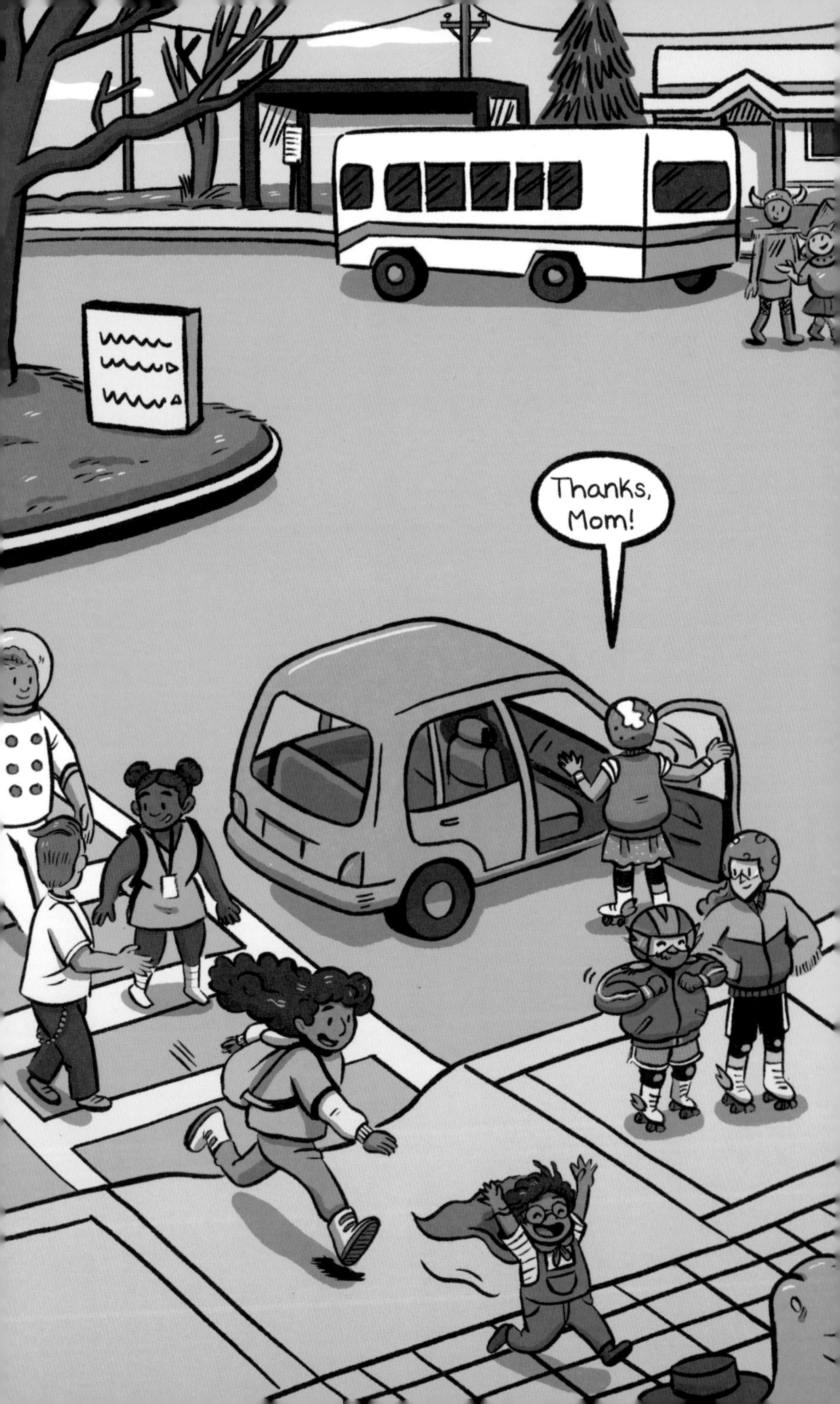
Thanks, Mom!

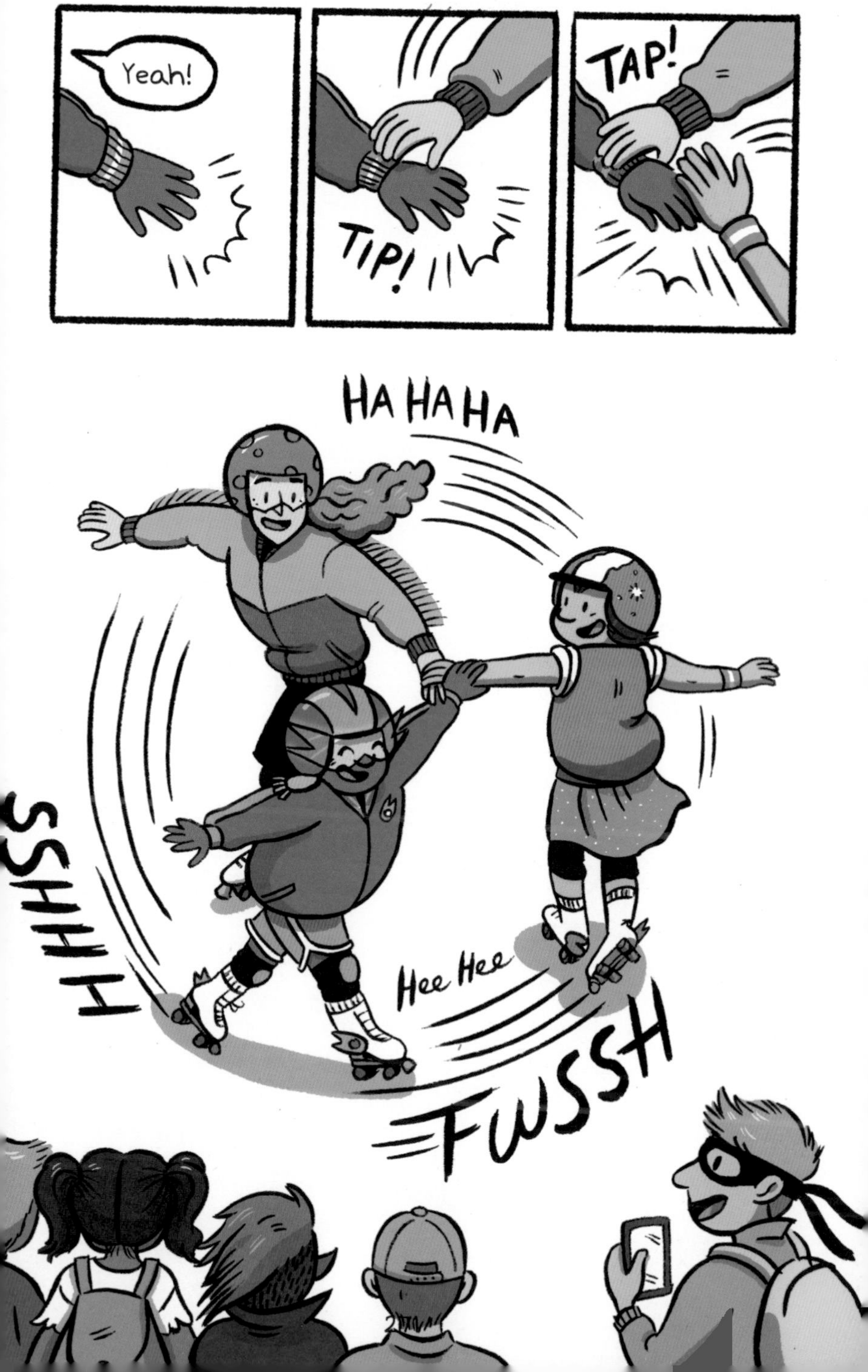
Yeah!
TIP!
TAP!
HA HA HA
HHHHSS
Hee Hee
FWSSH

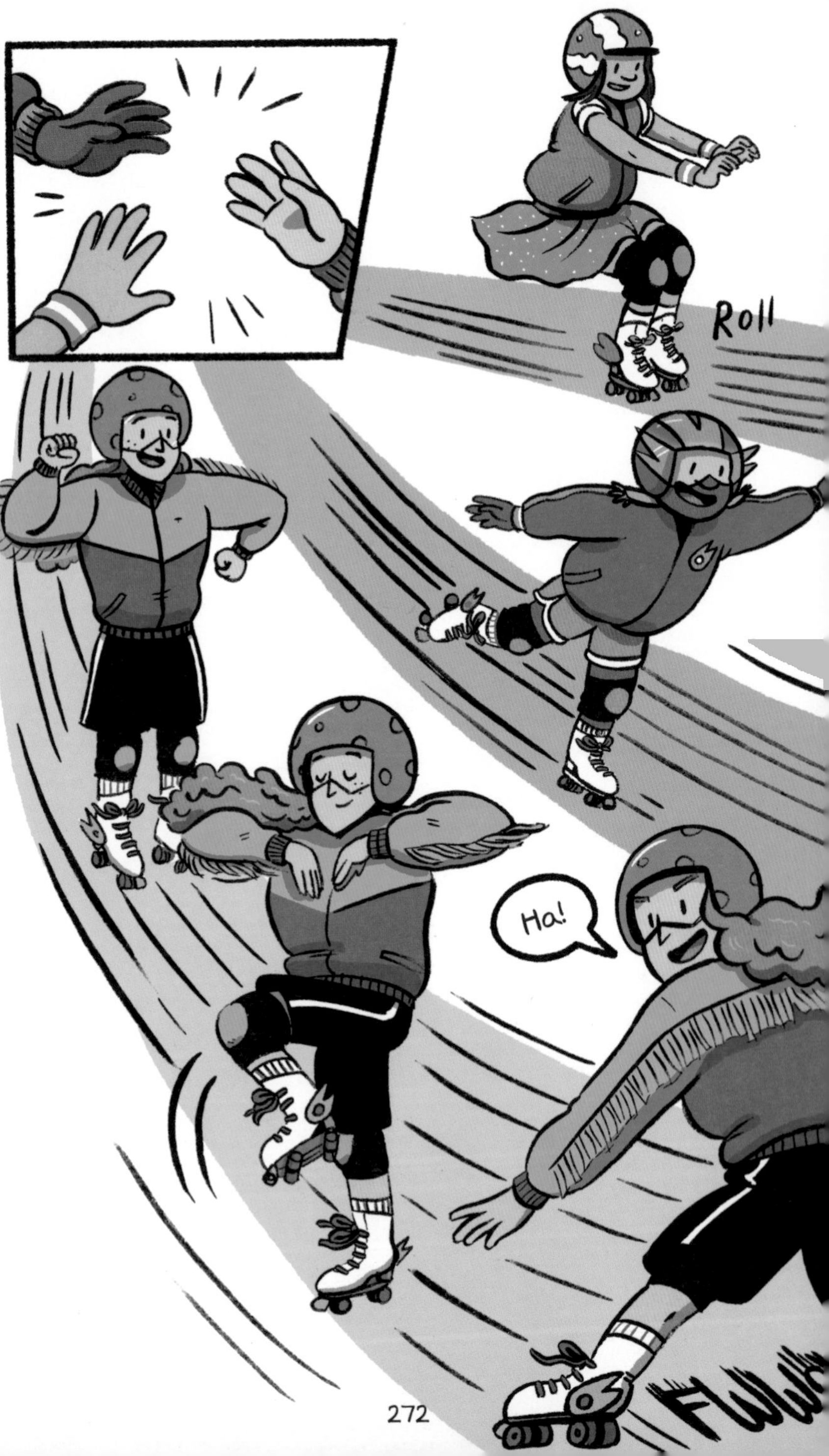
Roll
Ha!

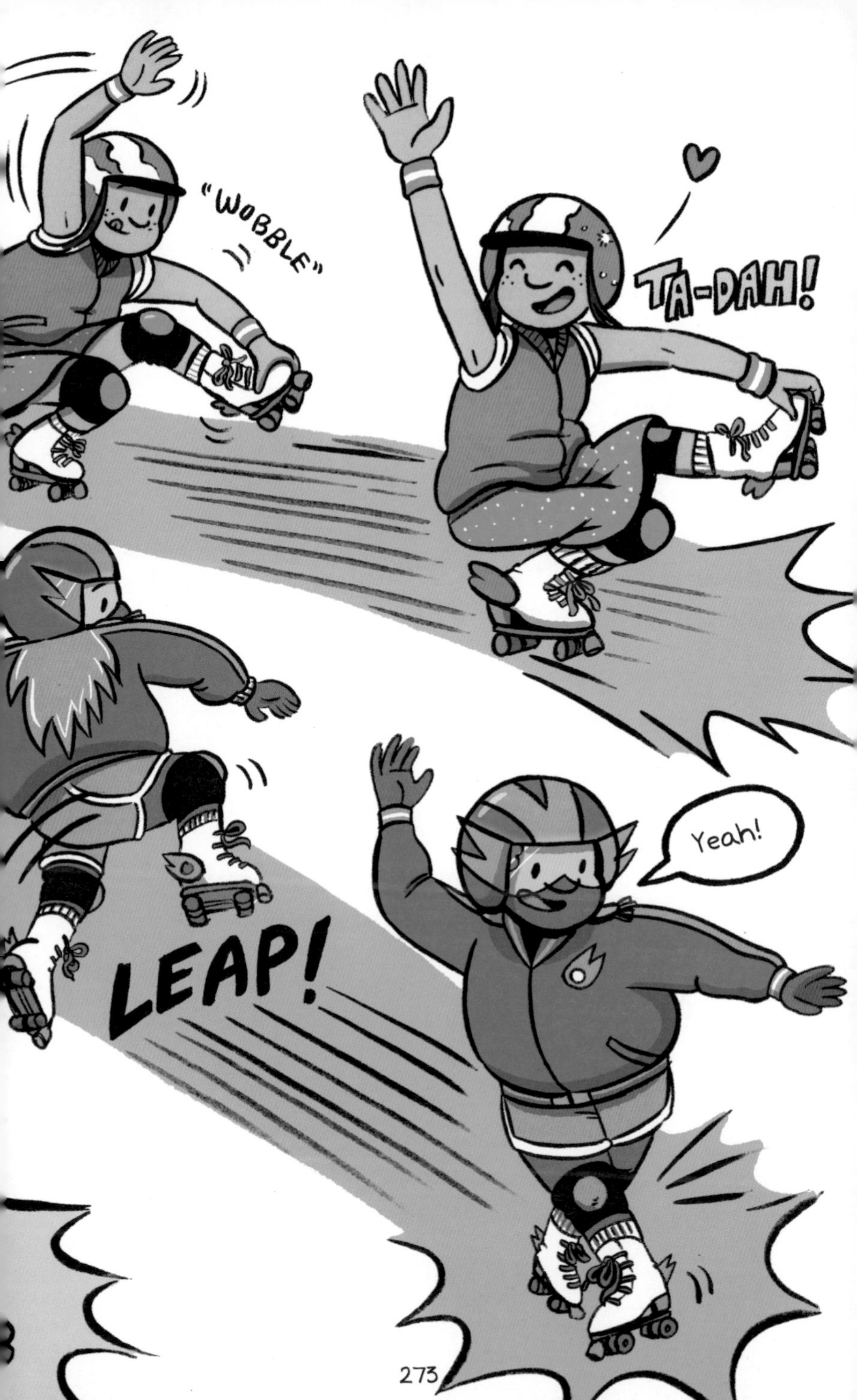
"WOBBLE"
TA-DAH!
LEAP!
Yeah!

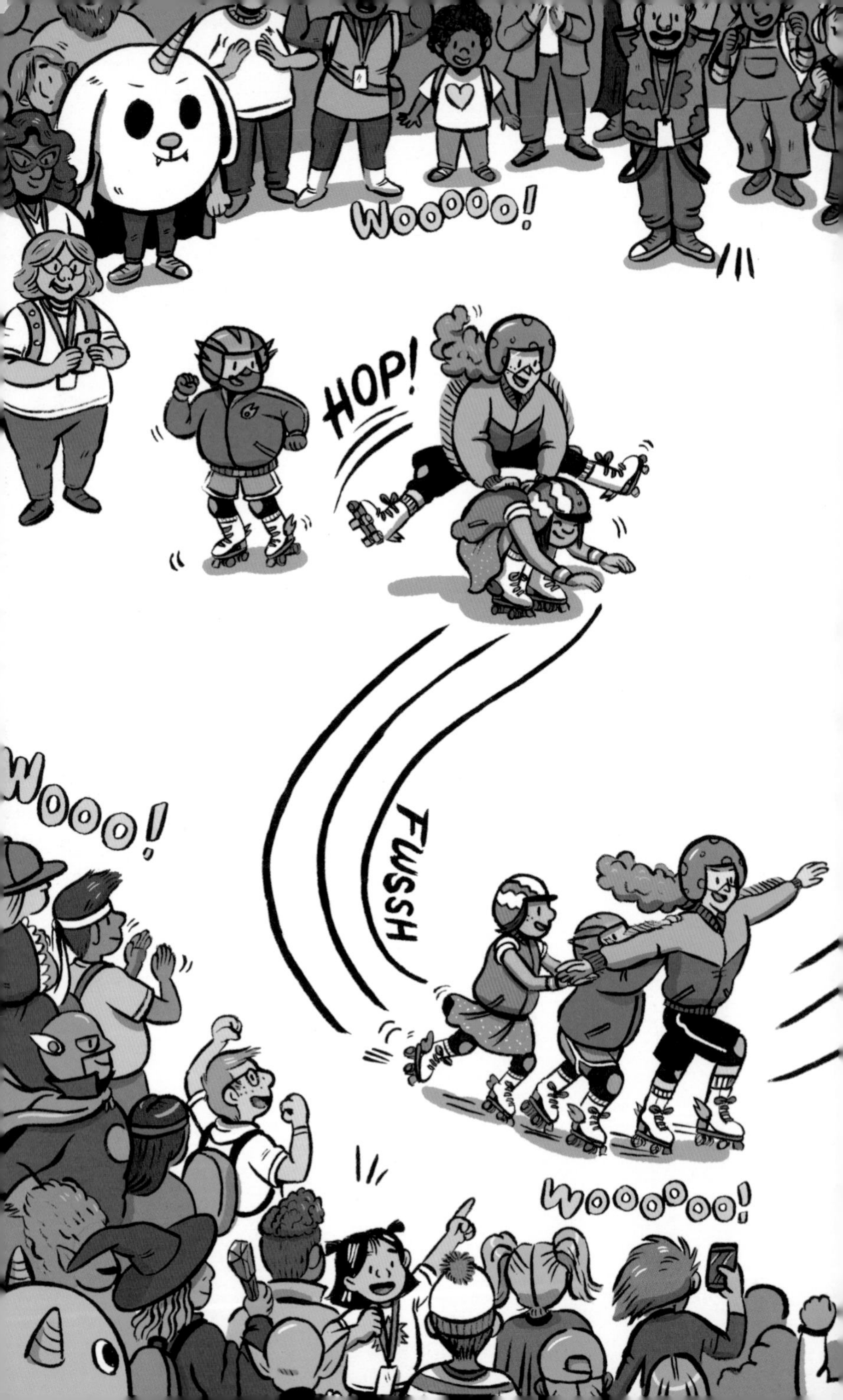
WOOOOO!
HOP!
FWSSH
WOOO!
WOOOOOO!

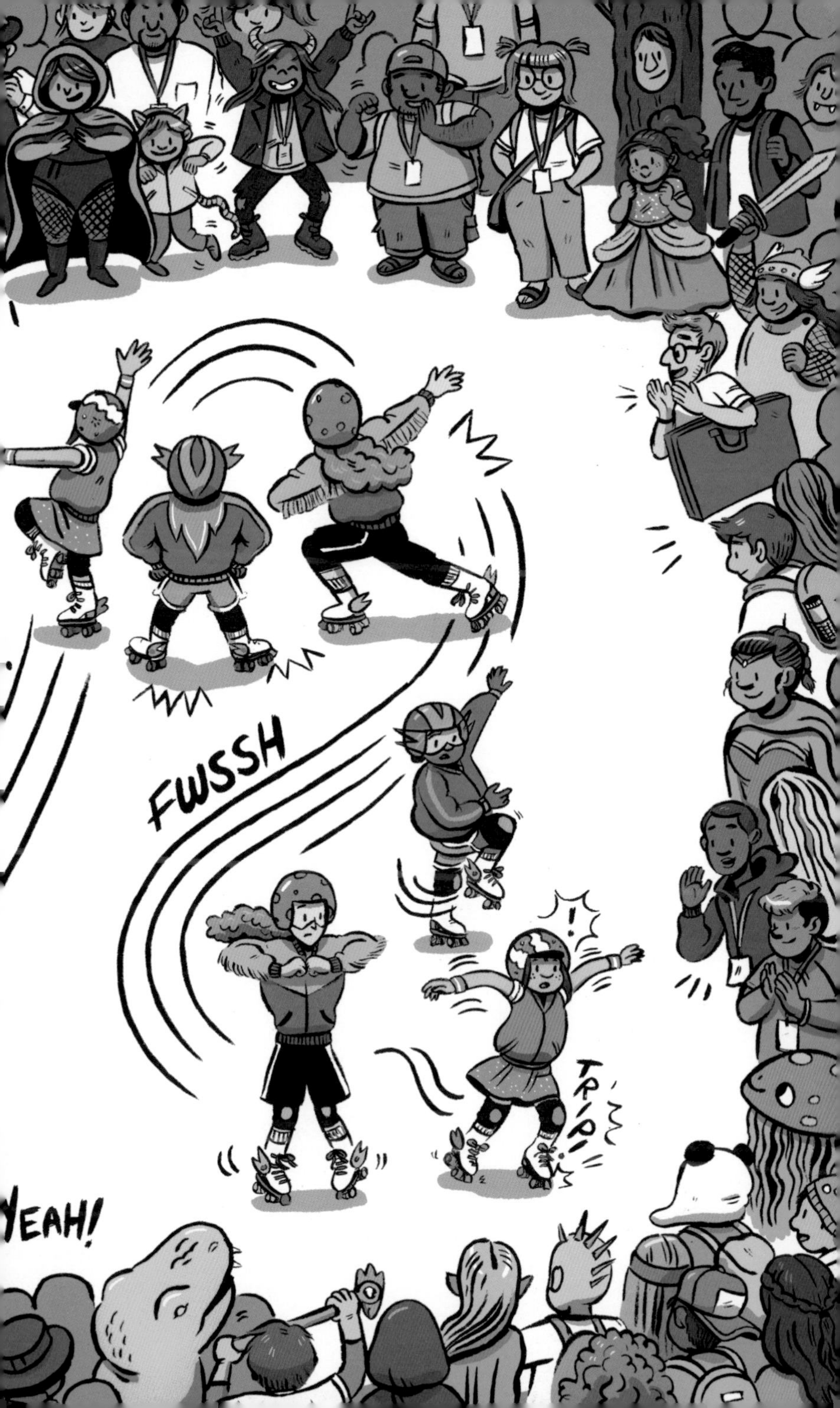
FWSSH
!
TRIP!
YEAH!

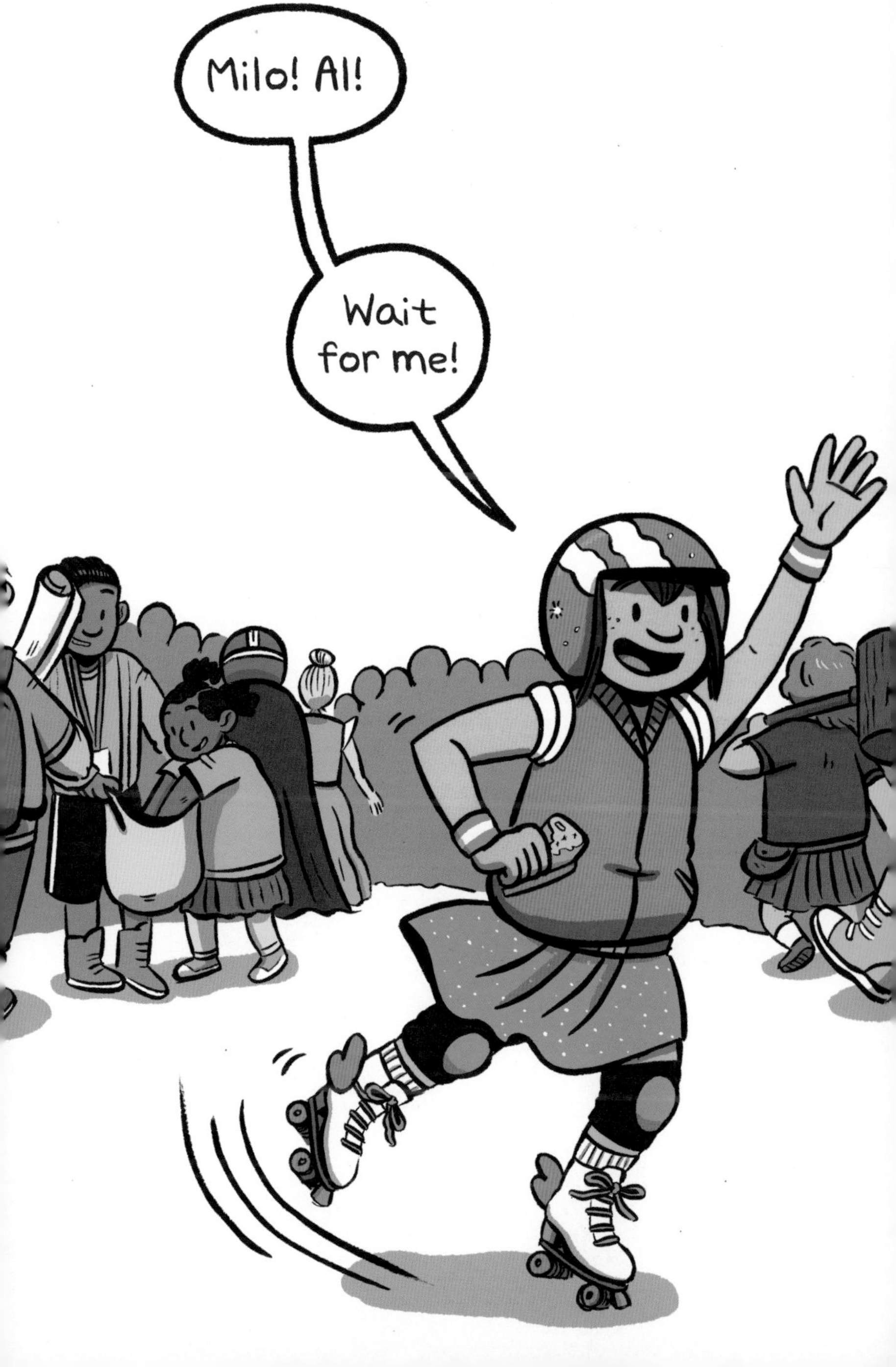
Milo! Al!
Wait for me!

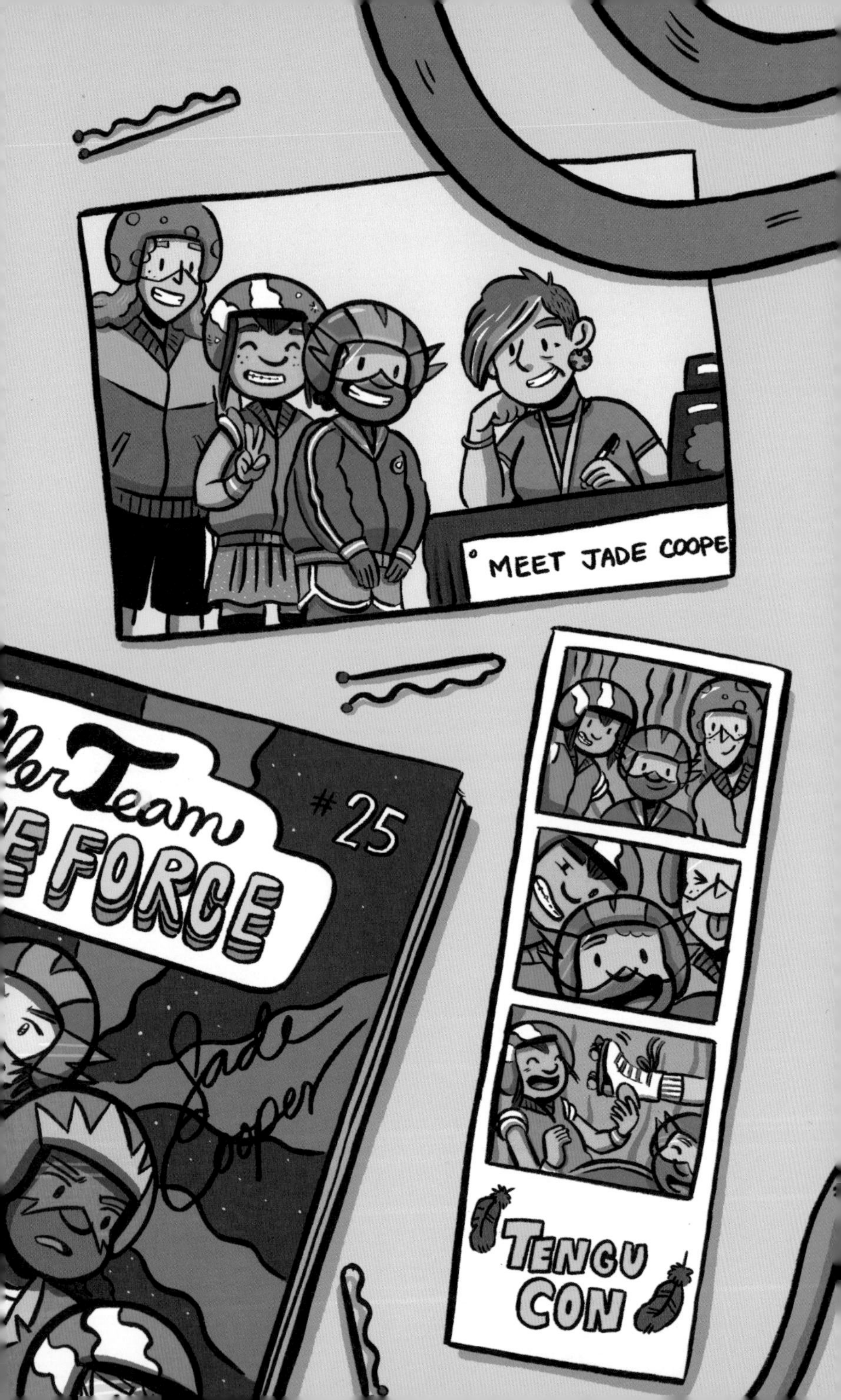
MEET JADE COOPE
ller Team
E FORCE
#25
Jade Cooper
TENGU CON

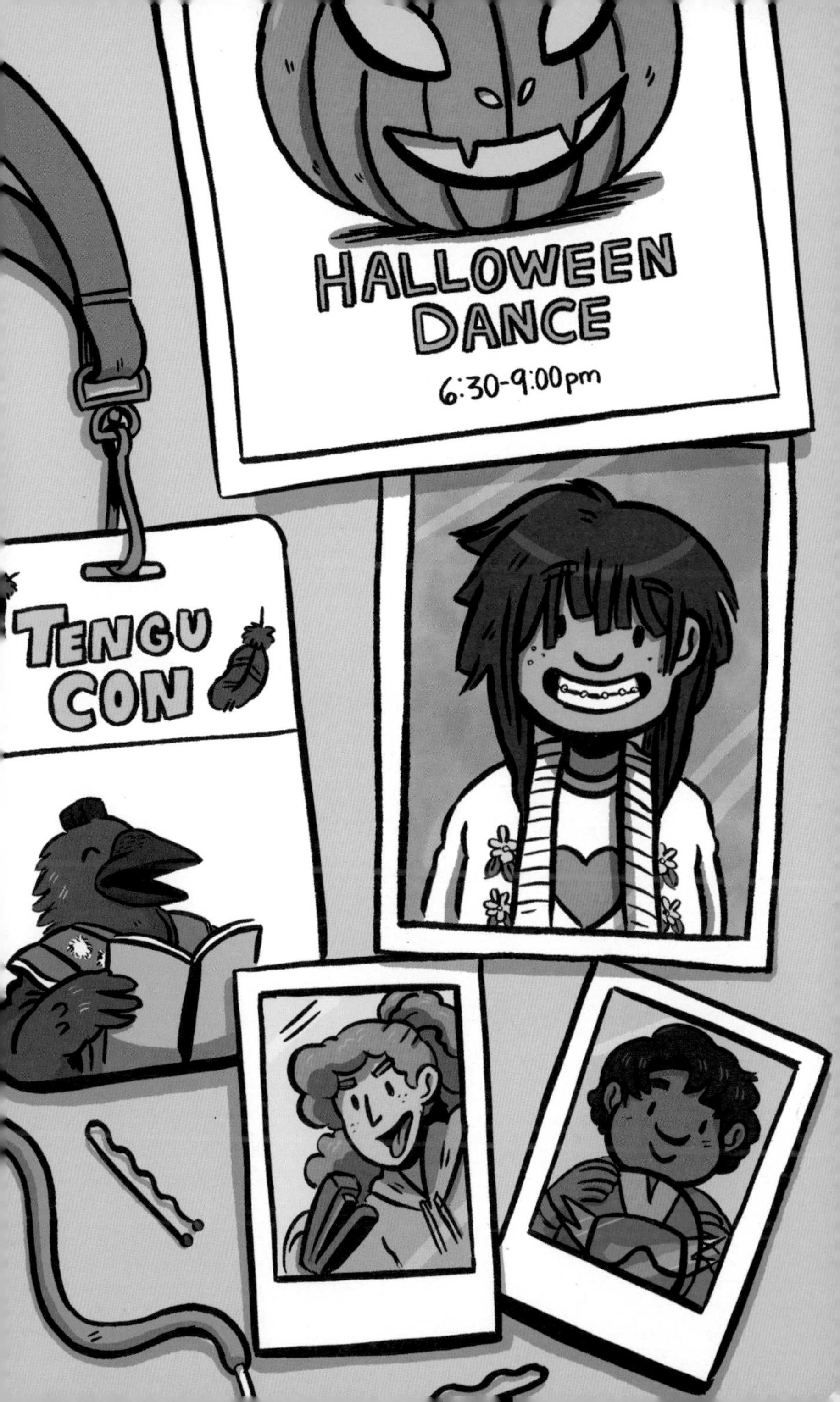
HALLOWEEN DANCE
6:30-9:00pm
TENGU CON

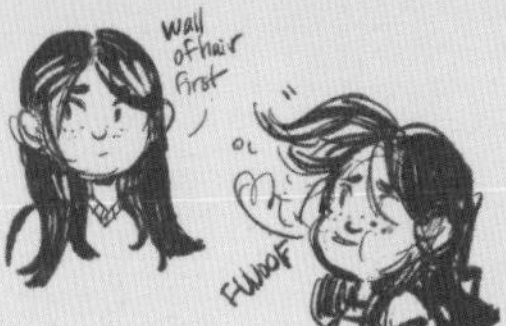
wall of hair first
FWOOF

AUTHOR'S NOTE

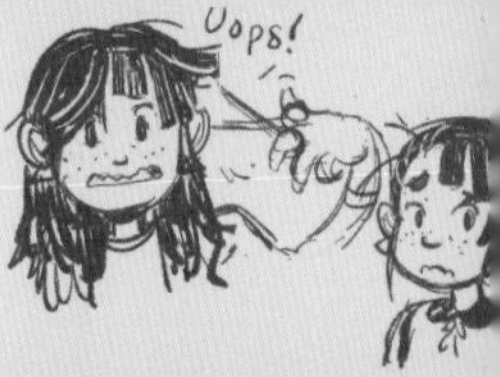
Oops!

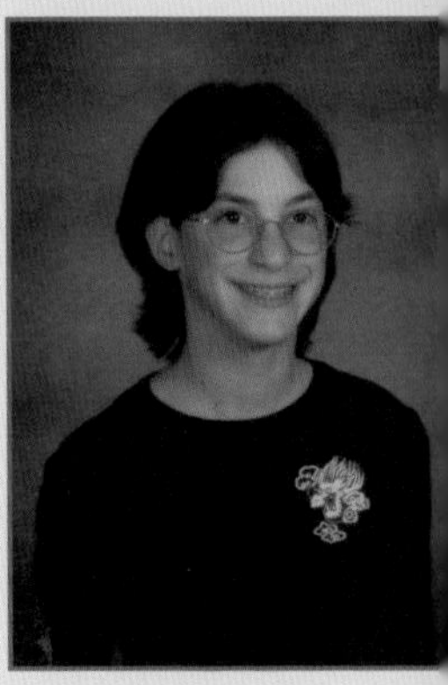

I was a kid who always loved to draw. Like Viv, Milo, and Al, I was inspired to create art and costumes fueled by the stories I loved. I could fill sketchbooks with original characters, but I always stopped short when it came to giving them their own stories. I thought of myself as someone who drew but didn't write, and at some point "didn't" changed to "can't." Whenever I thought about trying, I would get overwhelmed: How would I even know how to *start*? How would I even know what to *say*?

The idea for *Picture Day* came from an exercise I designed when I decided it was time to work through my feeling of "can't" and find my voice as a writer.

For an entire month, I wrote one sentence every day. Each sentence was from a random moment in a new story. Because it was a small task (just one sentence!), it felt achievable. At the end of the month, I had started 31 of my own stories! I printed out all my story pieces and placed them inside a tiny treasure chest.

During the next month, I did something fun and familiar: I drew the pictures! Each day I pulled a slip of paper out of the chest and drew a picture to go with it. I never knew what I was going to draw until prompted by the sentence—and figuring out the story as I drew was exhilarating. I was developing characters, building worlds. I was writing!

During that month, one of the story slices I created was this:

"Just a minute Mom" cried Dawn, "I'm almost ready to go…"

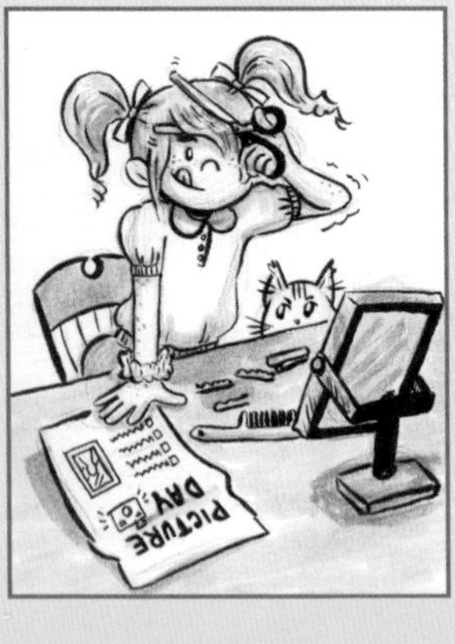
PICTURE DAY

When I drew this picture, I didn't know the character's name. All I knew was that she was about to cut off her hair on school picture day . . . and her mom didn't know about it! After asking myself a series of questions (What inspires her to make the cut? How do her friends feel about it? How does her *mom* feel about it?), I started to learn more. When I got stuck, I asked new questions and doodled to find the answers. Eventually, that one sketch became the beginning of *Picture Day*.

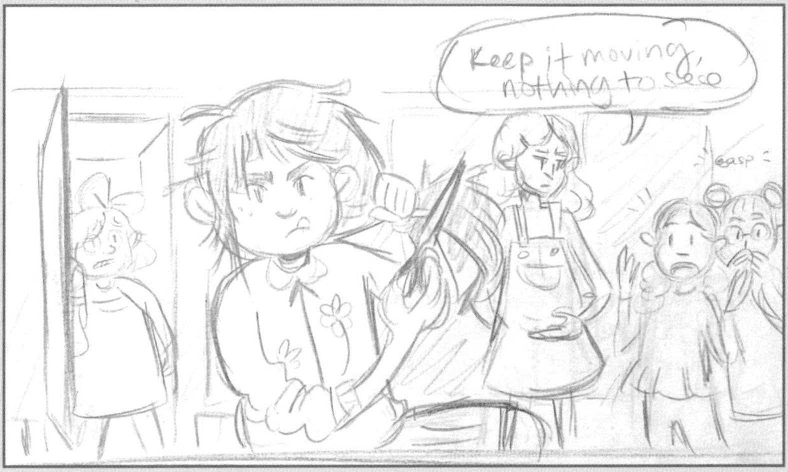
Keep it moving, nothing to see
gasp

I learned that my writing process required structure but with room for exploration. I needed a curious and open mind, and I needed to cultivate kindness toward my creations as they were developing.

It took a lot of time and confidence to find my voice as a writer, but I couldn't be happier that I finally took the leap.

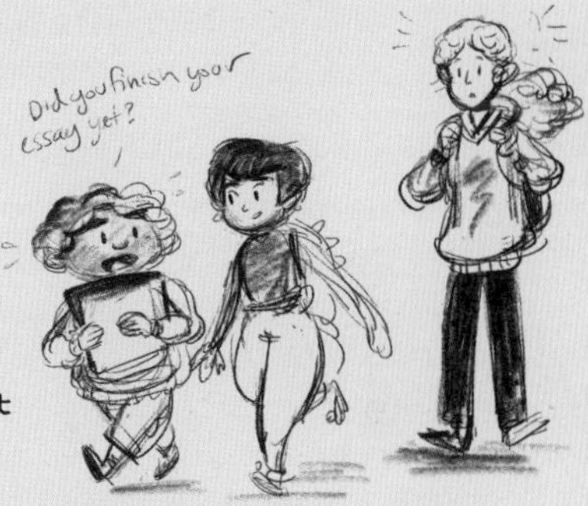
Did you finish your essay yet?

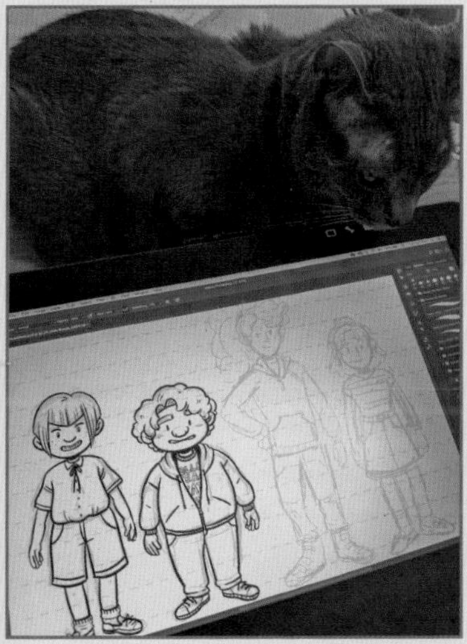

So if you are someone who thinks of themselves as a person who "can't" do something you really want to do, I hope this inspires you to start. Little by little, and with kindness toward yourself. I can't wait to see what you come up with.

—Sarah

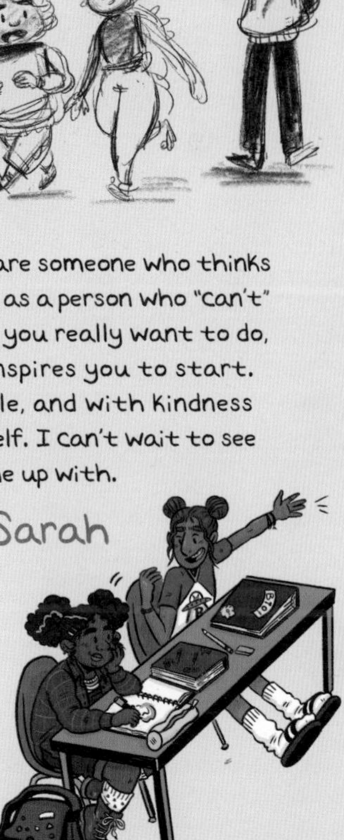

ACKNOWLEDGMENTS

Marisa DiNovis, I couldn't have asked for a more thoughtful and careful editor for this series! Thank you for never backing down from the hard questions that took my work to the next level. I always look forward to our collaborative chats. April Ward, your design work is top-notch. Thank you for making my art come to life! Jake Eldred, thank you for making my scheduling-spreadsheet dreams come true! To the rest of the Knopf and PRH team, thank you for your hard work, dedication, and enthusiasm in getting this book and series out into the world. An extra-special thanks for trusting me to lead you through extemporaneous creative activities!

Molly O'Neill, I'm so lucky to have you as my agent. You've coached me through finding my voice as a writer, and you are an unwavering champion of my work. Thank you for always being eager to hop on a call to brainstorm or answer my many questions about the publishing world. You are an integral part of my creative journey.

Thank you to my early readers, Jen de Oliveira and Elsa Vernon. Jen, you've known these characters and loved them as long as I have! Thank you for the comics/coffee chats, your careful feedback, and your friendship. I'm so glad that our books get to exist in the world together! Elsa, I'm so happy that we live in the same city again for all the reasons! Thank you for swooping in and giving me a crucial note that saved my ending.

To my Lumos Labbies community: I'm so thankful to have this wonderful group of people still in my life. Special thanks to Tyler Hinman, Ivy Ngo, Brendan Milos, Adrian Herbez, Gus Gutierrez, Matt Keefer, Bryan Young, Eli Delventhal, Shelby MacLeod, David Beavers, Aaron Kaluszka, and Bill Nega for brainstorming help with the RTSF theme song and Gabi's dance proposal puns.

Thank you to the entire team at Little Woodfords in Portland, Maine. This book was fueled by your cappuccinos and friendly conversations.

Mom, Dad, and Carrie: Thank you for instilling in me a love of reading and a love of comics, and for always enthusiastically encouraging my creative endeavors, no matter how strange (see: clicky pants). Leslie: Thank you for taking us in and giving me a space for my ideas to flourish after Luci's untimely demise.

Adam: This book truly wouldn't exist without your love and support. Thank you for everything from brainstorming plot points to building technical tools, from acting as my camera crew to cooking elaborate meals that nourish my soul. I love you and am grateful every day for such a loving partner and collaborator.